OPERATION
LIGHTNING STRIKE

Also by Nick Pope

Open Skies, Closed Minds
The Uninvited
Operation Thunder Child

OPERATION
LIGHTNING STRIKE

Nick Pope

SIMON & SCHUSTER
A VIACOM COMPANY

First published in Great Britain by Simon & Schuster UK Ltd, 2000
A Viacom Company

1 3 5 7 9 10 8 6 4 2

Simon & Schuster UK Ltd
Africa House
64–78 Kingsway
London WC2B 6AH

Simon & Schuster Australia
Sydney

A CIP catalogue record for this book is available from the British Library

This is predominantly a work of fiction. But although the story is set in
the near future, most of the locations and equipment depicted in this
novel actually exist, as do the majority of the political, civil, scientific and
military posts that feature. However, the characters associated with these
locations and posts are fictitious, and any resemblance to actual persons,
living or dead, is purely coincidental.

ISBN 0-684-85161-X

Typeset in Garamond 3 by SX Composing DTP, Rayleigh, Essex
Printed and bound in Great Britain by
Butler & Tanner Ltd, Frome and London

To Michèle.
With love and thanks . . .
Moo!

AUTHOR'S NOTE

A number of experts helped me while I was writing this book, supplementing my understanding of military and scientific matters with their own specialist knowledge. The assistance was priceless, and I am eternally grateful to them for being so generous with their insights and their time. These people have asked to remain anonymous, because being publicly associated with any speculation about the extraterrestrial nature of UFOs can be detrimental to career prospects. Although I will honour these authorities' requests for anonymity, it would be wrong of me not to pay tribute to them and I should like to take this opportunity to thank them all. Notwithstanding this specialist assistance, I have taken the decision to alter or obscure some of the technical details about weapons systems, defensive capabilities, and military doctrine, strategy and tactics, for obvious reasons of national security.

CONTENTS

ACKNOWLEDGEMENTS

As with all literary ventures, this book owes its existence to the dedication and efforts of a number of people. It would be impossible to single out everybody, but I should like to pay particular tribute to my literary agent, Andrew Lownie, for his ceaseless hard work on my behalf. I'd also like to thank Martin Fletcher, Editorial Director at Simon & Schuster UK Ltd, for his continued hard work and enthusiasm, together with Nick Austin and Rochelle Venables, whose input has considerably enhanced the project. Everybody at Simon & Schuster has worked very hard on this book, and I'm grateful to the entire team.

Family members and friends have helped in a variety of ways, as have numerous friends and colleagues at the Ministry of Defence. I'm particularly grateful to Brigitte Barclay and Georgina Bruni. But, as ever, the bulk of the burden has been shouldered by Michèle Kaczynski, to whom this book is dedicated. Her assistance has been priceless, and her friendship is beyond value.

GLOSSARY OF ABBREVIATIONS

AD	Air Defence
AEW	Airborne Early Warning
AMRAAM	Advanced Medium-Range Air-to-Air Missile
APS	Assistant Private Secretary
ASRAAM	Advanced Short-Range Air-to-Air Missile
ATC	Air Traffic Control
AWACS	Airborne Warning and Control System
BMD	Ballistic Missile Defence
BMEWS	Ballistic Missile Early-Warning System
BVRAAM	Beyond Visual Range Air-to-Air Missile
CAP	Combat Air Patrol
CAS	Chief of the Air Staff
CBDE	Chemical and Biological Defence Establishment
CDI	Chief of Defence Intelligence
CDS	Chief of the Defence Staff
C-in-C	Commander-in-Chief
CO	Commanding Officer
CPO	Chief Press Officer
CSA	Chief Scientific Adviser
DCMC	Defence Crisis Management Centre
DERA	Defence Evaluation and Research Agency
DIA	Defense Intelligence Agency
DIS	Defence Intelligence Staff
ECM	Electronic Countermeasures

FCO	Foreign and Commonwealth Office
FSB	Federal Security Bureau (formerly the KGB)
GCHQ	Government Communications Headquarters
HQSTC	Headquarters Strike Command
IFF	Identification Friend or Foe
Min(AF)	Minister of State for the Armed Forces
Min(DP)	Minister of State for Defence Procurement
MOD	Ministry of Defence
NASA	National Aeronautics and Space Administration
NATO	North Atlantic Treaty Organization
NBC	Nuclear, Biological and Chemical
NSA	National Security Agency
PAC	Public Accounts Committee
PJHQ	Permanent Joint Headquarters
PS	Private Secretary
Q/QRA	Quick Reaction Alert
RAF	Royal Air Force
ROE	Rules of Engagement
RPV	Remotely Piloted Vehicle
RV	Remote Viewing
SAM	Surface-to-Air Missile
SAR	Search and Rescue
SAS	Special Air Service
Sec(AS)	Secretariat (Air Staff)
SETI	Search for Extraterrestrial Intelligence
SHORAD	Short-Range Air Defence
S of S	Secretary of State
SOP	Standard Operating Procedure
THAAD	Theater High-Altitude Area Defense
UAV	Unmanned Aerial Vehicle
UFO	Unidentified Flying Object
UKADR	United Kingdom Air Defence Region
U/S	Unserviceable
USAF	United States Air Force
USAMRIID	United States Army Medical Research Institute of Infectious Diseases
US of S	Under-Secretary of State

PROLOGUE

Darkness. Not the comforting darkness of the womb, but a cold, empty blackness that struck a familiar chord in the deepest levels of the subconscious, stirring some primordial race memory. But any such thoughts were buried deep, for millennia had passed and humanity had come out of the darkness, into the light of technology. The terrors had been chased away. But now they were back. And they had a new face.

Isabelle Bentley looked down and saw unfamiliar controls. But she knew what to do, nonetheless. As one of the RAF's most skilled pilots, she'd been earmarked for this current mission long before she'd thought of volunteering. Aside from her courage, there was the fact that she was one of the few who had met this new enemy head-on. And survived. So the familiar cockpit of her Eurofighter Typhoon had given way to something more exotic and as she looked ahead, she saw not the comforting blue skies to which she was used but the blackness of space.

Out of the darkness came forth a light. At first, it seemed as if this light was just another star, but Bentley knew from her instruments that this was something else entirely and that she and her fellow pilots were closing in upon their quarry. The moment was approaching but for now all they could do was run through the final series of checks and wait until they reached the launch point. As the time drew nearer, the vastness of their target became apparent. It had been mentioned in the briefings, of course, but even the pilots' training in the simulator had not prepared them for the real thing. There were no words to describe its size adequately.

They were coming in blind. Intelligence on their target was scant but the enemy were undoubtedly employing both active and passive detection systems, watching for the attack that they knew was coming. So the fleet of craft moving in to strike used no radar systems or electronic jamming. They had known well in advance where to find their quarry, and had known its course. Earth was its target, and it was coming in on the same straight-line course that it had travelled for decades. There was nowhere else to go.

The target grew larger in Bentley's field of vision and she made a few mental calculations. Weapons release was moments away. At last, their quarry reacted to the threat that it had seen too late, and swarms of enemy scout craft filled the void between the attackers and the leviathan they were hunting. Pulses of plasma streaked towards them through the vacuum of space, in such vast numbers that survival seemed impossible. Some of these salvos found their targets and thinned out the attackers. Bentley saw none of this. The RAF forces were widely dispersed to present a difficult target and, though she knew that some of her comrades had been hit, any such destruction took place outside her field of view. She was entirely focused on her task and, although afraid, she knew that death – if it came – would be mercifully quick.

The attack run continued relentlessly. Orders had been given not to engage the scout ships, and not to be distracted by them. The pilots were to advance directly towards their target and release their weapons from maximum range. No other tactic was even possible: Bentley's craft – in common with all the others – carried only a single type of missile.

The moment was upon her. Two of her four weapons were

armed and released in seconds, with a minimum of effort. Two switches were thrown, a protective cap removed, and a button pressed. It was as simple as that — and yet these basic actions sent on their way a destructive power as potent as that of the stars she saw around her.

The missiles streaked ahead of Bentley, closing in on the monstrous vessel ahead. Their active systems came on briefly — to acquire the target — but then switched off, negating the possibility of jamming or any other electronic countermeasures. Once the target had been acquired, it was virtually impossible for the weapons to fail to hit home. It was inconceivable that they could go wide of something so huge. Bentley saw that her warhead had been joined by others, and knew that some of her fellow pilots had survived, though she didn't have time to wonder who. A volley streaked ahead of them. At this point the enemy scout craft switched tactics, targeting the missiles rather than the vessels that had fired them. This was a good sign. *They know they're vulnerable.* Some of the inbound rockets were struck, but neither time nor luck was on the side of the defenders.

The weapons had been specially adapted for the task in hand but, aside from that, were unremarkable. The nuclear warheads they carried had been set to explode at various different points. Some would detonate on impact, rupturing vast areas of the target's massive hull, but others would punch their way through its side, burrowing towards the heart of the ship to explode deep inside, destroying the critical systems that were at the very centre of the structure.

Bentley whooped with joy as she saw the first impacts — a series of flashes that seemed impossibly bright even to eyes shielded by a canopy and goggles that had been specially treated to deal with this very situation. She looked away and when she looked back she was able to see that the first wave of their attack had been devastatingly effective. The vast craft's hull was breached in several places, and a mass of material was coming away from the main body. And yet its size was such that even this series of cataclysmic nuclear explosions could not destroy the target totally.

Bentley marvelled at this and almost felt sorry for those on the receiving end of the onslaught.

Inside the ship, she knew, alien minds would be struggling to deal with the threat, directing the damage-control systems and trying to react to a situation that was fast deteriorating. Automatic defensive systems would be coming on-line, too, and a variety of measures would have to be taken, with one aim: survival. Bulkheads would be closing, fire-control systems would be kicking in and hard decisions would be being taken. Whole areas would have to be written off as entire levels were sacrificed, together with hundreds, probably thousands of lives.

It was time for the second phase of the attack. Ignoring the scout ships and defensive weapons that scored a few more hits on the inbound force, Bentley closed in and armed her two remaining missiles. It had been agreed that these would be aimed manually. Although the plan was complicated and depended upon the success of the first wave, the concept was a simple one: to target areas of weakness exposed by the first strike. Once more, Bentley watched in mesmerized fascination as a second – smaller – volley of missiles homed in on their crippled target.

In her mind Bentley could predict the result of this latest development. They'd all been briefed on the capabilities and design specifications of the alien ship and knew what to expect. But yet it seemed to Bentley that she was going beyond mere speculation and into a realm where – somehow – she could see in her mind's eye what was happening. Metal screamed and tore like paper as bulkheads failed, and hull integrity was breached in countless other areas. A chain reaction had been started, and critical infra-structures were now falling victim to the growing inferno raging at the very heart of the ship. The targeting of already damaged areas had been devastatingly effective, akin to turning a knife in an already painful wound. Computer systems that had strained to cope with the initial damage now found themselves unable to handle it. There were a number of actions that needed to be taken immediately, but the systems capable of doing these tasks were going progressively off-line. Alien minds in human bodies struggled to address the most crucial points, but key personnel were either dead or cut off from the action because communication links were being gradually severed.

When the end came, it was as sudden as it was spectacular. The ship began to break up and finally came apart altogether. Bentley knew that space was a vacuum and that there was no way that she would hear the final cataclysmic explosion. And yet she fancied that she *could* hear something. It was quiet at first but grew steadily, until it reached an almost unbearable volume. It was a cry of rage, fear, pain and anguish. It was the collective lament of a people who had sacrificed everything for a promise of paradise and died within sight of it, after an eternity of wandering the void. It was the screaming of a billion souls.

Bentley was screaming too as she awoke, sweat streaming from every pore of her body. When she stopped and analysed what had happened, she knew that it had been more than a dream. It had been a nightmare vision of the reality that she might soon have to face.

Chapter One

ALIEN DISCUSSIONS

Downing Street, Whitehall

'Good morning, ladies and gentlemen. It is no exaggeration to say that what we agree today, in this room, may decide the fate of the world and the destiny of the human race.' The Prime Minister's remark hadn't been scripted but could hardly have been more dramatic in its content and delivery. Politicians had a natural sense of drama, though, and much of political life revolved around punchy soundbites designed to grab attention. This remark certainly had the desired effect on the PM's guests.

There were four others in the room: the leader of the Opposition, who was the only other politician present, and three people from the Ministry of Defence – the Secretary of State for Defence, the Chief of the Defence Staff and the Chief Scientific Adviser. They listened intently as the Prime Minister made his introductory remarks. Their respective aides had withdrawn and it had been decided that the meeting was not to be minuted. There would be no written record of anything discussed in the room.

'We now have confirmation from NASA scientists about the uncorrelated target detected by the Hubble Space Telescope. This object is artificial and is heading for Earth. This would seem to provide us with independently verifiable evidence that corroborates statements made by former NSA Director Edwin Van Buren. It seems that this object is, indeed, an extraterrestrial craft. Now, this is a strictly informal brainstorming meeting, and I want everybody here to speak their mind.' This instruction was hardly necessary, given the strong-willed nature of those present, but the PM was leaving nothing to chance.

Despite the PM's desire to see an informal discussion, there was still a hierarchy by which the MOD contingent were clearly going to abide. It was Tom Willoughby, the Secretary of State who had proved his mettle during Operation Thunder Child, who spoke first, voicing a concern that he and CDS had talked over at some length. 'Thank you, Prime Minister. But before we discuss military options, can you give us a wider view on the political situation? If we're instructed to prepare offensive or defensive operational plans, then we can do that – we've already started the process, as a contingency. But to what extent is the UK going to be taking strategic decisions? Is this just a national operation? Surely not. Presumably the central question of how we respond to this threat is one that goes beyond the responsibility of any one nation. If we fight, do we fight alone, as part of NATO, or as one element of some sort of integrated UN force?'

'And if so,' chipped in CDS, 'under whose operational control?'

The PM sat back in his chair. He'd been expecting these questions and knew he didn't have any meaningful answers. 'All these elements have yet to be decided. I have to confer with our Allies – especially the Americans – and there'll have to be discussions at the UN. But I want to make one thing absolutely clear. We must reserve the right to take unilateral military action to protect our national interests.'

'I agree,' S of S responded. CDS, too, was nodding.

'I disagree.' It was Dr Barbara North, the Chief Scientific Adviser, who had spoken. She had already made her views known to S of S and CDS, but this was the first time she had had an opportunity to register her concerns with the PM.

'Explain.'

'Prime Minister,' CSA began, 'we really know *nothing* about this situation other than what we've been told by Van Buren, and he's lied so much in the past that I certainly wouldn't trust him.'

'He seems to be cooperating fully with the US authorities now,' the PM retorted. 'The President has reluctantly agreed to grant him immunity if he does. The same goes for the other members of this covert group – the Enterprise. So far, everything seems to check out.'

'Fair enough,' CSA continued. 'But, even so, I think we should treat all information from those people with extreme caution.' She paused and noticed that CDS was nodding his agreement. His face was impassive, but he'd made clear his opposition to granting immunity to anybody who'd been involved in covering up information that might have saved the lives of the military personnel who'd died during Operation Thunder Child. But he'd known that he could do nothing beyond offering a token protest. The PM had made it clear that this was a decision for the US to take and had gone along reluctantly with President Spencer's deal.

'As a scientist,' CSA went on, 'I have to go where the data takes me. In other words, we must differentiate between what we've been told, and what we've actually found out. Now, we've been *told* a lot of things by Van Buren, but what we actually *know* is a different matter. We have an unidentified but clearly artificial object heading for Earth. We have the remains of three small craft that are almost certainly extraterrestrial and we have the bodies of creatures that are non-human but essentially humanoid. As you know two of them survived for a while but then they died – we don't know why. I can tell you a fair bit about the craft but little about the entities, given that I can't autopsy them until we've resolved the moral question of how we treat their dead. Additionally, we have the remains of some sort of underground facility at Bentwaters, which was clearly being used by these beings but which has been destroyed so effectively that there's virtually nothing left. Finally, we have a mixture of photographs, gun-camera footage, radar tapes and eyewitness statements of contact with these craft. So we can say with a degree of certainty that we're dealing with extraterrestrials, but we really shouldn't kid ourselves that we know anything about their motives and their plans.'

'I agree.' It was CDS who spoke up in support of his scientific colleague. 'It's a basic rule of military intelligence that you should always differentiate between what you *think* and what you *know*. But it goes beyond that. You have to bear in mind that in the Gulf War and in the Kosovo crisis the actions of Saddam Hussein and Slobodan Milosevic were illogical from a military point of view. Even politically their actions made little sense. But now consider an enemy who is completely alien. If we find it virtually impossible to guess at the motives of our own terrestrial tyrants, what hope have we of fathoming what drives these . . . extraterrestrials?'

'Well, that's precisely my point,' CSA rejoined. 'We assume they're coming here to invade and we're making plans to fight. But violence must surely be our last resort. We need to *talk* to these entities, not fight them.'

'We tried that,' the leader of the Opposition interjected. 'It didn't work.'

'Maybe we went about it the wrong way, I don't know. But we can't give up on the option – not when there's so much at stake.'

'Nobody is giving up on the option,' the PM replied firmly. 'Nobody wants to pick a fight with an enemy who's almost certainly stronger and smarter than we are. But militarily we have to prepare for the worst. We'll try everything we can to come to a peaceful solution but, at the end of the day, we may have to fight. And so long as that possibility remains, however unpalatable it may be, we need to prepare for it.'

Farnham, Surrey

Richard Cody was probably Britain's best-known civilian expert on the UFO phenomenon and on the related mystery of alien abductions. He'd been investigating and writing about such matters for several decades, and even before the current crisis he had been viewed as the voice of reason in a field of study that attracted more than its fair share of cranks and cultists. The dapper widower had become a familiar face in the media over the past few weeks, and although he had been moderately well known before the current crisis, there were now very few people in the country who would have failed to recognize the retired barrister whose views were still, so it was rumoured, being sought by the Government. It was a testament to his modesty that he had taken to this new-found celebrity status with the characteristic quiet dignity that endeared him to people. Most other so-called ufologists had taken confirmation of first contact as a signal for a bout of smug, self-important posturing that boiled down to little more than an 'I told you so' attitude. This had gone hand in hand with a small-minded smear campaign that effectively became a witch-hunt of those ufologists who'd previously been sceptical of the extraterrestrial hypothesis. These same people had been vociferous in their condemnation of the government and, although they clearly had a point here, virtually none of their criticism was constructive.

Cody had disassociated himself from any of the public criticism. Together with a small group of more sober researchers – like the American academic, Elizabeth Krone – he'd concentrated his mind on the real issues. What were the implications of confirmed alien contact, and what response should humanity make? He'd also communicated his willingness to cooperate with the Government and offer what help and advice he might, with no linked demands for access to classified information or to the decision-making process.

In the room with Cody was another person who'd had a phenomenal amount of media exposure over the past few weeks. Jenny Thornton was somebody who had been making claims of alien abduction for some years. Recent events had turned her – in the mind of the public – from a harmless crank to a figure of intense interest. People looked to her for answers. But, like all those who had truly had an alien encounter, she didn't have any neat solutions to offer. Still, Thornton was not one to act like a passive victim. Although she'd been powerless to prevent the abductions, she'd wanted to make some sort of meaningful response to them. Accordingly, she'd become progressively more active in the UFO lobby and had herself begun researching and investigating both UFO sightings and abductions. Under Cody's careful patronage she'd built up a wealth of experience that she now used in the unofficial role of research assistant to Cody himself.

'What I'd like to know is whether we can truly trust the government in this matter? And if we can't, who speaks for the people?'

The person who had asked this question was Maxwell Henderson. Sixty-two years old but looking younger, Henderson had approached Cody ten days ago and asked him for a private briefing on the UFO phenomenon. Cody had received many such calls but had responded to this one immediately. This was not because of Henderson's money — myriad business interests meant that he was one of the wealthiest people in the country — but because of his influence. Henderson's varied career had included politics and although sensationalist media accounts of an adulterous relationship with a lap-dancer had wrecked his ambitions in the field, this was not before he had attained junior ministerial rank and further widened an already impressive network of contacts. He'd returned to the world of business, which had always been his first love. His was a name known to most people in the country and it was also known that he remained well connected to many of the key figures in the Establishment. It was this that had convinced Cody to co-operate with the man, coupled with the fact that he had approached him personally rather than through a secretary. Cody had surmised — incorrectly — that Henderson was being used as an intermediary by a cautious government that was wary of a direct approach.

'The government haven't been straight with us, that's true,' Cody replied, 'but I don't want to demonize them. They're fundamentally decent people, of that I have no doubt. Even people like Van Buren were probably acting from the best of motives, even if their actions were . . . misguided. They aren't evil, though.

I was a barrister, and in my time I represented some genuinely unsavoury characters.' His expression changed as unwelcome memories intruded. 'I know what evil is, Mr Henderson, believe me.'

'No, no,' Henderson shot back, holding out his hands, palms extended towards Cody. 'Please don't mistake my inference. I don't mean to imply that anybody's acting out of genuine malice. What I mean is – and here I speak as somebody who's been a politician – that the government are acting out of self-interest. And my question is this: is their self-interest compatible with the interests of the people?'

'The government's interest is in staying in power,' Cody ventured.

'Will they fight to keep it?' Henderson asked.

'They already have.' It was Thornton who replied and Henderson couldn't have been more pleased at the comment.

'Yeeees', Cody replied, without conviction. 'Perhaps. But it's equally possible that they fought simply because they were attacked.'

'What if I could prove to you otherwise?' Henderson leant forward and lowered his voice, as if afraid of being overheard. 'What if I told you that these . . . *visitors* . . . had made friendly overtures, years ago, and that this had been covered-up by a ruling élite who wanted their technology but feared the upheaval that would result from contact.'

Cody looked at Thornton, then back into Henderson's face, trying to read the man. 'Is that what you're telling me happened?'

'Yes.'

Downing Street, Whitehall

'Let's run through a few options here,' the PM ventured, casually. 'Suppose we get into a war-fighting situation and suppose I authorize you to carry out defensive operations only.' He turned his gaze on to CDS. 'You tell me that you've already begun drawing up contingency plans. Let's hear them.'

CDS looked uncomfortable and glanced at S of S's face, not

wanting to undermine his authority. But Willoughby's expression was impassive and he gave no indication that he'd been offended when the PM had posed the question directly to the military officer and not to his political boss.

'Defensively?' CDS began. 'Well, we already have our aircraft widely dispersed, either in hardened shelters or under camouflage nets. We're protecting these aircraft – and all key military installations – with various short-range air-defence assets such as Rapier, Javelin and Starstreak. Add to that several SAS units armed with Stinger ground-to-air missiles – some of those units are carrying out covert surveillance on the houses of known abductees. We have Typhoons carrying out constant Combat Air Patrols, with AWACS AEW aircraft providing top cover. Our ground-based radar installations are nearly repaired after the battering they took during Operation Thunder Child, and are running at around ninety per cent of normal capability – we hope to get that back up to a hundred within two weeks. The space-tracking radar at RAF Fylingdales is being repaired but won't be operational for another month, at least. But RAF Feltwell is up and running, and the Americans are sharing data.'

'Are we sure about that?' It was the leader of the Opposition who had asked this question, keen to be involved in both the discussion and the decision-making process and wanting to be seen making useful contributions.

'Yes, sir,' CDS responded. 'The new CO made a point of requesting the presence of a British liaison team at the facility. There's no operational reason for that: it's clearly a political offer, to show us they've got nothing to hide. We accepted the invitation, of course, and I'm told that our people have total access. The Americans are playing it straight.'

'OK, good,' the PM replied. 'But please tell us your estimation of the situation. If we're attacked, what are our chances?'

'OK, I'll answer that,' CDS began. 'But I want to qualify my reply. We really don't know the capabilities of our enemy, or the extent of their assets. Van Buren's given us *some* information but we can't be certain that he's been truthful. I understand they've asked him to take a polygraph test and that he's consented; we'll see. But here's an important point: even if he's not lying, who's to say his . . . *friends* . . . were being straight with him? Indeed, it's likely that he was deliberately misled in many ways and that he was given disinformation.'

'But Van Buren says he's been on the ship,' the leader of the Opposition interjected. 'So assuming he's telling the truth – and presumably the lie-detector test will resolve that issue – surely he'll be able to give us useful first-hand observations about their capabilities?'

CDS nodded slowly. 'That's true, but only up to a point. I could show you around an aircraft carrier but unless you were a naval man or knew what to look for I could give you a completely sanitized tour – and you'd never know. It's not what you show, it's what you *don't* show.'

'That's an interesting analogy, as it happens,' S of S interjected. 'In many ways that's what we're facing. If Van Buren is to be believed, these aliens are completely cut off from their source – once they left their home own planet, they had no further contact with it. They change their appearance, they adapt themselves to life on Earth and by the time they arrive, they're essentially human – their home world would be alien to them. And the journey's taken two or three generations, so it's the descendants of the original colonists who complete the journey.'

The Prime Minister encouraged these sorts of free-flowing discussions in all aspects of government business. They tended to become brainstorming sessions and often threw up interesting ideas. But he still hadn't had an answer to the key question, and decided it was time to refocus the group. 'Our chances, then?' Again, it was CDS, as the UK's senior military officer, to whom he turned his gaze.

'With defensive Rules of Engagement – lousy. They'd steadily degrade and diminish our capability until we were dead in the water. They'd probably start by taking out our satellites and then go to work on the radar network. After that, I guess they'd just keep hitting our military bases and keep chipping away, aircraft by aircraft, ship by ship . . .' CDS's voice trailed off, appalled at the thought.

'But we've had successes against them before. We adapted our tactics and managed to inflict some losses.' The PM was genuinely surprised that CDS was being so downbeat. The military had always struck him as being 'can-do' people.

'Yes, but at what cost?' CDS retorted, a little too sharply. 'Besides, all our analyses suggest they were hamstrung by their aim of protecting their base at Bentwaters: hitting us was never their primary aim. If it had been, they could have attacked Main Building or the PJHQ. Significant hits on either site would have crippled us. It's likely that much of the hostile action was – so far as they were concerned – little more than a test of strength. They were sizing us up.'

'So you're telling me we don't have a chance?' The PM stared hard at CDS.

'With defensive ROE, that's right. It's just a matter of time. But remember that aircraft carrier analogy, and run with it. If you're being attacked from a carrier, you can shoot down lots of their aircraft but still lose the battle. But if you sink the carrier – game over.'

S of S picked up this theme. 'CDS is right, Prime Minister. The fact that they're cut off from their source means they have no support. They're on their own, on just *one* ship. For all their power, that makes them *incredibly* vulnerable.'

'Do you have any ideas about how we might take the fight to the enemy?'

'Yes, Prime Minister.'

Farnham, Surrey

'Mr Cody, Ms Thornton, let me tell you the official history of our contact with extraterrestrials.' Maxwell Henderson leaned forward in his chair, made eye contact with his two hosts, and began his story. 'Several hundred years ago this planet was visited by extraterrestrials hungry for new worlds to colonize. Their species had outgrown their own planet, not just in terms of population density but also in a sort of psychological sense. It's difficult to explain, but it was as if they'd grown tired of it. They had controlled its environment and shaped it to their needs, but there were no more challenges to face and no more mysteries to explore. As a species, they were like children who awake one day to find that they're teenagers and suddenly realized that their toys meant nothing to them any more. They wanted something else, but they didn't quite know what.'

Cody and Thornton listened, captivated, as Henderson presented to them, on a plate, the very thing that they'd pursued so intently for decades.

'But to understand the aliens, you need first to understand humans in a way that few people do. I apologize if this sounds like a lecture, but you of all people deserve to know the truth. Most animals are driven by four basic needs: survival, nourishment, shelter and reproduction. But we live in a world where resources are scarce and demand outstrips supply, so we have aggression, as when animals fight over food or compete for a mate. Animals develop survival strategies, such as speed or strength, and evolution ensures that the weak are weeded out – the survival of the fittest, as they say.'

'Classical Darwinian theory' Cody observed.

'Precisely. Now, the churches used to say that humanity was unique and made in God's image, with consciousness representing some form of divine gift. Modern theory suggests otherwise, and postulates that intelligence is nothing more mysterious than a survival strategy. If we can't outrun or outfight the predator, we can *out-think* it. With intelligence comes consciousness, and then comes something else: curiosity; the need to explore; the urge to climb a mountain. At first glance this seems to offend against Darwinian theory since we don't climb mountains to look for food but *just because* they're there. We endanger ourselves needlessly. So it seems at first as if curiosity is an illogical trait.'

Thornton opened her mouth as if to say something, then thought better of it and let Henderson continue uninterrupted.

'Now consider the extraterrestrials and their predicament. They are masters of their own world, where they have eliminated most sources of danger. But any species confined to one environment is vulnerable, even on a planetary scale. An asteroid strike or a new virus could decimate or even destroy them. In any case, one day their sun will inevitably exhaust its supply of nuclear fuel and either explode or fizzle out. Either way, their existence is finite. To ensure survival, they must spread out from their planet and colonize new worlds – and that's where curiosity comes in. Curiosity, intelligence and consciousness are all inextricably linked.'

'So curiosity is . . . Darwinian . . . after all?' Thornton had struggled with the word but clearly had no difficulty understanding the concept.

'Yes. Curiosity led us to put a man on the moon and send probes to planets and satellites within our solar system. Several of our space probes have now left the solar system altogether, and NASA have been studying the possibility of an actual star mission for some years. The Hubble Space Telescope scans the heavens, while various SETI projects have used radio astronomy to listen for extraterrestrial transmissions. We are an outward-looking species – and so are the extraterrestrials. Ultimately, it's all about survival. The aliens aren't good and they aren't evil. They're driven by the same basic Darwinian principles that drive us and their thought processes are similar to our own. If the positions had been reversed, *we*'d be the alien invaders.'

Cody thought about it, and agreed that there was a certain logic to this idea. Since the human race had first developed, they'd always thrust onwards and outwards, aggressively pushing back the frontiers of their environment. Forests had been cut down, land had been brought under the plough, the oceans had been crossed, and now – as Henderson had pointed out – humanity was beginning to take its first tentative steps into space, fulfilling what seemed like an age-old destiny. People had always been fascinated by the moon and the stars, and celestial objects became objects of pagan veneration very early in humanity's history. But once science had identified the true nature of these celestial objects, people began to wonder about the possibility of life elsewhere in the universe. *But we didn't find them – they found us.*

'So that's the story of the aliens – who they are, and what motivates them. As you can see, there's nothing mysterious about it. Now let me tell you about how they first came here – and what happened next. The story of significant contact between aliens and humans goes back over a period of more than sixty years. It's a story of lies, deception and concealment – not on the part of the extraterrestrials, but on that of our own governments.'

Downing Street, Whitehall

CDS had everybody's attention as he began to outline a plan that had already been discussed in some detail within the walls of the MOD's headquarters building, known simply and rather unimaginatively as Main Building. 'We need to forget about these UFOs, scout craft, fighter craft – whatever it is that you want to call them. In a purely strategic sense, they don't matter. Only their main ship matters and our aim – if it comes to a fight – must be to destroy it. We can do this best with nuclear weapons.'

Although the PM and the leader of the Opposition were hearing this for the first time, neither of them raised any objections or looked remotely surprised. It was an entirely predictable strategy.

'Much depends on the defensive capabilities of the ship,' CDS continued. 'Are we under surveillance? Can they detect any spacecraft we launch? Would they spot a space shuttle heading for them, or a missile on an intercept course? These are questions that we need to consider. We need to wait until Van Buren takes his polygraph test and analyse the results. Then – allowing for the fact that he may have been fed disinformation, or that he simply won't know certain things – we need to get our own direct observational data, from Hubble and from other sources. This will get easier as the ship gets closer, but from Van Buren's initial debriefing sessions, and from our own initial analyses, we think we already have a rough idea what we're up against.'

'Go on,' the PM instructed.

CDS consulted his notes. Although a highly intelligent man,

the subject of their discussion was way outside his traditional expertise. The Defence Scientific Staff and the Defence Intelligence Staff had worked closely on an analysis, supplementing direct observational data with informed guesses where necessary. 'Einstein's Theory of General Relativity suggests that no object could be accelerated to a speed greater than that of light – that's around one hundred and eighty-six thousand miles per *second*. As you accelerate an object, its mass increases and time slows down.'

'How can time slow down?' the PM asked. It wasn't an unreasonable question for a man who, though gifted in many areas of study, had very little mathematics or physics. It was CSA who answered.

'It's a mistake to think of space and time as distinct, Prime Minister. If you think of them as linked – "space-time" is the phrase that's used – it's easier to grasp, because everything that you do has an effect on the physical world around you. You must try to see time as an integral part of that physical world, as opposed to a mere philosophical concept. This isn't just theoretical, by the way – it's been validated through experiments. Two atomic clocks were synchronized, and one was orbited around the Earth at high speed. When it was retrieved, it was slower than the clock that had stayed in the laboratory. The point is that if you accelerated something to anywhere near light speed, its mass would increase dramatically and time would slow right down. Before you could cross the light barrier, time would stop and the mass of the craft would become infinite. Therefore it's not possible to accelerate a craft to a speed faster than that of light.'

'OK, OK,' the PM conceded, wishing fervently that his scientific knowledge matched that he had of the arts.

'Anyway,' CDS continued, 'the scout craft seem to have got around this problem. We think – from examination of the crashed UFOs we have – that they use a focused gravity beam to warp space-time. Space-time already warps around any massive object, like a star. Imagine the way a waterbed would be distorted if you put a bowling ball on it. If you could amplify this effect, you'd have no need to accelerate at all. You would simply fold space-time until you'd dragged the location you wanted to your position.' Neither the PM nor the leader of the Opposition looked as if they understood, so CDS decided to demonstrate the proposition. He took a piece of paper and drew two points on it, labelling them A and B. 'What's the shortest distance between two points?' he asked.

'A straight line,' the PM ventured.

'Normally, yes,' CDS replied, drawing a line linking the two points. But look – suppose I do this.' He carefully folded the piece of paper, so that point A was superimposed on point B.

'Aaah, I *see*.'

'Well, it takes a lot of energy to do this, and only something with a small mass can travel in this way. The aliens' main vessel has a phenomenal mass and is therefore capable of only sub-light speed. We think that it managed to accelerate to somewhere between point three and point four of light speed, and that doesn't offend against any laws of physics. Indeed, NASA has publicly stated that a so-called star mission with such speeds should be feasible by the end of the twenty-first century. To achieve this, there are two possible means of propulsion. The first is nuclear fission, but the second, which is far more likely, is a propulsion system based on the mutual annihilation of matter and antimatter. And if that's the case, their ship has an Achilles' heel. Let me explain.'

Farnham, Surrey

'We don't know when the aliens first arrived,' Henderson explained, 'but it must have been several hundred years ago, because that's how long their ship's been on its way. We don't know where their home world is, but we *think* it's close, in galactic terms, and probably within fifty light years of our solar system.'

'Zeta Reticuli', Thornton interjected, suggesting a location long regarded by certain ufologists as being home to the beings known as the Greys. This theory stemmed from data retrieved through a hypnotic regression carried out on Betty Hill, an American woman who, together with her husband Barney, claimed to have had an experience in 1961 which was the first widely publicized account of what came to be known as an alien abduction. She'd drawn a map which she recalled having seen onboard the craft on to which she remembered having been taken, and an amateur astronomer had subsequently produced a controversial but widely reported theory that suggested Zeta Reticuli 1 or 2 might be the aliens' home world.

'Possibly,' Henderson nodded, 'but given the direction from which the mothership is coming, Epsilon Eridani or Tau Ceti are more likely. They're both sun-like stars, both around eleven light years away – very near in stellar terms, and over four times closer than Zeta Reculi. I'm sorry, I don't mean to sound patronizing, but my group have considered this in some detail. Anyway, there are numerous possibilities although in many ways this is irrelevant, because the colonists cut all links with their planet of origin, so working out its location presents us with nothing useful.'

'So,' Cody mused, 'they will receive no support from back home. They're on their own. That's interesting.'

'Yes, it is. And it's dangerous knowledge, because it just might convince our foolhardy leaders that they can destroy the ship.'

'Would that be a bad thing?' Thornton asked. She, after all, had suffered abuse at the hands of these entities.

Henderson looked at her, staring into her eyes. 'Ms Thornton, there are around *one billion* intelligent beings on that ship. Now, they may have done questionable things, but they're not coming here to wipe us out: they want to integrate themselves into our society. Would you sanction the deaths of one billion lives?' He held her gaze until she looked away.

Cody cleared his throat as if he was about to say something, but Henderson was already speaking. 'Let me continue, if I may, and give you a little history lesson. These entities discovered this planet on a scouting mission and declared it suitable for colonization. A ship was constructed and began its long voyage. Unlike the small craft, it travels at significantly less than light speed and the journey from its home world to Earth takes somewhere between fifty and a hundred years, the mission being completed by descendants of the entities who originally set out. This process is not unique. They have done it before and will do it again. Eventually, the worlds they colonize will do the same. One day, the ship the colonists arrive in will be used to take colonists from Earth to another world. There's something else: over the course of the voyage, they alter themselves, genetically, so that they look human. The Greys represent the intermediate stage in this transformation. The next generation are entirely human.'

'So they can pass among us unnoticed, infiltrate our institutions and take over the world.' Thornton's assessment was delivered with heavy sarcasm. She still didn't know whether to trust Henderson.

'No. So they can integrate into society without making us feel, ah, alienated – so to speak. Oh, don't get me wrong, they're not coming here to take menial jobs and live in ghettos. They're going to be the new ruling élite, but they're not going to kill anybody. Did either of you study history?'

Cody and Thornton were caught off balance by the unexpected question. 'A little,' Cody replied. Thornton gave a vague nod.

'It's not unlike the Norman Conquest, when viewed from the perspective of the average Anglo-Saxon serf. One ruling élite was replaced by another, and there was no adverse effect for the ordinary folks. They were certainly no worse off, and in the long term England benefited from these events and was significantly strengthened by them. England's emergence as a major European power in the Middle Ages had its roots in the Norman Conquest.'

'I see the analogy,' Cody conceded. 'But please tell us about these entities' dealings with our governments.'

'Once the ship was on its way, scout craft based on it made trips to and from Earth. This they could do almost instantaneously, as they are capable of faster-than-light travel. There were several reasons for those trips. They had to study us – learn our languages and our customs, examine our psychology to see how we'd react to their arrival, and gauge what resistance we might offer. They also, of course, had to take genetic samples so that they could begin to alter themselves and adapt their systems to life on Earth.' He looked apologetically at Thornton. 'That's where the abductions came in.'

Thornton exhaled in a drawn-out way that might have been a sigh, but made no other comment.

'They established some facilities here at various locations, some of which are names known to ufologists: Dulce, the El Yunque National Rain Forest in Puerto Rico, and, of course, Bentwaters. Most were abandoned in the 1980s and Bentwaters, as the whole world now knows, was destroyed a few weeks ago. That was their last operational facility.'

'And you're telling us that the government knew all about this?' Cody asked, trying to refocus the discussion on the matter that most interested him.

'Most certainly, yes. Whatever you may believe to the contrary, a UFO really *did* crash at Roswell. What happened next was precisely what happens after any *terrestrial* air crash; it's so logical I'm amazed no ufologist thought of it. Basically, *others* came to claim back their compatriots. They found a recovery operation under way, with the Americans thinking they'd found a Soviet aircraft and wondering if it had been trying to take out Roswell Army Air Field in a pre-emptive strike since it was home to the only atomic-bomb-capable squadron in the world, the famous 509th Bomb Group. Once the authorities found the bodies – thrown clear of the craft – it was obvious they weren't Soviet, so the extraterrestrials showed their hand.'

'And a deal was done?'

'Yes, Mr Cody. A mixture of threats and promises – mainly the latter, and largely concerning offers of technology: particularly attractive because of the Cold War. But, at the same time, the extraterrestrials knew that their ship would arrive in little over sixty years and they were genuinely surprised and frightened by the pace of our advancement. So they levelled with a few key officials and offered them partnership and global supremacy for the American Dream. The offer was readily accepted, and the world in which we live today is, to a great extent, a consequence of that alliance. Much "ufology" was devised by a small group of officials who knew that the best way to hide an alien presence that was becoming more intrusive was to drown it in a sea of nonsense. Revelation is disinformation; whistleblowers are either paid assets or patsies—'

'And all the time, the witnesses were discredited and the abductees were ridiculed,' Thornton observed bitterly.

'I'm afraid so. I'm sorry, I really am. Anyway, that's about it. There's lots that I don't know, and I can't guarantee I've got everything right – it's difficult trying to untangle sixty years of lies – but I'm convinced that you now have most of the key facts.'

'Mr Henderson, what exactly is your interest in this matter, and how come you know so much?' Thornton asked. She was naturally suspicious, and having just listened to an account that involved sustained and massive deception by various Establishment figures, she was understandably reluctant to accept the word of another such person – especially when she'd been one of the victims of the deception.

'I'm an influential figure.' It was delivered in a matter-of-fact way, with no trace of egotism. 'I'm well connected and have numerous contacts with politicians, business people and many other key individuals. There's an informal group of which I'm a member—' He stopped short when he saw the look on Thornton's face, and realized why she was anxious. Many ufologists were conspiracy theorists who feared the malign influence of secret organizations that had mysterious names like The Brotherhood or The Illuminati. Real organizations such as the Trilateral Commission and the Bilderberg Group had been tarred with this brush and were often portrayed as groups dedicated to bringing about a New World Order with a ruling élite in charge. Henderson had miscalculated, and needed to avert Thornton's suspicions. 'It's nothing sinister, I promise you. We act as a kind of think-tank, funding projects that the multinationals wouldn't touch and giving a voice to people who otherwise wouldn't have one. We sponsor research into disease control and run various environmental projects in the developing world. We fund several small publishing companies that handle New Age books, and we were a major force in setting up the Internet. We're generally left of centre but it's not a political organization, as such. We try to be a force for good in the world, and do things because— well, because they're worth doing. When NASA pulled the plug on the SETI project, we provided much of the private finance that kept it going. We've funded groups working on the threat posed to the Earth by comets and asteroids.'

'So what's your agenda now?' Cody asked.

'As I said, I'm very well connected with the Establishment. I have inside information about the current situation. Governments of the world are preparing to wage war on the extraterrestrials, simply to protect their own interests. But there are many of us who are appalled at the prospect and wonder whether there might not be another way. I know these aliens have done bad things, but haven't *we?*'

'What do you want from us? Cody asked.

'You both have great expertise in this field,' Henderson replied. 'So we'd like you to brief us on the whole UFO and abduction issue and help us sort out the wheat from the chaff. But we want you to do more than that. You're both well respected within a discipline where there are, quite frankly, a lot of cultists and crackpots. People know your names and your faces and they listen to what you have to say. We want your help in spreading our message of peace. We want you to help us stop a war.'

Downing Street, Whitehall

'As well as Van Buren's as yet unverified testimony about the construction of the alien craft, we can make certain assumptions about the ship,' CDS was explaining. 'We can reasonably suppose that it's constructed not unlike our naval vessels, with separate compartments that can be isolated from each other in case of trouble. That way, if there's a hull breach – perhaps caused by structural failure or asteroid strike – the overall integrity of the vessel isn't compromised.'

'Does the fact that space is a vacuum make any difference here?'

the PM asked. For a non-scientist, it was a perceptive question.

'To a certain extent, yes, Prime Minister. If we did breach the hull, the compartments behind would instantly depressurize. There wouldn't be fires and explosions, because there'd be no oxygen. The compartments affected would be destroyed, and the contents blown out into space, but we couldn't count on there being any sort of explosive chain reaction. And they're unlikely to have any critical systems near the hull – they'll be deep within the vessel, close to the core. Well protected.'

'With one exception? This Achilles' heel you mentioned?'

'Yes, Prime Minister. We believe that the ship uses a propulsion system powered by the annihilation of matter and antimatter. Specifically, one in which protons and antiprotons will be destroyed, producing massive amounts of energy. This destruction produces a vast quantity of short-lived particles called pions. These are manipulated by magnetic fields and converted into thrust. America's Jet Propulsion Laboratory has been carrying out theoretical research into this concept, so it's fairly well understood. The difficulty, of course, is in storing the antiprotons because, as I've said, if they come in contact with ordinary protons they'll be annihilated. Now, here's the thing: the antiprotons have to be combined with the protons under carefully controlled conditions, but this *must* happen right at the back of the craft, because that's where the pion stream must be ejected so as to create the thrust.' CDS paused, to gauge the expressions on the faces around him. He needed to see whether they understood.

'So,' the PM mused, 'if we can attack the rear of the craft, we might destroy whatever mechanism is keeping the antiprotons apart from the ordinary matter of which the ship's built. Controlled annihilation becomes uncontrolled.' The PM clearly did understand.

'That's right. We don't know how many antiprotons there are – many will have been used up during the flight – but we're guessing there'll be enough to do the job. We believe that if we can damage or destroy their containment mechanism, the antiprotons will fly off in all directions, obliterating matter as they go. The resultant damage would be vastly more powerful than the effects of nuclear blasts, and far more extensive. At the very least, we think we'd blow the entire end off the ship and this *might* be enough to destroy it altogether.'

'It sounds as if you've been doing a lot of work on this,' the leader of the Opposition observed. The PM had been careful to consult him during the events of Operation Thunder Child, to prevent the issue becoming political. Constitutionally, it was imperative that the leader of the Opposition should be involved in such momentous decisions. Now he was eager to ensure that he was fully included in the decision-making process – and concerned that he might have been sidelined.

'The MOD routinely plan for all contingencies, sir,' CDS replied. He saw what was troubling the man. 'This sort of planning goes on all the time, but we can't and won't take any action without political authority, not just from MOD Ministers but from the PM.'

'I'm hearing this briefing for the first time,' the PM interjected, defusing the situation. It was time to wrap things up. 'OK, thanks for the brief. I'll need to discuss this with Cabinet colleagues, then take it to Buckingham Palace for final approval. But let me make one thing clear: I regard this as a last option. If we can come to a peaceful solution we will. And I don't relish fighting this one alone, so I'll need to discuss this with our allies. Carry on refining this plan – do we have an op name yet?'

'Yes, Prime Minister,' CDS replied. 'We call it Operation Lightning Strike.'

The PM nodded grimly. It was a devilishly appropriate name for what they had in mind.

Farnham, Surrey

'What about what's just happened?' Cody asked. 'The UK's just got into a shooting war with these creatures. How did that happen?'

'We don't know, for certain,' Henderson replied. 'As you know from official announcements, it seems that we just got lucky – or, perhaps, *un*lucky – and stumbled upon the aliens' last efforts to evacuate their facility at Bentwaters. The RAF started to pay attention to transient radar signals that had previously been written off as spurious and decided to take a closer look. Their efforts were hindered by a small cabal of US officials who'd made a deal with the aliens. But this duplicity was exposed, and the US President brought the Americans in on our side.'

'So now what?' Thornton's question was all the more poignant because of its unpretentious simplicity.

'So now we try to mobilize public opinion against a continuation of violence. We build on my political contacts and start lobbying. We try to influence parliament and the press and, through them, public opinion. We might also try – through the scientific community – to make contact with the aliens ourselves.' He looked at Thornton. 'We might also try using the abductees to establish a line of communication.'

'Ahhh, so *that*'s what you want from me.' Thornton suddenly felt offended. It wasn't her expertise Henderson was after, it was her body – and, in a way, didn't that make him as bad as the aliens?

Henderson knew he'd made a mistake in raising this possibility so soon but tried subtly to turn it to his advantage. 'I'm sorry to sound so insensitive but I wanted to be truthful with you from the beginning, rather than spring it on you later.'

'OK, point taken.' A noncommittal response.

'The reason this is *so* important is because of the Americans – or rather, a small cabal within the US military and intelligence agencies. They accepted the deal they were offered and received technology in exchange for help in hiding the alien presence. But they wanted to keep their options open and began developing weapons that could be used against the aliens.'

'The Star Wars programme?' Cody asked.

'In part, yes. So now we have a formidable array of hardware, ranging from ground-based lasers to high-altitude missiles, which are *ostensibly* for anti-missile defence or for use in an anti-satellite role. Have you noticed how much talk there is these days about the threat to the Earth from comets and asteroids? Well, that's another front for the development of weapons and tactics that could be turned against the aliens.'

'Is this *entirely* a bad thing?' Cody asked. 'Doesn't it make sense to – as you put it – keep our options open?'

'Not really, no,' Henderson replied. 'We could make a nuisance of ourselves, I'm sure. We could dent their capability somewhat. But make no mistake, if we looked as though we presented a threat to the aliens' overall mission, their plans would change.'

'Oh?'

'They're not evil, and they'll work with us if they can. But they won't allow *anything* to jeopardize the ship. If we tried to move against them there, they'd forget about working with us – it'd be too risky. No, the moment we looked as if we posed a *real* threat, they'd wipe us out.'

Chapter Two

SECRETS AND LIES

MOD Main Building, Whitehall

Governments often think they can operate in a vacuum, believing that once a crisis has passed everything will return to normal. Experience should tell them otherwise but still they cling to the hope. In the weeks since the events of Operation Thunder Child, no further alien contact had been reported. Nothing unusual had been picked up on the radar, and no RAF aircraft had encountered anything untoward whilst flying on ever more extensive combat air patrols. But even though the skies were quiet, people didn't just forget about first contact with extraterrestrials, especially when people had died – and especially when governments had lied. And then there was the small matter of an alien vessel, now detectable on the Hubble Space Telescope and a handful of other terrestrial telescopes, heading for Earth. People don't forget such things, and there had been constant debates in parliament and saturation coverage in the media.

One man who had never deluded himself about any of this was Nick Templeton, head of Secretariat(Air Staff). In the normal course of business, Sec(AS) – as it was known – had a wide-ranging brief, looking after an assortment of air force matters covering everything from flight safety to the American presence in the UK. UFOs were just a small part of its varied portfolio – at least until recently. Before Operation Thunder Child, Templeton had had only one member of staff employed on the issue full time. The post had been regarded as one of the most interesting jobs in the Ministry: the desk officer's duties included not just researching and investigating UFO sightings and alien abductions, but everything else weird and wonderful that came to the department's attention. In the past, this had included crop circles, animal mutilations and even ghosts, leading to parallels being drawn with the fictional television series *The X-Files*.

But the Ministry's files on such phenomena were real, and now Templeton found himself heading what had become possibly the key division in the entire Ministry. He'd had – as the old saying went – a good war. Although relatively new in his post, he had an excellent grasp of his subject and always seemed well briefed. Although quite young for a Grade 5, he'd more than held his own among more senior and experienced colleagues, and had impressed Ministers and Chiefs of Staff with his hard work and his insightful analysis of the developing crisis. He'd been a key member of the Thunder Child team and, although this had won him a deserved promotion to the rank of Assistant Under-Secretary, there was no way that Ministers were going to risk losing his expertise. It all worked out rather well: Sec(AS) was restructured and all its other functions aside from those relevant to the crisis were transferred to the Command Secretary's division at HQ Strike Command at High Wycombe. New staff were posted in from various operational secretariats, with the aim of assembling a team of high-flyers with experience of crisis management. All these staff had to have been through the strictest Developed Vetting, on the understanding that they would need to be cleared for access to the most highly classified material in the Ministry. The new division needed to be headed by somebody with more rank than a Grade 5 and, as Templeton was to become an AUS, promoting him *in situ* was the obvious and ideal solution.

Templeton's first job had been to develop what amounted to a new division from the bottom up. He'd split his staff into sections responsible for discrete topics: one section investigated new reports of UFO sightings while another looked into the latest claims of alien abduction; there was a section devoted to searching old UFO files at the Public Record Office and elsewhere, and one that was tasked with monitoring data on the Internet. The largest of the sections had the unenviable task of ploughing through the civilian UFO literature, desperately trying to discover useful nuggets of information among numerous books and magazines. The final three sections dealt with media affairs, parliamentary business and overseas liaison respectively. Templeton, often working fourteen-hour days, tried to keep up to speed with all this work, trusting his deputies to deal with the day-to-day business but insisting on being briefed on any significant discoveries or developments.

This particular afternoon Templeton had a visitor who had himself been very much at the centre of events during Operation Thunder Child. Martin Blackmore was the Under-Secretary of State, which was the junior ministerial position at the MOD, reporting to S of S through a Minister of State. Technically speaking, Blackmore wasn't Templeton's boss – the civil servant had his own departmental chain of command – but it was working out that way in practice.

The Minister had just completed a walkabout of the new and improved Sec(AS), accompanied by his personal secretary, Sue Farthing. It was a rare opportunity for the Minister to meet the desk officers who prepared much of his briefing material, and he welcomed the chance to press the flesh and offer sincere thanks for all the hard work that he knew was being done. Blackmore was regarded as a safe pair of hands, and was well respected both within the MOD and among his fellow politicians. One reason for this was that he was prepared to listen to comments and ideas from whatever source, regardless of grade or rank. So he'd been pleased that some of the comparatively junior desk officers hadn't been afraid to voice their opinions as he'd toured the section.

With the tour over, Farthing had returned to the Minister's outer office, leaving Blackmore alone with Templeton. The two men sipped coffees that had been thoughtfully prepared by Templeton's private secretary. It was a rare and useful chance to talk things through privately, without the presence of anyone from the Air Staff or the Press Office.

'You've built up a good team here, Nick; they look a smart bunch, not afraid to speak their minds.'

'Thank you, Minister. There's a very steep learning curve, but everybody's doing well and working very hard.'

'I heard one or two interesting ideas on the shop floor'

'Oh yes?'

'Yes. There was a feeling that the division might benefit from having a couple of members of the Defence Scientific Staff seconded over to help out with the technical stuff. You're consulting them so frequently that it makes sense to have them here as part of the team. And there was a general feeling that we should be more proactive.'

'I agree on the first point. I'll take that forward. As for the second, well,' Templeton shrugged, 'it's difficult to know what to do. I'd venture to say that's more of a political issue.'

'Yes. As you know, there's to be a UN debate on the matter, but our most immediate problem is the demonstration.'

The Minister had raised an issue that had been troubling him somewhat. Scientific confirmation of the existence of a craft heading for Earth, coupled with the fact that since the destruction of the Bentwaters facility there had been no further instances of UFOs being detected on radar, had led to attention shifting away from the MOD. But now there was to be a demonstration outside Main Building, and this would have the unwelcome effect of putting the Department firmly back in the spotlight. The action had seemingly been organized on the Internet by a loose network of anarchists, peace groups and UFO organizations. It was being billed as 'a march for peace and truth', but the fact that the anonymous organizers weren't prepared to meet the police or provide stewards was not a good sign. Most of the attendees clearly would be well intentioned, but the Home Secretary had confirmed that the Security Service knew of a hard core of known troublemakers who were expected to attend.

'I've spoken to the Chief Press Officer about that and we agree that there'll be an upsurge of media interest generated by the demonstration,' Templeton began. 'But we've got very comprehensive defensive lines ready and are confident we'll be able to cope with the anticipated increase in press, radio and TV attention. There'll almost certainly be a knock-on political effect: we can expect to see the matter raised in Parliamentary Questions, and perhaps another debate.'

'Hmm. The PM may have to lead on that, depending on the wording of the motion. I'm not shrugging this off but we can't expect MOD to lead on the wider issues posed by this business.'

'No, Minister,' Templeton agreed, 'though doubtless the lion's share of the questions will be directed at us. What we do need to think about is what to do if programmes like *Newsnight* ask us to put up a Minister to go on the programme. I've had preliminary discussions about this with Jacqui Connolly.'

The Minister was relieved to discover that just because Sec(AS) now incorporated a media affairs section, he wasn't cutting the Chief Press Officer out of the loop. 'Your recommendation?'

'It depends who else is on the show. If they do a piece on the demonstration, we don't suggest you share a platform with some anarchist, especially if the demo is violent. But if things pass off peacefully, or if there's a discussion with scientists and other respectable figures, it would seem churlish not to take part – especially since one of the themes of the protest is open government. It would look bad if the piece ended: "We asked the MOD to take part in this programme, but they declined". It might make the demonstrators' point for them.'

'Hmm. We'll cross that bridge when we come to it.'

RAF Coningsby, Lincolnshire

'Hey, Izz, how's it going?'

'All quiet on the Eastern Front.' Flying Officer Isabelle

Bentley's humorous response raised a few chuckles in the crew-room, and her fellow pilots were pleased to see that one of the liveliest personalities on the squadron seemed to be returning to her normal cheery self. Bentley had been heavily involved in Operation Thunder Child and had flown as many combat missions as any of them, distinguishing herself in the process. One in particular had earned her the Distinguished Flying Cross – an award given to RAF officers who perform acts of gallantry while on active service. It had been an assignment involving an attempt to bring down a UFO and it might have succeeded – had the mission not been aborted when it had been revealed that there might have been American military personnel on the craft. But Bentley had undertaken a difficult assignment from which she'd known she might not return, and this had been justly rewarded. This was the mission described in her citation, but it was not one she dwelt on.

The operation that haunted Bentley was the one in which another RAF pilot – Stuart Coultart – had earned the Victoria Cross. His medal had been awarded posthumously, and Bentley had been badly affected by the death of the brave young pilot who had deliberately rammed one of the alien craft to save the seventeen crew members on board an AEW Sentry aircraft that had been under attack. Bentley was a naturally gregarious person with an outgoing personality, but she'd been hit hard by Coultart's death. She'd wondered whether this reaction might be due to a sense of guilt. Why hadn't she thought to do what he'd done? Or *had* she thought of it, subconsciously, but not been prepared to make the ultimate sacrifice? She'd done much soul-searching and her friends and colleagues had noticed her becoming more introspective. This was why her quip had been noticed and appreciated by the other pilots. It looked as if the old happy-go-lucky Isabelle Bentley might be back. They'd missed her.

'No contacts?' somebody asked. Bentley had just come back from a standard combat air patrol mission over the North Sea, as part of a two-ship formation. The pilot who'd asked the question was due to fly later and, although he'd receive a formal brief before he took off, nobody wasted an opportunity to get ahead of the game.

'Not a squeak,' Bentley replied. It had been this way for weeks now. They could almost believe the crisis was over, were it not that astronomers had confirmed the presence of an immense spacecraft heading for the Earth. It looked so tiny when pictured in newspapers and magazines. In truth it was just a point of light, indistinguishable from the background stars had it not been for the circles and arrows inserted by helpful picture editors. Some people were talking about extending the hand of friendship to what they chose to call 'the visitors'. Well, they'd tried that, hadn't they? Few of the RAF's elite Typhoon force had much time for such talk – hardly surprising, since some of them had seen 'the visitors' blow friends and colleagues out of the sky.

'I wish *something* would happen,' one of the less experienced pilots said. 'I wish the politicians and the scientists would work out what's going on and give us a mission.'

'Don't wish for something *too* hard; you may just get it.' This pearl of wisdom was offered by an old hand – a veteran of the Gulf War and the Kosovo crisis who had an instinctive feel for these things. He clearly felt it was only a matter of time before they'd be in action again. And nobody disagreed with his assessment.

The Pentagon, Virginia

It was a building in which coups had been plotted, wars planned and decisions taken that had touched the lives of millions. Ideas formulated within its walls had led to the fall of governments and the emergence of new leaders. Although policy decisions were taken at a higher level, much of the history of the modern world was the result of work done by anonymous desk officers working here for their political and military bosses. Lives lost, lives saved; if the building had had a heart, it would have been heavy with the burden of the secrets it knew.

One of the many interesting facts about the Pentagon was its status as the largest office block in the world. The sprawling headquarters of the US military and the Defense Department covered a site of nearly thirty acres, and its location in the Washington suburb of Arlington was a stone's throw from the political heart of America.

Now the Pentagon was to be the scene of an interrogation, of sorts. The man on the receiving end was the former National Security Agency Director, Edwin Van Buren. In the weeks that had passed since the exposure of his involvement in some sort of deal with the extraterrestrials, he had been kept under what amounted to house arrest. He was being held in what he recognized as the type of premises where – during the Cold War and on several more recent occasions – defectors had been taken to be debriefed. He was well treated but there were limits to his freedom, restricting although not entirely prohibiting his access to any means of communication. As ever, law, justice and the American constitution made uneasy bedfellows. There were military personnel on hand – for his own protection, he had been told.

The whole situation was a jurisdictional and legal nightmare; Van Buren had undoubtedly committed a number of offences, but nobody was entirely clear how the law applied to the situation in hand. Van Buren had waived the right to legal counsel, arguing that he had acted in the best interests of the country. The President had stepped in with an offer that she had only just sold to the key players: Van Buren would receive immunity from prosecution, on condition that he consented to an unlimited series of debriefings that would be validated by polygraph tests, hypnosis and drugs – the drugs to be administered under the supervision of a doctor to be nominated by Van Buren. If he cooperated, told no lies and held back no useful information, he would receive a signed statement from the President confirming that no legal action would be taken in respect of any offence committed prior to his debriefing. But if he once told a lie, gave a deliberately misleading answer or knowingly omitted any significant detail that subsequently emerged and that should reasonably have been declared, all bets were off.

Van Buren had agreed and was about to begin the first session, which was to be a preliminary discussion with just four interrogators: the US Secretary of State for Defense, the Chairman of the Joint Chiefs of Staff and two British officers – the Chief Scientific Adviser and the Chief of Defence Intelligence. The British had suffered the most deaths as a result of the recent alien activity, and while Van Buren continued to insist that this was not his fault and that he had acted in the best interests of his country – and, indeed, of the world – few people were inclined to be forgiving. The British had demanded full access to any debriefings and total cooperation from the US authorities in sharing any relevant data. The President had accepted this, managing to secure British agreement to the dropping of charges against Van Buren and the other members of The Enterprise – the small cabal of senior military and intelligence officers who had been working with Van Buren and who would in time be subjected to the same conditional debriefings as their boss.

Van Buren faced his inquisitors impassively, noting that the four of them covered all the relevant specializations: there was a politician, a military officer, a spook and a scientist. Van Buren knew and had dealt with his US colleagues and had met CDI before; General Sir Charles Crompton was known to his British colleagues as CC but such familiarity would not be tolerated here. Only CSA was new to him, and he correctly assumed that part of the reason for her presence was to keep him off balance by introducing somebody he didn't know. It was an old tactic, well known to anyone who'd ever been to spook school. The prime reason for Dr Barbara North's presence was to evaluate his testimony from a scientific standpoint.

CDI was sceptical about the usefulness of these sessions. As part of his training as an intelligence officer he'd studied the legendary interrogation of Sir Roger Hollis, the former Director-General of MI5 who'd been suspected by many of being a Soviet agent. Hollis had been 'invited' back to Leconfield House in Mayfair, four years or so after his retirement, where he'd been thoroughly grilled by a skilled and resourceful MI5 officer called John Day. The interrogation had spanned two days but the results had been inconclusive. The problem, of course, was that, innocent or guilty, Hollis knew the system too well and was conversant with all the tricks of the trade that had been used. CDI suspected that the same would apply here. They wouldn't be able to trip Van Buren up: either he'd tell the truth or he wouldn't.

Ministry of Defence, Moscow

'So, Yuri, tell me what you think is going on,' Petrov demanded.

Yuri Ivanov was the Russian Minister of Defence – a post that carried with it several of the most dire problems facing his country. In the days of the Cold War, it had been so very different. The Soviet military machine had been admired, feared and respected all over the world. Now Ivanov's prime purpose seemed to be to keep the lid on a situation that was threatening to boil over. Many troops hadn't been paid for months and only managed to make ends meet by hiring out their services to the Russian *mafiya*. The government had to turn a blind eye to this, on the basis that a large, unpaid and demoralized army was more dangerous to its political bosses than to its enemies. There were still major problems in Chechnya, lesser but still worrying ones elsewhere on the fringes of the Russian Federation, and the whole country continued to teeter on the brink of economic chaos. Many Russians looked back fondly to the days of the Cold War, and this was a growing concern for politicians both inside and outside Russia.

Sergei Petrov was mindful of all these concerns and the last thing he needed now was another problem. But this latest complication was one that couldn't be ignored, and the tall, gaunt President of the Russian Federation was determined to have some answers.

'Our scientists confirm the presence of an object that has entered the solar system and is heading for the Earth. It appears that the Americans have successfully kept the secret that lies behind this arrival for over sixty years.' Ivanov knew, as soon as the words had passed his lips, that he had made a mistake and laid himself open to criticism.

'How so? Why did we not discover this secret for ourselves?'

'The secret was known only to a handful of senior American personnel and was even successfully kept from their own government. We did look at the claims about Roswell and other incidents but decided they were false. We also carried out our own domestic studies into the UFO phenomenon. I have reviewed the files and cannot find fault with those involved. The cases we looked at were spurious. Real events – if any – are swamped by simple misidentifications of mundane objects. If mistakes have been made, they are honest ones, I'm certain.' Ivanov hated the fact that it sounded like an apology but knew this was the best way to defuse the President's anger.

Although prone to sudden and furious outbursts, Petrov was an intelligent man. His temper was kept for fools – and Ivanov was certainly no fool. There was no point in blaming people for mistakes that lay in the past, and even the President knew there were limits to his power. One did not lightly risk making an enemy of the Minister of Defence. 'How can we deal with this new threat?'

'Here around Moscow we have our ballistic missile defence system. This, as you know, comprises the Gorgon and Gazelle interceptors. The system is operational, but its effect could be limited against the sort of firepower we may be facing. Still, surface-to-air missiles such as the SA-3, SA-6 and SA-18 could thin out any attacking force, and even hand-held SAMs could be effective. Our intelligence reports suggest that the alien craft are fast but not invulnerable. They have good countermeasures but we can deal with that, so we think.' He didn't offer any technical details and Petrov clearly wasn't going to press him for them.

'Our air force?'

'We have MiG-29s and other fighters, but spare parts have been a problem and . . . the numbers of *operational* aircraft are not large.'

Petrov knew this already. 'The UN is to discuss this matter. If we fight *with* the Americans, what can they contribute?'

'Their anti-satellite technology is advanced,' Ivanov began, cautiously. He didn't like to highlight the growing technology gap but had no choice other than to give an accurate assessment. 'They have lasers and high-altitude missiles that could attack the aliens in space. It is conceivable they could configure their space shuttles for offensive military operations. Some analyses suggest this has already been done.' This elicited a grunt from the President. 'Their real strength lies in their air-to-air capability: they have stealth fighters armed with missiles such as Sparrow and Phoenix, together with other very capable fighters such as the F-14 Tomcat and the F-15 Eagle. These aircraft are old but still very effective. And we shouldn't forget other NATO nations – especially the British, who have combat experience with this new enemy. Their Typhoon Eurofighters are pretty good, and their pilots are well trained and well motivated. They too have advanced and effective air-to-air missile technology, with new systems like AMRAAM and BVRAAM.'

'So we have a chance?'

'Impossible to say; we lack detailed intelligence on the enemy's intentions and capability.' The answer was a little too sharp.

'From the preliminary analyses it seems to me that, unless we can destroy their ship in space, all we can really do is thin out the number of invaders. But if the Motherland is invaded, we shall resist – as we have always done. The size of our country will work for us, and eventually we shall triumph.'

Ivanov knew that his President was reciting orthodox military doctrine but felt that it simply wasn't applicable to the situation in hand. Still, he had one other card to play. 'Indeed so. But there is one area where our expertise is second to none – a capability that is not matched by the Americans and that may enable us to deliver a decisive blow to these new invaders.'

'Go on.'

'Our biological and chemical warfare programme has been reduced in size, as you know. But it need not be big to be effective, since so little is needed to be effective. As long as we have the necessary formulae, production facilities need not be large. And I tell you this – we *do* have these things and this could give us an advantage.'

'Then make this your top priority.'
'Very well.'

Rowledge, Surrey

Jenny Thornton had always had trouble sleeping, and knew precisely why. As a child, she'd called them the 'bad fairies' but now she knew them for what they really were. They often – though not always – came at night, and a lifetime of experiences had taught her to be wary of the darkness. *I'm not afraid of the dark – only of the things that hide in it*, she'd once written in a personal journal she'd kept for a while. Now, years later, these things seemed to be in the past. The abductions had stopped, not just for her but – if the data was to be believed – for everybody. Some people persisted in claiming they'd had such experiences and many new accounts were received. But most serious researchers felt these were spurious: there were good people involved in the phenomenon and when those people judged to be genuine said that abductions had stopped, the clear implication was that only the deluded or the fakers kept claiming they been kidnapped by aliens.

How could the researchers be so sure? Although the scientific establishment had never liked to address the situation, the fact was that a growing network of psychologists and psychiatrists had dealt with *thousands* of abduction cases in recent years, mainly in America but increasingly in Britain and elsewhere. Most of these therapists had worked on the situation in private, fearful of the damage to their reputations that might result from their association with a phenomenon that was by their own admission real yet unprovable in a strict, empirical sense. Many of these therapists were in touch with one another, and most shared data with those responsible UFO researchers who showed themselves committed to the concept of witness confidentiality. These therapists and researchers reckoned they could tell whether or not an abductee was being truthful, and were certain that it was the truthful ones who were claiming that the abductions had stopped. The alien agenda that had been served by these experiences was supposedly ended. The time for secrecy was over, and the whole world waited to see what would happen next.

Thornton's experiences might have ended but her nightmares hadn't stopped. This was why she existed on four or five hours of sleep each night and why, now, an unbidden memory intruded upon her consciousness. She had been about four or five years old and her parents had taken her out to Tilford, a pleasant village by the River Wey, not far from Rowledge. After going for a short walk along the river, they arrived at Hankley Common, one of many locations in the area that were used by the military. The site was used for parachute training and her parents had thought she'd like to see the soldiers tumbling towards the ground before opening their parachutes and drifting towards the target area. But unlike Salisbury Plain, which was used for more advanced training, involving jumps from C-130 Hercules transport aircraft, Hankley Common was used for basic training and the jumps were made from a converted barrage balloon.

An adult would have seen this for what it was and would have noticed that the balloon was tethered to the ground. But as Thornton had stared, transfixed, at the massive light grey structure, something strange had happened. She'd started to shake, then to cry. Her alarmed parents had looked in vain for the source of her discomfort, thinking that perhaps she'd been stung by a wasp. Then she'd started screaming, and had held tightly to her father's coat. It was at this point that her parents had noticed the look of terror on her face and had realized that fear and not pain was to blame. Her father remembered that the last thing they'd told her was to look at the soldiers jumping out of the balloon, and noticed that she was cowering behind him so that the balloon was not in her line of sight. He'd ushered her back to the car, vaguely aware that it was the balloon that was scaring her.

The journey home had passed in silence and Thornton's parents hadn't asked her why she'd been so upset – young children were prone to seemingly irrational behaviour, so perhaps they'd put the whole incident down to a childish tantrum or even to the memory of a bad dream. The child herself was unable to articulate her fear and was only vaguely aware that the barrage balloon had reminded her of something 'bad'. Now she knew what it was, of course, but at the time it had been just another incident in a lifetime of strange things that happened at the fringes of her awareness.

Thornton had bad dreams, but there were plenty of times when similar things happened during the day. But like dreams, the memories of these experiences soon faded and were forgotten. There was a general sense of unease sometimes, a feeling that all was not as it should be, but the source of her anguish was elusive. The incident with the barrage balloon had quickly been forgotten and was only recalled several years later when something else had happened: that was the night that the barrage balloon had been over their house and the bad little soldiers had come into her room.

Thornton sat up in bed and mulled over the event that she'd just recalled – the memory had been repressed – or perhaps suppressed – for years. Mindful of repeated requests from her mentor and friend Cody, she reached for the notebook and pencil that lay on top of her bedside table and jotted down a few notes. Ever the meticulous investigator of strange phenomena, Cody had asked that she keep a record not just of any abduction experiences but also of any memories of previous events that surfaced, either spontaneously or through dreams. Cody was a dedicated man but also a compassionate one, whose desire to crack the alien abduction mystery never once usurped his primary aim of helping the abductees come to terms with their experiences. As such, he'd told Thornton what he'd told all the abductees he'd worked with, namely that she was free to telephone him any time of day and night, should she need to talk.

Thornton was not tempted, since she considered that she was fulfilling a role that amounted to being Cody's research assistant. She took this very seriously, regarding one of the functions of this position as being to take some of the pressure off Cody, who she felt was working far too hard for his own good. The last thing she wanted to do was disturb his sleep. So she wrote up an account of what she recalled and went downstairs to pour herself a large gin and tonic. It would steady her nerves and might even relax her to the point at which she'd be able to go back to sleep. If there was a war going on, she told herself, she'd been one of its first casualties.

The Pentagon, Virginia

The session had been going on for about an hour. Little progress had been made. It wasn't that Van Buren was lying – so far as anyone could tell – but the lack of fresh developments was a simple consequence of his being so familiar with all the standard techniques used in debriefings. He was a careful man who paused before responding to a question and who never allowed himself to be provoked. When this technique had been tried, he'd smiled at his interrogator as if to say that he knew what was being attempted.

As one of the two military officers present, CDI had recognized these defensive techniques from the feared Combat After Capture course that he'd been put through early in his military career. The authorities had finally accepted that it was unrealistic to expect captured military personnel to confine themselves to revealing only their name, rank, number and date of birth – the so-called Big Four. Although the Geneva Convention was still officially in force, this rule had been flouted so frequently that it was becoming a joke. Hard lessons had been learned in the Gulf War and the terrible experiences of people like Andy McNab, John Nichol and John Peters had finally convinced the MOD that, in modern conflicts, captured UK personnel *would* be tortured and *would* talk. So the emphasis had shifted, and people had been taught how to waste time, evade questions and deploy a successful cover story. This new training had supplemented the climax to the dreaded Escape and Evasion course and was now standard practice in the UK.

The US ran similar courses and Van Buren was clearly deploying tactics that he'd learned in one of them. For all CDI knew, Van Buren might even have *designed* such a course – it was the sort of thing at which these spooks excelled. General Tom Johnson, the Chairman of the Joint Chiefs of Staff, was clearly getting as frustrated as CDI.

'You realize, of course, that this session will be followed by sessions using sodium pentothal and hypnosis. You further realize that your co-conspirators will be questioned using similar techniques. If there are any discrepancies between your accounts and theirs . . . if there are any differences between your testimony here and your testimony under drugs and hypnosis, you could be sent to jail for life. These are high stakes.'

'I appreciate that.' Van Buren was deliberately keeping his answers short – another tactic that the two military men recognized. The problem was that such a ploy demonstrated only a familiarity with the tactics of a sophisticated interrogation; it didn't mean Van Buren was actually lying.

'That doesn't worry you?'

'Why should it?'

Answering a question with a question was another classic technique, aimed at taking the initiative away from the questioners. Johnson ignored it. 'I'd like to ask you about loyalty.' It was a clever question.

'I'm loyal to my country. But above that loyalty comes a loyalty to the human race as a whole. Much of what you perceive as my disloyalty stems from a desire to safeguard humanity in its entirety.'

'And humanity is in danger?'

'Only if we arouse the wrath of those more powerful than us.'

'They would destroy us?'

'That is not their desire or their intention.'

'But they *could* destroy us?'

'If we provoke them sufficiently, yes.'

'So you recommend capitulation?

'Cooperation.'

'You mean surrender'

'I mean survival.'

CDI admired what Johnson had done. He knew that Van Buren could be provoked by accusations of disloyalty but appreciated the fact that Johnson pushed this button subtly and infrequently. Rapid-fire questions and answers were a gift to interrogators, because they denied the person on the receiving end the opportunity to stop and think before responding; it was the nearest they'd come to unbalancing Van Buren, and it was to the credit of the two civilians present that they saw what was happening and stayed silent.

'I know this is a dreadful cliché,' Johnson continued, 'but I assume you're familiar with the saying that it is better to die on your feet than to live on your knees?'

'It was a line spoken by a Spanish communist, Dolores Ibarruri, at the beginning of the Spanish Civil War. You're quoting communists now?'

'Do you agree with the sentiment?' Johnson ignored Van Buren's question.

'I wouldn't jeopardize the survival of the human race, no.'

'So you'd be quite happy to be subjugated?'

'No. But if the alternative was destruction, I'd choose subjugation.'

'You wouldn't fight?'

'We can't fight.'

'We have fought . . . or rather, our British allies have fought, and died, when your knowledge might have saved them.'

'I very much regret those few dozen deaths. But I was more concerned at the possibility of six billion deaths.'

There was a pause, and CDI realized that Van Buren had countered with an effective response. Johnson sighed – a pre-arranged signal that was a general invitation to the others to pitch in. CDI had a pre-prepared question that he now deployed, as much to keep Van Buren off balance as to elicit any revealing response. 'Who's the *real* enemy here?'

'The extraterrestrials. But we can't fight them without inviting our own destruction. So we must cooperate and ensure that the invaders don't ally themselves with those whose interests might be harmful to the West.'

'Ah, you're talking about the Russians.'

'The extraterrestrials offered to ally themselves with the USA at a time when we were confronting the former Soviet Union.'

'So your motivation in doing a deal was to win the Cold War?'

'The aliens offered to integrate themselves into our political system while simultaneously threatening to ally themselves with the Soviets. What should we have done? Should we have sat by and seen the whole world go communist?' Van Buren was still answering questions with questions, but his tone clearly revealed that he was rattled.

'But such concerns are a thing of the past, surely? The Russians are our allies, are they not? They have associate membership of NATO. Is now not the time for former enemies to become friends and unite against a common foe?'

'The Russian Federation is still a potential threat. Troops are sitting in barracks, unpaid, with only their work for the Russian *mafiya* to keep them occupied. There are those in their military who seriously believe that a return to the Cold War would be a good thing.'

'There are some in the West who agree.' Johnson's accusation was clever but ineffective.

'I don't think you appreciate just how great a problem we face,' Van Buren replied. 'The extraterrestrials may yet ally themselves with the Russians, if we prove uncooperative. They have announced their intention to fit in with *existing* political systems. Is this what you want – aliens entering into an alliance with the Russians, with us being squeezed out?'

'You trust the aliens, then? Do you not think that they might have made the same offer to other nations? Has it never crossed your mind that they may be playing countries off against each other in a divide-and-rule scenario?

'We would have known if anyone else had been approached. Our intelligence was that good.'

Johnson paused for thought. That last assertion was almost certainly correct. The KGB's study of the UFO phenomenon was well known to US intelligence agencies.

Johnson tried a different approach. 'What benefits have we derived from your cooperation with these extraterrestrials?'

Van Buren was momentarily perplexed at the sudden change of

direction, before he realized this was precisely what had been intended. He smiled at Johnson again to show him that he understood what had been attempted. 'The US acquired knowledge that was derived directly from extraterrestrial technology.' Van Buren glanced at Dr Barbara North, knowing that one of the reasons for the presence of the British MOD's Chief Scientific Adviser was to ensure that there was somebody able to evaluate any technical information he imparted. 'Lasers, fibre optics, stealth technology, even the integrated-circuit chip. All these things have their roots in alien technology.'

CSA's reaction surprised everyone – and delighted General Johnson. She laughed. 'This is sub-*X-Files* material, straight out of Colonel Corso's book *The Day After Roswell*. You're saying the Roswell crash happened, when you've previously claimed that this *deal* you struck was hammered out in 1980 after one of their craft got into difficulties in Rendlesham Forest?'

'There was a crash at Roswell, yes.'

'What happened?'

'*Something* crashed in the desert, and at first we thought it belonged to the Soviets. We thought it might have been a long-range spy plane – but another possibility was that it was a bomber, trying to carry out a pre-emptive strike on the 509th Bomb Group at Roswell Army Air Field. At the time they were the only atomic-bomb-capable squadron in the world, and if they'd been taken out, we'd have been in trouble.'

'Where was the wreckage taken?'

'To Wright-Patterson Air Force Base – or Wright Field as it was then known. The whole operation was carried out in strict secrecy, as you'd expect, given that one theory was that the Soviets were about to attack us. We went on to a higher state of alert, but it soon became apparent that the Soviets weren't doing anything. If this had been the first move in a war, there would have been other signs. In fact, there were none.'

'But it must have been obvious that this wasn't a Soviet aircraft.' CSA phrased it as a statement, not a question.

'Not at all. It had smashed into tiny pieces.'

'But the bodies?'

'Only found later, some distance from the craft. Anyway, to continue, once we'd determined that the craft could only be extraterrestrial, we set up a group to study the UFO phenomenon and to back-engineer the craft. But this was the time when alien activity really began to be noticed by the public, so our efforts had to blend a meticulous investigation of the phenomenon with a disinformation campaign aimed at preventing the public from taking the issue seriously. Remember that at this time all we knew was that we weren't alone. We had no overt contact, even after the crash, so we had no idea about the aliens' motivations.'

'So where does Corso fit in?' CSA asked. 'Was his book released with your sanction, or was he a whistle-blower?'

'American books like *The Day After Roswell* and British works such as *Open Skies, Closed Minds* and *The Uninvited* were part of a project initiated by The Enterprise, in anticipation of the situation we now face. They were authorized releases designed to acclimatize the public to an extraterrestrial reality, facilitating the peaceful integration of the two races.'

'Wait a minute,' CDI observed. 'You're bringing one of *our* people into this now. Are you saying that there were some in the UK who knew about this, and were part of the conspiracy?' If true, this was a potential disaster for the UK government and would expose them to all sorts of political problems.

Van Buren smiled. 'When it transpired that an MOD official with top-secret security clearances was having a relationship with the daughter of a member of The Enterprise, it was too good a chance to miss. At first we thought that you Brits might be on to us and that you'd set it up deliberately, to probe for information. But it checked out as one of those bizarre coincidences that do sometimes happen, even in our business. So we made our move, and a situation was engineered whereby the individual concerned was forcibly recruited into our organization. Once he'd been given a demonstration of the power we're up against, he agreed to co-operate. He was manoeuvred into a posting where he could help with our public-indoctrination programme. But he wasn't the first; the UK has its own dark little secrets here.'

All four interrogators recognized that this posed serious problems for the British. CDI and CSA – of course – were particularly irked by this revelation, but an obvious question occurred to both of them. Why had Van Buren implicated people who had not previously been under suspicion? Was he simply making a threat, making it clear that he could make damaging revelations, or were his motivations more complex? And how had The Enterprise manoeuvred their new recruit into Sec (AS) and the position of UFO desk officer? That could only have been done by senior MOD personnel, although as this was nearly twenty years ago, those concerned may well have retired. There were many new questions emerging.

'We'll come back to that,' CDI replied. This initial session was aimed at breadth rather than depth, and the aim was to expose as many new issues as possible so that they could be followed up in more detail later, once some checks had been made. It was going to be a slow process.

Salisbury Plain, Wiltshire

One soldier shot the lock off the door while the other – a fraction of a second later – kicked it in with his boot. The first soldier threw in a grenade, which promptly exploded with a hollow bang. The two figures quickly entered the room.

'Clear.'

They advanced through the various rooms, working almost as a single entity, one giving cover while the other went forward. Their dramatic entrance would have alerted any hostiles to their presence, but on this occasion stealth was not the aim. Each carried an M16 assault rifle, which had the advantage that it could be set for single-round fire or three-round bursts, as well as for a fully automatic mode. But the real reason this rather ancient weapon was still a favourite with the SAS had to do with what could be attached to the gun: an M203 grenade-launcher could be fixed to the underside of the weapon.

Stairs lay ahead. This was the obvious place for an ambush, so another grenade was used, with the throw timed just right so that it would explode while still in the air, at the top of the stairs, around waist height. There was another loud bang, and the two soldiers were up the stairs within seconds: even if a grenade failed to kill or injure the target, the sound or shock wave from an explosion within a confined space would almost certainly disorientate an enemy and this was the time to traverse any area where you were exposed. *Don't give an enemy time to think or react. Seize the initiative. Push ahead.* These were the tactics used by the SAS, and by special forces everywhere.

'Clear.'

'Clear.'

One room left. They hadn't known in advance, but things often worked out that way. The target was certainly more likely to be upstairs, although in this business you took nothing for granted. Doors were dangerous because they were choke points: you had to come through them, and that was where an enemy stood a chance of slotting you as you were silhouetted in the doorway. Normally you might consider coming through the window – or even the wall if it was thin enough. *Do the unexpected; hit hard; hit fast.* That wasn't an option this time. Most hostiles would go for a chest shot, or a head shot if they thought you'd be wearing body armour. So an enemy would instinctively be aiming high – perhaps three or four feet above the ground.

The two soldiers came in low, springing through the door in a crouch, all the time scanning for danger. Both of them saw the target at the same time. There was no mistaking the figure for a friendly: it was around three and a half feet tall, grey in colour, with a large head and huge black eyes. It was wearing a one-piece uniform of some sort – and it had something in its hand. The sound of two M16s – both set to automatic and firing simultaneously – was awesome. The target didn't so much drop as disintegrate.

'Clear.' The deadpan statement was followed by raucous laughter.

'Fucking outrageous!'

Jack West and Jane Vatch relaxed for a moment, now that this stage of the exercise was over. Both were veterans of Operation Thunder Child, although few people knew the details of West's mission. But, like all SAS Thunder Child veterans, they were now being used to train up other units and brief them on what to expect. It was a slow process, and they had to push themselves as hard as the people under their command. This was why they were still practising basic clearance tactics at the mock town that the army had built on a quiet corner of their massive training area on Salisbury Plain. Training or not, both of them knew that their bleepers could go off at any minute and that the next target they faced might not be made of hardboard. And it might shoot back.

The Pentagon, Virginia

Saul Weitzman had been a surprise choice for the post of Defense Secretary. He was an economist, and the US military establishment had been afraid that he'd been appointed to oversee a massive programme of cuts aimed at financing President Hilary Spencer's radical domestic overhaul of healthcare and social security. The fears had been justified, to a certain extent. But Weitzman had proved surprisingly popular with the Joint Chiefs, partly because of his honesty. His frank admissions that he was minded to recommend cuts in particular areas earned him the respect of senior military officers who were astute enough not to confuse the message with the man.

Weitzman was also respected for his intellect and his hard work. He got through briefing papers at a frightening rate, and it was clear that his analytical mind had taken in the issues. Shortly after his appointment he'd embarked upon a hectic schedule of visits, ensuring that he met not just the commanding officers but the young soldiers at the sharp end of the military machine. He was a quiet man, but when he had something to say it was worth listening to. He'd said little during the interrogation of Van Buren once the preliminary introductions were over, but now he interrupted with a seemingly bizarre question that caught even his fellow interrogators off guard. 'What can you tell me about the death of James Forrestal?'

The other interrogators consulted their notes but came up with nothing. General Johnson only knew that Forrestal had been the first US Secretary of Defense – a post that he'd held at the time the Roswell crash was supposed to have occurred. He'd resigned in March 1949 after having had a mental breakdown and had committed suicide two months later, jumping from a window in Bethesda Naval Hospital.

Van Buren's expression was something to behold. He looked as if he was going to explode with rage, and his face flushed with colour. It was the most extreme reaction that they'd seen: Weitzman had clearly found a very effective button to push. 'I don't know what you're insinuating but, as far as I know, it was suicide.'

'But he *had* been a member of a covert group set up to study the UFO phenomenon?'

'Yes.' Van Buren had regained his composure.

Johnson wanted to follow this up, but not until he and the others were better briefed on the background to this aspect. He shot Weitzman an apologetic look, and promptly changed direction again. 'We want you to tell us how best to attack the aliens' mothership.'

'I won't help you. As I've already explained, I won't take any action that might invite our destruction.'

'But you did try. Our anti-satellite missiles and lasers are the result of projects initiated by Enterprise members. And towards the end of Operation Thunder Child, when The Enterprise lost its grip on the secret, US forces engaged in hostile actions against the extraterrestrials. So they'll know that you plotted against them, and they'll know that you *acted* against them. Whether you like it or not, you're on our side.'

'It's true that we explored the possibility of developing a capability against them. Our first choice was the same as yours: resistance. But we came up short; there just wasn't time to develop a viable operational capability. With these people, unless you can be sure of stopping them, it's suicidal to try. Anyway, the next move is up to them. They're clearly taking stock, after the events of Operation Thunder Child, but I have no reason to doubt their commitment to the original plan. They have too much invested in it. But we'll find out soon enough. Now the secret's out, and now the mothership has been detected, the need for secrecy has gone.'

'So what happens next?'

'They'll be in touch.'

Chapter Three

FIRST CONTACT

MOD Main Building, Whitehall

'Minister, we have some new problems that I need to brief you on,' Nick Templeton announced grimly.

Martin Blackmore tried not to let his irritation show. There was no point in shooting the messenger, especially when the messenger was only doing his job and watching his boss's back. 'Forewarned is forearmed' had been the motto of the now defunct Royal Observer Corps, but it was an adage that was always in the mind of any good staff officer. 'Yes?'

'As you know, CDI and CSA are in America, sitting in on one of the initial debriefing sessions with Edwin Van Buren – well, sorry, they're doing a lot more than sitting in, they're – er—'

'Yes, yes,' the Minister cut in, impatiently. Templeton didn't usually stumble during an oral briefing but Blackmore was equally out of character in his sharpness. It was a sign of just how tired and stressed both men were.

'Well,' Templeton continued, composing himself, 'I'm being briefed by Wing Commander Terry Carpenter, who's out there as CDI's staff officer, and it appears there are now some indications that certain people in the UK may have been in on this conspiracy.'

'Who?'

When Templeton named the prime suspect, Blackmore nodded slowly. As a politician he'd suspected that The Enterprise must have had a contact in the UK, not least to ensure that information about the Rendlesham Forest incident was managed so as to prevent discovery of the now destroyed alien facility in the area. But the individual concerned had disappeared while piloting a light aircraft over the Channel several years ago and was widely presumed to be dead, although no body or wreckage had been found. Blackmore wondered, cynically, whether this revelation might be turned to the UK's advantage, if they could show the British member of The Enterprise as the victim of an American plot that had ultimately resulted in his death.

The thought had clearly already occurred to Templeton. 'While this might be manageable in itself, since it hardly reflects on the current administration, we can't rule out the possibility that a replacement was recruited. Although I understand that the initial recruitment was opportunistic, it may have proved sufficiently useful to justify seeking out somebody else.' He looked sheepish for a moment. 'And, technically, I'd have to be regarded as a prime suspect. If the mission is to shape UK public opinion on the UFO issue and to prevent the military and the politicians from discovering the truth, my position is the key post. I suggest that both my staff and I be subjected to an investigation.'

'Hmm. But anybody employed on the UFO issue has already gone through the most stringent Developed Vetting procedure, in view of the Top Secret information you handle. So if you've passed that, you'd pass a special investigation, wouldn't you?'

'Yes, Minister. But even though I *know* I'm loyal, and I have total confidence in my team, we can't ignore this, not least because we may have to show that we've taken action to address the possibility.'

'But we're getting ahead of ourselves anyway,' Blackmore retorted. 'We don't even know for sure if Van Buren's telling the truth. From what we know of him, he's a master of deception who's probably resistant to hypnosis and sodium pentothal. And threats of prison may not mean much to somebody of his age – especially if he's telling the truth about the threat we face. If he truly believes that he's acting in the best interests of the US and the planet as a whole, he's almost certainly sufficiently committed to face jail rather than jeopardize the plan.'

'He may be right, of course,' Templeton ventured.

'Yes, that's true. But it was never his decision to make. What else?' The Minister clearly wanted to move on.

'A tricky Parliamentary Question, from an Opposition MP.' Templeton glanced at his notepad, and read. ' "To ask the Secretary of State for Defence whether the Ministry of Defence has ever kept records detailing people who have reported alien abductions, and if so, when such data was first compiled; who authorized the decision and whether this data was passed to any third party." It's a pretty devious question, especially if it turns out that a former Sec(AS) desk officer was working for The Enterprise. But there's more. A journalist has filed a Freedom of Information Act request asking for details of abductees whose cases have been investigated by the Department. Now, we can withhold personal details – names and addresses – but we can't avoid confirming that we have these details on file, or giving some details of what we did.'

The Minister thought for a moment. These revelations might be embarrassing, but not catastrophically so. The PQ could be answered by saying that S of S would write to the MP concerned and place a copy of the response in the House of Commons library. This was a classic way of avoiding having to print the answer in *Hansard* – the parliamentary record – where the press and public might see it. It didn't rule out an MP leaking the information, but it made it less likely that the matter would be made public. It was typical of the damage-limitation philosophy applied by successive administrations over the last two or three decades. 'This is an interesting coincidence, isn't it, that these two approaches should come at the same time, and just as it's become apparent that the UK might have been involved in the conspiracy?'

Templeton looked uncomfortable. 'Yes, Minister. The PQ and the Freedom of Information request are almost certainly linked. But, as you say, it's the timing that's odd.'

'There's something here that we're not seeing,' Blackmore mused. 'Somebody's shifting the debate to the abductees. But who? And why?'

DERA, Farnborough

Dr Lisa Kaminsky had been busy since the events of Operation Thunder Child but had enjoyed every minute of it. She had been part of a large group of scientists brought in to study the wreckage of the downed alien craft and the few items salvaged from the destroyed alien base near Rendlesham Forest. Although DERA had 'untied' from the Ministry of Defence, it was still an MOD outfit in all but name and its scientists had signed the Official Secrets Act. Those involved with work on the alien technology had had to agree to more stringent security clearance but had willingly accepted the resultant intrusion into their private lives, in view of what was on offer. The chance to examine technology that originated on another world was a dream come true for any scientist, and Kaminsky was one of the privileged few. The limited numbers of those granted access was proving to be a contentious issue in itself, and the civilian scientific community was screaming for access, arguing – not unreasonably, perhaps – that widening the number of scientists involved would increase the chances of useful discoveries.

There was also a freedom-of-information issue at stake, and the international scientific community had reacted with fury at what they saw as a government attempt to exploit the technology for nationalistic purposes. They argued that the knowledge belonged to everyone. Curiously, this was a debate that had never taken off in the media – or, at least, not to the extent that the government had feared. In fact, the discoveries to be made from the wreckage and salvaged items seemed likely to be few. All the scientists agreed that the possibility of back-engineering a craft capable of interstellar travel was negligible for the time being.

But some quick results were possible in other fields. The alloy used to construct the craft was easy to analyse and would be something that could be used to build improved aircraft. And the directed-energy weapon had turned out to be comparatively simple to replicate. Kaminsky knew that the MOD had set a number of very tight deadlines for these items to be developed in the UK. The meaning of this was clear: the country was gearing up for war, and clearly wanted to use some of the aliens' technology against them.

RAF Oakhanger, Hampshire

Although nominally an RAF base, Oakhanger served as the focal point for all UK military satellite communications activities. The importance of communications could never be overstated by the military, and there was an old saying that the most devastating weapon known to any modern soldier was a radio. UK military satcom activity centred around a series of satellites in geostationary orbit, and the programme was known as SKYNET 5. The Space Squadron at Oakhanger ensured that the network functioned properly, and the result was that UK forces anywhere in the world had access to a secure and reliable communications system.

But since Operation Thunder Child, the Space Squadron had fulfilled another, more covert role. Additional security measures had been introduced, and behind the new perimeter fence, additional radomes and satcom dishes had been installed. RAF Oakhanger was doing more than monitoring UK-controlled satellites. Their communications dishes were pointing towards an area of the sky already targeted by most of the world's radio telescopes. The RAF was listening for something very specific and while it was unlikely to be transmitted in encrypted form, that was possible. And even if it wasn't so, the MOD needed to ensure that the message – if and when it came – was given to Ministers and Chiefs of Staff. Nobody would thank the RAF if news of first contact was picked up on the evening news, with the Department having to go cap in hand to civilian scientists at Jodrell Bank.

Flight Lieutenant Chris Wardell was an engineering graduate who'd drifted into the RAF after university and had never looked back. He'd specialized in satcom but had taken courses in astronomy, radio astronomy and cryptography. He'd been recruited into Operation Thunder Child in the closing stages of the operation, although in the event he'd had no direct involvement. Now he was one of a small team of watchkeepers, scanning for something artificial in the constant 'noise' of space radiation. It was an interesting situation, he thought. On the one hand, various governments had authorized the transmission of messages to the alien vessel. There could be little doubt that these signals were getting through. But there was no coordination of messages, and in advance of any United Nations effort to coordinate a unified response to the threat – something few people thought possible – there was a cacophony of nationalism spewing forth from Earth in a way that probably confused the extra-terrestrials.

Wardell had studied the early days of the SETI programme, when scientists had been excited by the possibility of communication with other civilizations. They generally listened at around the 21-centimetre frequency – 1420 megahertz. This was the frequency of the natural radio signal of the hydrogen atom and as such was considered a likely band on which any intelligent civilization might broadcast. Radio astronomers were so certain of this that the frequency was even now one on which terrestrial and satellite transmissions were banned. Wardell had also studied the famous incident in August 1977 when an unmistakably artificial signal had been detected by an astronomer working at the Ohio State Observatory. The astronomer had written 'Wow!' in the margin of the computer printout, but the signal had never repeated and the source remained unidentified.

When the new signal was first detected, Wardell was nearly sick. His pulse rate increased dramatically and his mouth felt dry – his emotions were all over the place. But he was ever the professional and instigated a series of checks that had been designed specifically for this moment. Yes, the signal was on the protected radio bandwidth of 21 centimetres; yes, it came through on a single channel, in line with predictions that an artificial communication would be a very narrow-band signal; yes, it was strong, coming in at over 170 times background noise. Most importantly, data from another receiver confirmed – through triangulation – that the signal wasn't terrestrial and came from the precise area of sky where optical telescopes had verified the presence of the alien mothership.

This moment had been anticipated, and a very precise course of action had been devised. Once Wardell had completed his checks – *once he was sure* – he lifted the secure telephone and spoke a pre-prepared and innocuous-sounding phrase. 'Sir, we have a confirmed code Sierra Yankee Foxtrot. I say again, Sierra Yankee Foxtrot. Do you acknowledge?'

'Sierra Yankee Foxtrot,' replied a voice. 'I acknowledge, thank you.'

Once that was out of the way, Wardell had one more watch-keeping task to complete. A signal had been prepared for this moment, with blank spaces for information such as the frequency and the signal strength. Wardell quickly but carefully filled in these basic facts, read through the final version and pressed the 'send' key on his secure computer terminal. A 'flash' signal was immediately sent to a pre-arranged distribution list that would ensure that the information got quickly to those who needed to know. Wardell then spent the next ten minutes telephoning the key registry staff, alerting them that flash signal traffic was on its way. Technically this shouldn't have been necessary, but it was an extra touch that would ensure nobody was caught napping.

Once Wardell had taken this action, he telephoned his own boss and suggested that he should come and see him. It was only when he'd done all this that he settled down to do what he'd wanted to do from the moment the signal had been detected – namely, to look at it and see whether it could be deciphered.

The Pentagon, Virginia
CDI and CSA were taking the opportunity afforded by a break in

the interrogation to confer and to swap notes. They'd had a joint session with the two US interrogators but the British and Americans had now drifted off into their respective national groups. It might have been an accidental thing but it served only to reinforce the suspicion that there were still secrets between the US and the UK.

'What do you think?' CDI asked bluntly.

'I don't know,' CSA replied cautiously. 'There's a possible discrepancy over what Van Buren said about stealth. He claims the technology is alien, but I know that some pioneering work was done at Farnborough, back in the 1950s.'

'It's not necessarily inconsistent,' CDI retorted, although he'd been genuinely surprised at the revelation. 'In fact, surely it would tie in quite nicely with the fact that the technology derived from the Roswell crash in 1947?'

'But not if the US weren't sharing data.'

'That's true,' CDI conceded. 'But suppose the Americans tried and failed to make sense of the technology and then brought us in, without telling us where it came from.'

'No.' CSA was sounding sure of herself. 'I've seen the files, and spoken to a few of the old hands. We came up with the concept but couldn't get it to work. When the US unveiled its stealth fighter the old sweats joked about it and said the technology was old hat.'

'Hmm. But a radar-invisible aircraft is an obvious goal once you've developed radar, so just because *we* tried and failed to develop stealth technology doesn't mean Van Buren's lying when he says the Americans acquired the technology from extraterrestrials – either through back-engineering or even as a trade.' CDI was thinking on his feet. 'If anything, it validates his point – we tried and failed. Our finest minds couldn't make it work, and suddenly the Americans produce a fully working operational stealth aircraft.'

'Not straightaway.'

'No, but long before its first public outing in the 1989 campaign to oust the rogue Panamanian general Manuel Noriega. I know for a fact that stealth aircraft were flying in the mid-1970s.'

'As prototypes or operationally?'

'There were – possibly – six aircraft flying by the late 1970s. Half a squadron, maybe.'

The discussion was bogging down, and although this was all useful background, both CDI and CSA realized they'd strayed off track. There were more important matters to probe. CSA picked one. 'A moment ago you mentioned the US trading with the aliens. But Van Buren hasn't admitted to that, has he? Or at least, not in the early years. He says Roswell happened but there was no follow-up; no direct contact. And yet much of the literature suggests otherwise and indicates a deal *was* done: technology in exchange for keeping the secret of the alien presence.'

'The *literature* talks about the Americans trading permission to abduct humans and mutilate cattle in exchange for stealth technology,' CDI retorted, a little sarcastically. 'Most of the *literature* is bullshit.'

'Or Enterprise disinformation.'

'Or both.'

'Yes,' CSA continued, desperately trying to marshal her thoughts. 'But here's my point: we know there was an alien base at Bentwaters, but we don't know for sure when it was set up or when the US authorities first found out. And we need to know.'

'At the showdown in Rendlesham Forest, Van Buren told the PM that the base predated the development of radar at Bawdsey Manor and that it was radar coverage that gave the aliens problems, by making it much more likely that we'd detect them. He described it as an accident of history that radar should have been developed a few miles from the alien base – or rather, one of several such bases. That makes sense – I can't believe a facility could have been set up in modern times. We'd have noticed.' CDI sounded sure of himself.

'Probably,' CSA agreed. 'But we must find out when the deal was done – after Roswell, or after the Rendlesham Forest incident. Van Buren claims that Roswell gave them proof that aliens existed, but that there was no contact at all until Rendlesham. Were they really in the dark for over thirty years? And what does this tell us about the alien agenda?'

'We need to probe this business of alien bases,' CDI mused, taking the discussion on to another issue. This was a tangible threat on which he could focus. 'How many were there? Where were they? Are any still active?' This last prospect horrified him.

'If any were still active, there might be scope to recover operational alien technology,' CSA enthused, putting a positive spin on CDI's fears. 'That could really—'

The wide-ranging discussion was cut short by CDI's bleeper and a message telling him to call London immediately on the secure line. CSA's bleeper went off a couple of minutes later, reassuring her that her outer office staff were on the ball. Just once, she thought to herself, it would be nice if her bleeper went off before those of her military colleagues. But most of the MOD watchkeepers would be military, and they'd always call the civvies last. CDI and CSA headed for the telephone in silence, wondering what could be sufficiently important to justify bleeping them when – for all anyone knew – they might have been in the middle of debriefing Van Buren. There was an old MOD saying that urgent calls seldom meant good news.

MOD Main Building, Whitehall

A meeting had been hurriedly arranged between US of S, CDS and the Chief Press Officer. Other senior MOD staff were being rounded up, but the matter under discussion would not wait.

'So what does it say?' Blackmore asked the obvious question.

It was CDS who responded. 'You're going to love this,' he said, his voice heavy with sarcasm. 'The message reads as follows: *We come to you as refugees and as friends. We seek your help, and in exchange offer you ours. We have much to learn from each other and much to trade. Decades ago we received assurances from certain nations that we would be welcome on Earth, but now you have responded with violence, attacking our emissaries and seeking to prevent the open dialogue we seek with all people of your planet. Accordingly, we are taking our message of peace over the heads of your leaders, and appealing directly to the people. We very much regret the deaths caused by our defensive actions, and hope that friendly relations can be restored.* What do you make of that?'

Blackmore thought for a moment. 'I assume the message wasn't encrypted?'

'No, Minister, it was actually transmitted in Morse code, of all things.'

Blackmore was a shrewd operator who immediately saw the significance of this. 'So it's a message for everybody – not just for governments, not just for the West.'

'Yes, Minister,' CDS replied. 'And it's clearly designed to cause trouble for us, and to put us under as much pressure as possible. Every radio telescope on the side of the Earth facing the alien ship will have heard that message. I estimate that we're among the first to have detected and read the message, but others will be doing so now and putting it out on television and radio, and on to the Internet. Even if we wanted to suppress it, we couldn't.'

'Jacqui?'

Jacqui Connolly, the MOD's Chief Press Officer, had been expecting the question. 'As you clearly recognize,' she began, 'this is straight out of the psychological warfare handbook.' She let the remark sink in for a moment. Psychological operations – psyops – were an increasingly important part of any modern military campaign. It could cover anything from the dropping of leaflets to the setting up of an Internet site. It covered other more shadowy practices, too, but, as with most things, the public only ever got to hear about the comparatively harmless and uncontroversial tactics.

Connolly went on: 'This message has the express aim of turning people against their governments. Note the way that they say "certain nations", but don't say who. That's a really clever touch, because it almost looks as if they're acting out of loyalty to allies and withholding the information to avoid implicating friends. It makes them look moral. Of course, what it *really* does is keep everybody off balance. Most people will assume that it's referring to Britain and America, but any other government that takes a hard line might find itself coming under suspicion of having made a deal. Note that making a deal is something inexcusable for us – because we had no right to, without consulting the people – but it's OK for the aliens, because they can say they acted in good faith and thought they were doing the right thing by coming to our leaders.'

'Calling themselves refugees is another interesting touch,' CDS observed, just as CAS and ACAS arrived, representing the Air Staff.

'Yes,' Connolly agreed. 'It's another very clever move on their part, and works on a number of levels. It evokes sympathy, and introduces a sense of vulnerability – this makes them seem less of a threat. But it also appeals to human arrogance, because it suggests that we might be able to help them. Notice they use the word "trade" – that's what equals do, and it's another clever touch because it appeals to businesspeople, who wouldn't want governments to destroy a potentially massive source of income.'

CAS had been impressed with Connolly's analysis but had a point of his own. 'It works on one more level,' he began. 'Fear. Calling themselves refugees implies that they're fleeing from something. So it plants in our minds the idea that there's somebody even more powerful out there, who might – conceivably – come after them. So it places additional pressure on us to welcome these invaders, to better protect ourselves against a future threat.'

'So what does all this tell us?' Blackmore had a few ideas himself but wanted to let his civil and military advisers follow their thoughts through to the logical conclusion.

'It tells us that they're well versed in psyops,' CDS replied firmly. 'But it also tells us that we're in a stronger position than we thought. They've put a lot of thought into this, and why should they bother unless they need to make trouble for us? And why make trouble for us if they can just press ahead regardless? Clearly, they fear that we *can* make an effective response.'

'So this is good news?'

'Potentially, yes, Minister.'

'Good. We can't reply unilaterally to this message. Any

response will need to be coordinated by the UN – although there's nothing we can do to stop individual nations and private citizens replying. But we do need to get a press line out right away, to show we're addressing the situation and to get our own message across. And once it's broadcast, chances are it'll get through to our visitors anyway.'

Connolly had been frantically scribbling away during the course of the short meeting. 'We need to sound conciliatory, otherwise we'll come across as the villains, and we need to avoid a direct denial of their accusations, because denials sound inherently negative. How about this: *We welcome the fact that open contact has finally been made, and are grateful for the regrets expressed about those of our people who were killed during previous attacks. We hope these actions were misunderstandings that can be rectified, and we look forward to open negotiation. We will be seeking urgent clarification about the alien intentions and demands, together with specific details of any deal they believe has been concluded on our behalf.* I think that strikes just about the right balance.'

There were appreciative nods of agreement from Connolly's military colleagues. It was a cleverly constructed piece of work. Some might have found it odd that the MOD were coordinating the government reaction and had been given responsibility for drafting the response to any message. The reason involved a bit of decidedly terrestrial psyops: putting the MOD in the lead sent a clear message to people that this was a defence and national security issue; it downplayed any idea that this was about benign contact with extraterrestrials and focused attention on the fact that this was being treated as an invasion. It also served to remind people of the casualties that the military had already suffered. 'Excellent.' Blackmore clearly agreed. 'Jacqui, please come with me. We'll bounce this off S of S and then clear it with the PM and the Palace. But it needs to go live as soon as possible – I'm sure we're taking calls about this already.'

Pyramid Heights, Westminster

It was a new development, completed in 2005, and was home to various MPs and businesspeople for whom proximity to Parliament was the deciding factor in where they lived. The block was located on Millbank, close to the Tate Gallery, and most of the flats had spectacular views of the Thames. Maxwell Henderson owned a flat on the seventh floor and all but two of his guests had now arrived.

Richard Cody and Jenny Thornton had been picked up from their homes in a car sent specially by their host. The chauffeur turned off Millbank and on to an entrance road reserved exclusively for visitors to Pyramid Heights. He stopped at a barrier, produced a swipe card, leaned out of the window and keyed in a PIN number. The barrier duly rose and the car descended into the underground car park.

To Cody's and Thornton's surprise there was a second barrier and this one was only raised when the attendant had examined the chauffeur's ID card, checked the car registration number and looked over the two bemused passengers. Once the car had been parked, the chauffeur escorted them into the foyer of the building. It reminded Cody of the reception area of a large hotel: the floor seemed to be made of marble, and there were various people milling around, looking after guests and taking delivery of letters and packages.

The chauffeur approached the massive desk and started chatting to one of the receptionists, whom he clearly knew. Cody and Thornton had to sign in and were directed to a lift and told to get off at the seventh floor. They were escorted to the lift by a burly security guard – one of four in the foyer – who ran a metal detector over their clothing and searched Thornton's handbag.

Two minutes later Cody and Thornton found themselves in Maxwell Henderson's luxury flat, where they accepted a glass of wine and some canapés.

'Thank you so much for joining us.' Henderson made the introductions and deliberately refrained from getting down to any serious discussion. Pyramid Heights was aptly named: the building itself was pyramid-shaped but in addition the main reception room of each of the flats was triangular and had floor-to-ceiling windows. This meant that there were stunning river views which were a major talking point among the guests, many of whom were clearly here for the first time and were as overawed as Cody and Thornton.

'Ladies, gentlemen.' The voice was not loud but it commanded attention. 'Thank you so very much for coming here today.' Henderson was a charming host. 'I've asked you here because I'd like to request your help. You're all either experts in various fields or people who have influence.'

Cody looked around at the assembled group. There were twelve of them, including their host. Even before the introductions Cody had recognized some of his fellow guests: a distinguished cosmologist who'd written a number of popular science books; three MPs, one from each of the three main parties; a high-profile businessperson, a very famous actor and – most interestingly, Cody thought – representatives from three major religions.

'I've asked you here today because I need your help. As I'm sure you've all heard by now, a message has just been received from the visitors – it seems to be a message of peace. My concern is that our leaders seem to be embarking upon a course that will lead to war. Narrow self-interest – specifically the desire to hold on to power – seems to be motivating our government, and others, to wage war upon the visitors. I do not say the visitors are good: the truth is that we simply don't know. But we need to find out; we need to negotiate. And, above all, we need to ensure that our leaders do not decide upon a route that will lead to a continuation of the violence that has already tainted what should be a profound, defining moment in the history of human development. Not all of you will agree. Let's talk.'

The subsequent discussion lasted for three and a half hours, and even then no consensus was reached. But most of those present agreed with one sentiment that had been expressed by Henderson on one or two occasions and which he stated again, as a summary of sorts. 'We've covered a lot of ground and I think we've all learned something new – I know I have. But if today's taught me one thing, it's this: we're not the only ones who want a say in how the powers that be respond to this situation – and we're not entirely powerless. There are some influential groups represented here, and we're blessed by the attendance of people who have clout and whose opinions count – or should count. There are voices here that should be listened to, and there are others who haven't been able to attend who feel as we feel. We have powerful allies.'

'What if our leaders don't see it that way?' The question came from the scientist.

'Then we must find new leaders.' Henderson replied.

Cody wasn't sure whether to applaud such a bullish response or to feel uneasy that he was in the presence of a man who, he was beginning to realize, just might be able to achieve such an aim.

Biopreparat Research Site, Omutninsk

In defiance of treaties, and beyond the gaze of most senior government officials, biological weapons were still being manufactured in Russia. This was because it was all but impossible to differentiate between an offensive and a defensive capability: developing a defence against a biological weapon involved producing a vaccine and the only way to produce a vaccine was to cultivate the biological agent itself, since a vaccine is little more than a mild dose of the agent against which protection is sought.

Governments had played this game for years, claiming that the stocks of biological agents they held were solely for self-protection, to immunize their own troops against the possibility that an enemy might deploy such a weapon. It was only the growing realization that other nations were developing frightening biological capabilities that had focused the minds of the superpowers on the need, finally, to curb these obscene weapons. The Aum Shrinrikyo cult had used the nerve gas Sarin on the Tokyo Underground, and Saddam Hussein would doubtless have used chemical and biological agents against Allied troops during the Gulf War had he not been quietly warned that the retaliation would be nuclear.

It was the danger of biological proliferation involving rogue states or cults that had finally led to renewed action on controlling biological weapons, and yet it was difficult for governments to give up the capability. It was for this reason that the last surviving doses of smallpox had still not been destroyed, despite the well-intentioned efforts of the World Health Organization. The truth was that neither America or Russia dared destroy their samples, in case some had been kept back. Without the sample, there could be no vaccine – especially if somebody produced a new strain.

In Russia, the body charged with actually producing the biological agents was known as Biopreparat. It had been created in 1973 (the year after the Soviet Union had signed the Biological Weapons Convention) to provide a civilian cover for military research into – and the development of – biological weapons. It was responsible not just for producing the biological agents but for weaponizing them and devising ever more effective means of delivery.

'I welcome you to this facility and am honoured by your presence,' stammered Colonel Mikhail Sokolov, the Director of the Omutninsk research and production facility. Sokolov was a hard taskmaster, feared by his subordinates, but it was his turn to feel cowed in the presence of his two distinguished guests – Biopreparat's chief, General Nikolai Yazov, and the Defence Minister himself, General Yuri Ivanov. The generals shook his hand, returned the greeting, and gestured at him to begin the tour.

For the next two hours Sokolov found himself on the receiving end of some very tough questions, but he was a hands-on manager who had made it his business to ensure that he was fully briefed on every aspect of the research and production taking place at his facility, even where this was outside his field of expertise. The generals were not ones to suffer fools gladly, and Yazov was pleased that his Director had held up so well under scrutiny. After the tour was over, they retired to Sokolov's office where tea was served by an aide who then withdrew, leaving the three men alone.

'You can guess why we are here,' Ivanov began. It seemed to be a statement more than a question.

'I—' Sokolov paused for a moment, wondering how best to

respond. In the old days it would have been best to say nothing, but now . . . 'The extraterrestrials,' he replied, firmly.

'Indeed so. Do not mistake me here,' Ivanov said, fixing Sokolov with a stare that carried a real sense of menace. 'I do not say we are planning an attack. That is not our wish. But we must put in hand some contingency measures.'

'I have given the matter some thought, sir,' Sokolov replied, a little too quickly. Seeing the look of alarm on the generals' faces, he quickly continued: 'I have done this by myself, purely as an intellectual exercise. I assure you I have committed nothing to paper and spoken to nobody about this matter.'

'Your assessment?' Ivanov demanded, bluntly.

'Sir, if the open-source material is correct, and if former NSA Director Van Buren is correct, these extraterrestrials have genetically modified their own physiology to incorporate human DNA. This would appear to have been the purpose of these . . . abductions. Accordingly, there is no reason to believe that our existing weapons will not be effective. In biological terms we should think of them as human, and susceptible to the same biological agents as humans. The British have recovered alien bodies kept – we believe – at their Porton Down facility. The Americans may have bodies themselves, if the stories about Roswell are to be believed. It would be helpful if the FSB could ascertain this and get me data, but if this is not possible, well, as I say, we must attack them as if we were attacking humans.'

Yazov clearly agreed. 'This seems logical. But in any case, we can plan on no other basis. If we were facing truly alien physiology, we would have no idea what agent might be effective – without obtaining a sample, and testing. This would be useful, though I doubt we have the means or the time—'

'What agents do you suggest we use?' Ivanov interrupted.

Sokolov deferred to his boss on that one. 'We have no clue as to what – if any – immunization programme the extraterrestrials have in place. Assuming they have good intelligence, they may know of our capabilities and may have taken steps to guard against them.' Yazov was being cautious in his analysis, qualifying his speculations where he could. 'Logically, we increase our chances by attacking with as many agents as possible. Specifically, we might use Ebola, Marburg, plague, anthrax, glanders, tularemia and smallpox. I certainly suggest that we should use both a bacterial and a viral weapon, so that we can attack on two different fronts.'

Sokolov nodded his agreement. 'None of this would pose a problem in terms of production. Biopreparat can manufacture any of these agents. The real problem is how to deploy these weapons effectively against the aliens.'

'You will leave that to us, for the time being,' Ivanov replied, rising. The visit was over.

Pyramid Heights, Westminster

After the meeting had broken up, Maxwell Henderson invited Cody and Thornton to stay behind, together with the MPs. Dinner was mentioned, but now, it transpired, they were having to sing for their supper. Henderson wanted their help in drawing up a series of parliamentary questions, designed to put the government on the spot over the whole issue. It was all being carefully orchestrated: while some of the questions were designed for immediate use, others were specifically engineered for certain contingencies and would only be deployed if certain courses of action were taken. Henderson had said that the aim of this was to facilitate a focused and informed debate, so that when Parliament debated the issue they would do so armed with the facts about UFOs and, in particular, facts about how the MOD had handled the subject over the years.

Cody was thrilled to think that, to a real extent, he was helping shape political opinion in a way that had not previously been possible. His mobile phone had rung several times, and he'd done a number of down-the-line interviews for radio stations who wanted his views on the latest developments. He'd arranged to do some television interviews later – ironically, from the Millbank studios that were less than five minutes' walk from Pyramid Heights. He'd turned down the offer of a courtesy car, explaining to the consequently panicked researchers that he was in the general area. He didn't let on precisely where.

Henderson didn't mind these interruptions. Indeed, he welcomed the opportunity that they presented, recognizing that in Cody he had someone who was already known to the press as perhaps the foremost civilian authority on the UFO issue. Cody knew his value to Henderson but was keeping his options open. He and Thornton had made it clear to Henderson that although they shared his view that the government was covering up information, they didn't necessarily accept his opinion that the aliens were benign. But by mutual agreement there was enough common ground to justify their working together, for the time being, and they certainly agreed with the twin aims of forcing the government to come clean on the issue and bringing about a peaceful dialogue with the aliens. Cody admired Henderson's ability to get things done, and the way in which he didn't try and force his opinions on them. At the same time he couldn't help but feel a little uneasy. The man seemed just a little bit *too* smooth.

Downing Street, Whitehall

'We're allowing ourselves to become bogged down in speculation and analysis.' The PM's assessment was blunt, but his use of the word 'we' instead of 'you're' was clever and defused the sense that any criticism was intended.

Tom Willoughby, the beleaguered Secretary of State for Defence, could only agree. 'Yes, Prime Minister.'

The PM let his briefing pack fall to the low table that separated the two men. 'Van Buren said this, we think that . . . the truth is, we don't know. But I *do* know we're wasting time on this. When these debriefing sessions were first proposed I thought it essential that we should be represented. But now I find two of our key people are away just when I need them here.'

'There is a secure link, Prime Minister—'

The PM cut short S of S's objection. 'You know my views on that. I'm not entirely convinced, given the Americans' track record, that there's any such thing as secure communications.

Even your own MOD analyses say it's impossible to be *certain* on this point – and we *need* to be certain.'

S of S nodded his agreement. 'CDI and CSA are on their way back, and for the time being their places at Van Buren's debriefing sessions will be taken by our Ambassador and Defence Attaché.'

'Very good. But Tom, listen, we really can't get engrossed in all this business with Van Buren and Roswell and every other story we've been told. The game's moved on, and we need to focus on what's happening *now*. If Van Buren can fill in a few gaps, and provide us with useful data, then fine. But for now we need to concentrate on what we actually *know*. We need a Gordian-knot solution to this problem – we must cut through the crap.'

S of S had no problem with what the PM was saying, and appreciated his directness. The PM had a reputation for being obsessed with the media and for speaking in soundbites, but in private, with his ministers and close confidants, he was a plain-speaking man who was quick to see to the heart of an issue. 'Yes, Prime Minister. Now, what should we do about issuing our media statement? Did you get a chance to look at what my people worked up?' S of S could be direct himself, and swiftly moved the discussion on to another area of concern.

'It's fine. I looked at it, and talked it through with my Press Secretary and your Chief Press Officer. We thrashed out a couple of minor changes, and it should go live any time now.'

'What's next?' S of S knew that the PM was in frequent touch with the Palace, the UN and other world leaders, and was grateful for the opportunity to be briefed on the latest thinking.

'I'll have to make a personal statement to Parliament, and I plan to address the nation later tonight. Tomorrow there'll be a debate at the UN, which will decide on an official response to the aliens' message. As you know, numerous individuals and a handful of nations are *already* responding, mostly saying friendly things and claiming that they want no part in any hostilities.'

'Hmm. The UN debate will involve everyone, I presume?'

'Oh, it has to,' the PM replied. 'Politically we'd be crucified if there was any hint of closed sessions, especially with some countries already trying to make peace deals on their own. But informal soundings suggest that all Security Council members are planning to hold the line that we'll try for a peaceful solution, but will fight anything that looks like an invasion.'

'I see a danger that the aliens will exploit this and try to break our resolve by playing up the idea that they have peaceful motives.' S of S offered his own analysis.

'I agree. If they succeed, they'll face a situation where many nations will offer no resistance, and even those that do will face opposition from their own citizens – the democratic nations, at least. Are you continuing to develop plans to destroy the ship?' The PM brought S of S back to his own area of responsibility.

'My people have continued to develop Operation Lightning Strike. As you know, we plan to attack the rear end of the vessel with nuclear weapons in an attempt to rupture the antiproton-containment field, so that matter and antimatter annihilate one another, blowing the entire back end off the ship. We now believe we have a workable plan but, as you know, only the Americans have the space shuttles that we'd need to do the job. We don't have time to build our own. So I need your permission to bring the Americans in. They'll have to fly the mission.'

The PM thought for a moment. 'OK. But I still don't know whether we can really trust the Americans. I'll want some of our own people on that mission.'

'I'm not sure there's time to train RAF pilots to fly shuttles, and the Americans only have a handful – they'll want experienced astronauts on board.'

'That's no good if they don't complete their missions. I want RAF people up there – as co-pilots, observers, whatever.' The PM's knowledge of the way in which shuttles were crewed was scant, but his intention was clear. 'The RAF can check that the job's being done properly, and we can have SAS troops up there to do something about it if it isn't.'

'I'll work that into our battle plan, but I think it's something you'll have to raise personally with President Spencer when you talk to her about Operation Lightning Strike. We have to convince her about the plan itself first, before we get into issues like this.'

'Very well. But I still—' the Prime Minister was interrupted by a knock at the door, which opened before any response was received. Few would dare to do this, especially when explicit instructions had been given that the meeting was not to be interrupted. *This must be important.*

'My apologies, Prime Minister, but you need to know about this immediately.' The PM's private secretary ushered in CDS, CAS and a younger RAF officer whom neither the PM nor S of S recognized.

'What is it?'

'This is Flight Lieutenant Chris Wardell from RAF Oakhanger,' CAS began. 'He's the watchkeeper who first detected the alien signal. He's a specialist in cryptography and has specialist knowledge of radio astronomy. I'll let him explain a critical new development.'

The PM admired the way that the military were prepared to let specialists – particularly such junior ones – brief on issues. It was certainly in line with his own philosophy that he wanted briefs from the experts who'd actually done the work, or made the analysis, rather than from their bosses who would paraphrase the data, perhaps misunderstanding it in the process and garbling the message. 'Go on.' It was offered in a friendly way, to put the young RAF man at ease.

'Prime Minister, when carrying out a follow-up analysis on the message, I detected another signal, piggybacking the original one. This message is encrypted, but with a code that was comparatively easy to break. We don't know who else knows about the coded message, but we're hoping that it's only us.'

Wardell paused, and the PM asked the obvious question. 'Have you decoded the message?'

'Yes, Prime Minister. They're asking for a meeting.'

Chapter Four

TALKS ABOUT TALKS

Aberporth Range, Cardigan Bay

The fighting might have stopped, but the training never did. This time the mission was different and was to be the first major live-firing exercise involving the latest addition to the RAF's armoury. The directed-energy weapon had been developed at DERA's Farnborough site and was the first piece of hardware that UK scientists had back-engineered from the downed alien craft. It was actually a comparatively simple device, and the beauty of it was that it didn't need to be integrated into complex machinery. It was, as the RAF said, a stand-alone piece of kit that was a useful add-on to existing systems. The weapon – which fired bursts of superheated plasma – was easy to fit to airframes and was being introduced to various different aircraft, either in a defensive or an offensive role. The priority was to fit them to the air defence force – the ageing Tornado F3s and their replacements, the Eurofighter Typhoons. Despite heavy losses, the Typhoons and their pilots had proved themselves in Operation Thunder Child, and the programme to replace the Tornados was being accelerated.

The Typhoons were formidable aircraft – easy to fly and highly manoeuvrable. They also packed quite a punch; they could be fitted with a mix of air-to-air missiles, including the ASRAAM, whose infra-red seeker could lock on to a target before or after launch, giving the pilot what was known as a fire-and-forget capability. But experience had shown that the aliens could break the lock-ons of these missiles by charging the hulls of their craft and shorting out the electronics. The alien hulls could also be cooled rapidly, which was another way in which these heat-seeking weapons could be fooled.

The Typhoons could also carry AMRAAMs or BVRAAMs for longer-range engagements. These were radar-guided but, again, the aliens seemed able to defeat the technology. This had led to an ironic realization: modern air-warfare doctrine stated that in air-to-air combat the best tactic was to engage your enemy from as far away as possible. American missiles such as Phoenix and Sparrow were particularly effective, but the BVRAAM – which stood for 'beyond visual range air-to-air missile' – was also a top-of-the-range weapon. But faced with an enemy who seemed able to defeat radar-guided and infra-red technology, the RAF had realized that their best hope was to get as close to the enemy as possible, and either fire their missiles from close in, before the enemy had time to activate their countermeasures, or even open fire with what had always been regarded as a last resort – the Mauser 27mm cannon.

The directed-energy weapon changed all that. The RAF would now be able to engage the enemy at long range but, it was hoped, with something that couldn't be deflected: it would either hit or miss. There had been numerous field tests before it had been customized for the RAF, and the decision had been taken – by the Prime Minister – to share this technology with the Americans, despite a strongly voiced and somewhat cynical observation that they probably had it already. It was difficult to say for sure, but rumours were circulating about how the weapon was being hurriedly added to the fleet of space shuttles. The Americans were clearly making their own preparations to resist an invasion, although the space shuttles gave them an offensive capability that the British didn't have.

Isabelle Bentley was in a group of four aircraft heading towards a remotely piloted target drone. The new weapon had been designated the Skystriker, and she noted with satisfaction the green light that showed that the system was on-line and functioning properly. The site of this live-firing exercise was Aberporth range – a DERA range that was essentially an area of Cardigan Bay in Wales that could be set aside for military use and closed to all other sea and air traffic.

'Red Two, this is Red Leader; I have a visual on the target and am commencing my attack run.' The incorporation of the new weapon had led to much hilarity among the RAF, and those whose aircraft had been fitted with the Skystriker had started giving themselves call signs from the *Star Wars* films, much to the consternation of the fighter controllers. It was typical pilot humour but senior commanders were allowing it because, as ever, it was the pilots who'd be taking most of the risks. Even high-ranking officers tended to cut people a lot of slack if they were putting their lives on the line.

Bentley activated her Head-Up Display and manoeuvred the green symbol that appeared in front of her until it was superimposed on the target drone. Her gloved hand flexed once, then depressed the button that engaged the Skystriker. Several bursts of superheated plasma shot away from her aircraft at high speed, approached the drone and . . . missed.

'Shit.'

Her headset crackled into life. 'Remember, Izz, use the Force!'

'Fuck off, Robbie!'

Bentley banked her aircraft to the left, allowing the next pilot to take his turn. She didn't have a visual on the target, but a few minutes later she heard a whoop of joy on her headset, followed by Robbie Skinner's voice announcing that he'd become the first RAF pilot to become a 'space ace'. Bentley was disappointed, as she'd desperately wanted to claim that particular honour. But they were having fun, albeit in the course of doing some very hard and very serious training. That had to be good, she told herself. Shooting at drones was great but, as they all reminded themselves, drones didn't shoot back.

MOD Main Building, Whitehall

'What do you think, Nick?'

Templeton was flattered that the Minister was seeking his opinion so often but was mindful of the responsibility that this entailed. His advice needed to be sound, not least because lives might well depend on it. Blackmore had asked for his views on the encrypted message. 'Well, clearly we have to play ball and meet with them,' Templeton began. 'For a start, we might actually find out what's going on, but politically, if one side offers talks and the other says no, well . . .' There was no need to finish the sentence. 'The key decision we have to make is whether to go public at this stage. Jacqui Connolly's been talking to the PM's Press Secretary, and he wants to make it public that we've detected an encrypted message. He wants us to be totally up front and make an open announcement.'

'Christ,' Blackmore exclaimed, a smile on his face. 'That'll be a first!' The two men chuckled, glad of the light relief. But it was a joke that only the Minister could have made; the cautious Templeton would never have dared. 'Go on.'

'The PM's Press Secretary is worried that the aliens are playing us for suckers. Their message already makes us out to be the bad guys, and he thinks they're setting something up that'll strengthen that view with our citizens. There's clearly a public perception that we've been covering up the truth about UFOs, so if it subsequently emerges that we're having secret discussions it'll just reinforce the belief that we're the bad guys, we're the ones with something to hide and we're the ones telling lies. That's his view. I don't agree.'

Blackmore reminded himself that this was why Templeton was so valuable to him. When he had an opinion on something, he wasn't afraid to speak his mind, even if it conflicted with the views of considerably more senior personnel. 'Continue.'

'Minister, the encrypted message is very clever. It asks whether representatives of the five permanent members of the UN Security Council would be prepared to meet in private with what they term "ambassadors of peace". So the Press Secretary's right when he says disclosure would make us look bad, but what he's not realized is the extent to which it would make the aliens look bad. Their *overt* message said that they had a message of peace for *all* the people of Earth and that they were going over the heads of the leaders, direct to the people. But their *covert* message contradicts that, and asks for talks with the big five.'

'Surely that's a good reason for making it public?' Blackmore retorted. 'Surely it'll completely undermine their efforts to portray themselves as the innocent party?'

'Ah, but that's the beauty of it,' Templeton replied. 'I think they've done this deliberately, as a sign of good faith. They're giving us something that's more damaging to them than to us, if it comes out, and something that's damaging to them *whenever* it comes out because it'll expose their overt message as a sham.'

'Why would they give us so valuable a weapon?'

'Minister, they're putting us in a situation where we have more to gain than to lose. I think it's to show us that they're *desperate* to talk, and that has to be a good sign: why talk if you can just take what you want? Conclusion: they want to cut a deal.'

'Hmm.' Blackmore thought for a moment. 'What do the military think?'

'They're still mulling it over and will want to discuss it with you later today. But most of the key players want to go for the meeting and keep it secret. There's another reason.'

'Oh?'

'It's possible that the aliens would want the talks in a place where they could have total control over security. Minister, this may be an opportunity to get on to their ship.'

Downing Street, Whitehall

As the Prime Minister emerged from the door of Number Ten, the media representatives saw that he was wearing no jacket and his

shirt was open at the neck. The impression – deliberately culti-
vated – created by this smart but casual look was that he looked
businesslike but relaxed. It was designed, in part, to put people at
ease. The spin doctors thought that ordinary men and women
often mistrusted someone wearing a collar and tie and felt that if
a politician wanted to be seen as one of the people they shouldn't
dress up like a bank manager or stockbroker. The old school
believed that a suit gave you authority but the prevailing view of
the modernists was that the *really* powerful people didn't need to
give themselves the appearance of authority by dressing up. It was
a typical piece of reverse psychology, they argued.

The Prime Minister approached the lectern and faced the
cameras. All the major networks were represented and those that
weren't had been promised free access by others who were present.
The price of access was silence: no questions would be taken. This
was an address to the nation, not a press conference. The Prime
Minister glanced at his notes and began.

'As many of you will know, we have now received a message
from the civilization that is *en route* to this planet. It is couched in
terms of peace and this gives us great hope. The communication
speaks of assurances given in the past and I should like to give *you*
an assurance: this country has *never* done a deal with these people.
If a deal *was* done, it was done by others; by individuals who had
no right to offer or make it. These entities call themselves
refugees. This country has always prided itself on welcoming
refugees, and it is our intention to offer the hand of friendship to
these newcomers. None of this should detract in any way from the
harm that has been done – in particular, the deaths of those brave
men and women who gave their lives in defensive operations to
counter what were – make no mistake – hostile, aggressive actions
against this country. Be that as it may, it is our fervent hope that
these attacks were the result of a misunderstanding – some
terrible, tragic mistake. It is our desire to see peaceful contact
between our peoples, and we are actively working towards this
aim.

'This is not a party political issue. I have had discussions with leaders of all the main political parties, and continue to consult with them as the situation evolves. Neither is this merely a national issue: the imminent arrival of these beings is something that will affect *all* the people of this planet, and it is for this reason that the United Nations is to debate the issue tomorrow and decide on an official response to the message we have received. On this point, we have been criticized for not having responded already, and indeed some nations and numerous private individuals *have* already sent their own replies. We understand their desire to make contact and resolve this situation peacefully. On the other hand, we also understand that first contact is a moment of unprecedented importance for the people of this planet. We believe it should not be rushed, and that our reply – when it comes – should be a considered one.

'What will we say? I have already had discussions with numerous world leaders and we are all agreed that our message will be one of peace. There are some pretty wild rumours flying around at the moment, but I stand before you this evening in hope. We are doing everything that we can to bring about a peaceful resolution of this situation. The message we have received talks about the possibilities that could result from contact and this is a sentiment that we share, wholeheartedly. Peaceful coexistence is not simply the *best* way forward – it is the *only* way forward. We have been working towards this aim, and we shall continue to do so. Thank you.'

BBC Television Studios, White City

Tom Willoughby had had very little notice of his *Newsnight* appearance. The PM's Press Secretary had telephoned him late in the day, and told him that the PM was going to address the nation in the early evening. *Newsnight* had been screaming for an interview ever since the message had been received and, given that the PM had talked about openness, it was judged that the time had come to put a government minister up to give an interview. Getting positive, high-profile coverage in the *Sun* and the *Mirror* might have been the best way to shape popular opinion, but if you needed to win over the Establishment it was generally acknowledged that there were three key media outlets that were pivotal to influencing the key decision-makers in the country. The front page of the *Daily Mail* was one, and Radio 4's *Today* programme was another. *Newsnight* was the third and was also the one that was generally regarded as the most problematic – due in no small part to the reputation of Marcus Rosental, the feared presenter whose abrasive style was popular with viewers but a potential disaster for politicians.

Willoughby went through the usual tiresome preliminaries of a television appearance, allowing the sound engineer to mike him up and test the levels before proceeding to a room where a young woman dabbed his face with make-up to stop him 'glowing' under the studio lights. The producer ran through the format of the show, and reminded him to switch off any mobile phone or bleeper that he might have been carrying.

It had been agreed that this would be a straight one-on-one interview, with no other studio guests to offer differing views. This was good news and bad news: while it meant that Willoughby wouldn't run the risk of being outperformed by another guest or bogged down in a three or four-way discussion, it meant that Rosental would be concentrating solely on him. There was no way of telling what sort of ride Rosental would give him and the producers gave the presenter so much leeway here that it often came down to his personal view on a subject or even on the interviewee. Rosental had interviewed Willoughby once before – on the subject of homosexuals in the armed forces – and had given him a hard time. But they'd had a friendly chat afterwards and Willoughby was reasonably confident that there was no personal animosity that might sour things now.

Although Willoughby was a little nervous – no one who wasn't a media professional ever *quite* got used to live television – he was reasonably confident. All government ministers now underwent formal media training, where they were put under enormous pressure by trained journalists poached by the Cabinet Office or the Central Office of Information. Willoughby's confidence also stemmed from the fact that he was well briefed. Although he'd delegated much of the day-to-day running of the crisis to his junior ministers, he'd made sure that he was involved in every key decision and informed of every significant development.

Furthermore, like all Defence ministers, Willoughby was sent constantly updated defensive press lines on every aspect of the crisis. Much of the brief had been written by his own people – mainly Jacqui Connolly and Nick Templeton – and approved by Willoughby himself, so he was familiar with the contents. The remainder had been prepared by other government departments and dealt with specific issues such as science and technology more generally. But all of these press briefs had been approved by the PM's Press Secretary to ensure that all those within Government were speaking with one voice. Willoughby hated the phrase 'on-message' but there was no denying the importance of unity, especially in times of national crisis: the government had to supply firm leadership on such occasions and this meant no mixed messages.

Willoughby was escorted to his seat by the floor manager and exchanged a brief greeting with Rosental before the producer warned them they'd be going live within thirty seconds. Moments later, a countdown was begun from ten seconds, the last three being notified silently with fingers extended. *Show time!*

Once the opening music was over, Rosental spoke directly to one of the cameras – the red light showing that it was live. He ran through the items that would be covered and, once that was over, launched directly into a scripted monologue about the current crisis, giving a general background briefing. There was then a pre-recorded segment, during which Rosental told Willoughby he'd be coming to him next. The red light on the camera reappeared, indicating that it was time.

'With me this evening is Tom Willoughby, the Secretary of State for Defence. Perhaps I can start by asking whether it is the Government's intention to seek a dialogue with these people?'

It was an easy question, giving Willoughby the chance to deploy a pre-prepared answer. 'It most certainly is. As the Prime Minister has explained, it is our hope that this situation can be resolved peacefully. As you know, the United Nations is to debate the situation tomorrow and agree a formal response to the message we've received. We—'

'Well, why, if you're talking about peaceful resolution of the crisis, is the Ministry of Defence still lead department?' Rosental's first question had been designed to start the interview smoothly but he knew Willoughby would have had a monologue prepared and he wasn't about to let him waste valuable time delivering it. Ministers were media-trained for such interviews and Rosental knew that the interviewee always tried to give as lengthy an answer as possible to reduce the number of questions asked.

'We're hoping for a peaceful resolution, but despite the fine words we've heard from these people, their actions so far have been hostile, and I need hardly remind you that men and women have been killed in defensive actions.' Willoughby had deliberately stressed the word 'defensive', and had made a point of reminding the audience that some of the military personnel killed had been women. Although women were fully integrated by now into the armed forces and took their chances along with their male counterparts, the *public* were still more squeamish about the deaths of women.

'So you're ready to fight if you have to?' Rosental asked.

'We hope we won't have to but, if we're attacked, we'll defend ourselves.' A short, factual answer, because it was an area Willoughby didn't want to discuss and it left no hook on which Rosental might hang a follow-up.

'This is a civilization capable of interstellar travel and one that may have the ability to destroy all life on Earth,' Rosental began, clearly speaking from script. Willoughby considered interrupting, a tactic ministers had been taught to use if it might disrupt what looked like a damaging, pre-prepared monologue. But Rosental would know what he was doing and this ploy might be counter-productive if it stung him into confrontation. 'How could you possibly mount any realistic defence? And if you did sting them into a response, might your actions not bring about the deaths of those you seek to protect?'

'Our previous responses to aggressive action have not been entirely without success,' Willoughby replied, cautiously. *Where is this going?* 'But, as I've said, our aim is for a peaceful resolution to this crisis and that is something that we're all working towards.'

'There is only one ship?' Rosental ventured.

'Yes.'

'If this ship were to be destroyed, the threat would disappear?'

'We don't know. They say they're refugees but we have no firm intelligence on where they come from or what other support systems they may have. It would be dangerous to make assumptions about such matters and, indeed, it would be singularly unhelpful to do so.'

'But presumably, despite your desire to avoid conflict, you're ready for it if it comes?'

'Yes.'

'So you have a contingency plan to destroy their ship?'

'You know that we never discuss such matters – and I must say that such questions are particularly unhelpful in a situation where we're trying to reach a peaceful settlement.' Willoughby delivered the standard reply and tried to suppress his mounting anger. Was Rosental trying to make him angry, to provoke him into a reaction?

'Who decides on our response?'

'As I've said, the United Nations will debate the issue—'

'Yes, but what about our own people? Do they get a say in all this? Your government is committed to holding a referendum on any issue of national importance. What if the people disagree with whatever response is proposed by their leaders?'

It was a question that the MOD had anticipated. 'We will consult the people if we can, although in times of national crisis a government sometimes has to take decisions on behalf of the people who elected it to power; sometimes, with the best will in the world, things happen which demand an immediate reaction.'

'How long until the alien ship arrives?'

'We don't know. That depends on its capabilities, and that's something on which we don't have firm intelligence.'

'If it maintains its current speed?'

'Its speed is not constant.'

'The consensus among scientific opinion is that it's decelerating at a fairly constant rate and that it will be in orbit around the Earth within two weeks. Do you disagree with that assessment?'

'I understand the reasoning behind this assumption,' Willoughby replied. 'But, as I say, it's an assumption and nothing more. It would be foolish to try and—'

'So you're saying that the vast majority of scientists who've studied this may be wrong?'

Willoughby thought about that for a moment. Rosental was clearly trying to trick him into a statement that would provoke angry denials from the scientific community. 'Of course not. I'm just saying that we can't make assumptions in this situation.'

'Do we have enough time left to carry out a referendum?'

Shit, this isn't going very well. Willoughby had been trained to be particularly wary of questions that sought yes-or-no answers and had been coached that the best way to respond was with another question. 'What question would you have me pose?'

'Should we use violence to resist an alien attack? I ask because opinion polls suggest an overwhelming desire for a peaceful solution.'

'That is meaningless. We will defend ourselves against attack but our aim is peace, and that is what we'll work towards.'

'Ah, but that's my point,' Rosental countered. 'Some people say that we *shouldn't* resist an attack, because it will result in our complete destruction.'

'Look, you can't expect me to discuss such matters when there are so many unknowns.'

'So the government doesn't *know* what's going on, or what it should do?' Rosental's question was deliberately provocative but at least Willoughby had manoeuvred him away from asking about a referendum.

'That's a cheap shot,' Willoughby countered. 'You know very well that it would be foolish to discuss such matters in an open forum.' The message was clear enough: the aliens were probably listening to this broadcast.

'I've noticed something interesting.' Rosental's expression was one of exaggerated puzzlement. 'Both you and the Prime Minister have used the phrase "these people" to describe the aliens. Is this deliberate policy? Nobody's used the word "alien" or "extraterrestrial". Is this something that's been agreed centrally?'

'We're certainly trying to avoid using loaded words like "alien" between of the negative implication that such words have.' Willoughby hadn't explicitly answered but he'd been forced to make a revelation of sorts, judging that this was better than evading the question and avoiding a follow-up. It was a clever line of enquiry.

'What about the issue of a cover-up?' Rosental changed the subject quickly, and his short question suggested to Willoughby that time was running out. Politicians always tried to look out for signs that the interview was nearly over so that they could end the session with a closing statement designed to give them the last word and allow them to end on a pre-prepared statement that got the message across to the audience.

'Much has been said about a cover-up,' Willoughby began. 'But there's really no evidence to support such a theory. We're examining these claims, of course, to see if they hold water, but our best assessment is that any such cover-up involved only a handful of people, acting without the knowledge or approval of their own governments.'

'Including people within the British government?'

'That has yet to be determined. Investigations are continuing, but—'

'What would happen to such people? Would they be tried in a court of law?'

'We would have to examine the circumstances of each case, and seek legal advice. It would be foolish to speculate on such matters without knowing the facts.' A clever although somewhat obvious response; say that something would be foolish and plant in the minds of viewers the thought that anyone who pursued such a line of enquiry was a fool.

'One final question. What is your message to those people who plan to demonstrate next week against MOD secrecy on UFOs?'

'I understand their concerns and I fully support their right to express their views,' Willoughby began in a suitably conciliatory tone. 'They have some questions they want answering and, frankly, so do we. We are still investigating the background to this situation in an attempt to find out who knew what. When we have that information we will make it public if we can. For now, we continue to work towards a peaceful resolution of this situation and look forward to an open dialogue with our visitors.'

'Thank you, Secretary of State. In line with the government's policy on openness and its desire to keep people informed, we trust that you'll be able to come on the programme again as the situation develops?'

Ah, that's why you eased up at the end, and even gave me warning about the last question. 'I hope so. We'll certainly be keeping people informed.'

'Well, we'll hold you to that. Thank you.'

Willoughby, remaining in his seat while Rosental went on to the next item, waited for its introduction pre-recorded segment to be broadcast. When it was, he exchanged a couple of words with Rosental before being led out by the floor manager. After having his make-up removed he was taken to his car and driven back to Central London where the PM's Press Secretary was waiting. The interview had been recorded, of course, and the two men would run through the tape together to see if there was anything on which they needed to brief the PM. Willoughby was pretty pleased with his performance, although the final question had been unexpected: they had traded a relatively easy ride for the promise of future interviews, although Willoughby was sure that his 'I hope so' left him sufficient room for manoeuvre. Rosental's 'We'll hold you to that' showed that he'd taken it as a promise, or rather – knowing Rosental – that he'd wanted to make it sound like one, even though he knew it wasn't. *The games we play.* Willoughby sighed to himself as he relaxed in the back of his ministerial car and tried to stop himself from falling asleep.

Farnham, Surrey

'Hi, Richard.' The call had been expected.

'Jenny, hi,' Cody replied. 'No need to ask what you've just been watching. What did you think?'

'Notice how they're not calling them aliens any more? He called them "these people" and the PM called them "newcomers" in his broadcast earlier this evening. But the big one – wow – he ended up by referring to them as "our visitors".'

Not for the first time, Cody was struck by Thornton's perceptive nature. As an indicator of government policy, few things were as important as the words you used, when you had a choice. As a former barrister, Cody knew this well from his personal experience but he knew it was equally important for politicians. Words were what you used to label people: good or bad; friend or foe. And now the government were using neutral or even positive words. That was good, wasn't it, provided it was from the heart, and not just spin? 'Yes, that *is* interesting, Jenny.'

'So the government's going to do a deal and not fight?'

'It looks that way, yes. How do you feel about that?'

'I don't know. These aliens made me and the others suffer for years and now they've killed people. But if Maxwell Henderson's right, well, maybe they thought they had the right to, if somebody made a deal and purported to represent us all. I don't want a war, Richard, especially if it's one we can't win.' Thornton paused and Cody was astute enough not to reply, suspecting she had more to say. 'But I do want an apology, from the government *and* from the *visitors*.' The last word was delivered with heavy sarcasm. 'I don't want what we went through swept under the carpet.'

'Of course not.' But even as Cody said it, he suspected that this was precisely what was happening. He'd thought that confirmation of an extraterrestrial presence would justify the claims of the abductees and ufologists and lead to their assertions being accepted by everyone. That had happened, to an extent, but was now an issue in danger of being lost in the margins of the larger story. 'Are you going to the demonstration?'

'I don't know. Maybe. How about you?'

'Probably not,' Cody admitted. 'I suspect it'll be hijacked by radical elements – and not just ufologists this time. I'd be careful.' He could hardly advise Thornton of all people not to go, but he was genuinely worried that the whole event would turn into a riot, with anarchist groups using it as an excuse for causing trouble.

'Yes, well, I haven't decided yet, anyway.'

They spoke for a few minutes more but there was little else to discuss. Events would move quickly now and were in the hands of others. As Cody replaced the telephone receiver he mulled over the developing situation. Matters would be debated in Parliament and discussed by the United Nations and a dialogue was to be opened with the aliens – he couldn't bring himself to call them anything else. Cody had always distrusted the MOD and the government on the UFO issue. But even if he could trust them now, could any of them trust the aliens? At least humans could relate to other humans and try to get a handle on their motivations. But did they have any way of gauging the alien agenda? It all came down to who you trusted more. And on that issue – conspiracy theorist or not – Cody had always been prepared to favour his fellow humans.

House of Commons, Westminster

It was actually rather a good time for a debate, the senior party figures had reasoned. The Speaker had been fairly bullish of late, and had spoken privately to a number of ministers, telling them that she would not tolerate a situation where she first heard about major policy initiatives in the media. It had been a long-running bone of contention, but this current Speaker was a stickler for procedure and had issued a number of embarrassing public rebukes when the convention had been flouted. Parliament, she had reminded the offenders, should be the first to be told. She had let it be known that she expected the Secretary of State for Defence or the Prime Minister to come to the House at least once a week to make a parliamentary statement, which would then be debated. She had also let it be known that, if this didn't happen, she would allow a Private Notice Question to be tabled, which would force the relevant minister to come to the House. This would have been an embarrassing way of doing business, so the government had cooperated with the Speaker's wishes.

The current debate had begun with a statement from Tom Willoughby, who had reiterated what the Prime Minister had said to the nation the night before and confirmed that the PM was *en route* to New York for discussions at the UN. The reason this had been judged to be a good time for a debate was that the government could largely fall back on a standard line about not wanting to pre-empt any decisions made by the UN. But, as often happened in parliamentary debates, an unexpected question could throw a spanner into the works, particularly if the Speaker was generous with the time available for the debate and the extent to which she was happy to allow a broad range of questions. Governments didn't like surprises.

'Madam Speaker, can the Right Honourable Gentleman give this House a categorical assurance that the government will honour whatever decision is reached by the *entire* United Nations and not come to a private agreement with the other permanent members of the Security Council?'

Willoughby knew the rules. You could refuse to answer, you could – to a certain extent – give an incomplete or ambiguous answer, but you could never lie. To tell a deliberate lie – especially to parliament – would result in the swift end of a political career; whatever the cynics and conspiracy theorists thought, lying really wasn't that common and when it was discovered it was harshly punished. 'It would be irresponsible of me to go into details about our response until the UN has debated the issue.'

'Answer the question.' The shouts came from several opposition members.

'Order.'

'I must press the Minister on this point. Will the government abide by whatever decision is reached by the UN, or will policy be decided in private by the Security Council? Maybe such a policy has already been formulated?' The fact that the Speaker had allowed the question to be restated was the clearest possible indication that she was sympathetic to the questioner.

'As I have said, I don't want to prejudge the UN debate or make any statement that would undermine that debate. When the debate has concluded, this government – in consultation with the main opposition parties – will consider the way forward.'

'Will you abide by the UN's decision?' Again, this was shouted by an MP from the opposition backbenches.

'Order. I will not tolerate any further interruptions from MPs in sedentary positions.' The Speaker called another MP and Willoughby hoped it would be a fresh question. The truth of the matter – which was logical, but not something to which the government wished to admit publicly – was that no government would allow itself to be bound by a UN decision with which it didn't agree. It might well be that the UN would agree a common policy but if it didn't, or if the majority view was unpalatable to the UK, then individual nations might well go their own ways. In either event, Willoughby knew full well that there would be numerous private discussions between the leaders of the five permanent members of the Security Council.

'Can the Right Honourable Gentleman say whether he will allow all the UFO files originating from his department or its predecessors to be made available to the public?' The UFO lobby had been pressing for this for several years, and even the less conspiracy-minded elements of this particular group had been surprised to find that some files were still not available, even under the Freedom of Information Act. This, they reasoned, proved that the MOD did indeed have highly classified information concerning official knowledge of an alien presence.

'Most of the files are already open,' Willoughby began. This question was one that had been anticipated. 'A small number have been withheld and will remain so for now, at least until such time as we have thoroughly reviewed all the data as part of our ongoing investigation into precisely who knew what.' He decided to go on the offensive. 'Several Honourable Members have pressed this government to examine these records to see if there are any indications of a conspiracy and I hope they will appreciate that we cannot make such material public until such time as these investigations are complete, not least because such a move might be prejudicial to any legal action.' Willoughby had fallen back on a contrived but essentially true defence: the matter wasn't technically *sub judice* but the possibility of legal action meant that Willoughby had an excuse not to open the files just yet.

The next question was also a legal one. But while the first part of the question had been anticipated, the second had not. 'As I understand the situation, the Right Honourable Member has indicated that criminal charges will be brought against any UK citizen found to have been part of a conspiracy to cover up knowledge about these aliens. Can he tell this House whether the same is true for any officials who had access to data that *should* have indicated an alien presence but who did nothing because of their own ignorance, prejudice, belief systems or whatever.'

'Hear, hear.' This came from several MPs on both sides of the Chamber.

'As to the first part of the question, we have already made it clear that such actions will be dealt with in accordance with the law. If there is a case to answer, one will be brought – this is a matter of law, not politics. The same would apply to the second part of your question, although my personal view is that such a course of action would be unlikely and unwarranted. I have every confidence in the abilities of my officials and their predecessors.' Willoughby hoped this would suffice but the Speaker allowed a supplementary question.

'The Right Honourable Member's loyalty to his officials is commendable but quite unjustified. We now know that a UFO landed in Rendlesham Forest in December 1980 and that it was seen by numerous United States Air Force personnel. We know that a UFO flew over RAF Cosford and RAF Shawbury in March 1993. We have numerous cases from the MOD's own files of UFOs being tracked on radar, of RAF jets being scrambled, of civilian and military pilots having near misses in UK airspace with these craft. And yet nothing was done, and ministers were briefed by their officials that these events were of no defence significance. How *can* such events have been of no defence significance?' This was turning into a speech, but there were enough cries of 'hear, hear' for the Speaker to justify allowing things to continue. 'Some officials within the Ministry of Defence wilfully ignored a threat to their county. Was this due to stupidity – or to something more sinister? And in *either* event, will he agree that criminal charges – up to and including the charge of treason – may be appropriate.'

The House erupted into a cacophony of noise, with cries of 'hear, hear' mixed in with cries of 'shame'. There was even some clapping from the Public Gallery, although this was lost in the general noise.

'Order. Order. Will members please resume their seats and let the Minister answer the question.' The noise subsided somewhat. 'Order. I will not tolerate behaviour of this sort, and it sets a very bad example for members to act in so rowdy a way, given the importance of the subject under discussion.'

Willoughby was at least grateful that the interruption gave him time to think through a response. He wanted to defend his officials but Nick Templeton had anticipated this sort of criticism and the minister's briefing pack had suggested a short, low-key response reiterating the legal point. On the basis that Templeton was in the front line over the accusation, Willoughby felt more comfortable in following his advice. 'As I have said, action against any officials will be determined in accordance with the law.' He was tempted to add to this but, as with television interviews, lengthy parliamentary replies tended to provoke supplementary questions because there was more likely to be a hook on which to hang one. Willoughby knew that Templeton must have been stung by the question, but had to admire the man's coolness under fire. Still, this was a potentially damaging new development, and Willoughby had a feeling that it wouldn't be the last they'd hear of it.

United Nations Headquarters, New York

'This isn't going very well.' The PM had already had a number of bilateral meetings with the US President and discussions with the leaders of the other permanent members of the Security Council –

France, China and the Russian Federation. By mutual agreement, other key nations had been privy to private discussions that had taken place outside the main debating chamber. This meant that Germany, Israel, Australia, Japan, Saudi Arabia and one or two other countries had also been involved.

'No, although that's no great surprise.' President Spencer agreed with the PM's assessment and decided to use this one-to-one discussion to test the resolve of her British counterpart. 'The smaller nations look to be carrying the day and have clearly had their own private discussions. There are several people singing off the same song-sheet, that's for sure.'

The PM nodded his agreement.

'But they're the nations who have the least to lose,' Spencer continued. 'They're probably buying into all sorts of New Age crap about redistribution of wealth, an end to poverty and disease, and so on. I think it's all nonsense. We're facing an invasion and the aliens are launching a PR offensive to try and weaken our resolve and destroy our unity by winning over as many of the smaller nations as they can. Divide and conquer, it's as simple as that. The question is, if they want to sue for peace, and the terms aren't favourable, will you fight?'

'Will *you*?' The PM took the easy option, and threw the question back at the President.

'Naturally, our first goal is peace,' Spencer began, cautiously. 'We'll certainly give the aliens a fair hearing at the talks. But we don't trust them, and if they come here it'll have to be on our terms. If that's not acceptable, then yes, we'll resist.'

'That's our position too,' the PM agreed. 'But when you say "on our terms", what precisely do you mean?'

'Well, specifically, we'd want to get our people up on to their ship before there were any landings. We'd want to inspect it fully and get firm data on how many of them are up there, and what other surprises they might have for us. We'd want to screen them medically to ensure there's no biological hazard and we'd want to ensure that they shared their technology with us. That's just for starters.'

'I agree. They'll have to hold in orbit while these issues are addressed. An unauthorized landing will be viewed as an act of war. On that point, though, do we really have sufficient resources to take them on and either win or, at the very least, force them to negotiate on our terms?'

'Yes, we do.' Spencer gave no further details, but her face suggested she wasn't bluffing. What were the Americans planning, the PM wondered, and would they share their plans with the UK?

Pyramid Heights, Westminster

Maxwell Henderson had trusted aides monitoring key developments in Parliament, at the UN and elsewhere. Their job was to brief him on major items of news as they happened. In addition, he had a number of television sets at his home, one of which was permanently displaying the news on Ceefax, while another was tuned to CNN. The arrangement was one that he'd adapted from his time as a government minister and it worked well. Two interesting items had just come to his attention and he was briefing a small group of associates – MPs, businesspeople and others in positions of authority – on these developments.

'One of our group, as planned, raised in Parliament the issue of treason charges against MOD officials. We'll push this – discreetly – with our media contacts and ensure that the story gets some coverage. This gives us another possible line of attack against the government, and we could look at the idea of bringing a private prosecution.'

'Bring in Cody on that?' someone suggested. 'He's a barrister by profession and knows as much about the UFO situation as anyone outside government.'

'Maybe,' Henderson allowed, not committing himself to any decision. 'The second piece of news concerns a second message from the ship. I'm reliably informed that it's medical in nature and that it seeks to explain some of their previous activities here as being connected with eliminating any biological hazard, either from us to them or vice versa. But they say that in the course of this process – which included studying all our diseases and immunizing themselves against them – they discovered cures and vaccines for some of them. They've sent formulae that we can use to manufacture these defences. This news has not yet been made public but it was openly transmitted. The story could break at any time. What does this tell us?'

'The timing's hardly accidental,' one of those present observed. 'The day of the UN debate – talks with the aliens happening any time now. It's got to be a hearts-and-minds exercise.'

'Or simply a sign of good faith,' Henderson countered. 'But there's another message implicit in what they've said.' Henderson scanned the faces but saw only blank looks. 'If certain governments were going to resist the aliens, one of the logical means of attack might be to use a biological agent. This new statement strikes me as a subtle warning on this point. They say they know all our diseases and have their own immunity. Now, that may or may not be true but, speaking as someone who's played the government game, I think the message is clear enough.'

'Why warn us if they have immunity?' It was a perceptive question and one that allowed Henderson to say what had really been on his mind.

'You generally only warn someone not to do something that you *are* worried about. This *could* be their Achilles heel.'

Chapter Five

MAKING PLANS

Fort Meade, Maryland

The NSA's primary mission was eavesdropping. They listened in on telephone conversations from all around the world, scarcely distinguishing between intelligence-gathering operations in hostile and friendly countries alike. They justified spying on the latter by pointing out – quite correctly – that the greatest danger to any state often lay in plans being made within the country concerned, whether by terrorists, criminals or intelligence officers from other countries. Civil rights activists complained that the technology was being abused and that the NSA was not averse to carrying out what amounted to industrial espionage, giving US companies details of competitors' bids in competitive tenders.

Whatever the truth of these accusations, the NSA had found itself under more scrutiny than it would have wished and the discovery that its former Director – Edwin Van Buren – had been involved in a conspiracy connected with the alien presence only added fuel to this particular fire. There had been questions asked on both sides of the Atlantic, and in Britain there had even been calls for the NSA site at Menwith Hill to be closed down altogether. That the NSA had ridden out this storm was a testament to the value of its work.

The system was codenamed ECHELON. Every e-mail, telex and fax, every telephone conversation on the planet, whether from a landline or a cellular phone, was listened to by the NSA, using computers that looked for so-called keywords. These ranged from obvious ones, such as the names of known criminals and words like 'bomb', 'drugs' and 'weapons' to less obvious words like 'package', 'delivery', 'shipment' and 'consignment' – it was a sign of the times that much of the agency's effort was being channelled into the fight against organized crime and, in particular, the war against drugs. The same was happening with the Security Service – traditionally known as MI5 – in the UK.

The NSA owned some of the most powerful supercomputers in the world and once a keyword, or more usually a combination of keywords, had been identified, a recording of the conversation would find its way to an analyst. Furthermore, some locations and specific lines were targeted for permanent monitoring. But there were limitations. Some conversations were made from secure telephones and even the skilled cryptographers at Fort Meade couldn't break every code, although they had access to many systems falsely believed by their users to be secure.

They didn't always need to hear the conversation to know what was being said. This was something of a cliché at the National Security Agency but it was true enough. What it meant was that occasionally it was enough to know that particular people were talking to one another. The somewhat jocular example of this given at the NSA's most basic training course was an exercise concerning a telephone call received by a fire brigade headquarters from a private address. Trainee analysts were given two minutes to decode the fictitious message. The codes were unbreakable but anyone who didn't answer along the lines of 'There's a fire, please come quickly' found themselves humiliated in front of their fellow trainees. This most basic of principles had resurfaced now and the NSA's new Director, Casper Goldwater, was going over some interesting new data with his deputy.

'Thank you for this report, and for your assessment. I've seen the raw data, together with your report, but I want you to sell it to me as if I were a sceptic.'

'Yes, sir. In the last three weeks there have been four telephone calls between Russian Defence Minister Ivanov and the Chief of Biopreparat. Furthermore, there have been *twelve* calls between the head of Biopreparat and the Director of the Omutninsk production facility.'

'How does this compare to normal traffic?'

'We backtracked and counted the number of calls during every single three-week period over the last three years. There was never more than one call between each party, and plenty of occasions when there were no calls at all.'

'But you don't yet have a complete read-out on what was discussed?'

'No sir; we're still working on cracking their latest encryption codes. But we have additional intelligence from CIA to indicate that both Ivanov and Yazov visited the Omutninsk facility. Our best guess is that the Russians are discussing a biological attack on the aliens.'

'I concur. Let's discuss this with Colonel Willett at USAMRIID.'

Old War Office Building, Whitehall

It was the blackest of black projects, and yet it was being co-ordinated in the heart of Whitehall by a man armed only with a blank sheet of paper, a pen and a tape recorder. It was called remote viewing. Some people called it psychic spying, while others favoured the old-fashioned term: ESP. Few people knew about the Ministry of Defence remote-viewing programme, which was probably no bad thing: the Public Accounts Committee would have had a collective fit if it had known that taxpayers' money was being spent on such a project. So, like so many other black projects, the MOD's remote-viewing – RV for short – programme was carried out by one private company who'd been subcontracted by another private company who'd been hired by people at the Defence Intelligence Staff.

It was a complicated chain, designed to ensure that there was no direct link between the MOD and an RV programme. And yet, it was nothing more than an agreeable piece of fiction designed to take the whole project outside scrutiny by people like the PAC or the House of Commons Defence Committee. The private companies were staffed by ex-military personnel and former intelligence officers from various agencies – and none of them would tell tales out of school.

It was the former Soviet Union that had taken the first steps in this most bizarre of areas. They had carried out research into various branches of parapsychology and there was some evidence to suggest that they had identified a number of individuals who possessed telekinetic powers. Experiments to see whether a subject could shatter glass at a distance, using only the power of the mind, seemed to have borne fruit. But little more was known and, despite persistent rumours, it wasn't clear if any form of offensive capability had been developed.

The Americans had followed suit, not out of any corporate belief in such things, but simply because they had to be sure that the Soviets hadn't developed a new capability. So they threw a few million dollars into various research projects, not expecting success but being delighted when it came. Much of this work had been done at the Stanford Research Institute and, although developing repeatable, workable telekinesis had proved beyond their capabilities, remote viewing had proved a worthy substitute. There had been four official US RV projects, codenamed Grill Flame, Center Lane, Sun Streak and Stargate. The initial work was done by the US Army but it was the CIA and the DIA who quickly stepped in to take over. The psychics were mainly military personnel selected after undergoing standard tests to judge whether they had psychic ability. Several hundred volunteers had gone through a test first designed in the 1930s by the American parapsychologist J.B. Rhine. The test involved an attempt to divine the five symbols printed on a set of so-called Zener Cards. Those few who consistently scored higher than chance would dictate were co-opted on to the programme. A few civilians were also invited to participate because of their reputations as psychics, although they were only allowed in if they passed the test.

The American RV programmes had had some high-profile successes, most notably in the locating of illegal drug shipments, but just as the programme looked as if it might acquire a degree of respectability a sceptical Congress looking to make defence cuts pulled the plug on the entire project. The US was officially out of the RV game, although the CIA was still running a small programme in the margins of a separate contract, in a barely legal way of getting around Congress.

Britain had been a comparatively late entrant into this particular game but it did have a small RV programme of its own. It had been used with varying success during the Cold War and was credited with having located a number of dead-letter drops. But it had been put on hold of late, with sceptics pointing out that the number of failures dwarfed the successes, suggesting that the successes had more to do with the laws of chance than with any genuine phenomenon. It was the Chief of Defence Intelligence himself who had reactivated the project, in the aftermath of Operation Thunder Child. CDI had become increasingly frustrated at the MOD's lack of intelligence about the alien vessel heading for Earth; the scientists could tell him how big it was and how fast it was going, but for anything further they had been dependent upon the testimony of former NSA Director Edwin Van Buren, whom CDI distrusted. So CDI had reactivated the RV programme, on the entirely logical basis that they had nothing to lose.

The man in charge was Wing Commander Terry Carpenter. Carpenter headed a small section in the DIS known as Defence Intelligence (Miscellaneous Projects). DI(MP)'s innocuous name hid the exotic nature of its business – it was the part of the DIS that assisted Sec(AS) in its research and investigation into UFOs, alien abductions, crop circles, animal mutilations and other mysterious phenomena. Its brief was simply to see whether there were any defence implications in any of these areas. As recent events had proved so dramatically, there clearly were.

There were two ways to 'run' a remote viewer, the first of which was to give them details of the target and get them to find it. The instruction might be given: 'Describe the office of the President of the Russian Federation'. The problem with this was that the remote viewers would have their own preconceptions, which might unduly influence the results. The second method was a so-called blind search, where only the coordinator knew the target and the remote viewers were left to describe what came into their minds. Carpenter, being a methodical man, was using both methods, with six separate remote viewers.

The final subject was now being put through her paces. Her name was Sharon Smith, and she had been a corporal in Signals before being co-opted on to the RV programme. The session had been under way for ten minutes and Carpenter had not been hopeful. Smith looked as if she was in a trance and had been speaking quietly about the ocean. She'd mentioned a submarine, then floated the idea that she was looking at an aircraft carrier.

'Just tell me what you see,' Carpenter prodded, gently. 'It's not a test – there are no right or wrong answers here.' But in his mind a connection had suddenly been made. *Didn't one of the analyses of the alien ship liken it to an aircraft carrier?*

'OK, I see a vast room of some sort. A flight deck, maybe. It's dark and very cold. There are aircraft lined up against the far wall – hundreds of them. This must be one of the biggest Russian carriers.'

'Take a closer look at those aircraft?' Carpenter phrased it as a question, with the merest hint of a request. He normally didn't interrupt this much – like all good spooks he knew the value of silence and realized that listening was more important than talking – but this was proving to be a difficult session. Smith was usually much more relaxed and this, as much as the description she was now giving, convinced Carpenter that she might just be on target.

'The wings are folded back, to save space. Packed real tight. Sleek; shiny; new; are they stealths? No, I . . . oh my God! I'm on the alien ship, aren't I?' Smith's breathing was suddenly very heavy.

Carpenter knew that any sudden shock could bring remote viewers out of . . . wherever it was they went. He had to calm Smith down. 'Uh-huh.' His voice was very relaxed.

'There are hundreds of small craft here, lined up against the one side of the wall. The room's so big I can hardly see the other side, but the room looks empty apart from the craft. I guess it's a flight deck, like on an aircraft carrier.'

Smith had a pad and a pen on the table in front of her, although she wasn't using them, Carpenter noted. Some remote viewers sketched what they saw as they went along, while others found that a distraction and only started making drawings afterwards. Carpenter was more than happy to see that she was completely focused on the task in hand.

They had reached an interesting point. It had started as a blind session but the viewer had successfully guessed the target, so Carpenter pulled out a pre-prepared list of questions. 'Now we know that, like an aircraft carrier, this craft will have a bow and a stern. Maybe you can orientate yourself? You may instinctively know which way to go and I'd like you to imagine yourself at the back of the ship. Can you do that for me?'

'Mmm, yes, I think so.' There was a long pause. 'I think I'm there. It was a long way. There's lots of machinery and piping, but nothing I recognize. There's a massive . . . chamber, I suppose, and I sense that there's stuff being made in there. Dangerous stuff. I . . . I don't like this place very much.'

'That's quite understandable. Now, do any of those pipes you mention lead into the chamber?'

'They all do.'

'Can you follow them back for me?'

'Er, well, they kind of . . . well, they go two different ways. Which one do you want me to follow?'

'Can you see, or maybe *feel*, any difference between one set of pipes and another?' Carpenter was conscious that he was asking leading questions but he had seen people come out of trances spontaneously and so wanted to make the most of a session that – he believed – was right on target.

'One set of pipes is thicker and feels . . . weird.'

'OK, now I want you to let your awareness follow the thick pipes back and see where they lead. Please make a special effort to judge the distance you're travelling.'

There was a long pause. 'I'm about a mile in. There's a massive room, with very thick walls and – oh my God, there are people here.'

'Are they humanoid?' Carpenter asked.

Smith seemed confused. 'No, no, they're not aliens, they're *people*. Like you and me . . . they can see me!' Smith convulsed in her seat, as if she'd received a powerful electric shock. Her breathing was heavy and she was sweating. After a few moments she had regained her composure but it was clear that she was no longer in a trance state. The look on her face was one of surprise as she stared hard at Carpenter. 'They could see me. I don't know how, but they could *see* me.'

Peterson Air Force Base, Colorado

Those military personnel working at Air Force Space Command HQ had had a rude awakening. The Defense Department had all but closed down the US Army's Space and Missile Defense Command and transferred its functions to the Air Force. However much any USAF officer might enjoy winning a turf war with the Army, the circumstances were troubling, to say the least. The general in charge of the Army's research effort had been exposed as a member of The Enterprise and it had emerged that the work his people had been doing had had two purposes, not just the one the government had known about. Ostensibly, their brief had been to design, test and bring on-line systems designed to destroy satellites and ballistic missiles. Then there had been talk of adapting the technology for use against any comet or asteroid deemed to pose a threat to Earth – a fear that, it now appeared, had been deliberately fuelled by a series of TV documentaries, magazine articles, books and blockbuster movies.

But behind these overt intentions had been a covert one: the development of a viable defensive – and possibly even offensive – capability against the aliens. Behind this had been The Enterprise, who had apparently been making deals with the aliens while simultaneously trying to develop the means to destroy them. So the Air Force was now lead service and that suited General Grant Meadows just fine. He'd never seen the logic of splitting responsibility for space policy among the services and believed the unification of command was long overdue.

'OK, what can this Command put into the field if we get into a shooting war with these people?'

The man to whom General Meadows addressed this question was Brigadier General Budd Enkleman, Commander of the Space Warfare Center. Neither man wanted a war but standard military doctrine meant that they had to assume the worst-case scenario and prepare for one.

'OK, whether we're conducting defensive or offensive operations, and whatever ROE we're using, we should attempt to engage them at the earliest opportunity and at the maximum range. So we have a multi-faceted response that starts out in space and comes progressively closer in. First up, we hit 'em with the space shuttles, sir. Now, NASA has six vehicles at present: *Columbia*, *Discovery*, *Atlantis* and *Endeavour*, together with the two new ones, *Exploration* and *Enterprise*.'

Enkleman paused after speaking this last word. It was an unfortunate irony that one of the new space shuttles shared the name of the shadowy cabal that had been covertly dealing with the aliens, but the decision had been made before that particular group had emerged into the light of day, and the letter-writing campaign by *Star Trek* fans had finally proved irresistible.

'So how are NASA handling the modifications?'

'They're on schedule sir. The plasma weapons and lasers are installed, together with the necessary targeting systems and software. Ditto with the missiles.'

'The crews?'

'Training is nearly complete, although, as you know, it's all been done on the simulators. That worries me, sir.'

'Me, too.' Meadows nodded his agreement, although both men knew only too well that the President herself had ordered that no space shuttle launch was to be carried out before negotiations with the extraterrestrials, lest it should be seen as unduly provocative.

'Now, here's the bad news, sir. Although this tactic offers the greatest possibility for overall mission success, it's also the most susceptible to hostile action. We only have six vehicles, so if even one goes u/s, our capability is seriously eroded. If we're attacked before a launch – well, one hit on Cape Canaveral and we're out of the game altogether. And if one of the vehicles should explode on take-off, either because of a malfunction or due to hostile action . . . hell, with what they'll be carrying . . .' Enkleman's voice trailed off, but the point was clear enough.

'And if we *do* get them up? Chances of success?'

'Not good, sir. I suspect it'll be a turkey shoot, with us as the turkeys.'

'How's morale?'

'Sir, the astronauts are fine about it, but they're about the only ones who are. The corporate view of NASA is very much against what we're doing. Although there's a lot of Air Force people and ex-military there, it's essentially a civilian agency and they're all for a peaceful solution.'

'So are we,' Meadows snapped back, a little too harshly.

'I know that, sir, but they don't.'

'OK. What's next?'

'KE-ASAT, MIRACL, THAAD and the 747 fleet.' To any outsider the reply would have been unintelligible but it made perfect sense to Meadows. 'Chances are that our kinetic-energy anti-satellite system would never get near anything. It's slow, and they're hardly likely to sit back and watch while we park it next to anything up there. They'd probably fry it before it got close. I also doubt that our high-altitude missiles will do well. Where we could score big is with our laser weapons.'

Meadows nodded. This had been his assessment too, although he'd wanted to hear it from Enkleman, who'd been far more involved in the day-to-day development of their plans. The problem was simply one of numbers. There was only a handful of the MIRACL ground-based lasers, and the much-vaunted fleet of modified Boeing 747s, equipped with iodine lasers, numbered far less than either man would have wanted.

'Sir, what it all comes down to is what we've discussed before,' Enkleman summarized. 'We've got a lot of things that might dent them some, but until we have hard intelligence on their strength we won't know how big that dent is. If we took out, say, a hundred small craft, we wouldn't know if we'd degraded their capability by ten per cent, one per cent or *point* one per cent. Fact is, sir, unless we can hit the mothership, we're screwed, and *only* the shuttles can do that.'

It had been a pessimistic brief but Meadows couldn't find fault with the analysis.

MOD Main Building, Whitehall
As Nick Templeton made his way into Martin Blackmore's office, he could see that the Minister was not in the best of moods.

'That mad cow in number eight is hassling me again,' US of S began.

Templeton winced. It was one of those desperately unlikely and very unfortunate coincidences that popped up from time to time in government business. The Minister lived in a plush flat in Knightsbridge, and it just so happened that one of his neighbours in the same block – Georgina Bruni – had written a book on the Rendlesham Forest incident. She'd turned up at his door one evening and had thrust a signed copy of her book at him, having recognized him from an article in one of the newspapers, shortly after the events of Operation Thunder Child. He'd tried to avoid her but had occasionally been cornered and put on the spot over both the incident itself and recent developments.

'What now?' Templeton asked, sympathetically.

'She's heard about what happened in parliament yesterday, with this department being criticized for having done nothing about the Rendlesham incident.'

'But we've been through this, Minister. The Americans misled us about these events.'

'Not good enough, Nick,' Blackmore snapped back. 'Those Americans who witnessed events were totally straight with us. The Deputy Base Commander sent us a report.'

'It didn't go into that much detail.'

'Well, we should have *asked* for that detail.'

'It's still not entirely clear what happened once we received it.'

'Well, I can tell you what some MPs are saying,' the Minister retorted. 'They're saying the MOD sat on it out of ignorance and prejudice; that people heard the word "UFO" and parroted the standard "no defence significance" mantra without even bothering to take a closer look. That report mentioned a metallic craft, for Christ's sake, not lights in the sky. Right next to the biggest stockpile of nukes anywhere in Europe.'

'We're still looking into what went wrong,' Templeton replied. But he knew it was a weak response.

'Look, I'm not having a go at you personally – I know it all happened long before you even joined the Ministry – but the department is vulnerable on this, not least because of Georgina Bruni's book. She has witness statements and documents in the appendices that aren't on our file, together with on-the-record comments from at least one USAF general. If I was coming to this cold, I'd be better briefed if I read her book instead of the MOD file, and that's a totally unacceptable position. I'm amazed that the press haven't followed this up before. But now there's this threat of legal action, it's bound to come out. When it does, people will draw one of two conclusions: either there was a cover-up and the truth was suppressed – possibly by The Enterprise – or we'll just look bloody incompetent. I hate to say it, but the cover-up conclusion would be the more attractive option.'

'Yes, Minister. We really are putting a lot of work into trying to unravel this. People are being interviewed, but this all happened nearly thirty years ago and—'

'I'm well aware of that, Nick, but it's the Civil Service that's looking pretty bloody exposed here, it seems to me. The Cabinet

Office is screaming for answers on this and although the view from the Treasury Solicitor is that legal action is unlikely, the law isn't entirely clear. So God knows what may happen. This is a potential embarrassment and a stick with which certain people may try to beat us. Either way, it's a distraction we don't need right now. I want some quick answers, Nick, so start kicking arses and taking names.'

Old War Office Building, Whitehall

'Christ, Terry, you've come to me with some pretty weird stuff in the past few months, but this has to take the biscuit.'

Wing Commander Terry Carpenter knew CDI well enough to say nothing in response. His boss was clearly running things through in his mind. It was a sign of Carpenter's pivotal role in events that a Wing Commander had this sort of direct access to CDI without the need to go through the usual chain of command. It was also a sign of the times that CDI knew – and used – his first name.

'I'll play devil's advocate.' CDI was clearly going to put Carpenter well and truly on the spot. 'You called in the remote viewers, but despite the session you're so excited about being a blind one, it might be a fairly reasonable assumption that we were after intelligence on the alien ship.'

'That's true, sir, but if that were the case I would have expected Smith to start seeing the ship straight away. But initially she thought she was looking at an aircraft carrier.'

'Hmm. OK, but pretty much everything she gave you is either in the public domain or a fairly logical guess. Lots of scout craft in the mother ship – it sounds pretty clichéd to me. Perhaps she was just making a series of informed guesses and giving you what she thought you wanted to hear.'

'That's not my assessment, sir. I agree with you about the scout craft, but not about the machinery at the stern of the ship.'

'Oh, come on,' CDI retorted. 'Pipes, chambers . . . how could there *not* be that sort of stuff up there? It's just the sort of thing you'd see in the engine room on a Navy ship. And, before I forget, you asked one hell of a leading question about whether there was a difference between the two sets of pipes. You practically told her what you were after and she gave it to you.' CDI's voice was raised somewhat, but this was a controlled exercise in putting the intelligence officer under pressure, to see if the analysis would stand up.

'Remote viewing isn't quite the same as regression hypnosis, sir' Carpenter began, conscious of the need not to sound as if he was lecturing his boss. 'In my experience you can't lead the witness in the same way, nor expect a witness to confabulate. But one of the most interesting things concerned the aliens. When I asked if they were humanoid, she described them as being completely human. Now, the public perception is that we're dealing with little grey aliens, despite what Van Buren says about most of them being indistinguishable from us. So if she was telling us what she thought we wanted to hear, or making informed guesses, surely she'd have seen one of these grey aliens? I think her testimony is for real, sir, not least because two of the other remote viewers came up with details that might tally, although these were outside views of what might be the ship.'

'OK. You may have something. But the problem is that in intelligence terms, it's unverifiable. I can take this to ministers, but only US of S has even been briefed on remote viewing as a technique. I hardly think this will cut much ice with S of S or the PM.'

'No, sir, probably not.'

'If you're wrong, well, it probably won't make much of a difference.' CDI was speaking in a whisper, and Carpenter correctly realized that the general was running things through in his own mind. 'But if you're right . . . my God, if you're right, we now know *exactly* where to target any attack on the mothership.'

Pyramid Heights, Westminster

'Mr Cody, do you know anything about the way in which the government classifies information?'

Cody wasn't sure what point Maxwell Henderson was trying to

make. But he'd noted that the man often asked a question knowing full well that the person to whom it was directed knew the answer. It was a technique he seemed to use when he had an important argument to make, so Cody was keen to see what his intriguing new acquaintance was driving at. 'As a matter of fact, I do. I've seen plenty of the MOD's UFO files, some at the Public Record Office and some obtained under the Freedom of Information Act. Furthermore, in the course of my research and investigation I've met a number of ex-military personnel who have briefed me on the different levels of classification, in general terms, of course.'

'Excellent. You know then that there's a sliding scale: unclassified, restricted, confidential, secret and top secret, and that information in these categories can be further limited by use of a caveat or a code word, such as Atomic or UK Eyes Only?'

'Yes.' Other people might have felt patronized by Henderson's methods but Cody recognized some of what he did from his own career as a barrister. Besides, Henderson was a genuinely fascinating man who had propelled Cody into a world he had previously only observed from afar. As a conspiracy theorist, Cody had often criticized the Establishment, yet now – through Henderson – he had accessed the very heart of it. Although he cautioned himself to be wary of being used, there was no denying that Henderson seemed to be cultivating him for his knowledge. But Cody was nobody's fool and realized that this was a two-way street.

'Have you ever heard the term "Super Secrets"?' Henderson asked the question quietly and Cody sensed that something important was coming.

'No, I can't say that I have.'

'A super secret, Mr Cody, is one that could start a war or bring down a government.'

'Uh-huh.' Cody was interested but didn't know where Henderson was going with this.

'It was a term invented during the Cold War by a political journalist. But such things do exist, as you can doubtless imagine.'

'Yes. I'm sure.'

'I know four super secrets, Mr Cody. One could start a war between two non-European countries. The other three might well bring down this current administration.'

Cody knew that his host was not one for idle boasts – and he also knew better than to ask about the actual secrets. There was a more important question. 'You intend to disclose these secrets?'

'Not unless I have to. But I hold them in reserve, as a threat, should it prove necessary. It is my hope that we will reach a peaceful accord with the visitors, but there are no guarantees here; people in authority will do a lot to stay in power. As an ex-politician I know this better than most.' Henderson smiled. 'The balance of power is changing, but our leaders may not accept this – they may seek to prevent it by plunging us into a conflict that can only result in our own destruction. I will not allow this.' There was steel in his voice. 'I say this not out of arrogance but out of love for my country and for my world. I have a family and friends, and I will not see them sacrificed by those who would risk everything to hold on to their positions. If our leaders can reach a peaceful settlement, fine. But if they cannot, I *will* bring down this government and we shall have new leaders who take a different view.'

It was not the first time Henderson had threatened such a course of action. Cody was now even more certain that Henderson might just be able to achieve his aim.

MOD Main Building, Whitehall

'We may have independent verification of something Van Buren told us about the aliens, but . . . well, you won't like the source of this information.' CDI may have been personally sceptical about some aspects of remote viewing but he wasn't in the habit of ignoring data and had taken the earliest opportunity to get the information to S of S. He briefed Willoughby about this latest development and Willoughby – though sceptical himself – promised that he'd get the information to the PM.

'The thing about this,' Willoughby mused, 'is that we'll know for sure when the talks take place. You know, I can hardly believe that we'll be meeting intelligent beings from another world. It changes everything we know.'

'Indeed.' Willoughby was becoming almost philosophical, but CDI needed him to focus. 'Now, this is where I put my analyst hat on. Most abduction reports describe the aliens as small, grey entities with large black almond-shaped eyes. The creatures are essentially humanoid but unmistakably alien. Most media speculation during and after Thunder Child has picked up on this theme. If the aliens are revealed to be indistinguishable from humans, we have an interesting situation.'

'Go on.' CDI had Willoughby's full attention.

'On the one hand, it validates the DIS remote-viewing data. It also validates Van Buren's testimony. But there's a big danger here. We must be wary of falling into a classic counter-intelligence trap. Suppose I tell you ten things, and you don't know whether to believe me. Then suppose you discover independently that one of the things I told you is definitely and undeniably true.'

'I see,' Willoughby replied. 'I assume that you're a reliable source and assess – perhaps wrongly – that the other nine things are also true.'

'Precisely. But I may have deliberately fed you one true fact, even if that's damaging to me. It's bait, if you like – I lose one of my genuine secrets. But in the long run, it's worth more to me that you believe the other nine – which are false.'

'So what you're saying is this: if our aliens look human, don't leap to the conclusion that the rest of what Van Buren told us is true.'

'Exactly.' CDI had got his point across. 'However, that's only one of the reasons I asked for this meeting.'

'Oh?'

'If the data from our remote viewers is correct, we have two new problems.'

This was the last thing that Willoughby wanted to hear right now. But CDI wasn't the sort of person to waste his time with trivia, especially at a time like this. 'Go on.'

'One of them said the aliens could see her. In the debriefing session she alternated between the word "see" and "sense", but the end result was the same – they were aware of her presence when, of course, she wasn't there in any physical sense. None of our viewers have encountered this before. If this is for real, it raises the possibility that the aliens possess some ESP abilities of their own.'

'Great.' Willoughby's comment was laced with bitter sarcasm. He saw the significance immediately. A player can't win at poker if their opponent knows what cards they have. 'Can we do anything about this? Especially during the talks?'

'I don't think so. Wing Commander Carpenter is trawling through the literature and taking a few discreet soundings. But the only thing I can advise for now is that you should bear in mind the possibility that they can read thoughts.'

'The gulf between them and us gets wider by the moment. I pray to God it doesn't come to a fight, because it seems to me less and less likely that we could win.'

'There's something else,' CDI ventured, cautiously. 'It sounds crazy – the stuff of science-fiction nightmares.'

'A few months ago I'd have said the same thing about UFOs,' Willoughby countered. 'Go on.'

'If the aliens are physically indistinguishable from humans, then is it possible that they have people down here already?' CDI phrased it as a question, but the answer to that question was clearly that it *was* possible. 'If I were them, placing some of their people here would have several advantages. Firstly, the opportunity to gather intelligence, but secondly – if you could get your people into place – the chance to influence our response.'

'So now you're saying that any of the key players in this crisis could be aliens – politicians, military personnel, civil servants . . .'

'I simply raise this as a worst-case scenario,' CDI replied. 'I'm sure it's most unlikely. It's very difficult to insert yourself into a potentially hostile environment where you don't speak the language or know the customs. Consider how hard it is for a sleeper agent to set up and maintain a plausible cover in another country then ask yourself how much harder it would be if you weren't just from another country, but another *world*.'

'But if they've been here since Roswell, or even further back than that . . . what could we do? How would we know?' Then a more focused question. 'How can we defend against this possibility, however unlikely it may be?'

CDI had thought about this. 'Aside from watching out for any unusual or out-of-character behaviour among key players, or any decision that would seem to favour the aliens, well . . . I'm not sure we can.'

Fort Detrick, Maryland

US Army Chemical and Biological Defense Command had enjoyed something of a renaissance in recent years. The public, it seemed, always needed something to worry about. Thirty years ago it had been the Cold War, with the attendant possibility of nuclear Armageddon. This had given way to concerns about rogue states or terrorists launching ballistic-missile attacks or using chemical and biological weapons. These concerns were not entirely unfounded: Saddam Hussein had threatened to use such weapons in the Gulf War and only the quiet promise of nuclear retaliation had dissuaded him. The Aum Shinrikyu cult had launched a sarin gas attack on the Tokyo subway, while diseases like the Ebola virus had broken out in cities such as Berlin. Even though the Berlin outbreak wasn't the result of terrorism, it certainly focused people's minds on the possibilities. Ebola was pretty much the scariest of the haemorrhaging fevers, the more so because the natural host remained unknown. The US government had once seriously considered negotiating with the government of Zaire to detonate a nuclear device in the small area considered by some to be the source of the Ebola virus.

The cutting edge of US Army Chemical and Biological Defense Command was a unit with the unwieldy title of the US Army Medical Research Institute of Infectious Diseases. Commonly known by its abbreviation, USAMRIID, the facility worked to develop vaccines against chemical and biological agents that might be used against the US by an enemy. Its civilian counterpart was the Center for Disease Control and Prevention, based in Atlanta, but the work done here in Maryland was more difficult and dangerous. The West was always trying to hold the high moral ground concerning such work, maintaining that its research was defensive. In reality, the only meaningful difference between defensive and offensive work was a delivery system: it was little appreciated that delivery of chemical or biological weapons was actually the hardest part of the process. Anybody could manufacture an agent but many of them were surprisingly short-lived in a non-laboratory environment. Contrary to popular belief, a CBW payload couldn't simply be attached to a missile because the resultant explosion would destroy it.

Colonel Scott Willett was the commanding officer of Fort Detrick and was hosting the meeting. His boss, General Hank Whitman, was also present. Whitman headed up US Army Chemical and Biological Defense Command. The third man was Casper Goldwater, the new Director of the NSA. It was he who now revealed information so sensitive that only a face-to-face meeting was judged appropriate, despite assurances about secure communications. The NSA Director was ideally placed to know that there were no guarantees where such things were claimed. It was fortunate, then, that both the NSA's headquarters and the USAMRIID were in Maryland. This meant a meeting could be arranged easily, without the need for anything more obvious than a brief and unobtrusive drive.

'We have developed intelligence suggesting that the Russian Federation is making contingency plans for a biological attack on the aliens.' Goldwater let the information sink in before continuing. 'We need to make an assessment of how effective such an attack might be, and consider what action to take.' Goldwater then handed over the transcripts of intercepted conversations that outlined what was being planned. The NSA had finally cracked the latest Russian encryption codes. Whitman and Willett took their time, reading the documents carefully and making some notes in the margins. Willett was glad his boss was present and waited for his general to respond before offering any views of his own.

'The Russian attack plan is based on a false assumption,' Whitman said, finally. 'The agents they're considering would be lethal enough but, as ever, it's *delivery* that's the problem.'

'Their idea to infect abductees?' Goldwater prompted.

'I suppose they were viewed as expendable assets.' Whitman's expression revealed what he thought about that. 'Well, your intercepts make it clear that the FSB have been going through their UFO files and drawing up a list of those people claiming close encounters. The theory's fine, but how are you going to do it in practice? Are people going to volunteer to be infected, for the good of their country? I doubt it. They might try to infect someone without their knowledge, but that would be very difficult. But there's a more fundamental problem: with the sort of bioagent the Russians are considering, anyone infected would get sick very quickly and would seek medical attention. Unless they happened to be abducted within twenty-four hours of infection, the plan would be useless. Longer than that and the person concerned would be hospitalized . . . or dead.'

'Yes,' Goldwater agreed. 'That was my assessment. And I very much doubt the aliens would abduct anyone showing obvious signs of illness. But there's another reason why the Russian plan won't work and it's one they don't seem to have realized yet, despite the fact that it's been revealed in open-source material.'

'Oh?'

'The abductions have stopped. The aliens have seemingly got what they wanted and terminated that particular project.'

'The aim of which was what?' Whitman enquired.

'The gathering of genetic material from specific bloodlines, if my predecessor is to be believed.'

'Why would they do this?' Whitman asked, realizing that the NSA man had not really answered his question.

'The initial assessment was that it was aimed at hybridization; that's certainly what the abductees and the ufologists had been claiming, quite openly, for decades. It seemed consistent with the data. Now we believe their aim was to genetically alter themselves to such an extent that they're as human as you and I, with the same DNA structure and the same genes.'

Whitman thought hard about that. Ten or even five years ago he would have said it was impossible but now, with recent advances in genetic modification, he wasn't so sure.

'That brings me to my next point,' Goldwater continued. 'Setting aside the Russian contingency plans, how would *you* launch an effective chemical or biological attack on the aliens?'

'Well, first off, I'm not sure I would,' Whitman shot back. 'Even if it were successful, you'd be most unlikely to kill them all. And if we sting them without destroying them, might they not wipe us out?'

'I'm asking for a contingency plan. Nothing more.'

'Setting aside the problem of how to deliver a chemical or biological agent – and, as I've said, that's the big problem – it's almost impossible to say what degree of success we might have. We don't know anything about their defences but I assume they've made some effort to immunize themselves against diseases. We don't know what vaccines they'd have, or what isolation procedures they might use should there be illness on board. We also know nothing about their air-filtration units, so we can't gauge how far an airborne virus might circulate. Finally, we don't know anything about their social structure . . . who interacts with who. So we couldn't say how quickly an infectious or contagious agent might spread.'

Goldwater nodded slowly. 'Anything else?'

'As a matter of fact, yes. Setting aside the issue of whether the aliens would wipe us out for launching such an attack, it may rebound on us anyway.'

'How so?'

'Even if we assume the aliens are genetically identical, there are still likely to be *some* physical or physiological differences between them and us. If there are, it makes it that much more likely that any disease we introduced to them would mutate into a new strain against which *we* might have no defence.'

'What about the Chimera Project?'

There was a silence. It was a testament to both Whitman's and Willett's self-control that neither asked how Goldwater had known about this most secret of new developments. The answer to that was clear enough.

Much of USAMRIID's recent work revolved not around existing diseases but newly created ones. They had, for example, researched the frightening possibility that somebody would use genetic engineering to develop an unstoppable bioweapon. New genes could be inserted into the DNA of an existing virus to create new, so-called designer diseases. There was also the possibility of an ethnically targeted weapon: a virus that could scan for specific genetic markers restricted to particular racial types and would only become active when it found them, inserting itself into the host DNA and destroying it before replicating in its own image.

Most terrifying of all was the possibility of combining existing diseases – and this was the aim of the Chimera Project. The chimera was a monster from Greek mythology. It had the head of a lion, the body of a goat and the tail of a snake. It was a particularly appropriate name for the project because its aim had been to combine material from two or more viruses. The basic principle was the insertion of the genes from one virus into another. The main difficulty with this was that the host virus would reject foreign genes, although it *was* possible if a compatible place could be found in the genome.

The Russians were known to have been working on producing a smallpox/Ebola weapon but this thinking had been ill-judged. The problem was that the resultant virus was *too* lethal. An effective bioweapon had to be both virulent and easily communicable. Ebola was the classic example, yet, perversely, it was its virulence that made it a less than ideal weapon. The speed with which it took hold meant that it would often kill its host before the host could pass it on. An outbreak would be detected almost immediately and countermeasures would be taken.

A truly effective bioweapon, therefore, certainly needed to be virulent and easily communicable but it also had to have a *slow* incubation period. So the initial ideas about combining diseases like Ebola and smallpox were abandoned. The really devious research focused on inserting viral material from diseases like smallpox or the plague into something more innocuous. The influenza virus was the favourite, because it had so many different strains – the trick was to find a really slow-burning one, because anyone infected might not feel sick or show any signs of illness for several days. They would go about their business quite happily for a week or more, during which time they would spread the disease far and wide. But then, when the influenza virus was finally broken down by the body's defences, the foreign genetic material would be released and whatever disease had been inserted would be unleashed.

'If we could find a way to deliver a chimera virus and introduce it on to the alien mothership, *could* such an attack succeed?' Goldwater's voice was level as he asked the question.

'I don't know.' Whitman's answer was little more than a whisper. 'Possibly.'

Chapter Six

PREPARATION

Cabinet Office, Whitehall

When the extraterrestrials had first sent an encrypted message about the possibility of holding talks, it had been seen as good news. But now the moment was approaching and, as the details had emerged, some people within government weren't so sure. There had been no dialogue, and encrypted messages transmitted at the alien vessel using military communications satellites had remained unanswered. One further communication had been received, stating simply that the leaders of the five permanent member nations of the UN Security Council were to go to a particular location at a particular time, where talks would be held. Senior members of the Cabinet were discussing the issue with the Chief of the Defence Staff, who had just been invited to speak.

'There are some obvious dangers, Prime Minister,' he began. 'It could be a trap, and the plan could be to assemble you all in one location and kill you. With the five key world leaders gone, the aliens might be counting on our command structure to fragment.'

'That seems unlikely,' the PM replied. 'Surely such a move would only serve to stiffen our resolve? It would expose their public statement of friendship as a lie and unite people in opposition against them.'

'That's true,' CDS acknowledged. 'But if they're as powerful as some of our analyses suggest, they may not need to win our hearts and minds. We can't be certain of their intentions.'

'If they don't need to win hearts and minds, why did they bother sending a message of friendship at all?' It was the Deputy Prime Minister who spoke up. 'Either it's a genuine message or it's a cynical attempt to manipulate public opinion – or even political opinion. But that's good news because, if they *need* to send it, it suggests they aren't powerful enough to take over just like that.'

There were appreciative nods from around the room. It was a pretty good point, and even CDS was forced to acknowledge it.

'I agree, up to a point. But suppose their charm offensive is designed *solely* to get us to agree to the meeting? And suppose the plan is to attack at the very moment they kill the world leaders? With the Commanders-in-Chief gone, there'll be a critical moment of vulnerability while we're all trying to work out what happened and what to do.'

'Everybody has deputies,' the Home Secretary chipped in. 'Surely the transition of command authority would be seamless?'

'In theory, yes,' CDS replied. 'But remember when President Reagan was shot, early in his presidency? There was absolute pandemonium – and there was even confusion over the where-abouts of the nuclear go-codes. If the leaders were killed and if communications were jammed so that nobody knew what was going on, the paralysis – however temporary – could give them a decisive military advantage in any attack.'

'I still think it's an encouraging sign that they think they'd *need* such an advantage,' the Deputy PM retorted. 'And surely if we're attacked we'll respond with force, with or without leaders in place. Even defensive Rules of Engagement allow that, in the UK or wherever.'

'I take your point,' CDS conceded. 'I'm just trying to sound a note of caution.'

The PM held up his hand for silence. 'I'm going.' The decision was made. 'I acknowledge there are risks in such a course of action, and we'll do our best to minimize them, not least by preparing for the possibility CDS mentions. We'll put our forces on maximum alert and look at whether we need to beef up our Rules of Engagement. But I judge that the risks in going are outweighed by those of *not* going. If this is our chance for a peaceful but acceptable settlement, we need to take it. And I can best do that by establishing a dialogue. I have to try, for all our sakes.'

CDS thought the PM's little speech was a bit melodramatic, but there was no doubting the man's logic. There was no doubting his courage either, and CDS found himself thinking back to the occasion when the PM had insisted on going to Rendlesham Forest in the face of CDS's protestations. Again the PM was planning to put himself in harm's way, only this time there were no clues as to what would await him.

'The administrative arrangements?' The PM's question focused CDS's attention on practical concerns, reinforcing the impression that an irrevocable decision had just been made.

'As you know, Prime Minister, Diego Garcia has been chosen as the location for the talks. We'll fly you in a Tristar from RAF Brize Norton but we'll need other aircraft in support. We'll have an AWACS giving top cover and you'll have fighter support. We'll need tankers for air-to-air refuelling and a Nimrod in the SAR role in case we run into trouble. We'll stage through RAF Akrotiri in Cyprus.'

'Other nations are doing similar things?' The question was from the leader of the Opposition, who had been involved in all key decisions in an attempt to stop the crisis becoming a party political issue.

'Yes,' the PM replied. 'They've all agreed to attend and are making similar arrangements.'

'Is there anything significant in the choice of location?' the Foreign Secretary asked. It was an insightful question which the PM invited CDS to take because of previous privately expressed concerns.

'It's an interesting bit of business, that's for sure. It's part of the

British Indian Ocean Territory and is the only inhabited island in the archipelago. That said, there's actually no UK presence there – there's a US military base which, as you may know, was used to stage B-52s during the Gulf War. It's actually a very clever choice, politically and militarily, and that's one of the reasons for my caution about the whole business. Its isolation makes it easy for the aliens to attack, because once we're there we're effectively cut off. You're all aware that the aliens have asked for a military exclusion zone, stipulating that all military personnel and equipment must be two hundred nautical miles from the island – including what's already at the US base. So if there's an attack, the military won't be able to intervene – at least, not soon enough to matter.'

'They could just be being cautious,' the Home Secretary suggested. 'If this whole thing has been a mistake, and if they're peaceful, they may be wary that *we'll* launch an attack. Don't forget, *their* leadership may be coming, too.' CDS admired her analysis. CDI had suggested this might be a possible scenario.

'That's quite possible,' CDS admitted. 'But the political angle does worry me. Diego Garcia is a wonderful choice if you're a conspiracy theorist. It's British territory occupied by Americans. Now, what sort of message does that send to the other three nations involved?'

'The French aren't bothered, but it's certainly caused problems with the Russians and the Chinese.' The Foreign Secretary's intervention was timely.

'Quite so,' CDS agreed. 'And isn't that a predictable response? It seems to me a deliberate move by the aliens to cast suspicion on Britain and America – the two nations involved in Thunder Child. In the minds of the Russians and the Chinese it must confirm suspicions that the US has been dealing covertly with the aliens and that the UK has been in on the conspiracy since day one.'

There was silence for a moment, broken by a question from the leader of the Opposition. 'What about security? Have we managed to keep this meeting secret?'

'So it seems,' CDS replied. 'Personally, though, I doubt that can last. I hope it won't leak from us, but with five nations involved, and so many preparations to make, *someone* will say something.'

'What about our press lines?' It was the leader of the Opposition again.

The Prime Minister took the question. 'We're working them up, between my office and the MOD. Frankly, we're working on a number of different versions of a press release, depending upon what happens. The defensive lines to take are even more wide-ranging and cover just about every conceivable eventuality. The thrust of them all, however, is that an invitation was received, together with a request to keep the matter secret. We complied with both requests in the hope of finding out what's going on and negotiating a mutually acceptable agreement.'

'If it does leak,' the Deputy PM observed, 'the location will work for us. The press will find it a difficult place to reach.'

'For the story of the century? They'll find a way, I'm sure,' the Home Secretary opined. 'What do we do about that? How do we stop some hack flying into the exclusion zone and starting a war of the worlds?'

CDS responded to that one. 'Despite the isolation and the short timescale, the Americans will have a carrier group there, centred on the USS *Oskar Schindler*. They'll be outside the exclusion zone themselves, of course, but one of their missions will be to use the ships and aircraft at their disposal to keep anyone else out. We'll be contributing our air assets to this carrier group, by the way. The presence of AWACS and Nimrod aircraft means we'll be able to spot any ship or aircraft coming anywhere near the exclusion zone, with more than enough time to warn them off or forcibly intercept them if necessary.'

'OK, so you can deal with the press,' the Home Secretary acknowledged, 'but could those forces do us any good if the aliens attempted to wipe out the world leaders?'

CDS looked uncomfortable. 'We'd see an attack coming. But no, we'd be pretty hard-pressed to do anything to prevent it. We're in their hands on this one. It's an issue of trust and faith.'

The assessment was an honest one and did little to make anyone feel good about the situation.

Gorky Park, Moscow

While some were talking peace, others were plotting a war. Defence Minister Yuri Ivanov had been surprised, a day previously, when he'd received a call on his secure line from somebody claiming to know about a recent visit he had made to a certain production facility, together with the reason for that visit. He'd been even more surprised to receive a request to meet his mystery caller in Gorky Park but had agreed nonetheless. Ivanov had been told to tell nobody about the meeting and to come alone. He'd thought hard about that but decided to comply. Anybody who knew about his visit to Omutninsk – and the reason for the visit – and had access to his secure telephone number was clearly a major player, and people like that didn't develop such good intelligence just to kill someone.

He'd suspected the caller was American. Although he spoke Russian well, there was the unmistakable trace of a foreign accent, and only the Americans – Ivanov reasoned – would have the means to intercept his calls. It was this that had first angered and then surprised him the most. That the Americans had been intercepting this most secure of lines was a disaster beyond calculation. Countless highly classified defence secrets had been discussed openly on this line, and now Ivanov had to assume that they had all been compromised despite the fact that they were encrypted. Worse still was the realization that if this supposedly secure line had been tapped, the chances were that other secure lines in Russia had been similarly bugged. The shock of this and the anger he felt soon gave way to surprise. His caller had just revealed a secret beyond value. Provided the information was true, countermeasures could be taken and the door could be closed on the eavesdroppers. Better still, counter-intelligence plans could be activated to feed the listeners disinformation. Was his caller after money? Ivanov wondered. Was he dealing with an American who had offered a free piece of intelligence and would then demand payment for more?

When he met the mystery man in the pre-arranged spot, he realized he'd been wide of the mark. He knew the name, though not the face, and when he stopped to think about it the man's identity was not the great surprise he'd anticipated.

NSA Director Casper Goldwater had taken a considerable risk in coming. For a start, his absence would almost certainly be noticed, despite a well-prepared cover story. More importantly, he couldn't be sure of Ivanov's reaction. He'd been sure he'd attend, but he couldn't be sure that he'd come alone. He wasn't particularly worried about his own safety but the prospect of arrest frightened him – Ivanov would be understandably furious to learn that the NSA had been listening in on his private calls. There was also the danger that Goldwater would be spotted by a journalist. He'd taken off his glasses and worn a hat to try and disguise himself, but he knew that his low public profile was probably his best protection. Despite these potential pitfalls, Goldwater judged that the stakes were too high to avoid the risk. There was only a small window of opportunity in which he might achieve his aim. As for Ivanov, Goldwater believed he could compensate the Russian for having intercepted his calls by offering him some-thing far more valuable. Introductions made, Goldwater rapidly came to the point.

'Some of us know of your plans to strike at the aliens with a biological weapon. I am here to tell you such a plan could never succeed. The agents with which you could attack are *too* lethal. They would take effect before they spread very far and you would bring down a terrible retribution on us all. Moreover, you have no means to deliver such an attack. In case you haven't yet realized, the abductions have stopped.'

In fact, Ivanov *had* realized this. Part of him had been dis-appointed, another part relieved – he had had no desire to infect his own citizens in the hope that they would be taken on board the mothership and he had also doubted that the aliens would take anybody showing signs of illness. Even if people could be persuaded to be infected, or could be infected without their knowledge, the time before they got ill and died would be so short that unless an abduction occurred within hours the plan would fail.

'You face two problems. Your biological agents are too fast-acting, and you have no means of delivery. Your plan is dead in the water.' Goldwater's scathing analysis was undeniably correct.

'You have a suggestion?'

'I have a solution. I have a virus that is deadly but that has a slow-burning fuse. If alien physiology really is the same as our own, it should be a week before those who are exposed first begin to show symptoms. By then it will have spread far and wide. There will be many deaths.'

'Then what's to stop them wiping us out? How can—' Ivanov stopped in mid-sentence and a smile spread over his face as he caught on. 'You have the vaccine.'

'Precisely. This will force them to the negotiating table, but on *our* terms.'

'Which are?'

'We get to board their ship in force. We take over enough critical systems to give us effective control. In other words, we neutralize the threat posed by the ship and rule out the possibility of force being used against us. Then we can discuss the terms on which we will allow them to settle here. But *we* remain in charge, and they fit into *our* social structures. They must also share their technology with us.'

'If they refuse?'

'How can they, when their very survival is at stake? They will negotiate or they will become extinct. I can conceive of no intelligent civilization that would choose the second option.'

'You're gambling a lot on the effectiveness of this biological agent. In fact, you're possibly gambling *everything* on it.'

'What are the alternatives? Do you really believe they've come all this way to fit voluntarily into our social structures? Do you think they're about to roll over and content themselves with – I don't know – being given Australia or something? No, they're coming here to take over – and that's one of the more benign scenarios. We *know* your own intelligence analysts concur.'

Goldwater let that sink in. 'The worst-case scenario – not one to be discounted – is that we will be exterminated. You only have to study human history to see what might happen. If we survive, it'll be as slaves or in reservations. Maybe some of us will be put in zoos. You say I'm gambling by suggesting this strategy. I admit it. But we gamble if we do nothing. We gamble if we trust these aliens. What do we *really* know about their motives? Do you trust them enough to *not* resist? Because unless we strike now, we lose our opportunity for ever.'

Ivanov thought for a moment. Goldwater's arguments were ones that he'd advocated himself. 'So what is this weapon of yours?'

Goldwater handed him a typed sheet of paper. 'This is the formula. The recipe, if you like. We know about your research into producing hybrid bioweapons and we know of your attempts to develop a smallpox/Ebola weapon. It was the discovery of this programme that accelerated our own research into such weapons so that we might have a vaccine if you succeeded. But, in researching this, our scientists had to keep one step ahead and consider what else you might develop. To produce our own vaccines, we had first to make our own weapons.'

'The kill is the cure,' Ivanov mused.

'Exactly. Well, we found a beauty. The formula I've just given you is something we call the Chimera virus. It's actually a generic name for a number of different agents, but the principle is the same – a *lethal* genetically modified agent encased in a *harmless* genetically modified agent.' Goldwater let that sink in. The expression on Ivanov's face showed that he understood. 'We find that plague and influenza are the best. This formula gives you a weapon with just the right mixture: slow enough to spread far and wide before it's noticed, lethal enough to kill once it takes hold. And it's so secret and so new that even if the aliens have immunized themselves against every disease on the planet it'll do them no good. It's sufficiently different from plague that even if they are protected from that – which is far from certain – it'll serve them no purpose. But I'm no monster. It's quite possible to implement a version of the plan that might not kill anybody at all.'

That stopped Ivanov in his tracks. But before he could think it through or say anything, Goldwater explained.

'Suppose we deliver the agent, then wait three or four days. We could then *tell* them what we'd done and offer them the vaccine before the disease took hold. Even if we did nothing and waited for some of them to die, casualties would be minimal if they agreed to our terms immediately. I'm not comfortable with this, for God's sake. In fact, it disgusts me. But I truly believe it's the only way to ensure the survival of the human race, and I'm afraid I'm prepared to do questionable things to achieve that aim.'

'I don't understand why you're telling me any of this,' Ivanov finally said. 'You have it all worked out. You're way ahead of us.' Such an admission did not come easily to the Russian Minister of Defence, but the time for posturing was over.

'Not so,' Goldwater replied. 'Only you can actually deliver the virus.'

'*Us?*' Ivanov was confused. 'But you said the abductions had stopped. How *can* we deliver the virus?'

'It's a political thing,' Goldwater said. 'I know how it can be delivered but I also know that I won't get political approval for it. America will never do it, for a number of reasons. Much depends on our president, and she's very . . . moral. Your president, I feel sure, won't have any such qualms. Or if he does, he won't let his sense of morality stop him from doing what's right.'

Both men chuckled at that and Ivanov wasn't about to disagree with the assessment. 'So how do we deliver the virus?'

Goldwater told him.

MOD Main Building, Whitehall

Just as the arrangements had been made, and just as the PM was about to begin his journey to Diego Garcia, another secure encrypted communication was received. The arrangements were to be changed and the location of the meeting was to be altered.

The new location had come as a shock to everybody and had

caused several problems for the MOD. RAF Machrihanish was situated on the west coast of Kintyre, in Scotland. It had been built amid great secrecy in the 1980s but had been abandoned at around the turn of the century. However, unlike other surplus MOD properties, it hadn't been sold but had been put on to what was known as 'care and maintenance'. In other words, a skeleton staff was still employed there and the base could be reactivated at a moment's notice. This was precisely what was happening now, and S of S had summoned US of S, his junior ministerial colleague, to update him on this new turn of events.

'It's good news and bad news,' Blackmore was explaining to his boss. 'On the plus side it gives us better control of the location. We're liaising with the Security Service about installing covert monitoring devices, but we'll have to play that one carefully. We don't know what countermeasures the aliens may have, and we don't want to get off on the wrong foot. So for now, we'll just scope it and see if it can be done. I guess we'll have to kick the final decision upstairs, though.'

'Uh-huh.' Willoughby grunted his agreement and nodded.

'But the location is bad news in other respects. Firstly, it's an administrative nightmare. As you know, the communication contained no details other than the new location, the date, time and the guest list. We don't know anything about the practical arrangements – simple things like dietary requirements. We're trying to guess every conceivable requirement on this and a whole range of other concerns to make sure we cover all the bases.'

'Fine. What else?'

'Security is the big problem. Although the area's very remote, it's not as isolated as Diego Garcia. Any increase in military activity will be noticed. We'll need to instigate an air exclusion zone, and this will mean rerouting civil flights into and out of Prestwick, as well as flights on the main transatlantic route. We're doing this now, but it's being noticed. Rumours are starting to fly. I have a D-notice ready for your consideration. It'll need to be cleared with Number Ten, of course, but on this I think we're all agreed that secrecy is necessary, in the wider national interest.'

'Quite. What about the Internet?' Willoughby knew that while a D-notice would restrain most of the responsible media the Internet was harder to control, not least because the whole issue of the Internet and the law was still unresolved.

'We'll monitor the situation and activate Operation Helper.' Operation Helper was one of the murkier secrets within government. It involved a handful of retired DIS and Security Service personnel who could be contracted to various government departments as the need arose. Nominally, they provided consultancy services in the field of Internet monitoring, looking out for sites and postings that might be of interest to the government. In practice, their activities went beyond monitoring: when a story appeared that was potentially damaging to the government, their job was to swamp the Internet with related stories designed to muddy the waters and throw people off the scent.

During Operation Thunder Child these veteran spooks had been used to great effect. When essentially correct accounts of UFO crashes in Alice Holt Forest and East Horton had been posted on the Internet, they had promptly posted fictitious accounts. Using numerous false identities they had posed as ufologists, serving military officers and concerned members of the public, posting totally bogus reports of UFO activity, crash retrievals, abductions and more besides. They had started rumours, 'leaked' non-existent secrets and caused so much confusion that the real data was swamped by a veritable sea of nonsense. It was classic disinformation technique – and highly effective.

'Anything else I should know?' Willoughby demanded.

'There's one more reason why the location is bad news for us. It just so happens that RAF Machrihanish is a location well known to conspiracy theorists. It has the longest runway of any RAF base in the country and in the 1990s it was claimed that it was used by various secret prototype aircraft like the Aurora. It was also claimed that Aurora itself was a cover for extraterrestrial activity. There was, as you know, a strong American presence at the base, including special-forces units such as US Navy SEALS. If the location is ever made public it'll reinforce suspicions that the UK and the US have been involved in a conspiracy to cover this whole business up.'

'This choice of location can hardly be a coincidence,' S of S observed.

'My view entirely,' Blackmore agreed. 'Either it's a deliberate attempt to cause trouble, or there really *was* something there. It could be that there was a facility there and that The Enterprise had something to do with it. We can ask Van Buren about that, but we still can't be sure that any information we get from him is valid.'

'OK, thanks for the update. Anything else?'

'One more thing. A request from CDI. He wants permission to deploy his team of remote viewers to Machrihanish, to see if they can pick up anything useful.'

S of S still wasn't sure what to make of the whole concept. 'OK, permission granted.'

The White House

'So, Madam President, that is the essence of the British plan.' Defense Secretary Saul Weitzman had just outlined Operation Lightning Strike to President Spencer.

'Would it work?' The president had a habit of asking very direct questions and this one was directed at the other person in the room, General Tom Johnson, the Chairman of the Joint Chiefs of Staff. Spencer was conscious that it might undermine Weitzman's authority but she needed a military opinion and so had no qualms about directing the question to Johnson.

'The attack strategy is fine, Madam President,' Johnson replied, 'but there are two provisos. First, we can't assume that any intelligence gleaned from remote viewing is accurate. We have our own RV programmes, but the results are inconclusive, to say the least – sometimes we're spot on but other times we're just plain wrong. The second problem is that we don't know what countermeasures the aliens may have. It's quite possible they'd detect a space shuttle launch and blow us out of space before we got to a position to launch our missiles. And I should add that even if we launched they might detect an inbound missile and destroy it before it got close enough to do any damage. Now those are some pretty big ifs. But to answer your question: *if* the RV intelligence is valid and *if* we can successfully prosecute an attack, then, yes, it could succeed.'

'And what about the moral issue? What if there are a billion intelligent humanoid entities on that ship?'

'Madam President, it depends upon their intentions. If they're benign, then we greet them with open arms. But if they're coming here to invade our planet and wipe us out, then I believe we're entitled to defend ourselves. There *are* six billion of us, after all.'

'This must be an option of last resort,' Spencer replied, firmly. 'But it's a last resort that I'd be foolish not to consider – we must develop the capability to do this thing, much as I hope it won't be necessary. Very well, continue liaising with the British and refine the plans. But command and control lies with us. It may be their idea, but we're the ones with the space shuttle fleet. We're the only ones who can strike at the alien ship before it gets into orbit.'

Rowledge, Surrey

Memories. Memories sometimes intruded, unbidden, taking Jenny Thornton back to when the nightmare first began. Even after years of experiences that she could recall all too vividly she sometimes remembered others that had been buried in her subconscious for many years. This time the memory had been triggered by a television programme about potholing. She had no interest in the subject but had caught the last five minutes of the documentary – it had been on television before a film she'd wanted to watch. As had happened often before, she'd had a feeling that there was something at the edge of her awareness, thrusting its way to the surface. She was in two minds about this. Part of her wanted to recapture the lost experience, as if this would return something that was rightfully hers and had been taken away. But another part of her guessed that it would be an unpleasant recollection, connected with her experiences. There was little choice, because once the seeds had been sown the memory would eventually surface. As it did now.

Thornton was six or seven and her parents were taking her on one of those interminable walks of which they'd been so fond. The usual haunts were Alice Holt Forest, Frensham Great Pond or Frensham Little Pond, or possibly the picturesque little village of Tilford. This time they'd said they had a treat for her and were going to take her somewhere rather odd. They'd parked the car near the ruins of Waverley Abbey and crossed the river before heading towards this new place where her parents had decided to go. They told her it was going to be a surprise. When they stopped walking her father told her solemnly that they'd arrived. Their destination was called Mother Ludlum's Cave.

Thornton's parents had told her the legend of Mother Ludlum who was variously described as a healer, an eccentric or – horror of horrors – a witch. The legend had it that she'd lived in a cave and whatever the truth of the matter, a large cauldron straight out of act four, scene one of *Macbeth* was kept in Frensham Church – a rare example of an artefact associated with witchcraft being displayed openly in a Christian church.

They'd all ventured into the cave, with Thornton's father waving around the torch that was more often used to explore the dark crevices of the loft at home. She'd been quite scared at the time, but had still managed to wander off and run ahead of her parents, wanting to see what was around the corner. And then . . . She didn't know what but she wasn't in the cave any more, even though she was *somewhere* dark, cold and menacing. She was aware of *something* but she didn't have the words to describe it. It was a feeling. It was like being underwater, or . . . something. It wasn't exactly unpleasant, but it was . . . different. Then she'd seen a light, walked towards it and found herself at the entrance of the cave again. For some reason her mother was crying but nothing was said and the rest of the walk took place in silence.

A few days later Thornton had a dream and told her parents excitedly that she'd met Mother Ludlum, who had big black eyes. Shortly after that, she'd written something on a piece of paper and left it on her bedside table: 'I'm not afraid of shadows – just the things that hide in them'. It had been a strange thing for a child to write. It wasn't there when she went to bed that night and, although nothing was said, she detected the faint smell of a match and was suddenly sure that her father had found it and burnt it. Memories.

Although completely unaware that talks with the aliens were scheduled to begin the following day, Jenny Thornton spent the evening mulling over the sort of issues that, unbeknownst to her, were being discussed by government ministers and military chiefs of staff. They were wondering whether the aliens could be trusted and what criteria, what independent verification could possibly be used to judge their veracity.

For Jenny Thornton, the issue was the same, although she articulated her thoughts in a different way. To her, it was simply that there was a world of difference between what the aliens said and what they did. As a child, when she'd first encountered them they'd told her that they wouldn't hurt her. But they had. Later, when she'd studied the phenomenon with Richard Cody, she'd been amazed to discover a huge range of cases where people who'd met the aliens in various ways had been told things that weren't true. The aliens had claimed to be from Mars, Venus, Saturn or wherever. They said that they'd come to warn people about the dangers of nuclear war and pollution. Some of these cases had been obvious hoaxes but Thornton and Cody both believed that the aliens were truly masters of deception, skilled in disinformation and deceit. She'd studied folklore and had learned about the fairy folk, the little people or whatever name they went by. Such reports were found all around the world and yet there were common themes – the entities were always tricksters.

Cody had written a paper suggesting that folkloric descriptions of fairies were actually accounts of alien abductions but described in the linguistic and cultural terms available to the contemporary witnesses. His paper had been scoffed at by most folklorists but had found favour within the world of ufology. Cody's central conclusion was that there had been an alien presence on Earth for longer than most students of the phenomenon believed and that this presence had always sought to conceal itself from humans while simultaneously exploiting them.

Cody had even put forward the idea that there was a symbiotic relationship of sorts between humans and aliens, who were dependent upon each other at some level. All Thornton knew for sure was that there was a world of difference between what the aliens said and what they did. They'd lied to her and they'd hurt her and, despite the conciliatory view being pushed by Cody and his new friend Maxwell Henderson, she wasn't about to forgive or forget the way in which her childhood had been taken from her. She'd written a paper of her own, comparing alien abduction to child abuse. It hadn't been as eloquent or as comprehensively referenced as Cody's paper on folklore but it had been written from the heart and had caused quite a stir among other ufologists.

RAF Machrihanish, Kintyre

The day that would in all probability decide the fate of the world dawned cold and – appropriately, perhaps – grey. The five world leaders – representing the five permanent member nations of the UN Security Council – had flown in the night before amid great secrecy and had conferred late into the night. Each of them had been endlessly briefed by various different officials and military advisers. The surprising thing, in view of the various political and cultural differences, was how similar these briefing sessions had been. Each nation wanted to use the occasion to gather first-hand intelligence on the aliens, and each nation wanted a resolution of the crisis that would have neutral or – better still – favourable consequences for their country. But there were differences between them because, while each country shared certain aims, there would always be different ways to achieve those aims.

The sea-and-air exclusion zone had been set up at the last minute, so as not to attract attention. It was being enforced by several naval vessels and a squadron of RAF Typhoons. The aircraft were unarmed, as were all military personnel on the base. This decision had caused great consternation among the military but the world leaders themselves had insisted on it. What lay behind the politicians' decision was fear of the accidental discharge of a weapon. The military thought that somebody had watched *The Day the Earth Stood Still* too many times. But the nightmare prospect of an interstellar war being triggered by a rogue shot was a frightening one and had led to this cautious stance.

Over Cumbria

Outside the exclusion zone, over the mainland, one of the RAF's Sentry AEW aircraft circled, monitoring the skies for anything unusual. The aircraft had a fighter escort but the defensive ROE made it abundantly clear that any intruder could only be engaged if it fired on the early-warning aircraft. The Sentry's crew scanned their screens carefully, their task made considerably easier by the exclusion zone: looking for an anomalous blip in an area cleared of all air traffic was clearly better than trying to separate it out from the electronic clutter of other aircrafts' signals.

'Possible contact.' The young fighter controller paused for a moment, then read off the coordinates. His boss checked the data.

'Confirmed.'

The signal was intermittent but clearly visible. The RAF had refined their procedures for interpreting radar data in the light of intelligence gleaned during Operation Thunder Child. It turned out that the alien vessels were not entirely stealthy, as had been initially believed. What they had going for them – and what had enabled them to operate with relative impunity for years – was the fact that they carried no IFF and behaved differently to conventional aircraft or UAVs. So when fighter controllers had picked up a weak and transitory signal, they'd written it off as a ghost return caused by a system malfunction or unusual meteorological conditions. All that had changed and, now the radar characteristics of the alien craft had been logged, a sophisticated new computer program had been designed to verify and then enhance the signals. That said, the fighter controllers still had a part to play, not least in the interpretation of the data. The computer might tell them that a possible target had been detected but it took a person with knowledge of tactics and procedures to evaluate the situation and make an assessment of the target's intentions.

'Estimate one craft, heading for the rendezvous point.'

'Any possibility we've got multiple targets, in close formation, trying to fool us into thinking it's just the one craft?' Fighter controllers are naturally suspicious people, especially when they've seen a tactic used themselves.

'Not likely, given the strength of the return. The filter programs concur.' Fighter controllers are also a proud, confident bunch: computers agree with them, not vice versa.

'Signal Control and tell them our guests are on time.'

'Roger.'

RAF Machrihanish, Kintyre

Confirmation of the approach of what was almost certainly an alien craft had different effects on different people.

Security personnel were in a flap, resenting the situation with which they had been presented while realizing they were powerless to prevent it. Five key world leaders gathered in one location, with an unknown enemy who had used force before and couldn't be evaluated by any human rules, approaching fast, was a nightmare scenario for any security detail to handle. SAS close-protection specialists had socialized with US Secret Service personnel and compared the situation. French, Russian and finally even Chinese security staff had also joined in. They soon realized they were united by their horror at the tactical situation and their absolute fury at being instructed to come unarmed.

Military advisers shared the concerns of the security personnel but were thinking on a larger scale, evaluating the strategic situation as well as the tactical one.

Civil servants reverted to type, going into an analytical mode that involved their playing out various possible scenarios in their minds and wondering if their political masters would stick to their briefs.

The five leaders were probably the least busy and therefore most relaxed personnel on base. Consequently they had time to think about the situation. Although they did so with different considerations in mind, they shared one emotion that most of the others had put to one side: excitement. They were going to see an extraterrestrial craft and meet intelligences from another world. So, while the leaders were feeling a mixture of emotions, there was not one of them who – at some level – wasn't thrilled by the situation.

Outsiders would doubtless have been shocked and surprised to learn that the world leaders weren't busily studying their briefs, conferring with officials or having last-minute discussions among themselves. But, in reality, all that could be done had been done. The only analogy that an outsider might have understood was that of the child studying for an exam: there comes a point when further revision is not only pointless but is actually counter-productive. You either know something or you don't and last-minute cramming is liable only to confuse you. The smart students know when to stop, and take care to approach the exam in a relaxed state of mind. Politicians behave the same way before negotiations and these were no exception.

There was another reason for what might have been seen as inactivity: the politicians realized – as few others did – that there was little they could do. They knew that the aliens had offered partnership, but they also knew that this would be a conditional offer. The aliens would have a list of demands and, while nobody knew the details, all knew that it would involve a large – if not total – degree of political control. Conversely, the leaders – no matter the nature of the political regime they headed – would know what was acceptable and what was not. There were, so to speak, lines in the sand and, while these lines had been drawn by different hands, they had all been drawn surprisingly close together.

The final administrative arrangements had been made by specialist protocol officers, whose duties more usually consisted of arranging inbound visits for ministers and chiefs of staff. Some might have found this bizarre, but if no one knew what to expect there was logic in planning for the most similar thing from past experience.

While the leaders were in a secure underground facility within the base – one concession to their security personnel – others were reacting to new developments. Data from the RAF's Sentry aircraft had now been correlated by the radar systems at the base itself. These fixed systems had been augmented by powerful mobile radars, ensuring that they had earliest possible notification of visitors. Given the speed of the craft, this notice was not particularly lengthy.

'Inbound target on the scopes, ETA two minutes. Stand by.' The assessment originated in the control tower but was rapidly relayed to other observers.

Everybody present was there because they had a key role or an important task but not everybody was busy at the same time. Consequently, as the craft made its final approach there were a number of people not actively engaged on any task who did what came naturally: they watched.

At first the alien vessel was just a faint speck in the sky but it was travelling so quickly that people soon got a better view. There were gasps of astonishment as people got their first close-up view of the craft. It approached at speed and then seemed to stop dead, hanging silently in mid-air, directly over the main runway. It was a delta-shaped object that the UFO lobby would have called a "flying triangle". It was about thirty metres in length and there were no wings or tail visible. It was this that most impressed the RAF personnel present, as they appreciated better than others the phenomenal power needed to keep such an object airborne, let alone for it to achieve the speed and manoeuvrability that it had demonstrated in its approach. The other thing that impressed the airmen present was the lack of noise. For an aircraft to hover – in the way that, for example, an RAF Harrier did – required the generation of a colossal amount of lift. The deafening roar of a Harrier's engines was always popular at airshows, but seeing as massive an object as this hovering without such noise was evidence of some still-unfathomable power source. Those close to the craft could discern a faint, low-frequency humming sound that they could feel as well as hear. It was a vaguely unpleasant sensation, not unlike standing too close to the speakers at a rock concert.

After a few seconds, the object descended slowly to the ground and appeared to touch down on the runway. No landing gear was visible, but a faint shimmering under the craft suggested that some unknown force was bearing its weight and keeping it just above the tarmac of the runway. An expectant hush fell and everybody waited to see what would happen next. After around twenty seconds it seemed that a section of the hull had vanished and that a doorway had appeared. Personnel had been instructed to keep at least thirty metres away from the craft but several key personnel had powerful binoculars and peered expectantly at it, trying to probe the blackness of its interior. Cameras had been mounted on tripods and were filming events. This was being done both to record the moment for posterity and – more immediately – to give intelligence officers data to analyse. One of the cameras was using an infra-red filter and the operator quickly relayed the message that there were no obvious heat signatures that might suggest the presence of occupants.

Whispered conversations took place and a tentative conclusion was reached: the aliens had sent an unmanned craft that would take the five world leaders to talks on the alien mothership. This had been considered by the analysts as one of two or three likely scenarios, and was therefore not something that came as any great surprise: it was, after all, quite logical that the aliens should want to retain absolute control of the environment, in order to minimize the amount of intelligence that could be gleaned. It had also been recalled that the disgraced NSA chief Edwin Van Buren claimed to have visited the ship, as part of a demonstration of the power that the aliens wielded. If this claim was true – and his interrogators believed it was – it was more than likely that the aliens would now want to use the same tactic.

Analysts concurred that if one of the aliens' key aims was to persuade Earth's governments not to use force against them, then giving the key world leaders a glimpse of what they'd be going up against was a likely tactic. It might mean that they gathered some intelligence on alien capabilities, but this was clearly a price worth paying if the result was that the world governments rolled over. Furthermore, any tour of the alien mothership would clearly be carefully controlled: they'd only be shown what the aliens wanted them to see.

The five leaders were escorted from the underground room where they'd been placed and were briefed about the situation. As the scenario had been anticipated, there was actually very little to discuss. After a few minutes the leaders strode purposefully out across one of the taxiways and approached the craft. The pace was brisk, and several people correctly deduced that there was more than a little pride at stake, with each leader wanting to be first on board the craft. It happened that the French President was first to reach it. Then he hesitated for a moment as if he was unsure whether manners dictated that he should go first or make a show of allowing President Spencer – the only woman present – to precede him.

While the Frenchman dithered and Spencer looked embarrassed, Sergei Petrov, the President of the Russian Federation, resolved the issue by striding past them both and getting on board first. The others followed him in and within seconds were out of sight. There was a smattering of applause from some of those present, but it was difficult to say whether this was generated by respect for the leaders' bravery or the simple relief of tension.

For a few minutes, nothing happened. Then, without anyone really seeing how, the opening in the side of the craft seemed to disappear. A few seconds later, the vessel rose slowly up in a vertical ascent until it was about a hundred metres above the ground. Then, to the amazement of those watching, the craft appeared almost to change its shape, at least at the edge, as if it was being stretched. Then, in a blur of motion, it streaked skywards and was lost from sight.

In the control tower the craft was being tracked by radar, with data gleaned from the base's systems and the AEW aircraft.

'Thirty thousand feet,' a fighter controller called out. 'Forty, fifty, sixty – what the hell – eighty, nine—' he stopped abruptly.

'They have achieved orbital height. I no longer have them.' He knew that other systems would be trying to follow their progress – the Deep Space Tracking Facility would be used, as would the powerful space-tracking radars at the Ballistic Missile Early Warning System. Telescopes would also be used. But all this monitoring could achieve little, and all those who knew about the historic rendezvous about to take place had no illusions about their own ability to control the situation. It was out of their hands. All they could do was wait and – if they were so inclined – pray.

Chapter Seven

TALKS

MOD Main Building, Whitehall

'Now what?' The moment Martin Blackmore had spoken, he realized it was hardly the most intelligent-sounding question he could have asked. In reality, though, there was little else to say. He doubted very much that Nick Templeton had any idea what would happen next, any more than he did himself.

Templeton paused for a moment, fighting the urge to say 'we wait' and trying instead to think of something more constructive than a clichéd platitude. As it happened, there *was* something to consider, depressing though the thought was. 'We knew they might be taken on to the ship, and we knew that one possible scenario was that they won't be coming back. We need to start thinking about what happens if they're kidnapped or killed.'

'The Deputy Prime Minister is acting for the PM in his absence, and will take over permanently if . . .' Blackmore's voice trailed off, as if he couldn't bring himself to articulate the thought. 'I'm sure the other nations have made similar arrangements.'

'Well, that's not quite what I meant, Minister,' Templeton

replied. 'I mean, if something happened, we'd need to consider what military response to make.'

'What, you mean a rescue?' Blackmore retorted. 'I don't see how.'

'No. I mean that if they killed our leaders, that would be tantamount to a declaration of war. We'd have to consider initiating Operation Lightning Strike.'

'What if they're just being held there?'

'Well, clearly the use of force is a *political* decision,' Templeton ventured carefully. 'But we may be faced with a situation in which we have to act very quickly indeed.'

'Rules of Engagement are safely in place, though,' the Minister retorted. 'If we're attacked, we can defend ourselves, meeting force with force in a proportional response. Lethal force can be met with lethal force. You're not suggesting that our ROE be more aggressive, are you, Nick?'

'No, Minister. I'm simply wondering what happens if – say – we don't hear anything for twenty-four hours. Or forty-eight. You see my point? We'll be hamstrung. Sooner or later – probably sooner – the whole story about the meeting will leak, or someone will simply twig that five world leaders are missing.' Templeton was thinking on his feet, but the more he developed this idea, the scarier it got. 'It's almost the worst scenario, because we wouldn't know what's going on, and we'll be coming under massive pressure from the press, the public and, most importantly, those other nations not privy to the negotiations. Could this have been a deliberate tactic?'

'You're beginning to sound like CDI,' the Minister responded. 'Next thing you'll be telling me that the world leaders might come back under mind control, or that they might have been substituted with aliens in human form.'

It had been meant as a light-hearted comment but, as ever, Templeton took it literally. 'Well, CDI was only doing his job when he put forward *those* sorts of possibilities. He's paid to have such suspicions. But even if mind control is possible, we operate by collective decision-making and the PM couldn't just order an unconditional surrender. And if he did, people would ask questions. As for aliens in human form, the possibility has been considered. The view from the DIS is that you couldn't duplicate the replaced humans' memories, so it would be readily apparent if a swap had taken place. And if they *could* replace people while acquiring the memories of those they replaced, well, we wouldn't be having this conversation. They'd have won and there'd be nothing we could do.'

Blackmore had been tempted to interrupt Templeton. But he realized that the value of the man was his ability to take a thought, run with it and produce some valuable insights. As it was, all he could do was agree with him. 'Yes, quite.'

The Alien Mothership

The five world leaders had been profoundly disappointed with their trip through space. The vessel into which they had climbed had been virtually featureless. There had been a ridge of sorts around the edge of the interior, which – they supposed – was meant to be sat upon. This they had done. They had known that a trip to the alien mothership was one possible scenario and this was something that had been covered in the interminable briefings that they had all received from their officials.

All had agreed to take the risk of making such a trip, if it was offered, even knowing that it could simply have been the culmination of a plan to gather the leaders in one place so that they could be removed – temporarily or permanently. To varying extents, all of them had harboured hopes that they *would* be taken to the ship – it was a logical tactic, after all – and had been looking forward to it. But if they had been mildly aggrieved at the Spartan nature of the interior of the craft that they'd boarded at RAF Machrihanish, they'd been really disappointed to discover that there were no windows. All had harboured a wish to see the Earth from space and to see the mothership as they approached. Indeed, their briefers had respectfully requested that they pay particular attention to the view, in the obvious hope that some useful intelligence could be culled. While the ship was visible from the

Hubble Space Telescope and other ground-based telescopes, few details could be discerned.

But, as it was, the whole experience had been somewhat akin to being in a lift: there had been the sense of acceleration, which had caused some discomfort, but this had been replaced by a feeling that was more difficult to describe. They all felt somewhat dizzy but were unsure whether this was a physical or psychological reaction to the situation in which they found themselves. After a journey that lasted twenty-seven minutes – they had timed it, as they had been asked to do by their military briefers – they felt a slight jolt, and assumed – correctly – that they had arrived at their destination. A door of some sort had opened, and beyond it a new world awaited.

The biggest surprise – though it had been anticipated in all the briefings – was that the aliens were indeed indistinguishable from humans. As the world leaders stepped forward, a little unsteady on their feet, though this was again probably more psychological than physical, they found themselves face to face with five very ordinary-looking men. There were other figures – all 'human' – in the background, but the aliens had clearly wanted to ensure that the meeting took place on equal terms, and this was taken as an encouraging sign.

Their surroundings could only be described as cavernous. There was not a great deal of ambient light, but it seemed clear that they were in a docking bay of some sort where the scout craft were kept. It seemed to stretch away as far as the eye could see in either direction, and though the details could not be readily discerned, there were vast numbers of these craft on show. Several of the humans wondered whether this was a deliberate show of strength, designed to demonstrate the aliens' resources.

By what seemed like mutual agreement on both sides, nothing was said, although a few smiles were exchanged in what was taken as another potentially encouraging sign. The rules of diplomacy were clearly well-understood, and no business was to be done until they had arrived at their final destination – wherever that might be. The British Prime Minister was not the only one wondering whether these five individuals were merely an escort party or alien leaders empowered to negotiate for their people. But the PM had something else on his mind: as they walked across the room – not down the line of craft but away from them, towards the other side of this vast space – he recalled the briefing that he'd been given on the remote viewing data. Although S of S and CDI had been at pains to stress the tentative nature of the information, there was no getting away from the fact that both the report he'd been given and the sketches he'd seen were uncannily similar to what he was now seeing. He cautioned himself not to become credulous, and recalled the warning that the remote-viewing data could simply be the result of logical deduction and guesswork.

It was certainly the case that the analogy between the alien mothership and an aircraft carrier was a logical one, and indeed one that had been circulating in the public domain. The remote viewer had been in the military, so it was perfectly possible that she better than most would know at some level that what the PM was now seeing was a predictable sight. That said, he desperately *wanted* it to be more than just guesswork and coincidence. He'd been sceptical about remote viewing but like all good politicians he wasn't one to reject something out of hand – especially if it might be useful. And this was certainly useful: if remote viewing did work, here was a way to gain all sorts of potentially useful intelligence. He made a mental note to order the immediate expansion of the remote-viewing programme – if he got back safely.

They were at the far end of the room, and all of them turned back to try and get some idea of perspective: they had walked for several minutes across a featureless space that they assumed was used for the maintenance of the small craft. The aircraft-carrier analogy was uppermost in all their minds and they all harboured images of this being an area normally full of people carrying out maintenance tasks on craft – a busy flight deck.

They were ushered through a door and into a featureless metallic corridor. They walked for about three minutes before coming to a junction where there was an entrance in the wall.

They were taken through and invited to sit in what was undoubtedly a monorail vehicle of some sort. When they were all safely enclosed within the pod-like structure, there was an unmistakable sense of acceleration that indicated they were being propelled forward at great speed. The nearest analogy any of them could think of was that of an underground train, though the US president also likened the experience to the motion of the various theme park rides that she'd taken over the years. Again, there were no windows, so there was nothing to see other than the functional interior of the capsule they were in. This form of transport was clearly a way to move quickly around the ship, and that was another indication of the vast size of the vessel, though this was something that observation with telescopes had already verified.

A sudden jolt told them that they had arrived, and moments later the capsule opened and everybody filtered through the exit. They were in another featureless corridor that was indistinguishable from the one where they'd entered the transportation device. Indeed, there had been nothing aside from the sensation of movement to indicate that they'd gone anywhere.

Another entrance was now visible, on their right, and the door slid rapidly to one side, revealing a large room. They stepped inside, and the door slid shut behind them. The room was dominated by a round table and six chairs, all of which looked as if they were made of wood – mahogany, perhaps. There were nameplates by all the places and the five world leaders quickly found their places and sat down. At each place were several sheets of paper and some pens, together with glasses filled with what all presumed to be water. There was what looked like a bulky folder of papers in front of each place. This was a setting that had clearly been designed to put them at ease – all were experienced with high-level meetings and had attended numerous such gatherings in their careers. The alien escort party withdrew.

'Welcome'. It began with this single word, and all eyes turned to the speaker. There was a nameplate in front of him, too, and this one identified the man as Harrison Clines. He was a tall man, aged about sixty as far as any of the world leaders could guess. He was black, with predominantly grey hair that was completely white in places. He had a craggy face and his forehead was lined. He looked tired but his eyes indicated a man who was both alert and intelligent. 'My name is Harrison Clines, and I speak for everyone on this vessel.'

Introductions were made, consisting of little more than an exchange of names. It was Clines who opened the real discussions.

'I am grateful to you all for your trust and understanding. It is no small thing that you have done to come here. Doubtless you all considered the possibility that this would be a one-way trip. Let me assure you that this is not the case. You may leave at any time, though I hope you will stay long enough to conclude our business. We shall conduct this meeting in English, as we know this to be a language in which you are all fluent. But the files in front of you are in your own languages.'

Clines paused for a moment, noting that none of the world leaders had so much as touched the dossiers placed so invitingly in front of them. 'Our discussions will be based around the contents of this file. It contains a detailed plan for the integration of our two societies. This plan is the result of many years' study, and covers every aspect of the changes that will be necessary, be they political, social, scientific, economic or military. Even so, this plan is not complete. Clearly there will be unforeseen issues that arise, or areas where our plan makes errors or misjudgements that will require additions or changes. Well, we *are* only human, after all.' His smile was met by neutral looks that betrayed no reaction.

'Notwithstanding these quibbles, we believe this plan is a constructive and clear blueprint for the forging of a new world order,' Clients went on. 'Naturally there are many uncertainties among your people. There are uncertainties among my people, too. But if we follow this plan and take the actions described therein, we believe there can be a peaceful and seamless transition to this new world order – a global system that will undoubtedly benefit both our races, as they join together. We offer you partnership and we offer you peace. Now, may I suggest you take a little time to read some of the plan. I shall withdraw and will return in one hour. Please use this time constructively. Read the Executive Summary at the beginning, and dip into the rest as time allows. But focus on the summary, because I shall need your acceptance of the basic assumptions therein before we proceed to any detailed discussions. The door will not be locked, but I ask you to remain in the room so that you use all the time studying the plan. The room is not bugged or monitored in any way. I realize you have no way of being sure on this point but I give you my word – which is something I do not break, as you will learn in time. You will have to take this on trust, but that is no bad beginning for the coming together of our peoples. I shall return in one hour.' Clines walked silently from the room. The door closed, leaving the leaders alone. It was Sergei Petrov, the President of the Russian Federation, who spoke first.

'Those were fine words, but clearly prepared ones. We were listening to a scripted speech. They've learned the art of diplomacy well enough, that is for certain.' There were nods of agreement from the others. Petrov promptly picked up his copy of the plan and made a point of turning to the final page, not the summary to which he'd been directed by Clines. The others picked up their copies and as the allotted hour went by their expressions alternated between amazement and disbelief. There was little discussion, mainly because all of them were trying to digest as much of the document as possible. All had read the Executive Summary, but rather than discussing it – perhaps because of suspicions that their comments would be overheard, despite the assurances they'd received – they used the time to check other areas that interested them.

Clines returned on time and found all the world leaders silently reading.

'I had hoped to find you in discussion, but perhaps this is a good sign. Perhaps you have discussed and agreed a response? We have many copies of this document, both in hard copy and on computer disk. It is entirely up to you how you share this data with your people. You may wish to restrict it to your key officials, or you may want to make it public. We recognize that your differing political systems might make this difficult, if some want it made public and some do not. Frankly, this is your problem. But the detailed and sometimes highly technical parts of the plan will need to be enacted in a coordinated fashion, so your key advisers will have to familiarize themselves with the relevant aspects of this document.'

Again, it was Petrov who spoke up. 'You say you were disappointed that we were not in discussion when you returned, but you correctly surmised the reason. We have indeed reached agreement on our response to your plan. Little discussion was needed on something so clear-cut. Let me put it plainly: this document is a blueprint for the subjugation of the human race. You demand what amounts to an unconditional surrender. You spoke to us of partnership, but that is not what you offer. If you are sincere in your talk of partnership, then fine: let us discuss this partnership. But let there be no doubt – the plan that you have presented to us is completely unacceptable to any of us, and quite beyond any suitable amendment.'

The PM thought he'd better say something at this point, not least because he felt that although Petrov had spoken well the Russian leader had been a little too aggressive, especially in his conclusion. Earlier in his career he'd been a minister at the Foreign and Commonwealth Office and the mandarins had taught him that, in negotiations, it was always best to end on a positive point. 'My friend speaks for us all, but I hope you realize we could never sign up to this plan. You say you've studied us: you'll know, then, that it's not in our nature to surrender. Very recently a number of British citizens lost their lives because they were fired at by your craft. You say this was a mistake, but this was not an isolated incident; it happened many times, over a series of weeks. Furthermore, we find that you actually had an underground facility on our territory – presumably not the only one on Earth – and that you were pursuing a clandestine agenda for decades, without declaring yourselves. None of these actions engenders the trust of which you speak. And what about your appearance? What about the grey creatures that pilot your ships and abduct our citizens?'

'We're in the final stages of modifying ourselves genetically so that we're indistinguishable from you. But our original physiology varies, much as there are slight genetic differences between certain races on Earth, or much as you have different blood groups. Certain of our . . . *bloodlines* . . . are less responsive to genetic modification, meaning that the process takes longer to complete. But most of us look entirely human now. In fact, it's probably true to say that we *are* human, in that our genome is identical to yours. Part of this is for practical reasons of compatibility with human infrastructure, but it's also an important part of the integration process; most human discrimination is visual, and we could well understand that our different appearance would impede our acceptance. But this will be much less of a problem now that we're indistinguishable from you. We're sexually compatible, of course, so within a few generations the integration will be truly complete.'

'This is fascinating, but it doesn't change the fact that you attacked us,' the PM retorted.

'We have said that this was a tragic mistake,' Clines replied. 'But you should look to your American friend for some answers on these points. Her government concluded a treaty with our people.'

'We did no such thing,' President Spencer interjected. 'If any deal was done, it was done illegally, by a cabal operating without any official authorization.'

Clines looked sternly at her for a moment. 'This may be so. But a treaty was concluded nonetheless, and the recent bloodshed arose simply because you broke the deal and began to interfere with our operations. We acted in good faith. We talked to representatives from your military and your intelligence agencies and we reached a mutually beneficial deal. This deal gave the US government access to alien technology that gave you a decisive advantage over the Soviet Union, which bankrupted itself in a futile attempt to keep up and fragmented as a result.'

'Whatever agreement – legal or not – that you made with the Americans has nothing to do with us. It cannot bind us. We knew nothing of this matter.' The Chinese President was a man of few words, but took the opportunity to put his case plainly and simply.

'The same applies to my country – and, indeed, to those countries not represented here.' The French President clearly agreed.

'Your globally fragmented political system is an unfortunate factor here,' Clines replied, 'but we cannot talk to everyone. How could we, when we would receive so many different responses? We're being bombarded even as we speak by a cacophony of voices, as nations, interest groups and individuals send us messages, most of which are conflicting. But this is irrelevant. Our hand was forced by what took place at Roswell and Rendlesham Forest.'

'Maybe so,' the PM agreed. 'But if you've studied us as thoroughly as you claim, you'll know that the sorts of people you've been talking to *can't* speak for entire nations. It's disingenuous of you to pretend otherwise. We're here negotiating with you because you speak for your people. We might choose to walk out of this room and talk to other people on this ship, but to do so would be meaningless. Negotiations take place between leaders. But let's not dwell on the past. We must address the current situation, and while we appreciate the hard work that you've done in putting together a plan, it remains unacceptable. It's very much *your* plan. If you truly offer partnership, then you'll see that any such plan can only be drawn up by both sides acting together, in a spirit of cooperation. I suggest we proceed on this basis and draw up something that will be acceptable to all of us.'

President Spencer thought the PM had spoken well and wanted to build on his comments, stressing the positive. 'I agree. And, by the way, we're not saying that there's *nothing* of value in your plan. While the fundamental principles are unacceptable, there may be much valuable material in it that can be adapted. Clearly we have much to learn from each other, and much to offer each other. We can certainly offer you a home. We welcome you to our world, and invite you to settle here. The influx of a billion settlers, if indeed that is how many of you there are, poses a massive social and economic challenge, but the additional pressure on resources will doubtless be offset by the technological advances that you will contribute.'

'It seems to me,' the French President interjected, 'that your ship might orbit the Earth while solutions to these problems are found. Gradually – as trust develops and as technology is shared – your people can be brought down, and the process of integration can begin. We must tread softly, though, and move cautiously. Any mass landing would doubtless cause a panic and create unfortunate repercussions for all of us. I'm sure you wouldn't want that, if – as you say – you come here with peaceful intentions.'

Clines sat impassively, listening to these speeches. 'You all speak well,' he acknowledged. 'But your arguments are based on a false assumption, which is that of equality. The basic principles of our plan are not negotiable, though doubtless there is room for manoeuvre at the edges. I don't wish to seem rude, but we do have technological superiority. We could overwhelm you in an instant, as you humans have done among yourselves many times in your history when a technologically advanced society has encountered a more primitive culture. But that is not our way. Though we could destroy you or enslave you, we choose neither path. We offer a partnership, it is true. But we have not come all this way and made the sacrifices we have simply to be treated as you treat immigrants into your own societies – as second-class citizens, denied the best jobs and housing, discriminated against by your police, and ending up at the bottom of the pile. We come here offering an alliance – but it's partnership on *our* terms, make no mistake about it.'

'A partnership implies equality,' the PM pointed out.

'Not so,' Clines retorted. 'NATO is a good example, as it happens. It exists as a military alliance, so in one sense it is a partnership. But it consists of member states with vastly differing military and economic resources, who exert influence within NATO in proportion to this power. America, Britain, France and Germany are the dominant powers within the alliance, and as such wield power over new members like Poland, Hungary and the Czech Republic. This is true, is it not?'

There were nods from around the table. 'You threaten us, then?' Again, it was the PM who took the lead.

'It is an ugly word, but speaking bluntly, yes. Ultimately, though, it is for your own good. The plans you would doubtless draw up, if you had a choice, would be narrow plans, dominated by nationalism and self-interest. They would be designed to preserve the status quo and keep power in the hands of those who currently wield it. And as I have said, we would come off second best, as happens with all immigrants on your world. Our plans, on the other hand, are drawn up on a global scale.'

'But your plan is equally driven by self-interest, is it not?' The Chinese President was barely concealing his anger.

'It might seem that the plan protects our interests and, indeed, this is true in the short term – of necessity. But in the medium and long term it will actually be of net benefit to most of the existing population of Earth. Let me explain. Your current system of government is fragmented and wasteful. Many resources are utilized in wars or deterrent measures designed to prevent wars. Economic systems are largely designed not to produce resources and raise the general standard of living but to generate profit for a tiny proportion of the population. The result of this is that poverty, hunger and disease are still rampant, when in reality a simple alteration of priorities could resolve these issues.'

'This sounds like a lecture on the evils of capitalism,' Spencer commented, a trace of sarcasm in her voice.

'Is it not an *obscenity* that people die of hunger every day while vast food surpluses are being stored only a few hundred miles away? Is that not a truly evil and repulsive thing?' Clines's voice was even and he stared at Spencer pointedly, with an expression on his face that was more one of pity than anger.

'It's not as simple as that,' she finally replied, weakly.

'Isn't it? Well, I think it's perfectly simple, so let me ask the question again. And this time, rather than hiding behind a glib soundbite, I want you to really focus and think carefully before answering. Is it not an *obscenity* that each day on this planet people die of hunger while food sits in warehouses and is thrown away in countries where waste is an everyday concept? Have you ever *seen* a child die of hunger, by the way? I have. We've studied your planet for many years, so that when we arrive we can quickly address some of the most pressing issues. Many of us have made study or acclimatization visits here, me included. I was in Ethiopia in 1983. I saw a child die, right in front of me. He was aged about four, though it was difficult to tell his precise age. He was so thin that I could see his bones, and yet his belly was bloated, as happens when one is literally starving. Liquid excrement was running down his legs, and yet he was too weak to cry. Then he vomited, coughing up blood which was a curious dark red – almost black. Then he died. Some time later the body was carried away and thrown into a pit to be burned, for fear of disease. I couldn't count how many bodies were in the pit. So I ask you again, is this not an obscenity?'

'Yes,' Spencer agreed, hoping her admission might help to defuse the situation.

'Yes,' Clines echoed, nodding his head slowly. 'And what have you done about this obscenity?'

'We have a massive aid budget that we spend on food programmes, we sponsor schemes to install wells supplying clean drinking water, and we—'

'But people are still dying. So what you're saying is that you choose to help some people but only so many. Not all? Would you stand by and watch your own child die like that?

'Of course not.'

'The child of your best friend?'

'No.'

'The child of someone who works as a cleaner in the White House?'

'No.'

'Why? Because you care, or because it would be bad PR? You see my point, of course. Where do you draw the line? Why is it acceptable to let some children, but not others, die in this way, when you have the resources to prevent *all* such deaths? Is it a question of nationality or religion? Colour, perhaps?' There was an awkward silence as they all stared at Clines. Was there some hidden message in the alien leader taking the form of a black man? Had the aliens done this deliberately?

'There simply aren't enough resources, and domestic expenditure must be our priority,' Spencer finally replied. She resented being put under pressure but somehow could not find it within herself to totally disagree with Clines, or to dislike him.

'Well, actually yes, there *are* enough resources, if you change your priorities. At the risk of being simplistic, if every child in America went without a computer games console, every child in the *world* could have enough food to survive.'

'You've said it yourself – it's a simplistic argument. In the real world, economic systems wouldn't support such a model, however worthy the cause – and don't get me wrong, I agree that it's worthy.'

'In our plan – that you're so quick to dismiss – there are sophisticated economic models that will help deal with these issues and bring about fundamental improvements in this area.'

'But such plans would inevitably involve sacrifices that people simply wouldn't be prepared to make.' The PM had intervened, partly to help Spencer and partly to ensure that he played as central a part as he could in these proceedings. 'What you say has great merit, but you've misjudged human nature. I believe that Earth's people are fundamentally decent, and you've only got to see how many of them give to charities or do voluntary work to realize that for yourself. But you're arguing for redistribution of wealth on a massive scale. If every taxpayer donated half of what they earned to charity, I'm sure we could address many of these problems. But the point is, they *won't* do that, however strong the argument for doing so. And it goes deeper than that. Our economic systems depend upon people spending their disposable income on goods and services. If they gave to charity instead, demand for these goods and services would fall and businesses would have to lay people off or fold altogether because they wouldn't be making enough money to thrive. Our society is a complex one and, while I'm sure your studies of us have been comprehensive, you are most unlikely to have made sufficient allowance for the human factor – your economic models may work on paper but you need to understand human psychology to truly understand economics.'

'Those are well-put arguments,' Clines acknowledged, 'but you're wrong. We *have* allowed for the human factor and we well understand the link between psychology and economics – your stock markets are an excellent example of this, as demonstrated by the way that share prices rise or fall as a result of confidence – or lack of confidence – that often has far more to do with state of mind than with hard economic data. But it's *greed* that's the real problem. You live in a world where a handful of multinational corporations wield a disproportionate amount of power. Some of these corporations have annual turnovers greater than those of many sovereign states. Entire economies can be wrecked by speculators with enough capital to force the devaluing of a currency. Can this be right? I think not.'

There was an awkward pause. Clines was lecturing at them as much as he was debating with them, but because of who he was his words held the leaders spellbound.

'But let's move on,' Clines said, his facial expression and tone of voice conveying a mixture of compassion and contempt. 'Let's see what else I can argue in support of radical changes. The environment might be a good place to start, and I say to you candidly that even the alarmists among you have underestimated the damage you're doing. Again, the problem is that so much of what you do is profit-driven, resulting in pollutants getting into the ecosystem and doing untold damage. Most serious is the atmospheric pollution, including the CFC and other emissions that deplete the ozone layer and lead to what will soon be dangerous levels of solar radiation not just over Antarctica and the Arctic as is the case now but over much of the populated area of the Earth. This will lead to widespread skin cancer and other problems. But the most important consequence of your failure to control your output of industrial wastes is that gases such as methane, nitrous oxide and ammonia are building up in the atmosphere in sufficient quantities to raise the global temperature by as much as two or three degrees over the next few *decades*. You understand the basic concept of global warming and know that the super-greenhouse gases I've mentioned contribute to this process, because they trap solar energy in a way that's thousands of times more efficient than carbon dioxide. But what most of your scientists *haven't* yet grasped is that the rate of increase of effect will be exponential. That's because when increased amounts of solar radiation reach the Earth's surface, evaporation of the oceans will increase too. The increased amounts of water vapour in the atmosphere accelerate the situation, and yet few of you have grasped the fact that water vapour is the most dangerous green-house gas of all. The situation is further aggravated by the sun itself, which is actually getting ever so slightly hotter. The one thing that could help you is to increase the number of trees and plants, because their photosynthesis process absorbs carbon dioxide – a natural greenhouse gas. But vast tracts of forest are being destroyed to make way for building projects which are similarly driven by profit.'

'They're driven by social need,' the PM retorted. 'If we build on green-field sites it's to build much-needed homes.'

'You should fill unoccupied homes and repair derelict ones before building new ones,' Clines replied. 'But Britain is not the main culprit here – the problems are actually more to do with what's going on in the developing world. The irony is that the rainforests being destroyed all over Earth also contain the natural resources that can best counter many of the diseases that plague you. Nature is all about balance, so for every poison there is an antidote – it's just a question of knowing where to look. Many of your indigenous peoples know this. Their shamans could tell you these things but you wouldn't listen: you're too busy putting perfume in the eyes of rabbits, or forcing them to smoke cigarettes.'

There was another awkward pause. Petrov looked as though he was about to say something but thought better of it.

'Perhaps we could talk about discrimination,' Clines ventured.

'In this world of yours that you're trying so hard to defend, people are killed for practising the *wrong* religion or supporting the *wrong* political party, or even being the *wrong* colour.'

'You're picking the worst aspects of our society,' the PM interjected. 'For every bad thing you cite, I could cite something positive. Look, I'm not saying there aren't issues that need to be addressed, because clearly there are. But we have the right to determine our own future.'

'You've lost that right. When you have the resources to address such issues but choose not to, you lose any moral right to govern. Besides, the threat of an environmental Armageddon demands immediate action that your own system will not and cannot take, not least because of the inertia inherent in all Earth's political structures. We must act immediately and radically if we are to reverse what will soon become an exponential increase in ozone depletion, pollution and species extinction.'

'So, at the end of the day, what happens if we refuse point-blank to go along with your plan?' It was Petrov who put the question uppermost in everybody's mind.

'If you refuse to cooperate, we shall implement our plan by force,' Clines responded. 'But such a course of action would be pointless and would result only in the deaths of as many of your military personnel as you might care to . . . *spend* on such resistance. We would take losses, too, so there would be considerable ill feeling on both sides. I don't propose to give away our battle strategies but I can safely say that, despite our wish for a peaceful implementation of our plan, we have – knowing the human propensity for violence – made contingencies for the other option. But we have no quarrel with the ordinary people of Earth and would make it clear to them that our only dispute was with their leadership. Even there, our plans would be largely defensive. But make no mistake, we can and will take every necessary measure to counter any threat that you pose to us and to neutralize any attack you choose to launch.'

'But surely the violence you speak of contradicts the fine words you've spoken about poverty and the other problems we face? It's no good talking about the evils of our world and with your next breath telling us that you're going to impose a new order on us, whether we like it or not. Many countries on Earth have democratically elected governments, and those that don't, aspire to that aim. The people have a right to choose – to make their own mistakes, yes, but to learn from them. What about democracy?' Spencer's point was sincere, but there was a noticeable sarcasm in her voice.

'What use is democracy when so many people are dying or suffering every day? Our plan can change that – it *really* can. Don't you love your planet enough to change it? Enough to save it? I've mentioned some of the problems that you have and that you seem unwilling or unable to solve. But I've not even touched on warfare and the arms trade, drugs, crime, or the threat from Near Earth Objects such as comets or asteroids. These are problems that *can* be solved, given a combination of the new technologies that we'll bring and the redistribution of existing resources.'

'The bottom line is that we can't trust you,' the PM replied. 'What you say has merit, but at the end of the day what you're really saying is, "Trust me, we're going to make it better". And you expect us to roll over and surrender control to you so that you can institute some sort of benign dictatorship that's going to take us into a new age. Well, excuse the cynicism, but we have the right to judge you on your actions and not your words.'

'We've covered this ground already,' Clines retorted. 'Time grows short indeed, and we need to start working on the implementation of the plan.'

'No. That's not going to happen.'

There was a long silence. 'Is that the view of you all?'

There were nods from around the table. 'That is most unfortunate and most unwise. You know the consequences and I regret to say that, unless you are prepared to change your minds, the plan will be implemented by force. I suggest you go away and discuss the matter with your officials. Give them the plan and talk it over with them. I promise that you'll come to see that there's wisdom in such a choice. But above all, take time to read it yourselves, in its entirety. There's much in there that will surprise you. The section on health, for example, contains data on cures and vaccines to help combat and eventually eradicate many diseases.'

'Bribes or lies,' Petrov exclaimed, in a decidedly undiplomatic outburst that took the other leaders by surprise.

'Your own doctors will soon demonstrate that the data is solid. And as for this being a bribe, that's not true. I won't pretend it's not in our own interest – we are as susceptible to disease as you, though we've been vaccinated against many of your diseases already. But this might best be described as a gift, from our people to yours. It's a gift that's given freely and in good faith. It will help the transformation of your world, eradicating a major source of death and suffering, freeing up resources for other social projects. But this is only one example of what's in the plan. Perhaps we should have written it differently, beginning with a list of all those things that we're *giving* you. But I thought to appeal to your reason and intelligence, believing you had a right to all the information. No intelligent, compassionate entity could possibly reject the society that we'll impose simply because they don't want to surrender the power or wealth that they have.

'But it goes beyond that. Even if you wouldn't trade your power and wealth for our new world order, surely you'd trade it for your survival? I say that because I wasn't bluffing when I spoke of an environmental Armageddon, and once again, the data in the plan will prove it. There are computer models that will verify what I told you earlier but show how to stop the slide. If you can't or won't do this, then we'll have to do it ourselves. Go away, think about it, talk about it, and then accept the inevitable. We *will* create this new world – our way simply makes the transitional phase quicker and easier.' Clines rose and, as he did so, the leaders rose too.

'What now?' Petrov asked suspiciously.

'Now you go home,' Clines replied. 'You know how to communicate with us, so please do so – and please come to the right decision, for all our sakes. The document you have doesn't go into details about forcible implementation of the plan, for obvious reasons, but your scientists know how soon this vessel will achieve orbit around Earth. When it does, the mass landings will begin immediately, so that our people can take control of key areas. You must already have a good idea of the timescale to which we're working. You have days, not weeks. But let's not part under the shadow of threats. We'll force the issue if we have to but I promise that, when you think about it logically, you'll see that our way is the better path. It won't create utopia, but it will give you a world of which we can all be truly proud.'

With that statement, Clines took his leave – and the leaders were taken back the way they'd come for a return journey that passed in near silence.

MOD Main Building, Whitehall

There was an air of suspense in the cavernous Defence Crisis Management Centre, located deep under Main Building. Duty officers monitored computers and people visibly flinched when telephones rang, as they did from time to time despite the late hour. It had been recognized that the absence of the world leaders had created a power vacuum, and some of the more suspicious-minded had suggested that this was a deliberate alien strategy to destabilize those nations most capable of mounting effective resistance. Some thought that the leaders would be killed or held hostage and these same people reasoned that, if this was true, any planned alien attack could well be made once the leaders were out of the picture.

Against that possibility, forces had been put on maximum alert and warned that an attack might be imminent. Radar operators were told to be particularly vigilant. The area around RAF Machrihanish was being monitored constantly and particularly closely. It was reasoned that while detecting multiple targets would clearly be a very bad sign, picking up a single target approaching Machrihanish would be reassuring because it would suggest that the leaders were being returned to their point of departure.

The call, when it came, was placed to a Group Captain who was in charge of the Air Force Operations Room. He promptly called a handful of ministers and service chiefs, relaying his message in a way that gave nothing away even though the telephones were secure. The meaning was clear enough. Flash signals containing a full report were being drafted even as he spoke, but his job was simply to tip off key personnel as quickly as possible to make sure they were ready to take any necessary action.

After a while, he came to the last number on the list, and relayed the message for the final time. 'It seems that our people are coming home.'

RAF Machrihanish, Kintyre

Base personnel watched in silence as the alien shuttle craft approached, hoping there would be no unpleasant surprises. Events mirrored in reverse that of the craft's arrival and within moments of touchdown everybody was relieved to see the five leaders disembark and walk – a little unsteadily – towards a specially designed structure that had been placed close to where the craft had landed.

There was, of course, a detailed plan for the return of the world leaders, a key part of which was to ensure their immediate isolation. This had been agreed in advance and the reasons were twofold. Firstly, it was to enable a thorough medical check of the politicians concerned against the possibility of a biological hazard. Though the aliens had given assurances on this point, nothing was being taken for granted and checks would be made to ensure that none of the leaders had been exposed – accidentally or otherwise – to any extraterrestrial microbes. The second reason for the isolation was somewhat more far-fetched, revolving around suspicions that the leaders might have been tampered with in some other way – or even substituted with lookalike aliens.

The structure which the politicians entered was a purpose-built decontamination unit. They'd all been briefed about this beforehand and knew what to do. Once inside the sealed structure, they walked under intense ultraviolet light that would kill most Earthly bacteria. Several more procedures followed. When these had been completed, they sat and waited for their officials.

'I have something to announce.' It was Petrov who broke the silence. 'We all agreed that the alien plan was unacceptable, even if it really does tell the truth about their real intentions. Of course, it's equally possible that the whole thing's a ruse, designed to make us lower our guard before they launch a massive attack. We are aware that some of you are developing contingency plans to strike at the aliens and, in particular, at their mothership. It's their mothership that must be destroyed or incapacitated if we are to remove the threat we face. There is a way that we can do this.' He proceeded to brief his colleagues on the existence of the chimera virus, though he said nothing about its source.

The PM looked sceptical. 'The problem with your virus, as with any other form of attack, is delivery. How would you deliver such a virus, when there's no guarantee that we'll ever get on to the ship again? The abductions seem to have stopped and, for all we know, the talks we've just had may be the last time any human sets foot on that vessel.'

'Indeed so,' Petrov agreed.

The French President was the first to realize what Petrov meant, but the expressions of horror on the faces of the other leaders soon showed that they too had worked it out.

'I agreed to be infected before coming here,' Petrov continued. 'My people here have the vaccine, and will administer it to me at once. You will all need to be treated, but this poses no problem. I apologize for having exposed you in this way and I regret not having forewarned you of this tactic. But there was no time to discuss it and, had you been aware of this matter, your behaviour might have inadvertently betrayed something.'

There was silence for a few moments while the others digested what they'd just been told. It was the PM who spoke. 'Then you've committed us to war, and possibly sealed all our fates. This is a tactic that should have been used only as a last resort and agreed between us all, not implemented unilaterally. Supposing we had reached agreement with the aliens? There'll be no negotiating after this.'

'Ah, but as you yourself have just said, that may well have been the last time anyone gets on to their ship. So when you speak of tactics of last resort, I say this *was* our last resort.'

'We have to tell them what we've done,' the French President said. 'We brief them on the situation, then offer the vaccine in exchange for access to their ship in sufficient force to control events. This is your plan, I presume?'

'Exactly,' Petrov replied. 'I have no desire to kill anybody. This was never an attempt to destroy them, not least because they would surely retaliate. No, the plan is to wait a while for the disease to spread and infect them in sufficient numbers, then to negotiate suitable terms that result in them getting the vaccine before the deaths start. They spoke of forcible implementation of their plan – and the military resources on that ship are indeed phenomenal. We've had a gun against our heads all along. Now we too have something to threaten them with. For the first time, we have parity. Now we can negotiate as equals.'

The PM looked around the room at the faces of the other leaders. Nobody was looking pleased, and even though there was an undeniable logic to Petrov's statement, the PM had a natural revulsion against the idea of a biological attack. It was a high-risk strategy, and he knew that Petrov had gambled everything on this one ploy. The stakes could not be higher – the fate of the world hung by a thread.

Chapter Eight

WAR OF WORDS

MOD Main Building, Whitehall

'That, then, is what the Russians have done.' It was S of S who gave the briefing to his ministerial colleagues on the defence team and the assembled group of senior military personnel and MOD civil servants.

'Then we need to go immediately to maximum alert,' CDS pointed out. 'Whatever might be decided about when to tell the aliens, there's a chance that they'll find out for themselves beforehand – and when they do, God help us. We know nothing about their psychology but, given that we've just unleashed a weapon of mass destruction against them, there's a good chance that they'll launch a massive retaliatory attack.'

'Aren't we pretty much on maximum alert now?' US of S asked.

'Pretty much, yes,' CDS agreed, 'but there are some additional actions that we can take: calling out the Reserves, upgrading Rules of Engagement and implementing a whole host of other preparatory measures from the War Books.'

'OK, we'll take that forward outside this meeting,' CDS agreed. 'These measures are going to attract some attention: they're not the sort of things we can hide.' He'd experienced this so-called 'transition to war' stage during a number of war games and knew what was involved.

Jacqui Connolly knew that she'd been put on the spot. As the Director General of Corporate Communication it was her job to advise Ministers and Chiefs of Staff about the presentational aspects of any MOD policy. 'We can portray the increased-readiness measures as being prudent defensive measures; the alien ship is getting very close, so the public might reasonably expect us to be on maximum alert. That's not our problem: our problem is that we've launched a weapon of mass destruction against them. That'll undermine any attempt to portray our stance as defensive.'

'So we say the Russians did it,' CAS suggested.

'Well, yes,' Connolly agreed. 'If that's politically acceptable that's precisely what we should say. We have to be truthful about it. We could say that this was a unilateral Russian action that was only notified to us after it had been taken.'

'And if we're asked whether we support it?' CAS asked.

'I recommend something neutral. We could say we understand why they did it but we certainly *don't* want to be seen endorsing or enthusing about a biological attack, so I suggest we distance ourselves from it somewhat. But, politically, we don't want to undermine the Russians either.' She looked at S of S for some help on this, as so much of what she was saying would have to be a political decision.

'OK, thanks,' S of S duly replied. 'I'll take that forward with the PM's Press Secretary. Any other thoughts?'

'We must make every effort to portray this not as an act of aggression but as a tactic to bring the aliens to the negotiating table. Also, as ever, much will depend on which way the press jump. The media still don't know how to call this situation but that'll change in the next day or so. There are only two ways they can go with this: they can represent things as a straight alien invasion and expect people to rally around the flag, or they can take the opposite stance and say that we should welcome the visitors. There's not much middle ground. The events of Operation Thunder Child make it more likely that the UK media will go for the first option. That said, the Russian biological attack is just the sort of thing that could change all that.'

'OK, good. Barbara, what can you tell us about the likely effects of this virus on the aliens?' S of S was controlling the meeting tightly.

As the MOD's Chief Scientific Advisor it fell to Dr Barbara North to make some sort of assessment on this point, despite the fact that there were so many unknowns. 'We've known for some time about the possibility of a chimera virus,' she began, cautiously 'The idea's been floating around for long enough and has been extensively covered in the literature – including open-source material. But though we believed such a thing to be theoretically possible, we never had any information to suggest it had been successfully done. Introducing the genes of one virus into another usually leads to rejection.' She was struggling to keep her comments as non-technical as possible but wanted to give the information to those people who could follow her.

'It's the same principle as blood groups – when you're giving a transfusion you usually need to use the same blood group. If you don't, the body rejects it. Well, we knew the Russians were trying for a smallpox/Ebola weapon, but the problem was always about of finding a compatible place in the genome to introduce the other virus so that it didn't get rejected.'

'So what'll it do to them?' S of S asked, conscious that North still hadn't answered his question.

'I don't know. If they're on the level when they claim to share our genome, then in theory it should affect them in exactly the same way as it would affect us. But the point is that we don't know how it would affect us. The Russians have given us the formula and the vaccine but other details are scant. We know nothing of how this was tested, or what data they have on how long it takes for the influenza virus to break down so that the plague material is released into the body.'

'The Russians claim it'll be a week before the aliens show

symptoms of the plague. What's your best guess on that point?'
S of S asked.

'Without data I can't second-guess the Russian assessment. But
although plague is fast-acting, it'll take a day or so before
symptoms appear. So if the Russians are claiming a week for that,
I'd say there might be five days before the influenza virus breaks
down and releases the plague into the body. But we honestly don't
know; the genetically modified aliens can share our genome and
still have some subtle genetic differences from us. All humans
share the same genome, after all, but all of us have genetic
differences that can result in varying susceptibility to disease.
Quite frankly, it's *possible* that it'll have no effect on them at all –
and it's equally possible that they're all dead already.'

'But your best assessment is the mid-point between those two
scenarios?' S of S asked.

'Yes. But let me once again stress that there are too many
variables to say for sure. Quite apart from any variations in alien
genetic make-up, the virus itself is highly unstable. The plague is
a new strain, and although the influenza strain used is more
commonplace, influenza is notorious for mutating very rapidly,
even in the course of one epidemic. The nightmare scenario is that
it'll mutate into something new and that the vaccine won't be able
to stop it.'

This was a sobering thought and one that clearly came as an
unpleasant shock to everybody around the table. 'Comments or
suggestions, anyone?' S of S asked, throwing the meeting open. 'I
don't want a debate on the morality of the Russians' action,
though,' he added tersely. 'Whatever we may think about it, it's
done.'

'I suggest we tell the aliens *immediately* and consider giving
them the vaccine without laying down any preconditions.' It was
Nick Templeton, the young Head of Sec(AS), who voiced this
opinion.

'Wouldn't that throw away our best chance of negotiating an
equitable settlement?' S of S retorted.

'Yes, but it would be a sign of our good faith. I don't think any of us – myself included – have *really* thought about the implications of the situation. We've all been treating this as if it were a conventional war with a conventional enemy. Most of what we're doing comes out of War Books designed decades ago to deal with a Soviet attack on NATO. We must face facts – one billion extraterrestrials are coming here with massive technological superiority. The old order will inevitably pass away, whether we like it or not.'

'So we just roll over?' CDS asked, sarcastically.

'Have you read their plan?' Templeton responded quickly. 'I'm going through it as fast as I can but I ask because there's actually some very good stuff in there.'

'If we can believe it,' CDS retorted.

'But there are things that can be quickly verified – the medical data on disease cures, for example.'

'But even if the data's genuine, the whole thing could be a ruse. After all, these things would be of little comfort to us if we were enslaved – and no use whatsoever if we were exterminated.' CDS was being fairly bullish, even though he admired Templeton for speaking out and didn't entirely disagree with him.

'OK, I accept that. I'm just saying that we shouldn't reject out of hand the idea of cooperating with the aliens. I say that not because I advocate surrender: in an ideal situation we'd be the ones dictating the terms. But we're not. As I've said, every indication is that they have massive technological superiority, and that means that they'll be able to make good their threat of implementing their plan by force. If that's the inevitable end result, why take action that'll only result in a lot of deaths?'

'A day ago I'd probably have agreed with you,' CDS replied. 'But whether we approve or not, the Russian attack has changed all that and may have given us a fighting chance.'

'A fighting chance to do what?' Templeton shot back. 'To wipe them out through plague, or to initiate Operation Lightning Strike and finish them off by blowing their ship apart when they're fatally weakened? We're talking about a billion intelligent beings who are apparently indistinguishable from us both in appearance and in genetics. Beings who come here bearing gifts of technology and innovative thinking that could make life on Earth very much better for everyone.'

'*If* they're to be trusted,' CDI chipped in. 'You advocate surrender on the basis of trust, and are seemingly prepared to gamble the world itself on the chance that you're right. Why not ask the families of those pilots killed during Operation Thunder Child and see if *they* think the aliens can be trusted?'

S of S held up his hand for silence. 'OK, OK, these are both valid points of view and the Cabinet will discuss all possible options. We don't want to kill any of the aliens if it can be helped, let alone endanger any of our own personnel. Operation Lightning Strike remains a tactic of last resort but, given the current situation, it would be foolish not to plan for such a last resort. But it seems to me that there *is* an acceptable compromise solution midway between all-out attack and unconditional surrender, involving allowing the ship into orbit and initiating a phased and controlled series of landings. But we must be on their ship, taking part in decisions. Doubtless there will be compromises on both sides, as there always are when two civilized societies negotiate with each other. But we must have a veto; we cannot allow others to dictate the future of this country or, indeed, of the entire world. Quite apart from anything else, we have a constitutional and political mandate to maintain existing political systems. As a democratically elected government we couldn't turn power over to outsiders – wherever they come from – even if we wanted to.'

The meeting ran on for another twenty minutes as various other issues were discussed. But Nick Templeton could not escape the thought that their discussions were irrelevant and that it was the aliens and not them who would decide the next move. Though few around the table were as forthright with their views, Templeton was certainly not the only one thinking along such lines.

The White House

'Madam President, I have Sergei Petrov for you on the hotline.'

Despite the fact that Spencer had been expecting the call, she was unsure of precisely what she was going to say. When Petrov had announced to her and the others what he'd done, she'd been horrified. She found the idea of chemical and biological warfare repugnant and had worked hard in the course of her presidency to secure further international treaties banning these obscene weapons. On occasion she had authorized military action against a number of production sites in countries where intelligence reports indicated that such weapons were still being developed. Now she faced a situation where a bioweapon had been used – and she was being asked not only to support this action but to capitalize upon it.

Spencer had discussed the matter with the Joint Chiefs of Staff, whose view had been coldly pragmatic. They'd agreed that the attack was unpleasant but she'd sensed in their voices and expressions a barely concealed admiration for the tactic. Intellectually, she was bound to agree with the assessment: it *had* been brilliantly conceived and flawlessly executed. She was too good a politician even to consider berating Petrov for what he'd done. Such a move was pointless now the deed was done and would serve only to rile the man. She had to concentrate on how to make the best of the situation.

'Sergei, hello. How are you?'

'I am fine, thank you. My doctors have given me the all-clear, and I see yours have confirmed that you're all right, too.'

'Yes,' Spencer replied, 'I am clear of the virus.' *Why does he remind me that he put me at risk in this way? This is hardly the most diplomatic of opening statements.*

'Good, good. Now, we must agree on a timescale for informing the aliens what we've done and agree also about what conditions we must impose on them in order to protect our interests. I suggest four days at least before we alert them so that the disease can take hold. We don't want to give them enough early warning for them to contain it themselves. In such a scenario we would have no bargaining power, and one billion very pissed-off aliens.'

'I disagree,' Spencer replied. 'We know very little of their physiology. Even though they claim to share our genome, there may be differences. The disease could be killing them right now. Imagine how you would feel if the positions were reversed. Once your people started dying in vast numbers, you might lash out in fury, even though logic should bring you to the negotiating table.'

'Not if my very survival were at stake,' Petrov replied. 'I would do *anything* to survive, especially if all my eggs were in one basket, as theirs are.'

'I believe it dangerous to assume that they think like us simply because they look like us.'

'Nonetheless, my way is best. The disease will be spreading, but having used a weapon like this we must have the resolve to see it through. We must be ruthless, up to a point. But if we let them off the hook now, we invite the very retaliation that you fear. We have done a dangerous thing, I agree. I also agree that it was an unpleasant thing that we did. But it has given us an opportunity to decide our own destiny. You heard what they said up there and you've seen their blueprint for a new world order. Even if they're to be believed, we'd be handing over power to them, totally and irrevocably. Now we don't have to.'

'I shall have to discuss this with others. but I tell you now, we reserve the right to take unilateral action here and communicate with the aliens.'

'That was the purpose of this call,' Petrov replied. 'To ensure that you do not do such a thing.'

Spencer thought it a strange choice of words for one fluent in English. 'You may *ask* that I refrain from taking this action, but you may not *ensure*. We decide our own fate.'

'But in this case, your fate and ours are tied together and the position is more precarious for us since it was I who, as it were, held the sword in my hand. I do not say you would do this, but there might be a temptation for you and others to distance yourselves from this action. Some might say it would be in your national interests to contact our friends and tell them that we did this thing. You might hope to curry favour with them for giving them early warning.'

'We would never seek to turn them against you, though it *is* a matter of undeniable fact that you took a unilateral decision here.'

'I do not doubt your good intentions. But now I must reveal something to you; something you will not like.'

'I'm listening.'

'There are many in your country who think as we do, and who doubtless support the action we've taken.'

Spencer knew this to be true from her meeting with the Joint Chiefs of Staff. 'I don't doubt it.'

'Earlier, I said that our fates were tied together by this action,' Petrov continued. 'But this is true in a way that you do not yet know. The attack was launched by Russia, that is true, but it was conceived by *your* people: chimera is an *American* virus.'

Spencer felt as if she was going to be sick. Few things in her interesting and complex life had shocked her as much as the few words that Petrov had just spoken. She paused momentarily, to gather her thoughts and decide a suitable response. She had to say something quickly. 'That is quite some claim. I presume it can be substantiated?'

'It can.' Petrov was giving nothing away.

'But you're not prepared to tell me the details? Well, then, your claim is meaningless. You could be lying to me.' This was not the language of diplomacy, but Spencer was trying to goad Petrov into revealing something. She was pretty sure he wouldn't make something like this up but she had to try and get him to open up somehow. A direct accusation of untruthfulness was as likely as anything to tempt Petrov into an indiscreet response.

'You can prove these claims for yourself, by confirming that the chimera virus is a US project. But I won't tell you who gave us this information. Their action has been of benefit to us all, and it may be that there is more business that can usefully be done. I do not want to shut the door on that possibility by revealing our source. What use would this person be, dismissed from office or arrested? In time, perhaps, this person will receive a medal of grateful recognition for giving us the means to negotiate a settlement on our terms and not on those of our mysterious visitors.'

'There will be no medals for those who betray their country.'

'That is your business, of course. It is of no concern to me. What *is* of concern is that you support our position in this matter and do nothing to jeopardize *our* proposed timescale for action.'

'And if I do not?'

'You know the answer to that, I think. Good day.'

Spencer thought about it for a moment. But there was no escaping the facts. If details of the biological attack were made public and it emerged that the US had been instrumental in planning the action, it could do untold harm to the national interest. And, much as she cursed herself for thinking along such selfish lines, she also had to admit that such a revelation could end her presidency. Even though the attack was carried out without her knowledge or approval, it would appear to others that she had lost control of the situation. The accusation would be that even if she *hadn't* known what was happening, she *should* have known.

'Madam President, I have General Hank Whitman from US Army Chemical and Biological Defense Command on the line. He says he needs to talk to you urgently.'

'I bet he does. Put him through please.'

'Madam President, I need to come and see you immediately. I've just been asked to verify the formula the Russians used and I'm afraid I have to report to you that it's an American one: *we* made that virus.'

The tone of his voice, Spencer noted, was that of a man who was genuinely shocked. But she reminded herself that Van Buren had been equally persuasive when telling a barefaced lie. Could Whitman be bluffing? Was he outraged at a breach of security or simply trying to cover himself? 'So I've just discovered,' she replied, carefully keeping her voice neutral. 'Any idea who's responsible?'

'Yes. It must have been NSA Director Casper Goldwater. I had a meeting with him only the other day at Fort Detrick. Colonel Willett, the CO, was present too. Goldwater showed us a transcript of an intercepted telephone call concerning Russian plans to use a bioweapon against the aliens. We discussed the possibilities, and that's when he revealed that he knew all about the chimera virus.'

'Is that thing even legal?' Spencer asked, coldly.

'We have no stocks of it, Madam President, just a formula that was developed in the course of research into how we might defend ourselves against the hybrid bioweapons that we know the Russians are working on. So we're not breaking any of the treaties or conventions.'

'Well, your harmless, defensive formula has just been used to make a weapon that's been used against the visitors and that might just goad them into wiping out all life on Earth. I'm ordering you to start mass production of the vaccine immediately. Do you understand?'

'Yes, Madam President.'

'Good. When you've set the wheels in motion I want you to come here and bring with you a clear and concise report on this virus, along with the formulae for both it and the vaccine. Clear?'

'Yes, Madam President.'

The call over, Spencer told one of her staff to get hold of the Director of the FBI. She thought it might be a good idea to work out how to arrest the Director of the NSA.

RAF Coningsby, Lincolnshire

It didn't take a genius to work out that an attack was expected. Isabelle Bentley and the rest of the Eurofighter Typhoon pilots had been given various sets of new instructions over the last couple of days, but the latest orders had been implemented with what seemed like desperate urgency. They went further than anything that had come before, even at the height of Operation Thunder Child.

All the aircraft were either in hardened air shelters or dispersed at various points around the runway, hidden under camouflage nets. Fuel and essential spares had been stockpiled at various secure locations around the base to guard against a successful attack on the usual storage sites degrading the aircrafts' combat capability. RAF Regiment personnel were deployed to Coningsby in force, in the short-range air-defence role, bringing with them their mobile Field Standard C Rapier missile systems. Though their regimental origin hadn't been announced, a tough-looking group of soldiers who were clearly SAS had also deployed, carrying various hand-held surface-to-air missiles like Javelins and Stingers. Similar measures had been taken at the other two RAF stations where Typhoons were based – Leeming and Leuchars – and at RAF Waddington, home to the RAF's Sentry airborne early-warning aircraft, as well as at the key radar installations.

The trouble with all this was that assets were now spread very thinly. There had even been talk of dispersing the Typhoons to other bases, but this was still being debated: it might make it more difficult to target the aircraft, but it would also make it more difficult to protect them.

If the precautions taken with equipment seemed excessive, those taken with the personnel who would use it seemed positively paranoid. The RAF knew only too well that its most prized assets were the pilots themselves – especially the Typhoon pilots, most of whom had already seen action against the aliens during Operation Thunder Child. Front-line aircraft could generally be replaced with ones from the in-use reserve, with a new airframe available in a matter of hours. And although the RAF had not yet taken delivery of all its 232 aircraft, the German, Italian and Spanish air forces also operated Typhoons and could doubtless be prevailed upon to loan some airframes if necessary. But it took years to train a fast-jet pilot and, although the total number of fully trained, combat-ready Typhoon pilots was classified, it was considerably less than the airframes available for them to fly.

There was a further factor: although the training programme had been accelerated, not all Typhoon pilots had had experience of using the RAF's new directed-energy weapon, the Skystriker. What this meant was that every effort was being made to protect the Skystriker-trained pilots. Those that lived in the Officer's Mess had been billeted elsewhere to guard against the possibility of one hit taking out a sizeable chunk of the force. They'd also been discouraged from taking their meals together or gathering in large groups in the bar after hours. The rationale was that while there might be some warning of an attack, it was possible that one could come with no notice at all. Analysis of previous engagements suggested that the alien craft might have appeared over the North Sea deliberately, to draw out the RAF. But if the abduction accounts were to be believed – which, apparently, they were – the alien craft certainly seemed to have the ability to enter the atmosphere and descend almost vertically. This would be very difficult to spot on conventional radar and, although RAF Feltwell and RAF Fylingdales possessed space-tracking radar that might detect such a move, the nightmare scenario was that the aliens might change their tactics and descend directly upon RAF Coningsby itself, launching a devastating attack before the RAF could even get into the air.

These were only theories but the strategic thinkers were always thinking of worst-case scenarios. In the current climate it would clearly have been foolish to dismiss such pessimistic assessments out of hand.

The inevitable consequence of these developments was a lot of bad feeling. Everybody was on maximum alert but nobody was quite sure why. There had been no hint of alien activity recently, although rumours were circulating about some sort of landing in Scotland, so the assumption was that ministers or Chiefs of Staff knew something they weren't passing down the line. That rankled, particularly with the Typhoon pilots who saw themselves as being very much at the sharp end and bitterly resented the fact that they weren't being kept fully briefed.

'Sir, it's crazy to expect us to perform at full potential if we don't know what's going on. It's obvious we're expecting trouble, but we don't know what form that's likely to take so we can't train for it and we can't prepare for it mentally.' Isabelle Bentley had been nominated by her fellow pilots to lobby the Station Commander. She was a distinguished veteran of Operation Thunder Child and it was felt that her view would carry as much weight as anyone's. And, as somebody who wasn't as rank-conscious as many, she had no qualms about pressing the CO for some answers.

'I know,' her boss replied, 'I agree with you. I'm not holding anything back, I promise. There's nothing I know about this whole situation that I haven't briefed you on. I'm pushing like crazy for answers, but all I know is that we've been ordered to maximum alert. The scientists say the alien ship is on its final approach now, so maybe it's just that this is seen as the most dangerous moment in this whole business.'

'But what are we supposed to do? Is this thing going to land and, if so, are we supposed to stop it?'

'I'm told there's no way their main ship *can* land – it's too big. It'll just orbit, so the scientists say. But it may be carrying God knows how many of the vessels you've already encountered.'

'But *how* many, sir? Are we talking hundreds? Thousands?'

'We simply don't know.'

'I thought the government were talking about a peaceful resolution of this? I thought the aliens had said it was all a horrendous mistake?'

'That's what I've been told. But we judge people – whoever or whatever they are – on what they do, not what they say. So even if all this talk about peace is encouraging, on past form it'd be crazy not to prepare for war.'

Downing Street, Whitehall

The perpetual problem of politics in the early twenty-first century was that of time. In the age of the Internet and of twenty-four-hour news programmes, there was simply not enough time to keep up with the world. So the spin doctors could practise their dark art to their heart's content, only to find that things had moved on and that a new story was already going out. The press offices of government departments were given larger and larger budgets, and more and more staff. Still, they found themselves in a perpetual game of catch-up where they were almost always being reactive, not proactive as their job descriptions demanded.

So it was that the PM strode into one of the main conference rooms, expecting to brief his key ministers on President Spencer's call from Petrov and planning to debate the issue of when to inform the aliens and what terms to demand. The conference room itself had changed in recent years, with the paintings replaced by TV screens constantly tuned to the most important channels. Two of the screens showed the homepages of Internet news sites. Even as the PM entered and saw his ministers gathered around the screen and not sitting at the table, he knew something big had happened.

'. . . content of the message – facts that we are trying to verify with the government.' Somebody had helpfully turned up the sound on one of the BBC news channels.

'What's happened?' the PM's Press Secretary asked.

'Shhh,' hissed an anonymous minister, to the amusement of one or two indiscreet souls who couldn't suppress a muffled laugh.

'Of the authenticity of the message itself, of course, there can be no doubt. After the proliferation of hoax messages once the existence of the ship had been confirmed, a scientific protocol was established for determining such matters and clarifying other disputed questions about the craft itself. Fortunately, scientists can very quickly determine the direction from which a broadcast comes by using radio telescopes. Either a message comes from Earth or it comes from space. This one comes from space, from the direction of the mothership itself.'

The Defence Secretary had broken away from the cluster of ministerial colleagues and told the PM what was going on, even though the PM had clearly worked it out for himself. 'They know,' Willoughby whispered. 'They know about the attack and have broadcast the details. Any chance we had of earning goodwill by telling them ourselves and telling them before the disease took hold has gone. We're out of options.'

'The plague has started to spread already?' the PM asked. 'How bad is it?'

'It's bad.'

A moment later they all realized that one of the Internet sites was showing the full text of the message itself. Everybody gathered around and even the PM had to push a few colleagues out of the way to get a clear view.

To the people of Earth we send our greetings once more, though in the most unhappy of circumstances. We had hoped by now to be negotiating the details of our arrival with your leaders. We sought to make our homes on Earth alongside you and, while we wanted to see some changes to existing power structures, these changes were primarily aimed at eliminating poverty and disease through the technology and medical knowledge that we bring. We met in secret with your world leaders, who were invited on to our ship for talks about how to negotiate a peaceful settlement that would be acceptable to everyone. Our proposals were rejected out of hand but while on board your leaders deliberately unleashed a biological terror weapon against us. The main constituent of this weapon is a new strain of plague. Thousands of our people are dead and thousands more are dying. Most of the victims are civilians; many of them are children. We have no quarrel with the ordinary people of Earth, who we suspect were not consulted about this attack and would not have approved such a cowardly action. But to those people who ordered, planned and launched this attack, we send due warning: you will pay for this act of terrorism. We shall take action against your chemical and biological warfare sites so that these evil weapons can never be used again. More generally, we will target your military facilities to degrade and diminish your ability to wage war against us. In carrying out these actions, we stress again that we have no quarrel with the people of Earth, and we give our assurance that we shall make every effort to minimize casualties. But we cannot allow this evil attack to go unpunished, and we intend to bring the perpetrators to justice, to answer for their crimes. Finally, despite everything, it is still our heartfelt wish to see a peaceful solution to this situation, so the hand of friendship remains extended to those who had no part in this unprovoked attack. It is still our intention to see our people united with yours, living alongside one another in peace and in prosperity.

'Oh shit.' The PM's comment was hardly the most eloquent of assessments but it summed up the situation well enough. 'Assuming it's genuine – and I suppose that's easy to check – how the hell do we counter it?'

'Prime Minister, we need to get you on television *immediately*. You need to address the nation. And in doing so, you need to address your remarks not just to our people but to *theirs*.' The Press Secretary inclined his head upwards, making his intention clear.

MOD Main Building, Whitehall

'Yo, Yo, UFO, people have a right to know!'

'CIA, CIA, how many people have you killed today?'

A demonstration had been planned originally for the following day but, as soon as the news of the alien broadcast had broken, people had started to show up. For once, unusually for demonstrations of this type, there had been no advance strategy, no orchestrated campaign on the Internet. It was genuinely spontaneous – and in danger of getting out of hand.

The newly refurbished Ministry of Defence headquarters on Whitehall was directly opposite Downing Street, so the demonstrators were able to vent their fury at the two most obvious targets from the same location. The police had them penned back behind hastily erected crash barriers across the road from Downing Street but more and more people were arriving all the time, streaming out of the Underground stations at Westminster and Embankment or arriving on the many buses that stopped in Whitehall itself. The police were frantically trying to arrange for the stations to be closed and were calling in reinforcements, but they were in danger of being swamped.

The situation was further exacerbated by the presence of numerous television crews who were arriving in a steady stream, some to cover the demonstration and some to cover the PM's imminent address to the nation. The only thing that worked in the police's favour the fact that a smaller demonstration outside the American Embassy had drawn away some protesters who might otherwise have gathered in Whitehall.

The more enterprising journalists had set up their cameras at the rear of Main Building in Victoria Embankment Gardens and were recording the views of some of those who had turned up. As the microphones were passed around it soon became clear that there was no shortage of people willing to offer an opinion.

'These people came in peace, and look what we've gone and done to them. What are they gonna do now, that's what I want to know. They've probably got nuclear weapons and God knows what else up there.'

'I'm ashamed of our government. I'm a patriot and I never thought I'd hear myself say this but I'm *ashamed*.'

'I'm a mother and I can't believe we've used those terrible, terrible weapons.'

'I tell you what, they can pick up TV signals, can't they? Well, if they're watching I hope they're watching this, and I hope they realize that it wasn't us what did this. OK?'

'I bet it was the Americans. I bet it was the fucking Americans!'

'Yeah, OK, mate. Keep it clean or we can't use it, yeah?'

Downing Street, Whitehall

'We can't do the broadcast outside, Prime Minister, there's too much noise from the demonstration. It'd totally undermine what we're trying to get across.' The PM's Press Secretary was stating the obvious.

'When am I on?'

'Whenever you're ready. All the main channels intend to run it live. Most of them are running specials already. *War of the Worlds* stuff, pretty much.'

'Great.'

'The demo could work for us if it turns violent.'

'I don't want to play that card,' the PM snapped back. 'Even if there are a few hotheads out there they're probably saying things that the ordinary person in the street would support. Which way are the media going to jump?'

'I'm not sure. Before this it was pretty mixed; some excitement, some scaremongering, lots of speculation – most of it pseudo-science or New Age crap. Now, I don't know. Their statement was a real piece of work; it's turned people against us. That's why there's so much riding on what you say. You can turn it around. Your broadcast will go out live, but it'll be used on *Newsnight* and Radio Four's *Today* programme tomorrow morning – we'll probably need to get the Defence Secretary on both those programmes, by the way; or the Deputy PM. The morning papers will go heavy on what you say, but the editors will go to conference immediately after your speech and decide how to play it, largely on the strength of your statement. But basically it's going to be a real black-or-white situation: the government or the aliens. Somebody has to be the bad guys.'

'Well, make sure it's not us. Brief them. Make sure you reinforce my key message. Make sure they know that lives may depend on how they play this. They *must* be made to see that the national interest's at stake.'

'I'll do my best. But I warn you, they're sending people out into the streets to take soundings and they're running telephone polls. If there's a public consensus, they'll go with *that* view, even if it means taking a pro-alien, anti-government line. They won't want to antagonize their readers.'

'Promise them access, exclusives, all the usual stuff. Pull out all the stops. It doesn't get any more important than this.'

'Yes, Prime Minister.'

RAF Coningsby, Lincolnshire

Despite instructions to avoid gathering in large groups, a number of Typhoon pilots had gathered around a television set in the Officers' Mess and were discussing the latest news.

'So did we do it, d'you think?'

'No way, it's gotta be a pile of crap.'

'I don't think so. If it was, there'd have been an instant denial. You know how it works.'

'Shit.'

'So how does this affect things?'

'It doesn't affect us at all; if we're tasked to fly, we fly.'

'Even if we did launch a bioweapon at them?'

There was an uncomfortable pause and, when the answer was

given, it was given in a tone that conveyed no enthusiasm whatsoever. 'Yes.'

Downing Street, Whitehall

The Prime Minister smiled and looked relaxed, even though he wasn't. The noise from the demonstration had obliged his staff to arrange for his address to the nation to be held in one of the Downing Street conference rooms. This was bad news for two reasons. Firstly, it would be readily apparent to all those media personnel present that the PM's people had been forced into this course of action: this would make the government seem as if it was very much on the defensive, putting across a view that ran counter to public opinion. Equally damaging was the effect that an indoor broadcast would have on how the address came across. Anything filmed indoors automatically looked like a party political broad-cast, whereas a much more dramatic and positive impression would have been created by the sight of the PM stepping confidently out of the front door of Number 10 and speaking to the media as flashbulbs went off around him. Such affairs looked less stage-managed, which was an important factor with a public increasingly cynical about spin-doctoring.

The PM was sporting a blue shirt, open at the neck. He wore no jacket and no tie, in an attempt to come across as less formal. The room was crowded, even though the media had been forced to adopt the pool system, sharing the footage that was taken by those who'd been given access. It had been announced beforehand that this was to be a straightforward address to the nation and not a press conference. Questions had been forbidden – though there was a likelihood that some enterprising journalist would shout something out afterwards, given the importance of the situation.

'Good evening. Many of you will by now have seen or heard about the latest message received from the alien vessel that is now just days away from us. The central theme of this message concerns an allegation that an attack, using germ warfare, was made against them during the course of talks held on their vessel. To clear up any confusion I should first say that scientists have verified the authenticity of the message itself: it does indeed come from the alien ship. As to the substance of the message, it is with great regret that I have to tell you that we have just learned that a biological attack was indeed launched against them. But let me make one thing abundantly clear: Britain had no prior knowledge of this attack and took absolutely no part in this action. Had we been consulted we would have done everything in our power to stop such a move. This government has consistently stated its opposition to the use of chemical and biological weapons, and indeed has been at the forefront of efforts to rid the world of these terrible devices.

'I want to explain to you exactly what has happened and give you the latest information that we have on the current situation. A short while ago, in addition to the open broadcast that we received from the alien vessel we detected an encrypted signal hidden within the original message. When this was decoded it turned out to be an invitation for face-to-face negotiations with the aliens. Even though we were disappointed that such a message had been sent covertly, there was no doubt in my mind that we had to accept the offer as it stood, not least because there was so much that we needed to discuss with these visitors. We, of course, had been making considerable efforts to contact the extra-terrestrials for some time, with a view to seeking an open dialogue. I was invited to these negotiations together with the leaders of the four other nations who are permanent members of the United Nations Security Council: America, Russia, China and France. It was unfortunate that other nations were not invited and it was also unfortunate that these negotiations were carried out in secret. If it had been up to me, that would not have happened. However, like the others who took part in the talks, I had little choice in the matter; our hosts were very much dictating the terms on which the negotiations were to take place and, while these terms were far from ideal, at least there was a chance for negotiation. We took that chance.

'We duly assembled at RAF Machrihanish in Scotland, whereupon an alien craft landed. It soon became apparent that this vessel was simply a means to take the five of us to the real location for the meeting: the alien's main ship itself. As you can imagine, we were somewhat nervous about this, but again – with so much at stake – I think we all felt that the risk was worth taking.

'There's not much I can tell you about the ship itself, simply because we saw so little of it. As for the aliens, they do seem to be indistinguishable from humans, though I understand that a small number of them are rather less so. But their claims of having genetically modified most of their number to look like us do seem to be true.

'The talks themselves were disappointing. Despite some cleverly scripted words and the promise of various technological gifts, it soon became apparent that the aliens were not really interested in negotiations. We were presented with a document that set out detailed plans for the dismantling of much of our system of government and its replacement with one of their own. While the aliens clearly had some innovative ideas and did seem to be offering us the chance of access to some of their scientific and medical knowledge, we were being asked to take all this on trust. There were no guarantees, no safeguards – in short, no way of verifying any of what they said. Nonetheless, it seemed to me that this might at least offer a start point for meaningful discussions. But this was not to be. The aliens made it clear that they were not the slightest bit interested in negotiation. We were presented with what amounted to an ultimatum: if we didn't agree their proposals, they would implement them by force. That hardly seemed consistent with their earlier statements about peace.

'I told you earlier that a biological attack had been launched. While I can confirm the basic fact that this happened, I can do little more at this stage. I only learned of this tactic a few hours ago and the facts are still unclear. Because they are unclear, and because we have yet to receive any firm data about what has occurred, I can say no more than this for now. What I *can* say is that I deplore this tactic; I repeat the categorical assurance that the UK government had no knowledge of this attack and played no part in it. Indeed, I shall be having urgent discussions with other world leaders with a view to ensuring that the vaccine for this disease is made available immediately and without precondition to the aliens.

'As horrible as this new development has been, it has not altered the basic situation in which we find ourselves. We are facing a powerful force whose previous actions have – whether intended or not – resulted in the deaths of a number of men and women serving in our armed forces. We have already said that we will do everything we can to seek a peaceful solution to this crisis. That remains our goal and, though the attack will undoubtedly make this more difficult, it continues to be our belief that any truly civilized society will recognize that, when threatened, humans sometimes lash out in fear. This should be met with understanding, not with aggressive revenge.

'We have a proud and lengthy tradition of democracy in this country, and that is a system which – in many varying forms – is found all around the world. I happen to believe this is something worth preserving; it is certainly not something that could or should be cast aside in hours, just because we receive promises or threats from beyond the stars. So our message to these new visitors is as follows: we welcome your arrival and believe it offers great opportunities for both our peoples. But we are equally passionate in our desire to preserve our democratic rights – including the right to self-government. We shall be steadfast in our defence of these civil liberties but we feel sure that, if you are indeed the peaceful civilization you claim to be, you will respect our rights and not seek to overthrow or destroy our society. The hand of friendship is still extended to you. I hope that you will take it. Thank you.'

RAF Feltwell, Norfolk
'Wow, that was some speech!'

'For sure!'

Staff at the Deep Space Tracking Facility had watched the PM's address to the nation with interest, knowing that they were very much in the front line. They'd been unaware of the recent turn of events and, though they'd all heard rumours, the aliens' statement and the PM's speech had come as a shock to them all. There had been deep unease over the suggestion that a biological weapon had been used and much speculation about who the guilty party had been and precisely how the weapon had been delivered.

There had been some changes at RAF Feltwell since the events of Operation Thunder Child. Though it seemed that the Americans had put their house in order, the British had insisted that more UK personnel should be deployed to facilities such as Feltwell and Menwith Hill: no longer would the US authorities be allowed to behave as if each US base on British soil was a little piece of America. The arrangements had worked well, engendering a new trust between Britain and America and going some way to repair the damage done by US involvement in the conspiracy to cover up details of the alien presence. There had been some residual bad feeling, of course, but government employees and service personnel well understood the need-to-know principle, recognizing that the cover-up had not been a corporate thing but was the doing of a cabal within various US agencies. Most Americans who knew the full extent of this deceit were appalled, and their vehement condemnation of it went a long way towards repairing the damaged special relationship between the US and the UK.

Feltwell itself had been central to the cover-up. The Deep Space Tracking Facility had had a legitimate role in tracking satellites, space debris and space probes. But in addition to this publicly declared role, The Enterprise had used the powerful space-tracking radar systems and the associated optical detection systems in an attempt to monitor UFO activity. But, while detection had proved possible to a certain extent, the data had never been passed to anybody else – even when the RAF found itself embroiled in hostilities with these UFOs. When the conspiracy had been exposed this changed and, free of Enterprise influence, Feltwell had passed raid warnings to the British – resulting in the base being targeted and hit by the very extra-terrestrials whom they had been secretly tracking for decades.

'Hey, look at this,' the duty watch officer suddenly called out. 'Are you getting this?' His screen was awash with what he took to be interference.

'Are we being jammed?' A colleague was getting a similar picture on an independent secondary system. That made equipment failure an unlikely explanation. All discussion of the PM's speech was forgotten, and staff struggled to make sense of the data.

'Run the filter program,' called out one of the supervisors. Such computer programs were designed to amplify real signals while eliminating returns like the ghost returns that often showed up on even the most sophisticated radar system. There was a pause while the software was inserted and the appropriate keys pressed.

'No, it's even worse. White-out.'

'But that doesn't make sense. Unless— oh, shit. Try to *de-enhance* the individual signals.'

'But that—' The operator cut off his objection as he realized his supervisor's line of reasoning. He keyed in the necessary instructions. It took longer to activate than the previous program because it wasn't normal procedure. The fact that the operator was shaking didn't help, either. Finally, the data was displayed.

'Holy shit.' There were gasps of astonishment from around the operations room as the operators looked at their screens. Now that the signals had been de-enhanced the interference had cleared up. There were *hundreds* of uncorrelated targets appearing over the North Sea, all heading for the British coast.

The watch supervisor lifted his secure telephone and placed a flash call to the Permanent Joint Headquarters. When he got through, he spoke quickly. 'We have a *major* raid in progress.'

Chapter Nine

DEGRADE AND DIMINISH

Over The North Sea

Isabelle Bentley had mixed feelings about the action that she knew was coming. The CO had called a briefing and she knew from the chat in the crewroom that there was some bad feeling about the situation. Everyone wanted to know more about the biological attack launched against the aliens and, although the PM's statement had made it clear that the UK was not involved, doubts remained.

As far as Bentley and her fellow pilots were concerned, biological weapons were an obscenity. Most of them had done at least one tour of duty in the Middle East, flying combat air patrols in the Iraqi no-fly zones as part of the wider effort to force the Iraqis to cease any attempt to resurrect their nuclear, biological and chemical weapons programmes. Indeed, sites suspected of being involved in such work were still being regularly bombed by British and American forces.

Given this, even a hint that UK forces might themselves be somehow caught up in an operation that had involved the use of such a weapon was distasteful in the extreme. 'Are we the bad guys now?' someone had casually remarked; it was a frightening prospect. The CO's briefing was to have been a forum in which such questions would doubtless have been aired. But the briefing never happened.

The harsh blare of klaxons announced what many had feared: vast numbers of alien craft had been detected over the North Sea. Their targets were unclear but the craft were on an inbound course, heading for the east coast. Bentley was sure that there were many differences between the human and alien cultures but she was equally sure that, whatever the aliens' thought processes and philosophy, a biological attack was bound to have stung them into action. There was a tragic inevitability about the whole situation and if the positions had been reversed she was sure she'd have felt the same way about it.

Readiness levels had been high. Some pilots had been on Quick Reaction Alert, fully suited-up and sitting in aircraft that were fuelled and ready for action. These aircraft had been launched immediately and had joined two that had been airborne already, flying combat air patrol over the North Sea against the very possibility that had now materialized. These aircraft in particular were badly exposed, so fighter controllers were trying to ensure that they could vector them back towards the coast, towards the aircraft that were even now struggling to catch up with these lead elements.

It was the fighter controllers who were having the most difficult job of it, because they were having to make sense of the radar data and trying to second-guess alien motives. It was possible that the attacking force was trying – and succeeding – to draw out the fighters in an attempt to thin out the numbers. But it was equally possible that they were luring them away from the mainland UK to take them out of the game. The alien craft were certainly capable of speeds and manoeuvres way in excess of anything the RAF could manage, so it was conceivable that they wouldn't bother engaging the Typhoon force at all. It was against this possibility that some of the aircraft from all three of the Typhoon bases had been held back and were flying combat air patrols over likely targets. What this meant was that the force was stretched thin.

Tactical experts at PJHQ had briefed all fighter controllers about some possible scenarios and were monitoring the wider tactical picture as it developed, ready to issue orders or offer advice if necessary. But they knew that only in the most extreme circumstances would they intervene and overrule a fighter controller. The fighter controllers were a highly competent group of men and women, and the PJHQ staff had to trust their people's abilities and let them get on with their jobs free of interference. Their task was a bit like some bizarre four-dimensional strategy game, only this time nobody knew if the opposition was even playing by the same rules.

Bentley and her colleagues in 29 Squadron had been split into what had originally been two groups of six Typhoons, while Coningsby's other Typhoons – those belonging to 5 Squadron – were being held back to protect the base itself. She was in the second wave of aircraft that now numbered just five because of a technical malfunction that had forced one pilot to return to base. This was unfortunate timing – it happened all the time but if the malfunction had occurred on the ground the pilot could have simply used one of the reserve aircraft. To have such a malfunction now was both dangerous and bad for the tactical situation.

Radio traffic was being kept to a minimum and this gave Bentley time to think – which, given the circumstances, was not necessarily a good thing. She was upset about the biological attack but tried to put it from her mind, reasoning that the UK had not even known about this development until it had been too late. She told herself that she knew too little of the overall picture to come to any firm view – it was not for her to feel pity or shame until she knew more. What Bentley did know was that she had lost friends and colleagues in previous engagements with the alien craft and she tried to focus on this, knowing that if she could channel her aggression she would perform better in the combat that almost certainly lay ahead. She replayed the details of these previous encounters, then comforted herself with the thought that they were all better equipped to deal with the threat this time around.

Each Typhoon was now equipped with three primary weapons systems. There were six BAe Meteor Beyond Visual Range Air-to-Air Missiles. These hadn't fared well during Operation Thunder Child, but DERA, in conjunction with BAe, had made some modifications that it was hoped might prove successful against the countermeasures that the alien vessels had deployed to defeat these missiles the first time around.

The second weapon system was the one that everybody was hoping would give the RAF a fighting chance: the Skystriker was a directed-energy weapon back-engineered from the alien craft downed in previous engagements. DERA had done a wonderful job with this new system that had proved surprisingly easy to produce and install. The RAF hadn't had as much training as they'd have liked, but the basic principle of the weapon was that it fired superheated pulses of plasma. DERA had configured the weapon to fire in two modes – narrow or wide.

The third weapon was the single 27mm cannon mounted in the Typhoon's nose, but this was only any use if the opposition closed to a short enough distance and became embroiled in a dogfight. The Typhoons carried a sophisticated array of countermeasures, including chaff, flares and jamming equipment – this was designed to defeat missiles and was not expected to be of any use in dealing with the directed-energy weapons that the aliens used. But the RAF pilots were a cautious bunch and since these items added little extra weight to the overall payload they were installed as usual.

Nobody had had much time to think about the aliens' intentions and, despite the PM's speech, the reality was that in such situations the military had to have authority to make instant decisions, simply because there was often no time to seek political authority for a particular course of action. Notwithstanding the peaceful sentiments being expressed by the PM, the aliens' message had spoken of degrading and diminishing the human capability to wage war. CDS and CAS had argued that this suggested an imminent attack on the military infrastructure and had successfully lobbied for the upgrading of Rules of Engagement, allowing the armed forces to open fire first if they believed an attack was imminent. This was why the Typhoon force was preparing to launch a volley of missiles before they could even see the alien craft. In the event, RAF commanders had managed to speak to the Defence Secretary, who had in turn spoken to the PM. Both had agreed with the military assessment that this mass and unannounced incursion could only be an attack and had accepted that the newly agreed ROE should be followed and that a pre-emptive missile launch was appropriate. Communications staff at RAF Oakhanger were even now sending a message to the alien mothership, asking them to turn back their attack and stating that, with regret, this was being viewed as a hostile act and would be treated as such. But as yet there had been no reply, and it seemed that the time for talking was over.

Bentley received instructions for a course change over her radio. Although there was no explanation she could guess the reason: there was a group of six Typhoons ahead of her group, who would be unable to fire their BVRAAMs if these aircraft were directly in front of them. The idea was to attack from different directions so that, as far as possible, the nightmare scenario of a 'blue on blue' – a fancy name for accidentally killing your own people – was eliminated.

As well as taking instructions from a nameless fighter controller, Bentley was able to make her own assessment of the overall tactical picture by looking at the data from her aircraft's airborne radar system. She thought it ironic that a few months ago the sort of signals she was now looking for would automatically have been dismissed as ghost returns. The 'If it doesn't behave like a conventional aircraft then there's nothing there' philosophy had been a triumph of narrow-mindedness over data. The pilots now knew that UFOs had been operating with impunity in British airspace for decades.

Bentley – like most of the RAF – blamed the MOD, who had parroted the 'no defence significance' mantra for years when asked about UFOs. While it was true that The Enterprise had played a part in suppressing the truth, old-fashioned ignorance and prejudice had played their parts too, as grey-suited bureaucrats had dismissed the data for no better reason than that it didn't fit their personal world-view or religious beliefs. Some MPs were mischievously pressing for treason charges to be brought against anyone who had wilfully ignored what, with hindsight, had been an obvious threat to the country.

While Bentley thought this went too far, she was certainly angry about the whole situation. Some anonymous 29 Squadron wag with more than a little artistic skill had placed a poster on the crewroom wall, depicting one of the alien craft firing streams of superheated plasma at a Typhoon. The caption at the bottom read 'UFOs – No Defence Significance?' Rumour had it that a copy had been sent anonymously to Sec(AS) with an additional hand-written message along the lines of: 'Thanks for the early warning on this. With love from your friends in the front line'. Though the sentiment was genuinely felt, such tales were, more likely than not, apocryphal.

Bentley received word that the attacking force had split into a number of smaller groups, and that one such was heading their way. The two elements of 29 Squadron were to attack this group simultaneously, as soon as they were in theoretical range of the BVRAAMs. Bentley and her colleagues learned that they were facing a force estimated at between ninety and one hundred craft. A smaller group was clearly not the same as a small group.

Bentley prepared to fire her missiles, making sure that they were all armed while releasing the protective cap that guarded against the possibility of an accidental discharge and shielded the button that would actually launch the missiles. As was her habit, she flexed her hand, clenching and unclenching her fist two or three times. It was a personal drill, more to do with mental preparation than with any physical need to circulate blood to her fingertips. Most pilots had little rituals or routines that weren't in the training manual and that might have struck outsiders as odd.

'Prepare to release missiles.' Bentley heard the voice of

Squadron Leader Mark Tomlinson in her earpiece. She flexed her gloved hand again, her finger hovering over the red firing button. *'Fire.'*

All six of her missiles worked perfectly, detaching from the aircraft and accelerating away into the distance at a speed of around Mach Five. One of the aircraft in her group reported a malfunction and only managed to fire five of its missiles: the other petulantly refused to detach. But such things happened and as with the aircraft forced to return to base, a pilot had to accept that it was a rare event when they were lucky enough to field all of their hardware at once. The technology was now so complex that there were a myriad possible malfunctions. The ground crews did a fantastic job to keep everything running but, in a world where one loose wire could ground a multimillion Pound jet, there were always going to be a number of non-runners.

'Weapons free,' Bentley called out, stating what was pretty obvious to everyone. Still, Tomlinson would need to keep track not just of his own actions but of the overall tactical picture, built up by seeing what everybody else was doing. *Rank has its privileges*, Bentley thought to herself.

A swarm of Meteor BVRAAMs was disappearing into the distance. Though these were known as 'fire-and-forget' missiles, this was a misnomer. What it really meant was that once fired, no further action was required from the pilot while the radar-guided missile sought to home in on its target. But there was clearly no way that a pilot was ever going to *forget* having fired a missile and, however much they were trained to put it from their minds, the temptation was to wonder whether or not it hit its target.

So it was that the Typhoon pilots studied the data from their airborne radars in an attempt to make sense of what was happening. The fact that there were so many hostile targets made this a tricky task. While fighter controllers had sophisticated computer programs that could make sense of the confused radar data, the Typhoons' airborne systems were showing the inbound craft as one big target. Bentley correctly assumed that this was because the alien craft were grouped so close together. She counted this as a piece of good luck: if the enemy were bunched up it made it more likely that the missiles would find their way to the kill zone. Furthermore, if the Typhoons started to get some hits in, fragments from an exploding alien craft might well take out some of the surrounding ones.

That Bentley had detected the alien craft at all was a good sign so far as the Meteors were concerned, as the missiles were radar-guided. Bentley had achieved what she thought was a brief lock-on before firing but, even if the lock was broken, the missiles' modifications meant that they stood a good chance of reacquiring a target – especially with the opposition bunching together as they were. They were clearly lousy tacticians but that suited Bentley just fine.

As their designation suggested, the BVRAAMs were designed to engage the enemy at the maximum possible distance. So it was inevitable that the first phase of this encounter would be difficult to evaluate and would have to be assessed from the data available through the airborne radar system.

Bentley was studying her screen intently, not just for any data she might be able to glean about the success of the missiles she'd fired, but also for any clue that the alien craft were close enough to pose a direct threat to the Typhoon force. The fighter controllers would relay such information themselves when they'd studied data from the ground-radar systems, which gave far better coverage than Bentley's small airborne system. But pilots detested the idea that they were dependent upon others, and were smart enough to want to check the data themselves. Bentley wasn't sure what was happening with the RAF's Sentry airborne early-warning fleet; she was fairly certain that one was in the air at all times but, given the way that one of these aircraft had been targeted during Operation Thunder Child, she was guessing that they were being kept out of harm's way. She didn't mind that: it wasn't as if they were short on radar data with so many craft coming their way.

Bentley reminded herself to keep an eye on what was going on outside her aircraft. This might have sounded strange to an outsider but, with aircraft as sophisticated as the Typhoon there was a danger that pilots would veer too far towards a state of being what the RAF called 'cockpit aware'. This was even more of a danger with a one-person aircraft such as a Typhoon, where the entire workload fell on the pilot instead of being split between a pilot and a navigator. While it was essential to monitor instruments continuously it was also important to be 'outside aware', especially for a pilot flying with other aircraft and needing to check their separation distances. This was doubly true if a pilot was expecting trouble: radar wasn't infallible and good pilots knew that using their eyes was equally important.

Bentley was trying to strike a balance between checking her instruments and monitoring her outside environment but found herself increasingly mesmerized by the game that was playing itself out on her radar screen. There were sufficient numbers of BVRAAMs in the air for them to register as a discrete target on her radar and she watched with fascination as they sped towards their target. She was concerned that the missiles were so bunched up because she recalled what had happened during Operation Thunder Child. Then the alien craft had opened fire on the missiles that had been so close together and some of them, when they'd exploded, had taken out other missiles that had not yet been hit. She'd raised this concern at a tactical briefing a few days ago, and suggested that the missiles should be fired off in two or three separate salvos. There had been much debate about this, resulting in individual commanders being given discretion and authorized to make their own decisions depending on the tactical situation. In the event, Mark Tomlinson had decided that because the alien craft were themselves so tightly bunched they presented too good an opportunity to pass up. In the circumstances, Bentley was forced to agree.

The distance between the BVRAAMs and the alien craft was getting progressively shorter. Bentley was amazed that the craft hadn't taken any evasive manoeuvres; they were certainly capable of sudden acceleration and not to try this tactic or break formation and disperse seemed crazy, as if they were oblivious to the missiles.

It was then that Bentley recalled the modifications that had been made. She wondered whether the alien craft had been confidently relying on countermeasures, only to find – with luck, too late – that they were no longer effective. She smiled at the thought, which gave her new confidence.

Bentley's radar screen indicated that the missiles had now reached the alien craft. But, although logic suggested they were scoring some hits, her airborne radar was simply not powerful enough to produce data sufficiently clear to make a meaningful assessment. She did some rapid mental arithmetic: 29 Squadron had had two aircraft airborne on CAP and had launched twelve more, though one had promptly gone u/s and returned to base. So that meant there were thirteen aircraft that had each fired six missiles, though one missile hadn't fired. She duly came up with the figure of seventy-seven missiles. Since the fighter controllers had suggested they were facing a group of between ninety and one hundred craft, there would clearly be enemies left even if every missile hit and destroyed a target. But such a scenario was unlikely in the extreme; even the most optimistic projections suggested that a one-in-four kill rate was about the best they'd be likely to manage. About the only piece of good news was that the aliens had clearly been so busy trying to get their countermeasures to work that they'd forgotten to target the missiles with their directed-energy weapons.

'Golf Charlie One to Alpha Foxtrot One and Alpha Foxtrot Two, we assess you have between ten and fifteen hits. Well done and good hunting.'

Bentley wasn't sure whether this was good news or not. Her rough calculations had suggested that twenty kills was a possibility even if the directed-energy weapon had been used – something that hadn't apparently happened. It was still pretty impressive, but left anywhere between seventy-five and ninety alien craft heading their way, with all the Typhoons' missiles fired. If they'd known the craft were going to bunch up the way they had, they might have risked committing 5 Squadron as well: double the number of hits they'd recorded really would have been impressive. But she reminded herself that this was hardly fair to everyone else, and would have left the base itself – or whatever other targets the aliens might attack – badly exposed.

Given that the Typhoons and the alien craft were flying towards each other, the closing speed was phenomenal: Bentley and her fellow pilots knew that they'd be in visual range in a matter of minutes.

'Ready the Skystrikers.' Tomlinson's voice was calm, deliberately so: it was designed to put the others at ease. Bentley had been checking the status of her Typhoon's weapon already and was sure that the others had been doing the same. But Tomlinson's command had not been superfluous: in a combat scenario, hearing one's commander in this way was invaluable.

'Skystriker enabled,' Bentley duly acknowledged.

'I have a red light – wait, I— oh. OK. Enabled.' Clearly somebody wasn't finding arming their Skystriker quite so straightforward, although the problem seemed to have been resolved. Sometimes it was irritating to listen to everyone's cockpit chat but most times it was a comforting reminder that you weren't alone and that there were other people looking out for you. The second point was the vital one, as any one of your colleagues might spot something vital that you'd missed.

'Set Skystriker to wide-burst mode and fire as soon as you see the opposition.' Tomlinson's calm, professional voice came through clearly on Bentley's headset and she duly checked that her weapon was set in the correct mode. Like the others, she'd been initially sceptical about incorporating alien technology into the Typhoons. But she had changed her mind when she'd been briefed on how simple the technology actually was and when she'd seen it in action and had a chance to test it herself. She recalled her irritation at having missed the chance to become the first RAF pilot to successfully destroy a target drone with Skystriker during training, especially when Robbie Skinner – a friend with whom she had a long-running but good-natured rivalry – had destroyed it with the next shot. Robbie was also in 29 Squadron but was in the other group of Typhoons. Bentley wondered whether she might get her own back by becoming the first pilot to score a hard kill with the Skystriker but then thought that the anticipated engagement would probably be too messy to determine who had hit what and when. It was at this point that she thought of something that she'd managed to put from her mind for most of the time since she'd taken off: namely that she might be dead in little more than a minute.

All fast-jet pilots thought about death and most of them had lost friends, either in peacetime training accidents or in actual operations. Bentley reminded herself that death could come suddenly to *anyone*, whether through a car crash or heart attack. Indeed, she'd often thought how terrible it would be to live to be very old, getting more and more decrepit, or to die of a disease like leukaemia that slowly robbed someone of their life-force.

But, while she thought there was something to be said for a quick death, Bentley wasn't ready to go just yet. She wasn't sure if she was scared of death as such but she didn't want to die before she'd really had the chance to live. She wasn't conventionally religious, although she did believe in the immortality of the soul and in reincarnation, despite being dismissive of much of the New Age nonsense that had evolved around the concepts in recent years. What she was really afraid of was burning to death in her aircraft, or drowning if it came down at sea without her being able to escape from the cockpit and deploy her inflatable life raft. If she had to die up here, she hoped it would be a quick and painless death – a direct hit that would blow her and her aircraft apart in an instant.

Running through these thoughts filled Bentley with new purpose. She told herself that she *wasn't* going to die; she was going to fight and she was going to live. After all, she reminded herself, she'd been here before and she knew that she possessed the two qualities that pilots most needed: she was skilful and she was lucky.

'Target in sight; one o'clock high.' She didn't recognize the voice immediately, although she thought it sounded like Tom Crookes, a popular member of 29 Squadron known to everyone as TC.

'OK, that's confirmed. Well spotted.' Tomlinson knew the value of a carefully doled-out bit of praise. 'Watch out for our own people,' he added, reminding everybody that there were six other Typhoons out there, which were, with luck, about to launch their own attack with Skystrikers.

Even as he spoke Bentley saw flashes on the horizon, indicating that the second group of Typhoons was already engaging the alien craft. Her first thought was that she was seeing the plasma bolts themselves but she soon realized this was impossible, given the distance. Then she realized that she must be seeing explosions. She felt an icy chill at the possibility that it might be Typhoons exploding, but knew enough about the location and approach pattern of the other jets to work out that this wasn't the case. This was more good news, although she realized that she wouldn't even be in the running when the debate started over who'd first brought down an alien craft with a Skystriker.

Moments later, Bentley was close enough to make out individual craft. Tomlinson gave a few terse orders but, while there might have been an initial attack plan, such a concept soon broke down since modern combat was reactive, depending on a constantly evolving tactical picture. Targets of opportunity might arise and nobody wanted to pass up such possibilities just to adhere to a plan. This was a fancy way of saying what every combat pilot knew: namely, once pilots engaged any enemy at close quarters, it very quickly became a scrappy dogfight.

The Typhoons were spaced out nicely now and Bentley checked that nobody was so close that they might inadvertently stray in front of her aircraft. Once she was satisfied on this point she aligned her sight for the centre of the fast-approaching mass of alien craft, flipped off the protective cap and thumbed the button that activated her Skystriker.

DERA had adapted the alien technology and improved on it. Instead of firing a plasma pulse every few seconds, pulses were being spat out at a phenomenal rate. What was more, though the new weapon could be reasonably accurate against a single target in narrow mode, the wide mode they'd selected was better suited for the non-specific targeting of a large number of craft: the effect was rather like that of a machine gun, where the aim is to ensure that the bullets spread over a wide area. Bentley thought the effect was not unlike a firework display and watched with fascination as what seemed like a swarm of iridescent purple bees rushed out to meet the approaching alien craft, some of which were already falling to the Skystriker attack being launched by the other Typhoons.

Even as Bentley saw more craft explode in front of her she realized that the favour was being returned: a mass of purple bolts was heading straight for her position. The closing speed was phenomenal, and it was all but impossible to tell whether any individual shot was heading directly for her. Of all the ways to go, being hit because you'd actually steered *into* the path of one of these bolts would be particularly galling, she thought to herself. But since most of the pulses seemed to be heading to the port side of her position, she decided to bank her aircraft and head into the clear airspace to her starboard side. This was where she had to be particularly mindful of the position of her fellow pilots and she was careful to check that there was nobody in her path before she executed the manoeuvre.

Bentley determined to bring her aircraft around in a loop and re-engage from the side: it took a moment to orient herself and when she did she realized that she was some way from the action. She accelerated rapidly to try and put herself back in the game, all the time trying to take in as much of the battle as she could in an attempt to get an overview. This was done not out of curiosity but from a very real need to know where best to put her aircraft: whilst all the time alert to the risk of a collision, she had to see if there were some particularly vulnerable targets or, conversely, whether there was a fellow pilot who needed her assistance. Ideally, as well, she had to do her best to ensure that she wasn't duplicating effort by engaging a target that was already being attacked. Aerial combat could certainly be a complicated business, especially when these assessments and decisions had to be made in seconds: time was one thing a pilot didn't have much of in a high-tech, high-Mach dogfight.

Partly by skill, partly through luck, Bentley found herself in a combat pilot's ideal position: directly behind the opposition, able to fire on them without being in danger of being hit herself. Unless – she cautioned herself – some of the alien craft had split off from the main group and were even now bearing down on her position. But she'd checked carefully and, although there were always blind spots, she was convinced she was in the clear. This suited her just fine: the opposition were doing just about everything wrong – they'd relied on their countermeasures defeating the BVRAAMs and not twigged until too late that the missiles were still locked on. Then, to compound the error, they'd stayed bunched up and presented an unmissable target for the Skystrikers. Finally, and most bizarrely of all, they weren't exploiting their numerical superiority by breaking formation and engaging the Typhoons one by one.

Bentley depressed the firing button for her Skystriker system and watched as the bursts of plasma streaked ahead of her Typhoon towards the alien craft. She had the satisfaction of seeing two craft succumb to hits; neither of them exploded but both went into steep dives and were clearly out of the game. But even as she fired again, she realized that her targets were accelerating away and would soon be out of range completely. Fast though the Typhoons were, they were clearly no match for the alien craft whose propulsion system was still way beyond DERA's capacity to back-engineer.

The engagement was over before Bentley had time to assess what had occurred. She could see a couple of other Typhoons but the squadron had clearly got pretty spread out, having dispersed when fired on. The radio chat started and it was only then that Bentley learned that two Typhoons – both from her group – had been destroyed. Nobody had seen parachutes and nobody had picked up a distress call. It appeared that both aircraft had fallen to direct hits from the directed-energy weapon and had exploded in mid-air before the pilots could eject. One of the dead was Tom Crookes and the other was David Talbot.

The realization that two members of 29 Squadron had almost certainly been killed hit Bentley hard. The Typhoons had thinned out the opposition considerably, with a total of what would later be estimated as between thirty and forty hard kills. To inflict such losses on the enemy with the loss of just two of your own aircraft was, on paper, a success beyond hope or expectation. But when the people lost were friends with whom you'd trained and socialized for months, if not years, balance sheets of kills and losses suddenly counted for nothing. This was no time for tears, a luxury that no airborne pilot could afford, given the importance of good vision. But the tears would come in time, on the ground, as they would come for all the pilots who had lost friends.

Tomlinson's voice reminded her that she still had a job to do: fighter controllers were hoping that the Typhoons might get back to the assessed targets before the action was over, or that they might be able to ambush the alien craft on the return leg of their journey. Tomlinson rapidly ordered the nine surviving aircraft of 29 Squadron to head for home. Their own base was the aliens' likely target and this news certainly focused the pilots' minds: surviving with most of their aircraft intact would be little use if there was no base from which to operate them.

The Typhoons headed purposefully back towards where the action was now shifting and as they did so a thought occurred to Bentley: did the aliens have so many craft that they could afford to take losses of this magnitude? Her initial thought had been that the RAF's tactics had taken them by surprise, though she doubted they'd be caught that way twice. But was it possible that they simply didn't care? Did the intelligence directing the alien scout craft have enough of them to spend them so casually? It was a chilling thought.

RAF Coningsby, Lincolnshire

'Our radar data shows multiple inbound targets; the assessment is that they're heading our way.' The news was delivered to the small group of SAS troopers by an out-of-breath RAF Regiment corporal who'd been tasked with keeping the special forces informed.

'No shit,' somebody called out from the back of the group, to the irritation of Sergeant Jack West. West questioned the corporal on the estimated time of arrival, size of the force and direction of approach. When he'd gone West outlined a plan and threw it open to his squad to debate. Though he'd have the final say, he was smart enough to call on the expertise of his colleagues and not so insecure that he couldn't take argument or criticism if it came. But his instincts were sound and, though a couple of modifications were suggested and adopted, his plan was implemented pretty much as he'd outlined initially.

West's basic idea was to spread his team around the perimeter of the base and engage the aliens as they came in for an attack run. Previous experience during Operation Thunder Child suggested that the alien craft were most effective from close range, so they'd have to fly in directly over the base itself. Ideally, West and his team would get some hits in before the craft reached their targets. But, given the numbers involved, it was inevitable that most would get through; the SAS force hoped to thin out the numbers some more as the intruders left.

On past form West was reasonably sure that the attacking craft wouldn't bother engaging a single person but would concentrate instead on the base's fixed assets: the control tower, the buildings, the hardened air shelters and perhaps – if they were tactically smart – the runway itself. So his plan was to split his squad up and place all eight soldiers at points on or even beyond the perimeter fence, spread out somewhat but with most of them positioned at the side from which the craft were approaching. West felt this would maximize their chances of targeting the craft while minimizing the possibility that they'd take casualties if the key facilities were hit. Staying away from the targets was always a smart move, he reminded himself. *But not so far away that you can't protect them.*

West and his team weren't the only ones tasked with defending the base. That was the primary responsibility of the RAF Regiment. There was some good-natured rivalry between them and the SAS, but it would have been a very foolish Regiment soldier who didn't welcome the presence of the SAS with their Stinger and Javelin missiles. The Regiment's main weapon was the Rapier Field Standard C missile system, which had its own built-in radar system to acquire and target any intruder. These had been carefully positioned around the base, using the same concept that West had used to position his team. Underneath the rivalry and the occasional insults they were all professionals at heart.

As ever, the biggest single problem was that of avoiding a blue-on-blue incident. West had argued that the air-defence aircraft should be kept out of the engagement altogether. That way there'd be no danger of taking out one of the RAF's aircraft instead of one of the alien craft: if the RAF were out of the way, everything in the sky could legitimately be assumed to be hostile and engaged without second thought. But while that had been a successfully used tactic during Operation Thunder Child, the RAF were understandably keen to get their own air-defence aircraft into the action, especially now that they were armed with the new Skystriker weapon system. Judging from reports even now being received from PJHQ, it seemed that the Skystriker was performing well enough to justify the confidence placed in it by senior service personnel.

West still wasn't convinced and although there were some technical and highly classified ways to avoid missiles taking out friendly aircraft – through interrogating the IFF signal emitted from the RAF jets – it wasn't a foolproof situation, especially if the skies were crowded with a mêlée of friends and foes. Mindful of the risks, West briefed his people carefully and told them to be sure of their targets before firing.

Klaxons sounded to announce the imminent arrival of the hostile forces – a routine that hadn't changed since the Second World War. West knew they were supposed to be helpful but he wished they wouldn't keep the things on for the duration; he found the noise grating and it interrupted his concentration.

There was a loud roar from somewhere behind West and his first thought was that the base had been hit. Seconds later he realized that he'd been mistaken and that what he'd heard was the sound of a Rapier missile being fired from a nearby launcher. Wave after wave of the missiles streaked into the sky towards targets that

West could not yet see. The missiles were coming from various locations, giving West an idea of the way in which they'd been spread carefully around the base. The noise continued relentlessly for several minutes as more and more missiles came off the launchers.

Suddenly West saw a mass of incandescent purple specks directly overhead, and correctly surmised that the alien craft were on their final approach and had launched a salvo of their own weapons. The superheated plasma was totally unlike conventional weapons but still had a devastating effect on anything it hit, causing explosions of sorts – though not the spectacular fireballs that would result from missiles with explosive warheads. But after several more salvos of the aliens' weapons the base *was* rocked by a series of massive blasts. West guessed correctly that some flammable stores must have been hit – although such things were well protected as a matter of course, there was no escaping the fact that a working military base needed to have a ready supply of fuel and was also criss-crossed by gas pipes. The wail of sirens indicated that fire trucks were on their way to deal with the situation. West didn't envy the crews, who in order to deal with the very real danger posed by fire had to drive into harm's way and place themselves at the very facilities that were presumably the main target of the aliens.

West already had his Stinger missile up and ready and was scanning for targets. As yet he could see none, despite having positioned himself on a relatively high piece of ground in the hope that it would afford him a better view of the action and give him an improved chance of spotting and engaging any enemy craft that came close enough. There was no guarantee that they would, of course, but intelligence suggested that the aliens had to attack from relatively close range. West was slightly surprised that he hadn't seen the craft that had launched the attack but guessed that it had come in very low from the other side of the base. The unmistakable sound of a Stinger launch bore out his theory as he realized that one of his team on the far side of the base had found something to shoot at.

As ever in such situations West had to fight down his curiosity and concentrate on his own part of the battle. It was a natural human reaction to be curious about how everybody else was doing: commanders in particular had to contend with the additional factor that they were in charge of the other people and responsible for them. But nobody would thank West if an intruding craft came over his position without him getting a shot off simply because he was distracted by other parts of the battle. Good commanders have to learn to trust their people to do their jobs, and not interfere.

It wasn't as if West didn't have a difficult job. There was a popular misconception about the size of RAF bases, and few people realized just how vast they were – precisely so that they could soak up a large number of hits and still remain operational. A main runway might be around 7,000 feet long, but there would be another secondary runway running parallel to this and numerous other taxiways. The support facilities were also spread over a wide area, to make it difficult to inflict major damage on the operational capability of the base itself.

West had been moving his Stinger unit backwards and forwards in expansive sweeps in an attempt to pick up a signal. He'd been doing this for several minutes while the battle went on around him and had been getting increasingly frustrated. Every few moments he paused and had a really thorough scan of the horizon, straining his eyes to see if he could make out a target. There was a sudden massive roaring sound from above as something passed very low over his head. Momentarily deafened, West looked up to see that the sound had come from a Typhoon, its unmistakable delta shape visible in the distance as it banked and started to turn again towards the base. West wasn't sure if it was hunter or hunted but before he could decide he spotted what looked very much like an approaching alien craft. It was Stinger time.

The Stinger was a remarkable missile by anyone's standards. Although the British Army's favoured surface-to-air missile was the Javelin, the SAS always preferred the American Stinger missiles, mainly because – unlike Javelin – they required no further action on the part of the operator once there were fired. They were classic 'fire-and-forget' missiles, which suited the SAS just fine because their *modus operandi* seldom involved their hanging around to see how their attacks had fared. Stinger was an American invention but it had been the Soviet invasion of Afghanistan that had made the weapon a household name around the world. Armed with Stingers supplied by the CIA and the SAS, the Afghan resistance – the mujahedin – had inflicted terrible losses upon the Soviets, who had ultimately been forced to withdraw from Afghanistan, thanks in no small part to the crippling losses of transport aircraft that had been supposed to keep the occupying forces supplied with men and equipment.

The heart of a Stinger was the reusable gripstock, to which was attached a disposable unit containing the missile in a launcher tube. The missile package was a pre-sealed, one-shot weapon that came with its own battery. The only difficulty was that the battery's life was very limited so the user had to be sure they had a target before switching on. Suddenly, West was sure. He spotted one of the enemy craft coming directly for his position, firing purple bolts of plasma as it came. The fact that West was in its direct line of fire was both a blessing and a curse; it made targeting easy but the downside was that the plasma bolts seemed to be passing directly over his head, with little clearance. Explosions well behind him suggested that he wasn't the target, but it was off-putting in the extreme when these pulses of destruction were so close.

West clicked the trigger, activating the missile. He now had about a minute and a half of battery life so he had to make it count. He had no trouble centring the optical sight on the approaching craft and the infra-red seeker on the missile did its job. The audio signal switched from a low hum to a high-pitched squeal, letting West know that it had locked on to a heat signature from the craft's hull. He depressed the trigger once more, launching the missile. The Stinger was a recoilless weapon so, as ever, he was mindful of the danger from the ignition of the solid fuel and was careful to ensure that the launch angle was not so steep that the backblast bounced up off the ground and covered him in flames. Weapons like this were dangerous in the hands of anyone who wasn't fully trained in their use. Even as West fired he heard a roar from somewhere off to his right and realized that one of his colleagues had fired another Stinger at the same target. He discarded the used launcher tube and quickly fitted another, ready for a second shot if one was necessary – or possible.

The heat signature from the alien craft was not large, and certainly not as obvious a target as that presented by the exhaust plume of a jet fighter. But this factor was outweighed by the short distance at which the alien craft were being engaged. Strategists had assessed that at this range the aliens were likely to have little or no chance to use any countermeasures – previous intelligence suggested they could charge their hulls and change their temperatures to confuse any infra-red targeting system – to defeat the missiles. Indeed, at this short range it was unlikely that they'd have time to detect a missile lock-on, let alone react to it.

Although the Stinger was a fire-and-forget missile system, West wasn't likely ever to forget that he'd just launched a heat-seeking missile at an alien spacecraft. He hadn't forgotten, of course: it was just that he was too professional to stop and stare at the result of his first shot if there was a chance of a second. Once he'd fitted another launcher tube to the gripstock he looked skywards once more. But, even as he looked, he realized there was no time for a second shot: the craft had clearly been hit, and even as he thought about switching the weapon on to try and reacquire the target, his quarry passed almost directly over his head, trailing smoke. There was a thunderous explosion as it hit the ground somewhere behind him.

West was unsure what to think about that. At least the downed craft hadn't crashed on to his own position – a not-impossible outcome when engaging a target already in the shallow dive of its attack run – but it had crashed somewhere on the base. This could easily have done more damage than might have been done had it carried out its attack unmolested. For all West knew it could have crashed on to one of the main fuel dumps, or killed a bunch of the

RAF Regiment soldiers. But he couldn't afford to think like that: all he knew was that there was one less enemy to contend with. That one, at least, wouldn't be back.

There was another roar from above and West saw two Typhoons flying overhead, firing their own plasma weapons at a target he couldn't see. He also heard the unmistakable sound of an M16 assault rifle. This again clearly showed that his own people were in action – the SAS preferred M16s to the British Army's standard rifle, the SA-80. The only mystery was why this weapon was being used at all. West assumed – correctly as it turned out – that somebody was having technical problems with their Stingers. Again, for all the professionalism of the soldiers, they were increasingly at the mercy of technology and, like it or not, equipment malfunctions were a part of their working life.

The engagement was over in a matter of minutes. West still had a Stinger assembled and to hand, in case it was needed, but when nothing happened for another couple of minutes he risked a brief radio check. All of his team had survived and although there wasn't time for a proper debriefing – that would come later – he did pick up a few pieces of information.

The missile West had heard his colleague launch was the only other Stinger that had been fired. This had resulted in a hit but, as he'd feared, the stricken craft had done considerable damage when it had crashed, taking out a fuel-storage tank in an explosion that had also damaged and set fire to some of the administration block. Another soldier had achieved lock-on but his missile had refused to launch. He'd opened fire with his rifle but couldn't say whether his rounds had hit the craft. The RAF Regiment were maintaining that their Rapiers had shot down three craft on their approach but West knew all about how kill claims became exaggerated in the heat of combat and would believe the claim when he saw the wreckage. Somebody had seen a Typhoon go down but there were reports that the Typhoons had themselves accounted for a couple of the enemy. The base itself had absorbed a lot of hits, with considerable damage to the infrastructure. Nobody had details of casualties but the fact that so much of the base was still burning suggested that they'd be lucky to have emerged from the battle with no dead or injured.

West instructed his people to wait for a follow-up attack but it never came and after another fifteen minutes the all-clear was sounded. He told his troops to rendezvous at a pre-arranged point for debriefing. Their data would then be forwarded up the chain of command along with everybody else's so that an accurate assessment could be made of the overall battle.

As West set off to meet his team he was already mulling the details of the battle over in his mind. He'd been surprised that he'd seen so little of the action and even more surprised that more of his colleagues hadn't managed to acquire any targets of their own. His first thought was that he'd positioned his people too far out. It was only later that he found out that only two alien craft had got past the Rapiers and the Typhoons to manoeuvre into position and launch an attack on the base itself. West was elated and thought this meant that 29 Squadron must have all but wiped out the incoming craft before they reached the Coningsby. Then he found out that this wasn't the case; the craft that had got past 29 Squadron had split into two groups. West was stunned to find out that his battle had been nothing more than a minor skirmish in the overall scheme of things: the main focus of the alien attack had been elsewhere.

Chapter Ten

FIRE IN THE SKY

Farnham, Surrey

As Richard Cody was the country's leading expert on UFOs, his life had been dominated in recent days by media appearances on various television and radio shows. He was well known to the programmes' researchers and was at the top of all their lists when they needed people who could talk with authority on the subject. The fact that he was retired meant there was no problem with his availability and living reasonably close to London was another factor that made him a popular choice for media outlets that wanted to get a UFO expert into their studios. Cody was an experienced interviewee who knew his subject inside out, was articulate and knew that producers wanted soundbites and not waffle.

The only problem of late had been one of overexposure: since Cody had appeared on so many of the major shows there was a danger that programmes that now sought to use him would look a little second-hand. But within ufology there were few people as authoritative as him and producers were worried that they'd book somebody who'd turn out to be a crank: there were plenty of *them* around and the sudden and explosive turn of events was certainly bringing more than a few out of the woodwork. Even so, the media appearances were easing off a little and Cody found himself doing work that was more akin to that of a consultant: he'd be sounded out about other ufologists who might be relied upon to make a helpful contribution to a programme. He'd suggested Jenny Thornton, who as well as being his research assistant was a much respected investigator in her own right.

An added attraction for the media in having Jenny Thornton on a programme was that she was an abductee, somebody who'd had her own experiences with the extraterrestrials. The current crisis had certainly resulted in the rehabilitation of the abductees, who were now viewed as pioneers and not cranks. But, needless to say, not all those claiming to have been abducted were genuine and the media were careful to choose people who'd been talking about their experiences long before the alien presence had been publicly confirmed. Indeed, it was an irony of actual alien contact that it had pretty much disproved most of the claims about UFOs and alien abductions that had previously been made.

This was particularly true of the New Age material, much of which had been 'channelled' by psychics claiming telepathic contact with beings from this or that star system. Real life suggested that alien contact was unlike most of what had been claimed, though some ufologists pointed out that such material could easily have been alien disinformation – genuine alien contact but with an entirely fabricated content, designed to be so bizarre that it served to discredit ufology in the eyes of the scientific establishment.

But now Cody and Thornton faced a problem. Neither were the sort of New Age types who automatically described the aliens as 'visitors', and their previous stance on the UFO and abduction phenomena was that they were fundamentally negative experiences. This was particularly true of the abductions that were described by Cody – who was a retired barrister – as non-consensual criminal acts. The phrase 'crimes against humanity' had been used by them both, and was actually the title of Cody's best-selling book on alien abduction. So, on the face of it, Cody and Thornton might have been expected to welcome some of the recent developments. Their controversial views, which had been attacked or simply dismissed by most, were now accepted as fact. And as well as vindication had come retribution, when the RAF had squared up to the aliens during the events of Operation Thunder Child.

At first glance what was happening was precisely what Cody and Thornton had lobbied for over the years: the government was treating the UFO issue seriously and taking active measures to protect its citizens from whatever the aliens were doing. But the moment the RAF started taking casualties, it stopped being a matter of simple debate. To some it might have seemed strange that this didn't harden the attitudes of people like Cody and Thornton, who might have been expected to welcome military action being taken against the perpetrators of these 'crimes against humanity'.

But such a view was simplistic. Cody, for example, had always argued that whatever the true nature of the alien agenda, two intelligent civilizations had much to teach each other. Indeed, the conclusion to his book had argued against viewing the aliens as bad simply because of what they did. Were scientists bad, he argued, simply because they shot animals with tranquillizer darts, fitted them with electronic tags and released them into the wild? Did these scientists stop to think how the animals felt about this? Cody had maintained that even if the aliens were humanity's *technological* superiors we might still have things to teach them. Our art, music, literature and poetry were unique, he'd argued, and might be a suitable gift for the aliens. Perhaps they would give us some scientific data in exchange.

So, on the face of it, recent events should have hardened Cody's and Thornton's views, convincing them more than ever that the aliens were bad and that humans held the high moral ground. But what happened when the 'alien invaders' weren't bug-eyed monsters coming to destroy the planet? What happened when the aliens looked just like us and offered to share their technology?

And what happened when it was your own side that launched a pre-emptive attack, using one of the most obscene and indiscriminate weapons ever devised? Simplistic concepts of a good versus evil struggle were meaningless.

This was the dilemma that Cody and Thornton faced. Choosing sides was normally such a simple concept – either someone was for something or against it. But recent events suggested that there might be arguments on both sides. The aliens claimed that there had been a deal struck with agencies of government – and wasn't that precisely what Cody and other conspiracy theorists had argued all along? They'd accused governments of covering up the truth about Roswell and Rendlesham Forest, and now it seemed that they'd been spot on with such allegations. The trouble with this was that it suggested that the aliens' claim that they'd had consent for what they'd been doing had been true, and in such circumstances it was harder to blame them. How could anyone choose when both sides were in the right? Conversely, how can anyone choose sides when both parties have been equally deceitful?

And yet, time to choose it was. Maxwell Henderson was lobbying for support and planning moves that he claimed might bring down the government. Cody was unsure precisely what was planned but he knew Henderson had previously threatened to release certain information that would shake the Establishment to its core. Henderson had spent decades in politics and business, and was the sort of well-connected power broker who probably really did know where a lot of bodies were buried. Although Henderson was no longer in Parliament himself, Cody had seen at first hand how a number of MPs were seemingly at the man's beck and call. Might he force a vote of no confidence in the House and bring the government down that way? Cody was sceptical about such a move and although he didn't know the nature of the secrets Henderson knew, he doubted it could force a change of government. That would need an election, and the present administration had a sizeable majority.

But Cody knew there was another factor and thought that, for all his undoubted political skills, Henderson might have mis-judged the situation. While people had undoubtedly found the biological attack on the aliens repugnant, it was something in which the UK genuinely seemed to have played no part. Had the aliens done nothing by way of response, public sympathy might have swung their way and Henderson might have been able to make good his threats. But the aliens had attacked in force and, though they had been undeniably provoked to such a course of action, reports were coming in from all around the country of deaths at military bases under sustained attack from the aliens. And, despite some dissenters, the press had spoken. The tabloids in particular, which were so crucial in shaping public opinion, had followed the traditional line: my country, right or wrong. They knew that whatever the complexities of the situation, there was one undeniable fact about conflict: in time of war, people will rally around the flag.

Cody had discussed the situation with Thornton and was adamant that they had little choice but to follow suit. After all, when 'our boys' – and an increasing number of 'our girls' – were fighting and dying for their country, those who were seen to side with the enemy would at best be ignored or at worst be branded as traitors. To a certain extent, Cody argued, they had to go with the flow of public opinion and slip in what mention they could of a more conciliatory approach. The alternative, as Cody saw it, was to risk losing the unprecedented media access and influence that they had built up recently. Real life, as he knew only too well from his career as a barrister, was seldom as black and white as the media portrayed it. But for the time being they were in a media-led situation where it was inconceivable to side against the government. He made his decision – but he didn't feel pleased with it.

House of Commons, Westminster

The Prime Minister's initial statement had been met with the customary silence as – to a lesser extent – had been the next speech, made by the leader of the Opposition. The PM was flanked by the

Foreign Secretary and the Secretary of State for Defence, and it was the latter who gave a detailed account of the military situation, describing how Britain had suffered a wave of attacks on key military bases. The speech was understandably short on detail – the military still regarded information on battle-damage assessment as classified – not least because the government was keen to downplay the military action and eager to talk up its peaceful intentions.

But once the debate was thrown open to backbenchers, cracks began to appear in the façade of unity that traditionally bound government to Opposition in time of war. MPs began to get more and more vociferous, mainly because of the frustration that stemmed from there being so many questions that the government could not or would not answer. Many voiced concern about the biological attack and demanded that those responsible be removed from office and face criminal trial. The government's only response to such demands was to restate that the UK had no prior knowledge of or involvement in the attack, and to say that what had happened was an internal matter that was the sole responsibility of those concerned. The MOD had insisted on classifying as much of the information about this as possible, to the fury of MPs who were demanding information. The interventions, in particular, became quite lively.

'On a point of order, Madam Speaker, is it acceptable for the government to be playing up its peaceful intentions in public while in private the Prime Minister's Press Secretary is briefing journalists in altogether more bullish terms, telling them not to trust anything that the extraterrestrials say? The phrase "the alien lie machine" has been used. Can you tell us, Madam Speaker, whether it is proper for the government to have two policies – a private one and a public one?'

'That is not a legitimate point of order, but the honourable gentleman has made his point well enough and I'm sure it has been noted in appropriate places.'

'Further to that point of order, are such comments appropriate when the only lie machine we recognize is the Downing Street press office and the spin doctors who—'

'Order. That is *not* a proper point of order. Will the honourable gentleman please resume his seat.'

'On a point of order, Madam Speaker, will you agree that the previous comment is particularly distasteful and inappropriate in time of war, when in previous wars such comments might be viewed as tantamount to treason.' The House erupted at this, with cries of 'Shame' and 'Withdraw' aimed at the hapless backbencher who'd made the comment.

'Order. These are not matters for this Chair. Will honourable members please remember that time wasted on bogus points of order is time that cannot be spent on the debate itself. I can see a considerable number of honourable members who are trying to catch my eye, so that they can make a contribution. This is a matter of huge importance and interest, and this sort of raucous behaviour does a disservice to this House. Many people are watching what happens here today, and they will not be impressed to see time being wasted in this way.'

The debate continued but, despite the Speaker's plea, there were further incidents that showed just how much bad feeling there was over the handling of the whole situation.

MOD Main Building, Whitehall

CDS had asked CDI to drop in for a private chat, to take stock of latest developments on the intelligence front. CDI was born to his job, being conspiratorially minded and a master of strategy. He would have been a worthy head of either the Security Service or the Secret Intelligence Service, but there was a strict agreement that neither MI5 nor MI6 could poach from the military or the Civil Service – though the occasional secondment was authorized. CDI had been at the heart of Operation Thunder Child and was equally heavily involved in the current crisis. He was also one of the few people cleared to see all the data, which made him one of only a handful of those with whom CDS could have a totally open discussion about the latest state of play.

'The latest news isn't good,' CDS began.

'Oh?' CDI was cleared for all the information, but CDS was still in the position to hear it before anyone else.

'In many ways the alien strategy is not unlike our own. They're carrying out a systematic programme to degrade and diminish our military capability. They're doing to us what we did to Saddam Hussein and to Milosevic. It's the UKADGE that's been hardest hit so far. Saxa Vord, Buchan, Boulmer . . . they've all been hit hard. Most primary radars have been destroyed or damaged and we're now largely dependent on the secondary systems. We've got mobile radars deployed, dispersed and guarded by Rapier and other ground-to-air systems, but it isn't enough. We're being worn down, and for all I know the enemy have virtually unlimited resources. The AD force is being hit hard too, and it won't be long before they're in the spotlight. As ever, it's the pilots more than the aircraft . . .'

'If their tactics are something we recognize, we should be able to figure out the wider strategic picture,' CDI observed. 'Understand their doctrine . . . set some traps?'

'Yes, we're already doing that,' CDS replied, a little testily. 'We've had some successes. A few craft have been brought down. No survivors, but here's an interesting thing – the occupants were "greys", if that's the term we're supposed to use. Not human at all. CSA has an interesting theory about that, reinforced by statements from Van Buren and from Clines himself: she says that the greys represent the penultimate stage in the aliens' transformative process to make themselves human. She thinks that it's taken two or three generations to complete the change and that, if these greys had offspring, they'd be completely human in appearance and would share our genetic make-up entirely. Although these *things* look alien, their genome is virtually identical to ours. She even thinks that these creatures are being used for the difficult and dangerous jobs. On Earth they won't fit in, so they're being used – like a resource.'

'Hmm.' CDI thought for a moment. 'Did it ever cross her mind that they might *all* look like that, except for a handful of individuals genetically modified to look human? On a planet-wide basis, the more that people think they're human, the less likely it is that they'll want to fight. And can you really comprehend a species wanting to change itself into something else? Would we modify ourselves so that we had tentacles instead of arms, just so we could handle the cutlery on Mars?'

'No, probably not, but we can't hope to guess at their thought processes. What I want now are some radical ideas. How can we fight back, before we have nothing left to fight back with?'

'You know the answer to that,' CDI replied calmly. 'Once we used the bioweapon, we committed ourselves. There are no half measures now. As has been said, we could bring down a thousand of their fighter craft without denting their capability to any significant extent. No, the only option left is to finish the job we started and go for their mothership. It's the only tactic that gives us any realistic chance of success. One knockout punch to end the war. We need to initiate Operation Lightning Strike.'

White Sands Missile Range, New Mexico

The Americans were having their own problems. All around the world, it seemed that those powers implicated in the biological attack on the alien ship found themselves the target of retribution. Protestations of innocence were ignored, and attack after attack was launched. But only on the military. For the most part, then, this meant the war – if that was the right word – was something remote from the experience of most civilians, something that, given the nature of the enemy, could almost be denied.

In a way the Americans were just as innocent as anyone else because, while the attack had been delivered by the Russians and suggested by the Americans, neither nation had embarked upon such a course of action as a matter of national policy. The attack had been instigated by The Enterprise – a private venture, despite the fact that at its core were highly placed members of various US government agencies. But military strategists had pointed out an obvious fact to the political leadership – it was no good complaining that a war had started by accident if your opponents were seemingly uninterested in such protestations. So, while attempts at dialogue and reconciliation continued, there was still the matter of defending oneself against attack. That was something which was stretching the Americans to their limits, but an integrated military action was now being planned with the aim of inflicting serious losses on the enemy and bringing them to the negotiating table.

Central to the attack plan was White Sands Missile Base in the New Mexico desert. Over several decades it had been the place where new weapons technologies had been developed and tested. Along with its sister facilities it had been at the forefront of efforts to build aircraft and missiles with capabilities that would have astounded even the experts.

With a deafening roar, six missiles were launched from their silos and streaked skywards at high speed. These were no ordinary weapons. Known to the military as Theater High-Altitude Area Defense missiles, and abbreviated to the equally unglamorous acronym THAAD, they had not yet entered operational service. The publicly stated reason for their development had been to provide a defence against ballistic missiles fired against the US by traditional 'rogue' states like Iran and Iraq. The military – themselves the victims of careful manipulation from The Enterprise – had been stoking such fears with the public for years to get funding for the project known by some as 'Son of Star Wars'. Cold War enemies had been carefully replaced in the public's mind by new foes – rogue states, or terrorists with the insane aim of launching a *jihad* against America. In truth, such enemies were more imagined than real, and while there were doubtless those who would carry out such attacks if they could, the ability to strike at the continental United States was something way beyond the capability of a real enemy. There was one exception to this, and this was the very enemy they now faced. The Enterprise – notwithstanding the deal they'd struck with the aliens – had striven to develop a viable defence against them, as a measure of last resort. This technology was now being used.

The THAADs were joined by another volley of missiles. Known as the Kinetic Energy Anti-Satellite System and abbreviated to KE-ASAT, these weapons were equally cutting-edge. A veritable swarm of them was now heading for a position high in the atmosphere where vast numbers of alien craft had been detected. It seemed that the aliens concentrated their craft at such high levels before moving off to attack various targets. It wasn't clear why they did this, but it presented the military with what they called a 'target-rich environment'. It was an opportunity to hit the enemy hard and they weren't about to pass that up.

'Bunching up like that is lousy strategy,' one of the military officers observed dryly.

'Yeah,' somebody agreed. 'I guess they figure they're out of range.'

'But we can only catch them by surprise once,' the first officer pointed out. 'After that they'll adapt their strategy and move to counter the threat.'

'Let's hope once is all it takes. Hit them hard enough to stop them in their tracks . . .' He didn't sound as if he believed his own analysis.

The White House

'The attack is under way, Madam President.' Defense Secretary Saul Weitzman delivered the news in a deadpan voice that gave little away.

'Any news yet?'

'Not yet.'

The President thought for a moment. She was a lawyer by training but had an instinctive understanding of strategy in its wider sense. 'How come they haven't hit White Sands? Or the Skunk Works, or Dreamland? Surely they must know that such places are home to the best of our technology and that they therefore represent the greatest threat to their mission?'

It was a smart question. Weitzman deferred to the other person present, General Tom Johnson, Chairman of the Joint Chiefs of Staff.

'Madam President, there's only one answer we've been able to think of. They're thinking *beyond* the war. If they thought the outcome was in the slightest doubt, they'd have concentrated on those facilities from day one. So the only answer that makes any sense is that they want those places themselves. When you consider that, according to The Enterprise, some of our most advanced bits of hardware are derived from alien technology, it's not impossible to suppose that we've gone beyond them in some respects. We may have capabilities and technology that they don't have. Aside from interstellar travel – which does them no good against us in a strategic sense – they don't have technology which is that far ahead of us. If we hit their craft, we bring them down.'

'You're implying that we can beat them?'

'Presumably The Enterprise thought so, to risk their attack.'

'The Enterprise are themselves split on the issue. They were all working towards trying to stop the aliens, but were divided over whether they'd reached the point where we could do that. Aside from the question of resources, the alien and human technologies are in many respects about equal. As you know, in military terms, fighting an offensive campaign is more difficult than a defensive one.'

'I believe that in numerical terms a three-to-one advantage is generally required for an attack to stand a reasonable chance of success.' President Spencer had been reading up on the doctrine of war.

'Indeed so,' Johnson replied. 'But a part of that equation relates to lines of supply. Here, that factor doesn't apply, since they're cut off from their source. They have with them everything they need. But their greatest asset is also their greatest liability.'

'The mothership.'

'We're operating from multiple bases and can disperse our assets, moving them out of harm's way. They have just one.'

'But so do we, in a sense,' Weitzman objected. 'The Earth itself, I mean.'

'Yes,' Johnson agreed. 'But the aliens need that asset as much as we do. Generations of them have slowly adapted themselves for life here. Their mothership can only travel at sub-light speed. They have nowhere else to go. The Earth itself is safe.'

'It all comes back to the mothership,' Spencer agreed. 'You want me to authorize Operation Lightning Strike, don't you?'

'Yes, Madam President. My analysis about why they've spared White Sands may only hold so far. Ironically, the more successful we are with our current attack the more likely they are to write off the possibility of gaining those assets themselves and simply take them out. It's not White Sands that we need, of course, but Cape Canaveral. If that's hit, Lightning Strike is dead in the water.'

'You're asking me to commit genocide.'

'With the aim of saving the human race.'

'Assuming they want to exterminate us. That may not be their intention.'

'That's *not* a gamble we can afford to take.' Johnson paused for breath, realizing that he'd raised his voice to the President. 'I apologize, Madam President, but when the survival of the human race is at stake, I don't think we can make assumptions about alien motives. If there was any other way, I'd advocate it, but . . . well, once The Enterprise used bioweapons, the die was cast. Even if the aliens had peaceful intentions initially, they've realized that we represent a mortal threat to them. If the positions were reversed, I'd come in with all guns blazing.'

'Couldn't we . . .' Weitzman began to say something but then thought better of it, his voice trailing away limply. There were no more ideas. There was only one option left.

'Initiate Operation Lightning Strike,' the President ordered. 'But be ready to abort at a moment's notice should the position change.'

'Yes, Madam President,' Johnson acknowledged, a look of grim determination on his face. He'd got what he wanted, but he took no pleasure from the thought of what might be achieved. He was fairly sure the mission would fail. If it did, a group of brave American astronauts would die, and the aliens – realising the nature of their mission – would have another reason to wipe out humanity. But if the mission succeeded, Johnson knew that the President had been right – it *would* be genocide, and on an unprecedented scale: a billion colonists were said to be on board

the alien ship. Indistinguishable from humans, they claimed to be
settlers on the final leg of an epic journey; immigrants wanting to
make a new life here on Earth, bringing with them new skills and
new ideas. Johnson cleared his mind of these thoughts. He had to
focus on the mission. As for the rest, who could say what was right
or wrong? God would judge him.

White Sands Missile Range, New Mexico

Deep in a bunker below the sprawling facility, military officers
studied their radar screens, trying to make sense of the data. They
were using a mixture of conventional and space-tracking radars,
since the targets being monitored were at the very edge of the
Earth's atmosphere. The missiles streaking up towards the cluster
of targets were big enough to show up as separate blips
themselves, and not for the first time several of the radar operators
allowed themselves to think of the drama unfolding on their
screens as being somewhat akin to an arcade game. Symbols closed
in upon symbols, with several appearing to merge before
disappearing altogether. Whoops of joy went up from the control
centre when this happened – they were getting some hits in.

As ever in warfare, there were consequences, and even as five
alien fighter craft were blown apart by a threat that they hadn't
anticipated, the rest turned to deal with the source of the danger.
They came screaming down on to the facility, firing blindly as
they went, but homing in inexorably on the silos from which –
even now – the controllers were launching the last of their
missiles, knowing their secret was out and that they wouldn't get
another chance. Fully fifty craft were involved in the attack, and
the USAF officers watched calmly as they came ever closer. Exactly
as planned.

The MIRACL lasers had been designed as anti-satellite
weapons and had proved their worth in several trials. Contrary to
the public perception of such weapons, they weren't yet capable of
cutting through metal in the way so beloved of science fiction
writers, though that would doubtless come in a few years. While
such things could be done in a laboratory, at close range, the

MIRACL weapon worked in a different though no less effective way. Essentially, it had been designed to hit satellites with a high-energy beam that was still too weak to damage the structure of a solid object but would render it useless by shorting out any sensitive electronics. The satellites against which it had been tested had overloaded and been turned into floating junk. Now it was time to use the weapon in anger.

There were a total of ten lasers, but one had malfunctioned and couldn't be brought back on-line, despite the frantic efforts of technicians. Each of them was about six metres high and looked rather like a large telescope. If such weapons hit the alien craft there was little doubt they would bring them down. But hitting them was easier said than done. The problem was that the lasers could only be manoeuvred slowly, and although they'd been pre-positioned to point at the angle from which an alien attack was thought likely to come, the real-life operational picture was evolving quickly. Although designed to hit satellites, which flew on predictable courses, there was no reason why the lasers shouldn't be effective against the alien craft.

The plan had been to use all the exotic new weapons at once, in one attack, to catch the aliens by surprise. It was hoped that the military would be able to hit them hard and convince them that these were standard front-line weapons in the US inventory. It was a deception, of course, and everybody knew that the weapons were prototypes, not yet in operational service. But if the aliens could be persuaded otherwise, they might think they were dealing with defenders considerably better able to protect themselves than had been thought. The military planners termed this tactic 'kidology', and realized that the more damage they did, the more likely it was that the deception would work. Ironically, the planners felt this represented the best chance for peace. There was a certain logic to that: if somebody thought they'd bitten off more than they could chew, they just might sue for peace. So went the theory.

The first of the lasers fired but the beam went well wide of any targets. Other lasers powered up and were fired. There was scant time for acquiring any of the craft, let alone achieving anything like a 'lock-on'. The lasers consumed a phenomenal amount of power, but once on-line could fire a steady burst of energy sky-wards. If it had been possible to move the lasers at a reasonable speed, they would have been truly devastating weapons, capable of blotting numerous enemy craft out of the sky with little difficulty. But the lasers were bulky affairs and were capable only of very slow movement. They stood little chance of success against fast-moving targets. But that had been anticipated.

Tactical experts watched with satisfaction as the lasers did their work. It was only visible on one computer screen, which showed a three-dimensional pattern of the airspace above White Sands. The battle was unfolding as planned and even as the alien fighters closed in on the facility, they reacted to the laser beams, manoeuvring to avoid them. What the USAF officers could see – and what the aliens had clearly missed – was that the laser beams had been fired at a very wide angle, which was steadily being reduced. To avoid intersecting the beams, therefore, the alien craft had to move in a certain direction, pre-selected by the USAF. It was rather like rounding up cattle, going wide of the herd to bring them back to a central position, where they were nicely bunched up and easily controlled. The lasers still hadn't recorded a single hit and only the USAF knew that this was the way this particular engagement had been planned. The trap was about to be sprung. The cavalry was about to arrive.

Over White Sands

Captain Tom Buckmeister looked with satisfaction at the data gathered by his on-board radar and knew that his fellow pilots would be seeing the same thing. Attracted by the high-tech missiles capable of hitting the opposition when they were virtually in space, the opposition itself was closing in to eliminate the source of this new threat. Then they'd detected the laser beams and had manoeuvred to avoid them. But in doing so they'd bunched up and been corralled into a preordained 'kill-box' that would be saturated with fire from Buckmeister and his fellow pilots. The aliens wouldn't cooperate for much longer, he thought.

They'd see the trap and disperse. That was why the strike had to be quick and intense. They'd never get a better chance to inflict such losses because this wasn't the sort of thing that could ever work twice. It needed a very special sort of pilot to pull something like this off, and a very special aircraft. That wasn't a problem.

The Aurora was America's most advanced operational aircraft and although even more exotic craft were being developed and test-flown in prototype form, Aurora was operational and had been for some years. Funded from the black budget and hidden within the publicly declared Stealth programmes, it had been developed in relative secrecy until – ironically – it had been 'outed' by ufologists who thought it might be evidence of back-engineered alien technology. Curiously enough, this theory was actually correct, though The Enterprise managed to swamp the legitimate stories with its own increasingly wild accounts, discrediting the whole concept – at least with most aviation journalists.

But some of the stories *had* been true, and Aurora had indeed flown between various locations in America and its forward base at RAF Machrihanish in Scotland. Despite the fact that Aurora was a 'deep black' programme, the whole project had nearly unravelled in September 1994 when one of the aircraft had crashed on landing at Boscombe Down in Wiltshire.

The Enterprise had designed Aurora for reconnaissance of alien activity, intending to use it as a fighter if necessary. But the cover story for the majority of the black-project staff – who had no knowledge of The Enterprise – was that it was the replacement for the SR-71 Blackbird. Almost completely stealthy and capable of speeds of around 3,500 m.p.h., Aurora was a remarkable aircraft by any standards. And if some of the hardware seemed a little exotic, nobody questioned it too closely. The Skunk Works – and places like it – could do some truly amazing things, but all the pilots cared about was performance – and survival.

Buckmeister and his fellow pilots were based at Cannon Air Force Base in New Mexico and had been briefed on their mission only a few hours before. They all regarded their task as a long-overdue payback.

Contrary to the view of Hollywood producers, aerial combat in the modern era was usually very brief and fought at distances where aircrews didn't even see the enemy. In one respect, the forthcoming air battle would conform to type: the Auroras would make one pass and one pass only, before dispersing and heading back to base.

Buckmeister steadied his breathing and looked at his head-up display, noting with satisfaction that they were about to enter a target-rich environment. Normally the Auroras would carry a mixture of Sidewinder, Sparrow and Phoenix air-to-air missiles, but this time they carried only the new plasma weapon, back-engineered by the British. The British called it Skystriker, but the US military had designated it Firestreak. It was, however, essentially the same weapon, and fired pulses of superheated plasma. It was the Americans who had improved upon the initial British design and attained an increased fire rate that spewed out plasma with a wide dispersal rate, not unlike a machine gun. Accuracy was replaced with the ability to saturate a wide area – a capability that was massively enhanced when several aircraft were deployed at the same time in the same area.

A couple of the pilots had wondered out loud whether it was a mistake to leave their normal payload behind. It was Buckmeister who had pointed out the tactical folly of such a move – even though the missiles could accelerate to speeds of around Mach 5, the plasma bolts were faster and were deemed to be more effective weapons for the planned scenario. This being the case, the missiles couldn't be allowed to arrive at the kill zone before the plasma bolts – they either had to arrive later or at the same time. But given the relative speeds of the two weapons systems, the missiles would have to be fired *first*.

When Buckmeister explained this, they all understood why it was pointless to carry the missiles: fire them first, and they'd only be hit by plasma bolts, and every bolt that hit was one that *could* have hit an alien fighter. Buckmeister had gone on to explain that not being weighed down would give them advantages in terms of speed and manoeuvrability, and would add to the chances that they'd survive in the event that they were hit by the aliens before any of their missiles had been launched.

White Sands itself was taking quite a battering: the alien fighters were in a steep attack dive, and were firing their own plasma weapons as they went. But this too had been anticipated, and personnel had been deployed to secondary command centres deep underground.

The USAF had deployed decoy aircraft – plastic models – on some of the runways, and had erected Portakabins at various points around the facility. These Portakabins were filled with powerful but entirely superfluous equipment, the sole function of which was to generate powerful – and, with luck, detectable – EM fields. The aliens, it was hoped, would think this was the focus of the attack against them. Each dummy aircraft and Portakabin was packed with fuel drums, so that when they were hit there would be a powerful explosion. There were officers who specialized in such deception and they had pulled out all the stops on this one.

Real parts of the facility were also being hit, of course, but the decoys were drawing much of the fire. The deception served another purpose apart from the obvious one of lessening the likely impact on important parts of the facility: it served as a target marker for Buckmeister and his Aurora force, aiding them in their efforts to acquire their targets visually on their final approach.

The six Auroras were flying in formation, each having been assigned a certain part of the kill zone. Buckmeister removed the protective cap from his Firestreak weapons system and aimed the directed-energy device at his assigned area. By now he could see the facility itself, far below, lit up by explosions. And there, in front of him, was the attacking force, advertising their presence even further by their own weapons system. Radio silence had been maintained until that point and when Buckmeister broke it there was only one word to say.

'Fire.'

All six Auroras opened fire, their Firestreaks having been pre-set to the fully automatic mode. The air ahead of them turned purple with hundreds of energy bolts, fanning out ahead of them in a tightly-packed mass so dense that it looked like a purple fog reaching out for the enemy. The wave broke over the formation of alien craft, exploding many of them immediately in what was soon a near-total rout.

The Auroras broke formation and dived for the relative safety of the ground, with operators of the MIRACL lasers ensuring that the beams were momentarily switched off as the friendly aircraft came screaming above the base. But even as the Auroras turned for home, a second wave of aircraft attacked: F-117 stealth fighters appeared, firing a volley of Phoenix and Sidewinder missiles before they, too, turned for home. There had been no plans for the stealth aircraft to use Firestreak, not least because only a handful of them had yet been equipped with the new weapon.

White Sands Missile Range, New Mexico
There were whoops of joy from around the room. Nobody yet knew precisely how many alien craft had been destroyed but everybody knew it was a lot. The base itself was no longer under attack and space-tracking radars suggested that the aliens had retreated out of the atmosphere altogether, backing away from any further fight.

'We certainly kicked some butt today,' one of the radar technicians observed, a satisfied grin on his face. 'It should set them back a bit and maybe even make them think twice about messing with us at all, if they suddenly realize we can hit them at those sorts of ranges and with that level of kill-rate.'

'Maybe,' somebody replied. 'But maybe it'll just make them even *more* pissed off with us . . . and then what?'

Over RAF Waddington
The RAF was in the process of learning the truth of what senior officers had always maintained: in time of war, to have just seven airborne early-warning aircraft was simply not enough. What made it worse was that one had been undergoing third-line maintenance when the current crisis had started, and was effectively out of action. Another had been undergoing the less intensive

second-line maintenance and had been rushed back into service. All were normally based at RAF Waddington, although they'd been dispersed of late to avoid the possibility that several could be taken out at once in a successful enemy attack. But two were still based at Waddington, and the RAF's aim had been to keep one airborne at all times. It put enormous pressure on the aircrew but was a vital factor in maintaining comprehensive radar coverage over the UKADR – especially now that so many primary radar heads were being damaged or destroyed in what was clearly a sustained attack to blind the RAF. The aliens, unlike Hitler decades before them, were smart enough to realize that the only way to win a war was to establish air superiority – if not air supremacy – by systematically destroying your enemy's ability to wage war in the air.

The RAF had realized that the Sentry AEW aircraft were going to be a prime target, so they never flew without a massive fighter escort. But this just made it more obvious to the opposition just how priceless the Sentries were and some cynics suspected this might even to contribute to the expected attack – an attack that was even now under way.

The RAF fighters spread out to meet the offensive. A number of different units were involved in the defence: the RAF had been hit hard by a steady rate of losses among the Typhoon force. To keep the three squadrons at full strength, replacement aircraft were being brought forward from the in-use reserve. More serious were the losses among pilots, not least because not all the AD force had yet undergone conversion training from the older Tornado F3s to the newer Eurofighter Typhoons. So the RAF's three prestige AD squadrons were now being augmented with older, less capable aircraft and with less experienced pilots. Never a good combination. But peacetime cuts had hit the RAF hard and the problems ran too deep to be fixed by a few augmentees.

The truth was that with the break-up of the old Soviet Union and the Warsaw Pact the armed forces as a whole had been cut back to the bone, equipped well enough – just – to fight a limited conflict or peacekeeping operation but ill-equipped for a full-scale war. The RAF simply didn't have enough aircraft or pilots for the current crisis, and although negotiations were under way to borrow assets from other countries, not all wanted to embroil themselves in a conflict they deemed unwinnable. Those countries that might have been willing to help were generally under attack themselves. The RAF would have to make do with what it had got. This meant that other aircraft types such as Jaguars and Harriers, normally deployed in the ground-attack role, had been converted to an AD role and pressed into service. It was backs-to-the-wall stuff.

Isabelle Bentley was certainly feeling the pressure. She loosed a couple of Meteor BVRAAMs and banked her aircraft hard to avoid an alien craft that had appeared seemingly out of nowhere, firing its plasma weapon as it came. As she reorientated herself after the manoeuvre she saw that the tactical position had gone to pieces. What had started out as a controlled engagement had degenerated into the sort of aerial battle that her training syllabus had said was a thing of the past – individual dogfights were taking place and once it got to that point she knew that losses were going to be fairly steady on both sides.

What concerned Bentley was the location of the AEW aircraft. At the first sign of trouble the Sentry had gone into a steep dive, heading for the relative safety of the ground. But Waddington itself was under attack and a landing had been adjudged too dangerous. It was diverting to her own home base of Coningsby, a few miles to the south-east. But Bentley realized this was tactically dangerous: the RAF could ill afford to leave the Sentry unguarded, though by breaking off from the main combat they might draw attention to the very thing they were trying to protect. Furthermore, leading it away from the area would mean that the escorting aircraft would be angled away from the main body of alien craft and vulnerable to attack from the rear.

But even as Bentley thought matters through, the decision was made for her as she saw an alien craft break off from attacking a Tornado F3 and reposition itself for an attack run on the fleeing Sentry. She turned sharply and activated her Skystriker, firing pulses of superheated plasma at the enemy craft. Her salvo missed, but she hadn't expected a hit: she'd had no time to aim properly and had been guided by the overriding need to fire her weapon quickly so that the alien fighter would respond to the new threat. It had been within an instant of lining itself up directly with the Sentry and she knew that once it did it would open fire. The Sentry was a large and not very manoeuvrable aircraft: once fired on for any significant length of time, a hit – and the aircraft's consequent destruction – was inevitable.

Bentley's salvo passed over the alien craft, but even as she tried for another shot she realized that she was constrained in her angles of approach by the need to avoid hitting the Sentry herself. She had to attack from the side, not the rear, and that meant it would take longer than she'd like to come round for another pass. This one would have to count. But even as she came in for a second pass, a salvo of plasma bolts passed in front of her – she was being fired on herself. Normally she'd have reacted instantly and thrown her aircraft into a violent evasive manoeuvre but this time she hesitated for an instant, concerned that breaking off her attack would prove fatal for the Sentry.

In time of war, compassion has consequences. There was a loud bang and Bentley realized with a mixture of surprise, fear and anger that her aircraft had been hit. She'd been trained for such an eventuality and had undergone simulations, but in reality nothing could come even close. Above everything else it was the noise – her aircraft was breaking up around her. She pressed the eject button and exploded out of her disintegrating aircraft into a world of sound, light and pain.

Chapter Eleven

LIGHTNING STRIKE

MOD Main Building, Whitehall

'You mean that the bodies haven't been recovered? I don't understand – how is that unusual?' Under-Secretary of State Martin Blackmore was quizzing CAS on the latest engagement.

'No, Minister, I mean they *disappeared* altogether. We lost nine aircraft over Waddington – including the Sentry – but no bodies were found and no signals from their personal locator beacons have been detected.'

'But doesn't that simply mean that they died instantaneously, blown to pieces in their aircraft?' The Minister didn't like using such terminology in front of an RAF officer but couldn't think of a more tactful way to express himself.

'Almost certainly not, Minister,' CAS replied. 'Death – even with a direct hit from any weapon – is seldom instantaneous. More often than not people have time to eject and to activate their PLBs. For this to happen with none of our aircraft losses in this latest engagement is . . . extraordinary.'

The Minister thought for a moment, before asking his next question. 'Might this simply mean that the aliens are using a new and more potent weapon? One where death *is* instantaneous?'

'Possibly. But the Navy are recovering the aircraft and some of them look relatively intact. In fact, some of them look rather *too* intact.'

'Meaning what?'

At this point CAS turned to Head of Sec(AS), and invited him to put forward his own theory about what was going on. 'Nick?'

'Thank you,' Templeton replied. 'Minister, it's my belief that the reason we haven't found any bodies or picked up any signals is that our pilots were removed from their aircraft immediately after or perhaps in some cases *before* their destruction.'

CDS and CDI were also present and it was CDI who interrupted with the logical objection. 'Well, hold on a moment, if they can do *that*, why bother engaging us at all? They've taken quite a few losses, so surely they wouldn't have taken *any* if they could just beam our pilots out of their cockpits.' This last observation was delivered with more than a trace of sarcasm.

Templeton nodded. 'I take the point and I'm not saying it makes sense in *our* terms.' He paused to let the distinction sink in. 'But when you look at the circumstances, I fail to see what other option there is. We know that abductees were taken from their beds and their cars by being drawn up through a beam of light. We know that they were somehow taken through solid objects. Is it so hard to suppose that this is precisely what's happened to our pilots?'

'Well, setting that aside for the time being, what about CDI's point?' the Minister asked. 'Why haven't they used this tactic before in the recent engagements?'

'I honestly don't know. Maybe it's a strategic decision to suddenly go after the pilots. We've speculated previously that the aliens were trying to draw us out into combat situations, either to evaluate our capability or to systematically take out our aircraft. Well, maybe the evaluation's complete. Or maybe they were prepared to take losses up to a certain point that has now been reached. I don't know. We can't get inside their heads.'

'Wouldn't someone have seen something? Did anything strange

show up on radar?' Blackmore had a great many questions and chose to fire off two in quick succession.

CAS stepped in to answer these points. 'In a combat situation everybody's incredibly focused on their individual position. You try to keep an eye on the wider tactical situation, but . . .' His voice trailed away. 'As for radar,' he continued, 'nothing. But the situation was very confused and our overall capability has been degraded significantly over the last couple of days. Maybe that's the answer to CDI's question – maybe they can only do this when our radar coverage isn't so effective.'

'The real question isn't how – it's *why*.' Templeton had been thinking hard and was adamant that everybody was at least going to hear his theory. As Head of Sec(AS) he knew more about UFOs and alien abductions than anyone in government and had been able to subject all the latest developments to a really informed analysis.

'As a sign of good faith, perhaps? Maybe they're tired of all the killing and are trying to send us a message.' The Minister's guess was born more out of hope than anything else.

'Maybe to interrogate the pilots, to find out about our new weapons and tactics. Skystriker is hitting them hard and it must be galling to have your own weapons used against you. And don't forget the reports we're getting about the Americans getting some big hits in on the opposition.' CDI's view typified his natural caution.

'I think the answer is simpler than that,' Templeton replied. 'What we have to ask ourselves in the first instance is this: where have the pilots been taken? There's only one possible answer, it seems to me, and that's the mothership. The real question, though, is *why* take them to the mothership?'

'To show them the effects of the bioweapon, maybe? Then send them back and hope that we'll lose our will to fight.' CDS's theory was logical enough.

'I don't think so,' Templeton replied. 'If they wanted to stop the war all they have to do is cease hostilities. We have extremely limited opportunities to take the fight to them. In any case, why not invite or abduct the politicians? Or the senior commanders? Those people who actually make policy decisions – those would be the logical ones to take. No, it seems to me that the reason they're taking our pilots is because they know we value them – they're *hostages*, put on the mothership to deter any attack on it.'

'Then we might expect to hear from the opposition, and we might also expect this tactic to be continued. In fact, developing this line of thought, we might expect children to be abducted in large numbers so that the mothership is packed with those whom we value most . . . those they'd never believe we'd attack.' CDS liked Templeton's direct approach and was building on his analysis, his thinking developing rapidly as he worked up a viable hypothesis.

'Of course, this tells us something very interesting,' Templeton added cautiously. 'If the aliens are using them as human shields, it tells us that they feel vulnerable – no, more than that: that they *are* vulnerable. The biological attack may really have hit them hard and degraded their ability to fight. They've almost certainly taken massive casualties and lost key people. Systems may be down, all but essential activities cut back – and all at the most crucial moment: the final approach, as the ship goes through the last phase of its deceleration, prior to entering orbit.'

'My remote viewers support such a view,' CDI interjected, 'though I realize the data gleaned through remote viewing isn't highly thought of in certain quarters.'

'OK,' Templeton continued, 'but for what it's worth, *I* certainly think remote viewing works. Sec(AS) has always had a watching brief on anything paranormal and I'm aware that some pretty convincing studies have been done over the years – not just here but also in America and Russia. But be that as it may, I don't think the aliens would have any *need* to take hostages unless they were genuinely worried that there's a serious threat to the mothership.'

'So you think this is good news?' Blackmore asked.

'In a way, yes. It doesn't prove that we're winning but it certainly suggests they're worried about losing.'

'Well, we can't really attack the mothership now,' Blackmore retorted. 'Not when it would mean killing our own people.'

There was a silence. Neither Templeton nor even CAS or CDI dared offer a view on this. CDS was the only person who could really offer an opinion – and he did so. 'If it's the only way, and if there's political agreement, then with great regret we – or rather the Americans – would launch an attack. Such a tactic now represents not our best but our *only* chance of stopping the aliens. If Nick's theory is right – and I think it is – tactically the aliens have made a huge mistake, because they've advertised their vulnerability. But here's the thing: they're doubtless aware how much we value human life and have factored this into their strategy. But what they clearly may *not* have realized is how we sometimes sacrifice the very lives that we value so much, for the greater good.'

CDI added some thoughts of his own. 'We need to check whether this is happening elsewhere in the world. It makes sense for them to target aircrew because, as well as being good hostages, it diminishes our capability to wage war. So if aircrew *are* being targeted, we need to watch out that our people aren't simply taken from their barracks before they can get into action.'

'Wait a minute.' CDS was clearly thinking this through and everybody stayed silent, recognizing that he was marshalling his thoughts. 'Wait a minute. If pilots are being targeted we can turn it to our advantage. It worked once before, during Thunder Child. We have a number of SAS troops trained to resist the hypnosis the aliens use as a means of control. They wear contact lenses designed to filter out the blue light that also seems to play a part in the control process. We could get them into the pilots' accomodation and hope that they're taken. If they are, we get on to the mothership. And then . . .'

Trimmingham, Norfolk

Nobody could really understand how it had survived at all but survive it had, even though it was surrounded by craters. RAF Neatishead played the central role in coordinating what was known as the recognized air picture of the UK's air defence region, using data from radar systems all around the country. But

Neatishead's own radar wasn't actually at the base at all: it was located ten miles away on the Norfolk coast at Trimmingham. The massive radome housed a sophisticated Type 93 radar that had been attacked on two occasions without being hit. Neatishead itself had sustained heavy damage but the Trimmingham site was still operational.

With the damage done to Neatishead and other radar stations, and with the loss of one of the priceless Sentry aircraft, Trimmingham was becoming increasingly important. Although the radar could – in theory – be moved, it had become clear that the aliens were able to detect the location of an operating radar, so moving it would serve no useful purpose. Although it had survived, the cost had been steep. A battery of Rapier missiles and their RAF regiment operators had been hit before they'd managed to launch any missiles. There had been no survivors. The attacks had been beaten off by Jaguars from the nearby RAF base at Coltishall and Typhoons from RAF Coningsby. But the Jaguars had never been designed as air defence aircraft and had not proved as capable as the agile Typhoons. The radome at Trimmingham was unscathed, though three Jaguars had been lost. But the SAS were still getting some hits in with Stinger and Javelin missiles, and were even now taking up position as another raid came in.

But even as the Rapier squadron tried to acquire targets on their own radar, to engage the attacking craft before they could open fire, there was a deafening roar as three craft came in at low level, under the radar coverage. There was no warning at all and before anyone could react destruction rained down upon the facility as bolt after bolt of superheated plasma was unleashed. Most missed their targets, but with three craft in an attack and so many bolts being fired, some hit home. The RAF Regiment tried to lock on their Rapier missiles to counter the new threat, but couldn't acquire any targets. They were wary of being hit before they could launch, so they tried to reacquire the main body of craft that were still a short distance away. They didn't have a solid lock-on but decided to launch anyway, gambling that they might hit something.

Missiles roared off the launcher and into the sky, towards the area from which the main attack was expected. But the real danger came from the three craft that had got under the wire. SAS Sergeant Jack West managed to get a Stinger away but swore as he saw it go wide. Everyone was getting data on the wider tactical picture and it seemed that although jets had been scrambled to try and intercept the intruders, these defending aircraft were themselves under furious and sustained attack: a major assault was clearly under way and it was difficult to tell which if any location was the prime target. But the message to everyone at Trimmingham was clear: they were on their own.

The three alien craft had split up after their first pass and approached from different angles for their second attack run. Again, they came in so low that it was hard to spot them until the last moment, making it difficult to launch missiles. But even if the craft were spotted, coming in at ultra-low level made people think twice about firing their missiles, for fear of hitting their own people: firing a heat-seeking missile was fine if you had a target high in the sky, but if missiles were fired at a near-horizontal angle they were likely to pick up other heat sources on the ground, such as the engine in a vehicle – or even the heat from a building. Even though the SAS had a reputation for bravado, they would never risk a shot unless they were sure that no friendlies were in the way. Seeing this, West and his fellow SAS troopers had decided they stood a better chance of engaging the enemy with small arms, and the air was filled with the clatter of M16s in automatic-fire mode. For all the skill of the SAS, such a move was unlikely to succeed, and although some rounds did hit the attacking craft, none did any significant damage.

It was only a matter of time, especially as the attackers seemed to be ignoring all other targets bar the primary. A hail of plasma bolts converged on the giant radome and struck it full on, blowing it apart. Having achieved their aim, the intruders turned tail and departed, the main body of attackers turning away from Trimmingham without even firing a shot, clearly seeing no point in engaging Rapier units or individual soldiers. A volley of

Rapiers followed the craft out, but none found their target and the craft left to join another part of the fight.

Everybody was in a foul mood, none more than the SAS. The enemy had adapted their tactics and achieved their aim, without loss. The SAS hated the idea of losing and felt as if they'd failed, even though such an idea was perverse, given the difficulty in defending a fixed target from sustained attack. Orders came through for them to pull out, the reason for their presence now having been reduced to smoking rubble.

'Where next, boss?' asked a grim-faced Jane Vatch. She was feeling particularly aggrieved as she'd seen rounds from her M16 hit the underside of a craft without doing any appreciable damage. She tried to form an image of it trailing smoke and crashing into the sea but realized this was nothing more than wishful thinking.

'Back to Coningsby – or what's left of it,' West replied, having just received his orders.

'I suppose somebody has to look after the RAF,' she quipped, trying to lighten the mood.

'Maybe so, but that's not our mission.' West was looking sombre.

'Oh?'

'Let's just say we'll be going on a little journey.'

Number Ten

'That's it, then? They've launched the op without consulting us?' S of S stared at the Prime Minister intently, but knew he had neither misheard nor misunderstood.

'Yes. President Spencer informed me twenty minutes ago. The space shuttle fleet was launched from Cape Canaveral an hour ago. So far, no action has been taken against them.'

'Surely the aliens will blast them out of space well before they approach the mothership?' S of S's question was aimed at CDS, as if he somehow expected him to have insights into alien psychology and tactics.

'That would certainly be logical,' CDS ventured, cautiously. 'But now we know that some of our own people are up there – and more importantly, now they know we know – they may not be expecting any further attack. They know how much we value human life, so it may be inconceivable that we'd launch an attack.'

'But *our* people are up there,' the PM objected. 'How can the Americans . . . I should tell them to stop. It's Operation Lightning Strike they've initiated. It was our idea . . . our operation. I should tell them no. I should . . .'

'Prime Minister,' CDS said, calmly, 'the Americans will not have taken such a decision lightly. You know President Spencer. She's a good woman. But like us, she's been backed up against the wall with no room to manoeuvre. Once the Russians, or The Enterprise – it really doesn't matter who – launched the bio-weapon, there was no turning back. Like it or not, we were committed. The aliens weren't just going to take that.'

'So you're saying that we have to throw away the chance of peace? Throw away our chance of cancer cures and God knows what else? And we have to stand by and watch as the Americans commit genocide against a civilization that may very well have been sincere in its statements about their peaceful intentions?'

'I'm afraid so, Prime Minister. As we've said before, we all want to believe that the aliens have peaceful intentions, but we simply *can't* gamble that they're being truthful when they make such claims. If we're wrong, we lose everything: the human race will be extinguished. Even now, of course, we're experiencing a devastating onslaught. Our people are dying out there.'

'Only because of the biological attack, surely?' The PM was desperate for a way out because he knew what was coming next.

'We'll probably never know for sure,' CDS replied. 'But we have to put that from our minds. I wish to God that attack had never been launched but it was and, once it was, we were effectively committed to war.'

'So we sit by and watch the Americans initiate Lightning Strike?'

'No, Prime Minister,' CDS replied, 'We have to do more than that, I'm afraid. The biological attack committed us to all-out war, even though that wouldn't have been our choice. Operation

Lightning Strike reinforces that and places the whole issue beyond debate. We can just about claim that the biological attack was designed to force the aliens to the negotiating table. They may buy that, they may not – probably not. But Lightning Strike is something else entirely. If it fails, the aliens will have absolutely no doubt that we intended to wipe them out totally, and they'll almost certainly wipe *us* out. We'll have shown ourselves to be too great a threat. So we have to do more than sit by and wish the Americans luck. We have to launch our own adapted version of Lightning Strike and actively help them destroy the mothership.'

'But we don't have any way of getting at it, do we?'

'Until a day ago, the answer to that would have been no. But we now think there's a way we can get some of our people on board.'

'And then what?' the PM demanded.

'Prime Minister, have you heard of a weapon called RA-115?'

'No. What's that?' The PM's voice betrayed his irritation.

'It was developed by the Soviets during the Cold War,' CDS replied. 'Essentially, it's a nuclear bomb. But it's the size of a suitcase. If it could be got on to the mothership – and we believe it could – and if we could get it to the rear of the ship where we believe the matter/antimatter drive is located, then . . . well, even if the Americans fail altogether, we believe we could destroy the mothership ourselves.'

Pyramid Heights, Westminster

When Maxwell Henderson let it be known that he was to hold a press conference 'to reveal something of international importance concerning the alien presence' the media were understandably interested. Henderson was a recognized figure and, though he was no longer directly involved in politics, few doubted that his influence made itself felt in many places in Whitehall, Westminster and far beyond. He had money and charisma in equal amounts and though he was not necessarily a popular figure, he was certainly what the papers called 'a player'. An invitation from him was not something to be refused and even his methodology in gaining an audience was subtly done: friends of his had spent the previous day targeting key figures in the media, letting it be known that something big was about to break and that Henderson was involved. This had set up an atmosphere of tense expectancy, which was reinforced when news came of the press conference.

But Henderson was astute enough to avoid simply inviting every journalist or correspondent he could find: invitations were carefully dispensed to only the most influential players. In that way, recipients felt that while nobody got an exclusive, they were nonetheless part of a privileged group of insiders. Henderson would sweep up the other media outlets with a press release, but for now, his luxurious penthouse played host to journalists from all of the broadsheets and most of the tabloids, together with correspondents from the main national radio and television news programmes. Henderson's personal assistant had made it clear, however, that the room was not to be cluttered with television cameras and radio microphones. Just one of each had been allowed, on the condition that all present would have access to the feed.

Some networks had decided to run the material live, even though none knew what was to be revealed, while others had cleared space in programmes later in the day. Predictably, this activity had come to the attention of the government, not least through journalists who occasionally did the odd favour for the Security Service in exchange for the occasional story – when it was in the national interest that some tasty titbit be leaked with official approval. The Prime Minister's Press Secretary had telephoned Henderson to see what he could smoke out and to remind him in fairly blunt terms that as a former Minister he was still bound by the terms of the Official Secrets Act. Henderson had been unforthcoming about his statement and had replied in general terms only. The Press Secretary had gone away unsatisfied, to make some contingency plans of his own.

The Alien Mothership
'I'm Navy,' the man was explaining, in a typically Southern drawl. 'I fly the F-14 Tomcat, and we were right in the middle of

a big battle, when – well, I don't know for sure – there was a bright light and I felt kinda light-headed. Thought I'd been hit by their plasma weapon but my aircraft was still there, intact. But it was like I was under water or something.' He frowned, searching for the right analogy. 'I felt sick and my body felt so heavy I could hardly move. Next thing, I swear to God, I'm coming outta my aircraft, right through it. I tell myself it must be a dream or that that's what happens when you die. That's it – I really thought I'd died; that my immortal soul was leaving my body, you know. And then this. Well, one thing I do know for sure – and I mean this as no disrespect to present company – but this sure ain't heaven.'

'Maybe it's hell,' someone added, with a grin.

'Didn't somebody once say "Hell is other people"?' another voice chipped in.

'That was you, just then,' somebody replied, prompting a one-fingered gesture.

The original speaker looked around him. There wasn't much to see. There were about fifty people present, most of whom were wearing military aviators' gear. The US Navy pilot recognized most but not all of the uniforms. As for the room itself, it was about twenty metres square in size, dull grey in colour and absolutely featureless, with not the slightest hint of doors or windows. 'There's only one answer that makes any sense, as I'm sure you must by now realize. We're on the mothership, and it's clear from this room that we're prisoners rather than guests.'

Several of them had already tried to break out, but had made not the slightest impact on the walls. Others had shouted for somebody to come, but nobody had. The Navy pilot's assessment seemed spot-on.

'There's nothing to be done for the time being, so we might as well get to know each other. Aside from passing the time and being the friendly thing to do, it might throw up some useful information.' With that, he turned to the pilot nearest him. 'I'm Mitch Cooper, US Navy' he said, by way of introduction.

'Isabelle Bentley, Royal Air Force. Pleased to meet you, Navy!'

Downing Street, Whitehall

'What's he playing at? And, more importantly, what can we do to stop him, should the need arise?' The PM had enough on his plate without the antics of some maverick ex-Minister and was quizzing his Press Secretary about Henderson's imminent broadcast.

'None of our usual contacts and sources have been able to say *what* he's planning – only that it's something big. Or so he says. It could just be bullshit.' The Press Secretary was one of a very few people who could – and frequently did – swear in front of the PM.

'Well, what's his public position on the situation?'

'That's the interesting thing: he doesn't seem to have one. There have been rumours of meetings and suchlike and a suspicion that he's been behind some of the backbench troublemaking, but there's nothing concrete.'

'So what can we do?'

'As you know, we've issued D-notices covering a number of aspects of the current situation. The media can't report any operational details or indeed anything else that might jeopardize national security. Although the system's voluntary, editors are pretty hot on it, especially in times of crisis. The reporting of this war has been pretty good in that respect, with one or two notable exceptions. Generally speaking, there's been little mention of specific losses or damage – anything that might help the enemy. In exchange we give the journos access to various bits of film footage and interviews that we know they'll like. But my point is that we probably don't need to – they're more reliable than we give them credit for and, as ever, they'll rally around the flag.'

'What about the specifics?' Nothing in his Press Secretary's analysis was new to the PM who wanted answers, not platitudes.

'We have the Defence Press and Broadcasting Advisory Committee, staffed by various journos but fronted by an admiral at the MOD. They could kill a story.'

'I don't want to know about a fucking committee,' the PM exploded, 'I want to know what we can do to pull the plug if Henderson blurts out something damaging there and then. What can we do *now*?'

'Very little. If he really went OTT we could hope the networks would pull the plug themselves. Some of them might, but if one doesn't the damage is done. And once the story's out it's more and more likely other outlets will run it, because they can say that the information is in the public domain so any damage has already been done. But the other factor to consider is the Internet: once the story's out somewhere, it'll get on to the Net. He might even put it there himself.'

'So we're stuck.'

'Yes, Prime Minister. We'll have to wait and see what happens. It may just be a whinge on behalf of the peace lobby.'

'Let's hope so.' The Prime Minister didn't sound convinced.

Space Shuttle Enterprise

The irony of the situation was lost on none of the astronauts. *Star Trek* fans had finally got their wish some years ago, as one of the latest of NASA's expanding space shuttle fleet was given the name that the fans had lobbied so hard for. Now it turned out that it had also been named for a shadowy group of conspirators who really *had* been dealing with a new life and a new civilization.

In some circles, suspicions remained about this: might The Enterprise have had a hand in naming the shuttle, aware that it might have a role to play in dealing with the alien presence, whether in partnership or conflict? But conflict it was, and what The Enterprise had started, the eponymous space shuttle would attempt to finish. The US Government had been committed to war by forces they even now couldn't understand: the Russians had launched the attack but fellow Americans had made this possible. And behind it all, The Enterprise themselves – a shadowy group whose influence was great, but whose reach and motives were still the subject of debate and investigation. Supposedly formed after the Roswell crash to manage information about the alien presence, they'd been implicated in numerous wars, conflicts and dirty operations all around the world for the last few decades. Nobody was sure whether this was done as part of a deliberate policy or whether it was simply a consequence of individual members pursuing a private agenda for monetary gain.

Whatever the truth, The Enterprise had been involved in drug running, arms dealing and much, much worse. The odd thing was that, contrary to popular opinion, The Enterprise *hadn't* been entirely unknown prior to confirmation of the alien presence: conspiracy theorists had known about them for years and a quick search on the Internet – if you could get beyond the myriad mentions of the Enterprise in its *Star Trek* context – would have revealed quite a few details and names of those involved – or, rather, of those who had either been caught or implicated. This struck some as curious, but analysts pointed out that just as the best place to hide a book was in a library, the best place to hide a conspiracy was within another conspiracy. People had known about The Enterprise for years without guessing their *real* agenda.

'I don't feel great about this, you know.'

'Nor me, but if we mess this up, there may not be an Earth for us to go back to – at least, not the Earth we know and love. I don't want to blow these guys up either, Tom, but it's a them-or-us situation now.'

The shuttle was at the front of a widely spread arrow-shaped formation. They negotiated the increasingly crowded region of space just beyond the Earth's atmosphere, avoiding satellites and glimpsing in the distance the International Space Station, still only partially built but now evacuated against the possibility of destruction that, to the surprise of many, had not come. Some saw this as a sign of friendship, but other more cynical commentators pointed out that it could simply be a case of 'to the victor belong the spoils of the enemy'.

'You realize that, technically speaking, we're breaking the law? The Outer Space Treaty of 1967 prohibits the weaponization of space, and *particularly* prohibits weapons of mass destruction like the ones we're carrying.'

'So sue me.'

'I'm being serious. And it's probably against NASA's Charter as well. Look, I'm not wimping out on you, I'm just saying, OK?'

'OK. But actually you're wrong about the Outer Space Treaty . . . I checked. It says we can't put nukes in orbit, or put them on moons or planets, or station them in outer space. But we're not doing any of those things, we're just using them in a one-shot deal. OK, put it this way – a giant asteroid is heading for the Earth and if it hits, game over. You wanna hold off and say "Sorry, man, we *could* nuke it and save the world, but I think it might violate some law"?'

'Of course not. I was just saying.'

'Yeah, well – *don't*. It wouldn't go down very well with our back-seat passengers. I know everyone on the programme but I don't recognize those guys. Haven't you figured out who they are?'

'Well, I guess they're . . . mission specialists? I dunno, this was all thrown together so damn' quick.'

'Mission specialists! Yeah, *right*.' The sarcasm was unmistakable. 'Their *mission* is to make sure we carry out *our* mission and, if we don't, you can bet they're not going to just sit back and admire the view.'

'Shit.'

Pyramid Heights, Westminster

'Thank you for coming here today. I have some things to say about the visitors, the ongoing hostilities and the imminent arrival of the mothership.' Henderson had everyone's attention. 'I also have some things to say about the government's handling of the UFO phenomenon, with particular reference to what they did and didn't tell you about this over the years. As you can see, I'm not speaking from prepared notes, though after I've spoken I'll be handing out a written statement that sets out the key facts. I'll also be happy to take your questions, but only after the statement, please.'

Somebody coughed, but apart from that there was silence as the assembled group of journalists and commentators awaited what they fervently hoped would be exciting revelations – though with a giant alien ship just hours from Earth now, and spectacular pictures available from Hubble and just about every major observatory in the world, it was going to take a lot to steal the front pages.

'Let me first of all say that my statements are in no way meant to be disloyal. I fully appreciate that brave men and women are fighting the visitors on a number of fronts even as we speak, and that some have paid the ultimate price. But let us be clear about this: the visitors have been attacked with a biological weapon of mass destruction – these weapons are deemed so repugnant that they are outlawed by treaties signed by this government and others. Faced with aggression on this scale against a ship that is crewed predominantly by civilians, the visitors have said that they have no option but to meet force with force by depriving us of the means to wage war.'

There were one or two muttered comments from commentators who felt this was little more than a defence of the alien position. Henderson was astute enough to pick up on the fact that his remarks were not being well received in certain quarters. Yet he was a skilled public speaker and his carefully measured words were certainly striking a chord with two-thirds of the audience. He held up his hands, palms outwards.

'I know how this may sound to some of you,' he acknowledged. 'But I'm simply trying to put the recent aggression by the visitors into context. I do not ask you to condone it – that would be ridiculous. But I *can* ask you to try and understand it: if the positions were reversed and it was us who had been attacked with a potent biological weapon, who among us would not urge the powers that be to strike back against those who had attacked our families?' Henderson paused to let his remarks sink in. 'Notwithstanding that argument, you might ask what guarantee we had that the visitors had honourable intentions. Many have pointed out what they see as the folly of trusting these visitors, and I understand this point. But it seems to me that if the visitors were going to wipe us out, they would have done so by now. This government uses the terms "proportionality" to describe the military force that we deploy in response to aggression: self-evidently, this means that when we are attacked, we respond in a similar way, meeting force with force in a way designed to ensure that the threat is removed without escalating the situation. And yet, one might argue that the visitors have been more restrained than we would have been had the situations been reversed. A biological strike seemingly aimed at genocide in a literal sense has been met not with weapons of mass destruction but with limited action against our military forces. Those people living away from military installations would be unaware that there was a conflict at all, were it not for the media. Then there is the question of the knowledge the visitors have offered to share with us – or rather, the knowledge they have *already* shared with us. Scientists are already confirming the validity of some of the medical data that's been handed over. I put it to you that such gestures make a nonsense of the suggestion that the visitors are here to wipe out the human race. The information was freely given, and I know that much, *much* more has been given than the government has revealed. After this statement, I'll be handing over some of this actual data so you can see for yourselves. The government has tried to classify some of this material but such action is unwarranted and unconstitutional: the information is not theirs to classify. It is given freely, not to any power groupings but to *all* the people of Earth.'

Those present were certainly interested by that and none had any doubt that Henderson was talking about alien scientific knowledge, though he had not said so specifically.

Downing Street, Whitehall

'How the hell did he get hold of *that?*'

'How the hell did he get hold of *what*, Prime Minister?

The PM and his Press Secretary were watching Henderson's statement on one of the networks carrying it live. But it was apparent that there were still some secrets that the PM had not shared with his most trusted and powerful confidant.

'There's a great deal of data being offered,' the PM explained. 'But it would be foolish to release it before it can be evaluated.'

Pyramid Heights, Westminster

Henderson proceeded to set out the history of humanity's contact with the extraterrestrials, explaining about the Roswell crash, the underground facilities, the Rendlesham Forest incident and much more besides. He detailed the role of The Enterprise and its attempts to cover up the alien presence while simultaneously trying to back-engineer their technology and develop a capability against it. He named several members of The Enterprise who were in the United Kingdom. The name of one had been known to some, but the names of the others were not. The final name drew gasps of astonishment: it was that of a prominent member of the Cabinet.

'Please,' Henderson said, 'allow me to finish. I have all the documentary proof you could require. There really *is* an operation code-named Majestic, and I have some of the MOD papers that prove it. Parliament and the public have been systematically misled about the nature of the UFO issue for years. But let me make it clear that I'm not accusing anyone other than a few Enterprise members of this deception. Most of the politicians and civil servants who parroted the party line about UFOs being of no defence significance were not involved in the deception except as victims. They too were duped by The Enterprise and if they're guilty of anything it's only of allowing their own closed-minded belief systems to triumph over data about UFOs and alien abductions that they often refused even to read. But ignorance and prejudice are not crimes: if they were, Whitehall and Westminster would be very empty places and Dartmoor and Pentonville would be even fuller than they are.' This last remark was delivered with a mischievous grin and a tone of voice that was devoid of malice. It elicited a laugh from most of those present.

'Now to the purpose of this meeting. As you will doubtless know, I have numerous contacts in government and elsewhere. I say this not as a boast but as a statement of fact. I know that the biological attack on the visitors' mothership is part of a wider conspiracy to commit genocide against this intelligent extra-terrestrial civilization. The biological attack has weakened them considerably and now there are those who wish to finish the job. Some of The Enterprise are so obsessed with clinging to power and are so twisted with hatred against the visitors that they would commit mass murder to keep their positions and destroy something that they regard as evil for no reason other than that they are outsiders. I do not know the details of what they are planning, but I would urge anyone involved in such a plan to cease their activities, which are illegal, immoral and would stand in the annals of human history as a crime beyond even the Holocaust.'

Downing Street, Whitehall

'Christ, this is powerful stuff.' The PM's Press Secretary had not been a fan of Henderson's politics but there was no denying his political skills. 'Just look at the audience – there's Marcus Rosental from *Newsnight*, and Nicky Straw from the *Today* programme. He's really got some movers and shakers in the audience – this has been very well planned. It's targeted at the people who can really influence public opinion.'

The Prime Minister nodded in agreement. 'And the sad thing is that he's right, in a sense. I don't disagree with anything that he's saying. It's just, well . . . we're *committed*.' The PM was stating one of the great truths of modern warfare – once plans were made and once troops were committed, there came a point of no return when the sheer momentum of events made hostilities inevitable. The reason for this were in part psychological but scientific studies had been done that really did seem to bear out such a theory. Several Gulf War generals, for example, had privately expressed the view that once the build-up of troops reached a critical point it was virtually inconceivable that a peaceful resolution would be found. It was as if the drawstring of a great bow had been slowly pulled back and the incredible tension could only be released by the firing of an arrow.

Pyramid Heights, Westminster

'But to stop the genocide, it is insufficient simply to appeal to people's good nature. History shows the truth and tragedy of this:

from the insanity of the Somme to the evil of Auschwitz, we know how difficult it is for ordinary people to disobey orders, however mad or repugnant those orders may be. Fear for one's own life, fear of being branded a coward – there are many reasons why the most monstrous things happen, often because decent people simply cannot stop what truly evil people have started.'

Henderson's audience was highly intelligent and politically astute. Whether they had ever thought about matters in this way or not, most recognized the fundamental truth of what he was saying.

'In such a situation, we should make a stand, and try to stop what many might feel to be inevitable. To do so, we must bring down the decision-makers and replace them with level-headed people who will do good. I am not saying the government is comprised of evil people. Far from it: the majority of them *are* decent and honest men and women who genuinely believe they are doing the right thing for the right reasons. They are not. They are being manoeuvred into attacking the visitors by forces they can neither understand nor control. But when the few evil ones are so embedded in the system that they cannot be identified, let alone removed, regrettably the whole system needs to be brought down. To give an analogy, if quality-control checks reveal that a batch of fizzy drinks has been contaminated with poisonous chemicals, but the manufacturers do not know where the batch concerned has been sent, then *all* cans of the product must be removed from supermarket shelves, all over the country. We must bring down this government, even though most of its members are . . . uncontaminated.'

Space Shuttle Enterprise

'Target in sight – Holy Christ, will you look at that!'

The alien mothership was a truly awesome sight. Scientists had always said that if humans ever built a spacecraft capable of interstellar travel – at least, one that obeyed Einstein's laws of relativity – it would have to have a rotating living unit at the front, to simulate gravity. The alien mothership had no need to simulate gravity, which it possessed by nature of its mass. At the core of the ship was an asteroid, the size of a small moon but made of dense, massive elements such as nickel and iron. The aliens had clearly used this asteroid as a foundation, and built upon and into it the most stupendous structure any of the astronauts had seen. The final result was an object so vast and yet so engineered that it defied description. There was simply nothing to which it could be compared.

'How long until weapons release?'

'Two minutes. Target is locked on.' The moments dragged.

'Do you think . . .' The remark was never finished.

'Weapons release on my mark. Ten, nine . . .'

'Oh God, please forgive me.'

'Three, two, one – fire. Weapons are free, I say again, weapons are free.' If there had been a camera on the man speaking, it would have shown he was crying.

Pyramid Heights, Westminster

'I can play a small part in this, perhaps. Since my departure from politics I have not been idle. I have been a collector of information. I have secrets to tell, all of which can be backed up with documents that you of all people will have the expertise to verify. I shall tell you secrets about the Falklands War, and the Gulf War, and the Kosovo campaign, and about a certain fatal car crash that was not entirely accidental. And when I have told you these things, you will perhaps put the actions of the visitors into perspective as they seek to remove a threat to them in a way that impacts least upon ordinary men and women. And tomorrow a political friend in the Commons – a brave person prepared to sacrifice a political career for a greater good – will table a vote of no confidence in the government. It is my hope that this vote will be passed, and that a new coalition government will be formed – one that will immediately cease hostilities against the visitors and bring about a just and prosperous peace.'

Henderson sipped from his glass of water, and began his concluding remarks. 'Many of you, doubtless, are asking yourselves how I know these things. That is a fair question. In response, I say this: I know because I have been at the centre of many of the events that have taken place. I am a member of The Enterprise.'

Farnham, Surrey

'You two-faced little fuck!' Jenny Thornton was furious, and vented fury on the image on the television screen.

'I don't know what to say.' Richard Cody was a little more restrained in his analysis of what he'd just learned.

'He was using us. All the time he . . .'

'Maybe he had his reasons, Jenny. And who can say he's wrong? What he says sounds . . . well, it sounds *right*.'

Pyramid Heights, Westminster

'What I want more than anything is peace. Peace between our two races. Is that too much to ask? Must we lash out against those we don't understand, when they have so much – so *very* much – to offer? I think not. I think that we can reach out across the void of space with the hand of friendship.'

Space Shuttle Enterprise

All the missiles had now been fired. Their launch had taken place from the maximum possible distance since nobody wanted to reveal the space shuttle to the aliens as a target. The missiles themselves homed in on the mothership, pre-programmed to strike the rear of the craft where analyses suggested that the matter/antimatter drive was located. If the controlled blending of protons and antiprotons could be disrupted, and if sufficient quantities could be brought together at once, the mutual annihilation would very likely prove to be catastrophic for the mothership. But a few missiles were targeted on other parts of the ship, in case the analyses were wrong.

'Ready to arm missiles.'

'Ready, on my mark.' Missiles were to be armed only at the last moment because if an armed missile was hit, the resultant explosion might take out other missiles nearby. A few seconds before impact, the weapons would be little more than inert cylinders of metal. But, once armed, they would bring destruction on an unimaginable scale.

'Missiles armed. Impact is imminent.'

Chapter Twelve

THUNDER AND LIGHTNING

The Alien Mothership

Isabelle Bentley noticed a man and a woman in RAF uniform and went over to introduce herself. The world of fast-jet pilots was still comparatively male-dominated and she didn't recognize the woman.

'Hi. Isabelle Bentley. 29 Squadron, RAF Coningsby. Who are you?'

The man and woman looked at each other warily. 'We're Army,' the man replied.

'But you're in RAF flying suits,' Bentley objected.

'When the head sheds heard about pilots being taken from their aircraft and barracks, they decided to infiltrate a few soldiers to gather intel and maybe see about a rescue.' The man smiled.

Head shed? That's SAS talk. 'OK. Er, what's that?' Bentley pointed to a small black briefcase that was handcuffed to the man's wrist. She didn't like where this was heading.

'That's my bag of tricks – stuff to pick locks, a camera, that sort of thing. Thought it'd come up with me!'

'Great,' Bentley replied. *Liar.*

Space Shuttle Enterprise

'Both our missiles are armed and locked on to their targets.'

'How's everyone else doing?'

'*Discovery* reports one missile hung up . . . they're trying to free it, but they're not hopeful. Looks like an electrical problem. Er, *Columbia* has not launched at all. I – er – I think I heard gunshots and now they've gone off the air.'

'Say again? Did you say *gunshots?*'

'Er, roger that.'

The astronauts from various shuttles were swapping notes and trying to get a sense of the wider tactical position. The captain of the *Enterprise* was trying to be businesslike, but it was difficult, especially given what was going on aboard *Columbia*. He guessed that the crew had refused to launch their missiles on moral grounds, only to find that their 'passengers' had other ideas. He had no way of telling what was going on for sure, though, and there was absolutely nothing he could do about the situation anyway. He had other things to do.

'OK, missiles on final approach.' Everybody was wearing protective goggles to guard their eyes against the glare from the anticipated nuclear explosions. Tactically, they should have turned tail the moment they'd fired their missiles, but mission control wanted them on the spot for battle-damage assessment. When the crews had argued that Hubble could do this, they'd been told that they were closer and would get a better view. One of their number had pointed out the folly of this and said that either the mothership would be destroyed or it wouldn't be, with no middle ground between those two scenarios. He'd been waved away and told that they might be required to make another attack run with secondary weapon systems. But as these consisted of conventional missiles and the Firestreak plasma-weapon system, nobody held out much hope that this would succeed.

'Whoa – we have a detonation. Did we hit them?'

'No, that's too soon. They're onto us. Stand by to take evasive action on my mark.'

But there was no need. The aliens were tactically astute enough to realize that all their efforts had to be put into targeting the missiles locked on to their ship. The space-shuttle astronauts looked on in awe as what seemed like thousands of plasma bolts shot out from the mothership, turning the darkness of space bright purple. Other detonations followed, as more of the inbound missiles were struck. But for all of this activity, the aggressors had the advantage: the astronauts realized the aliens had discovered the attack late in the day – perhaps their early-warning systems were poor because such an attack had not been anticipated. Alternatively, early-warning and defensive systems might not be fully automated and, if they were dependent upon living operators, the biological attack might well have killed key personnel and degraded their capabilities.

Thirteen missiles had been fired in all and the astronauts watched as the count dropped. The aliens were steadily reducing the number of missiles, which were now down to seven. But the missiles were travelling very quickly, aided by the vacuum of space. Furthermore, they were comparatively small, being just a couples of metres in length and quite narrow: a difficult target to hit at the best of times.

Six . . . Now just five. It was just like an arcade game, but with the Earth itself as the prize. Four.

'Ain't gonna happen for us. We're running outta missiles.'

'Yeah, but they're running outta time.'

Three.

Two.

It was going to be a very close thing. But somebody's luck was going to run out.

The Alien Mothership

When the ship had begun its long journey, the inhabitants of the planet that was to be their destination had only just developed powered flight. No threat was anticipated, even allowing for the technological advance that would almost inevitably take place on the destination planet during the long years of the journey. But defensive systems were fitted to the ship in any case, as much to guard against the possibility that they might – on their way – encounter another spacefaring civilization. The systems were also designed to cope with the possibility that the craft might be struck by a piece of space debris that the navigators failed to spot.

All these defensive systems had been brought on-line. Some of the aliens' efforts were being spent on trying to destroy the inbound missiles but other activity was dedicated to coping with the consequences of a hit: emergency bulkheads were closed and personnel instructed to go to designated safe areas at the heart of the ship, furthest from the hull. But for all that, they knew their greatest vulnerability and took action to minimize the threat. Frantic orders were given to shut down the main propulsion system and to vent all but small reserves of antiprotons.

Space Shuttle Enterprise

'We have missile impact and nuclear detonation on the mothership . . . and another. OK, we have two – I say again, *two* confirmed hits on the mothership. One on the centre and one on the primary target zone at the rear.'

None of the astronauts cheered.

The Alien Mothership

Two massive explosions shook the ship, vaporizing vast amounts of rock instantly and doing catastrophic damage to the areas hit. If the ship had been an artificial structure, the inevitable hull breaches would have ensured its immediate destruction. But the mothership was built around and into a massive asteroid and much of its mass was solid rock. The aliens had burrowed into it and added on to it, but much of the ship was still protected by millions of tons of rock, and sections had been built independently of neighbouring sections so that the loss of one would not necessarily mean the loss of another. Still, a nuclear strike had not been anticipated and, for all its protective mass, the safety of the ship could not now be guaranteed – its fate lay in the balance.

Operation Lightning Strike had been devilishly planned. But for all its cunning and its surprisingly accurate guesses about the propulsion system being an Achilles heel for the aliens, it was always going to face the problem that an attack could only be launched at the very end of the mothership's voyage, meaning that its supply of antiprotons – depleted further by last-minute venting – had probably been very nearly exhausted.

This proved to be so and was something that would doubtless help the aliens who now had only to manoeuvre their ship into orbit. Indeed, prior to the attack, the few remaining antiprotons were being used to decelerate the ship in this final phase – a job that would now have to be done with secondary and more conventional propulsion systems.

Farnham, Surrey

Richard Cody and Jenny Thornton were doing what people normally do at times of national crisis – they were watching television. They'd been watching Maxwell Henderson's statement and had been discussing their own involvement with this charismatic character who was even now threatening to bring down the government. Thornton felt cheated but Cody was rather more sympathetic to Henderson and his views. The broadcast had just been terminated and they were looking at a grim-faced presenter who was clearly getting instructions from his producer.

'Ready on five. Which camera? Oh, OK.' You could always tell when a really big story was about to break, because organization dissolved into chaos and even the well-oiled media machine came off its tracks. 'Are we on?'

The presenter looked directly into camera and spoke, his tone firm and serious. 'Good afternoon. We are receiving unconfirmed reports of a number of explosions – possibly nuclear explosions – on or around the alien mothership. We hope to have pictures shortly . . . er, OK, there's one shot now.' The presenter paused for a moment and looked at the image that was showing up on the monitor. 'Well, I have to say you can't tell very much from that. That's a still picture, I'm being told, taken from Lick Observatory. We're trying to get some pictures from Hubble but NASA isn't talking to anyone right now. We're also trying to get some sort of official confirmation of what's going on – we've asked the government for a statement but nobody's saying anything at the moment. We'll let you know as soon as we can. What I can tell you is that there are a number of things that we can't broadcast at the moment – we've been privately aware of certain events for a while but . . . er, as responsible broadcasters we clearly have no desire to jeopardize national security and put lives at risk.'

'Does it look as if the mothership is under attack?' the other presenter asked.

'Well, it's possible some . . . accident has occurred. Although scientists have made some informed guesses, we don't really know anything about how the ship is powered, for example. But I have to say that sounds unlikely, so, yes, an attack may well have taken place.'

'And can we see from those photographs the extent of the damage? We're talking about damage, are we, as opposed to complete destruction?'

'Penny, it's very difficult to make out very much from these photographs. We're getting calls from amateur astronomers who reported seeing some flashes, but apart from that, it's difficult to tell.'

'Is it possible that the flashes were actually caused by the mothership launching weapons against us?' There was a pause after that question. Cody and Thornton looked at each other worriedly – they, like the television presenter to whom this question was addressed, had not considered this possibility.

'Er, that's a possibility, yes.' Another lengthy pause. 'OK, the Prime Minister's office has just confirmed that an attack *has* been launched against the mothership, in response to continued alien aggression. They've refused to give any further details and won't comment on the suggestion that nuclear weapons have been used. They have, however, confirmed that UK forces weren't involved in the attack. We're trying to get an interview with a government minister, but obviously this story is just breaking so – well, perhaps in the meantime we can go back to Maxwell Henderson and get a comment? Do we still have that link? OK.'

'—consequences of which we can only guess at.' Henderson's face betrayed his anger and he was clearly in the middle of making a statement. 'We can't hope to understand their psychology, but it seems likely that this will simply bring down upon us the most furious retribution. But it's no good our just condemning this action – we need to do something as individuals. We need to do something constructive. I don't know how widely this is being broadcast – it may even be that the visitors are monitoring this signal. If they are, let me assure you that we the people utterly dissociate ourselves from this attack. Please do not condemn us because of the actions of governments – or of a small cabal within government. I am a member of this group – The Enterprise – myself, but I can promise you that I wish you no harm. The Enterprise was split on the whole issue, and while most of us wanted to accommodate you, some prosecuted their own war on their own initiative. To radio astronomers anywhere in the world I say this: get out there and broadcast to the mothership. Tell them that this attack was not carried out by the people of Earth but by a small cabal. Broadcast a message of peace – our very existence may depend on that message getting through.'

Cody poured himself a large whisky and handed the bottle to Thornton, who poured herself an even larger measure. Cody's telephone rang, and he gave a brief down-the-line interview to a radio station. Shortly afterwards his mobile telephone rang. 'Yes? Yes, OK.' He turned to Thornton. 'The BBC want to get us in for their live coverage, to make a contribution or two. They're pretty much running with this on a twenty-four-hour basis anyway. I think we should go.'

'I'm not necessarily going to agree with your views, Richard. Some of us are a little more wary of the aliens than you . . . or Henderson. Maybe this is payback time.'

'Genocide?' Cody snapped back sharply. 'There are a billion people on that ship.'

'So they say. But they're not *people*. We're *people* . . . and there are *six* billion of us.'

The Alien Mothership

The assembled company of captured pilots were in mid-conversation about how they'd performed in combat – with the exception of West and Vatch who were studying the faint joins that they thought might be a door. Vatch had some lock-picking equipment that she was trying to use, while West was using his boot to try and break out.

'We tried that,' somebody called over, a little sarcastically.

'Well, maybe you didn't try hard enough.'

At that moment the room was plunged into darkness and the room began to vibrate. There were some strange sounds in the distance. After a few minutes the room began to get a little lighter – the glow seemed to come from the walls themselves – but it was fainter than before and kept varying in intensity.

'What the fuck was that?'

'Did we hit something?'

'Yeah, right: "Watch out for the moon". "What moon?" "Bang!" No, we didn't hit something; something hit us.'

'Well, that's good, isn't it? It means we're getting some hits in on the mothership.' The man who'd asked the question didn't look convinced.

'Yeah, that's really great – except for the fact that we're *on* the mothership. Hell, they probably don't even realize we're here.'

'Of course they do.'

'Hey, the door's open,' West called out. 'When the power cut out it must have unlocked.'

Everybody made their way to where West was standing and saw that the hairline slit they'd seen had now widened into a gap of about five centimetres, running from the floor to the ceiling. West locked his fingers around the edge of the gap and pulled hard, forcing the door open more. Others joined him and between them they pulled the door open even wider until the gap was big enough to pass through.

'OK,' somebody asked. 'What now?'

'We try and get back home, I guess.'

'Yeah, how you gonna manage that? I don't think this is like

Independence Day, where Will Smith gets into one of those alien spacecraft and just flies it off, you know?'

'Yeah, but maybe—'

'Can I say something?' West cut in, loudly and aggressively. When he had everyone's attention he spoke quickly and to the point. 'Jane here and me – we're Special Forces. Now, in case you've all forgotten, we're at war right now and I've lost some good friends – I'm sure we all have. We're on the mothership and somebody's managed to get some hits in, somehow. I don't know how – maybe it's NASA with space shuttles, or maybe there are other groups like us and one of them managed to bust out and cause some damage. But look, we're all military personnel and it's our duty to use this opportunity to help everyone back home by taking the war to the enemy. We must use the opportunity to do as much damage up here as we can.'

'Yeah? What with?' somebody asked.

'Like I said, we're Special Forces. We slept in an RAF barracks to get ourselves up here and we didn't do it for fun. I've got a bomb in this case.' West replied, holding up the briefcase that was still handcuffed to his wrist. 'A nuclear bomb'.

'Fuckin' A' one of the Americans remarked.

'Anyway,' West continued. 'First off, I suggest we get the fuck out of here, before the guards or whatever figure out that the power going off buggered up the locks.' They filed out into a deserted corridor.

'What do we do if we're challenged?' someone asked.

West had been carefully briefed on this and, though the strategy was based on a series of assumptions, it had sounded plausible. 'We form up into a squad and walk around as if we know what we're doing. If intel's right, most of them up here look human, so we shouldn't look out of place. If they're wrong, we'll know soon enough. Intel thinks each alien will be assigned to a particular country, so they'll speak one language each. Whatever is said to us, pretend we can't understand and just ignore them.'

'But won't they all share their . . . you know, their *alien* language?'

'Look, I never said I had all the answers,' West retorted. 'Like I say, just ignore anyone we meet and carry on. Either we'll fit in or we won't. If we don't, we're screwed, but if we do, it's a matter of psychology – unless somebody looks out of place or suspicious you don't pay much attention. Anyway, it's very unlikely that everyone here carries weapons. This is a *society* here – they'll have their military and their police, I guess, but they'll also have their doctors, their bank managers, their . . . I dunno, their *plumbers*, I suppose.' That elicited a laugh. 'And if push comes to shove, Jane and I are armed.' West pulled out his US-made Browning 9mm semi-automatic pistol. 'We came prepared for this, don't forget.'

'So what are you gonna do with that bomb?' one of the Americans asked nervously. 'Is it armed?'

'I'm gonna arm it now and set it on a timer, in case we're jumped. But my aim is to get it to a critical point and detonate it with enough time for us to get clear.'

'You're lyin', man. If you've got a nuke, you're aiming to *destroy* the ship, not damage it. Like the guy said, this ain't *Independence Day*. We can't just hitch a ride outta here, and if we're on the ship when you detonate the bomb . . . game over, man.'

'OK, what do you want me to say?' West retorted. 'You're right. But I don't know if we *can* destroy the ship, anyway. An attack's already been launched, either by NASA or by another team like Jane and me – I thought we were the only ones but it makes sense that there'd be back-up, I suppose. Either way, the attack would have been nuclear – but we're still here. So who knows? I'll give us time to get clear if I can. But if any of you want to go your own way . . . try and bust out somehow or try and do some damage of your own, feel free. Tactically that might not be such a bad idea, anyway.'

MOD Main Building, Whitehall

An emergency briefing was being held in S of S's office to discuss the latest developments. CDS was speaking to the assembled company.

'I can confirm that the Americans have initiated Operation

Lightning Strike. Preliminary indications are that two of the missiles did get through on-board defences and detonated either against or actually inside the mothership. It's not clear whether they exploded on impact or whether they managed to penetrate before exploding, as we'd hoped. It's also possible they were exploded by defensive systems just short of the ship but, even if that was the case, they would still have damaged it.'

'Let me be clear on this,' S of S asked. 'You're saying the ship is damaged but not destroyed?'

'That's right. The space-shuttle fleet has been ordered to make another attack but they need to get in close to do that. They've got a few non-nuclear missiles – but high-explosive nonetheless – and Skystriker. But they're much bigger than the nuclear missiles they fired earlier and, frankly, I think it's a suicide mission, especially now the aliens are wise to the attack. They've been ordered to strike the areas that look most damaged, but . . . well, I suspect it's more to give damage assessment than anything else.'

'Well, what next?' US of S asked. 'Now we've *really* pissed them off.'

'We have one more card to play,' CDS retorted and promptly explained how Jack West and Jane Vatch had been infiltrated on to the mothership.

'But for all we know, they could be dead already – killed by the aliens or even by the NASA attack itself.' It was CAS who raised this possibility.

'Yes, maybe. We don't know.'

'So we can't recall them . . . cancel their mission?' Nick Templeton asked.

'No. Why would we want to?'

'Because using force like that is a *political* decision, not a military one and, with respect to S of S and US of S, there's to be a vote of no confidence that may result in a new administration not minded to see through the attack. The media coverage is changing markedly and is now shifting against the war.' Templeton glanced at the Press Secretary who promptly nodded her agreement.

S of S was taken aback by Templeton's remarks. 'Well, I take your point. But, even if there *were* to be a new administration, there's no way to stop the attack if we can't communicate with the team. It's no different from dropping a bomb – once it's dropped, that's it. Doesn't matter if the pilot has a change of heart. In any case, losing a confidence vote doesn't necessarily lead to a new administration – the convention is simply that an election is called. But in time of war things may be very different. There's no real precedent for this and it may be that the national interest is best served by continuity.'

'What do you think the aliens will do to us now we've nuked them?' US of S asked, addressing his question to nobody in particular.

'I suspect it'll provoke them,' CDI replied. 'I think we'd better all hope and pray that our SAS people do manage to complete their mission. This is a them-or-us situation . . . more than ever, now.'

At that moment CAS's Principal Staff Officer opened the door without knocking and made an announcement that chilled them all. 'Radar has detected enemy craft heading for London. Air Defence aircraft are moving to intercept, but Main Building is one of a number of possible targets. Recommend we evacuate or go to bomb shelter areas, sir.'

'What about everyone else?' S of S asked.

'Security Control will make an announcement ordering all staff to secure areas, sir.'

'Then I hardly think *we* should run away,' S of S retorted.

'Agreed,' CDS added. 'I suggest we go to the DCMC.'

The Alien Mothership

The group of kidnapped pilots made their way down corridors that were deserted. Jack West led the way, while Jane Vatch brought up the rear. That way, at least, the armed SAS troops might stand some chance of reacting to any danger that presented itself.

'Any idea where we're headed?' someone asked West.

'Nope.'

'Well, what's your plan?'

'Intel reckons the ship's powered by a sort of matter/antimatter thing. They come together in a controlled way and it creates huge amounts of energy. If we can hit that system and bring the matter and antimatter together in an *un*controlled way – bang!'

'So do you have any idea where this "thing" is?'

'It's at the back of the ship. Trouble is, I don't know where the back is. So we'll keep going until we find it, or until we find another likely-looking place. Detonating it deep inside the ship, somewhere near the core, might also do the trick. We just need to get ourselves orientated.'

They rounded a corner and found themselves face to face with a group of about seven men, all entirely human-looking and dressed in dull-coloured but otherwise unremarkable clothes. Remembering what they'd been told, the kidnapped pilots and SAS personnel kept going and tried to avoid making eye contact. They waited for the others to voice a challenge . . . but it never came. Within a few seconds they were clear, and a casual glance back from Vatch revealed that the aliens they'd seen had gone.

'Either they're as cool as we are and they're reporting us now, or we made it,' Vatch whispered to those near her. 'Whichever, now we know intel were right: they *do* look just like us. You've just seen your first aliens.'

'Makes it kinda hard, though, doesn't it? Wanting to nuke them all, I mean?' The questioner was one of the US Navy pilots.

'Don't let appearances fool you – they're aliens in human form. It's like that old sci-fi series, *The Invaders*. You know, architect David Vincent, and all that. But these are the guys who've been beating up on us. They've killed hundreds, and now they've nearly reached Earth. Once they get into orbit, well, forget *The Invaders* . . . we're talking *Independence Day*. We have to stop that.'

Then they found the little girl. They came to a junction, took a right-hand turn and there she was. She looked about ten years old and was entirely human-looking. She was crying.

'I'm lost,' she said, in between sobs. 'Can you help me?'

West and Vatch were the only ones who'd had detailed briefings on the aliens and it was they who moved to deal with the situation. Vatch thought that the presence of a woman might be reassuring, although she had no way of telling whether or not what worked with human children would work here.

'Where are you supposed to be?' Vatch asked. Answering a question with another question was a classic tactic when you wanted to keep somebody off balance and not say something that might give you away.

'In the shelters, of course,' the girl replied, a touch of petulance in her voice.

'Weren't you with people?' Vatch was playing this coolly and saying as little as possible. *Less to get wrong.*

'My mummy and daddy got sick and died when the *bad* people came. I was sent somewhere else but they didn't care about me. I ran off to play and then—' Her voice broke down, and she sobbed quietly for a minute or so. Vatch put her hand lightly on the girl's shoulder. 'Then the *bad* people came back and we have to get to a safe zone and I don't know where the nearest safe zone is.'

'It's that way,' Vatch replied calmly, pointing the way they'd just come. The girl ran off, after a brief word of thanks.

'What the fuck do you mean, "*It's that way*"?' one of the Americans demanded to know.

'You think an adult wouldn't know where the nearest shelter is?' Vatch responded. 'Now that really *would* have looked suspicious. Anyway, chances are she'll run into someone – maybe those same guys we saw. It was the safest thing for us to do without compromising ourselves.'

Not the safest, West thought to himself, relaxing his grip on his pistol.

'*The bad people*? Is that how they think of us?' Isabelle Bentley was appalled. 'How many of them did we kill?' Her question was aimed at nobody in particular. And nobody had an answer.

MOD Main Building, Whitehall

'This is security control. This is security control. We have received information concerning a possible threat to Main Building. All staff are to proceed immediately to bomb-shelter areas. This is security control . . .'

Ministers and Chiefs of Staff gathered in the Defence Crisis Management Centre, deep below Main Building. It was said that the building went down as far as it went up, which was no exaggeration. The atmosphere was tense as they waited for further news of the inbound raid. This was the first time London had been targeted and the military realized the significance of the switch from tactical to strategic targets.

'Are the Royal Family safe?' Blackmore asked, loyally.

'They and the Prime Minister are being evacuated as we speak,' CDS confirmed.

There was an awkward silence as the assembled company waited for news from the RAF duty officers who were busily collating information from both the Permanent Joint Headquarters and from Strike Command.

'How did it come to this?' Blackmore asked wistfully. 'Biological attacks . . . nuclear strikes. Who are the bad guys here?'

'The Enterprise. The Russians . . . the Americans, even?' S of S was groping for a satisfactory answer but didn't have one.

'Or *us*, for letting it happen?' Templeton suggested. Few civil servants would have dared speak so boldly in front of the highest-ranking people in the department, but Templeton had a reputation for speaking his mind. 'We can't use The Enterprise as some sort of universal bogeyman, there to blame for all our mistakes and wrongdoing. We have to take responsibility *ourselves*. *We* did these things, or at least we went along with what others said.'

'The aliens are the bad guys here, surely?' CDI, at least, was prepared to mount a defence of their position.

'Are they?' Templeton replied. 'Don't get me wrong, I'm not saying they come out of this particularly well, either. But I'm saying this isn't the simple good-versus-evil struggle that we thought it would be, or that the media says it is. What if there is no right or wrong here?'

'It's irrelevant now,' CDI retorted. 'The die is cast. Our SAS troops are on the mothership and will doubtless let off their weapon soon. Added to the damage already done by Operation Lightning Strike, the blow will prove fatal.'

'They may yet fail,' Templeton retorted. 'While I respect their bravery . . . well, maybe they *should* fail. The mothership has already been hit by two nuclear explosions and yet it survives.'

'They detonated against its side, whereas *our* bomb is inside. We don't know where, precisely, but it's inside and that should prove decisive. But what we haven't told our people – what we *couldn't* tell them – is just how *powerful* the weapon is. We had to allow them some hope of escape – some hope that they might manage to simply cripple the ship or to escape before it was destroyed,' CDI explained.

'They knew,' CGS interjected. 'I would have told them myself, only I didn't need to. People like that, they may not have university degrees, but they're smart. They knew, all right. I saw it in their eyes when I gave them the mission. They knew it was a one-way ticket.'

'What do you mean?' Blackmore demanded. 'This is one of these so-called suitcase bombs, isn't it? These are the things that Alexander Lebed warned us about back in 1997, aren't they? They're tactical weapons designed to be carried by the old Soviet special forces, the Spetznaz. I didn't think they were that powerful.'

'They weren't,' CGS replied. 'You're talking about the RA-115. It weighed around thirty kilograms and was designed to be used against tactical targets like warehouses and control points. Lebed spoke out because he thought some had fallen into terrorist hands after the break-up of the Soviet Union. Anyway, the point is that Lebed was already behind the times. You think the Americans didn't have their own version? You think they didn't improve on the potency? Well, they did. They made one much smaller than thirty kilograms, that's for sure, and much more powerful. *That's* the bomb our people have infiltrated on to the mothership and, if it goes off anywhere near the core, the mothership will be destroyed. Of that, there is *absolutely* no doubt.'

Space Shuttle Enterprise

'They still want us to go in?'

'Yeah'

'It's a fuckin' suicide mission, man. Their guard is up now. The element of surprise is gone and they're expecting us. And I don't think they're gonna be pleased to see us after what we just did to them.'

'We hit 'em hard, though . . . no doubt about it. Maybe we hit 'em so hard they won't be able to fight back.'

'You'd better hope.'

The *Enterprise* and the other space shuttles – except for *Columbia*, which appeared to be drifting in space – homed in on the crippled mothership. They launched their remaining missiles, knowing even as they fired them that they would hardly scratch the ship, severely damaged though it was. But there was no point in delaying the launch, especially if it increased the chances that shuttle and missiles alike would be destroyed. They moved in for a final attack run, preparing to fire their plasma weapons in a last desperate attempt to inflict further damage. But, even as the first bolts were fired, thousands of similar bolts rushed out to meet them. And while missiles were small and difficult to hit, the shuttles were not.

Victoria Embankment Gardens, Whitehall

'Behind me you can see the Ministry of Defence Main Building, where even now plans are doubtless being made to deal with the latest developments and to counter the threat – if indeed that's what it is – from a massive alien craft that is now just days or perhaps just hours away.'

Victoria Embankment Gardens lay between Main Building and the Thames, and was a favourite spot for television film crews who wished to shoot interviews with the MOD's headquarters building in the background. A BBC crew had set up and were filming a brief interview with Cody and Thornton that would be used to trail a forthcoming live debate.

The presenter faced the camera, his expression serious, and

spoke. 'Much has been heard in the past few days from military commentators, politicians and scientists. They have all had some interesting and sometimes very controversial things to say. But this has obscured the people who in a very real sense were in at the beginning of the crisis. These people were seen as cranks or self-publicists, and yet history has proved them right. They stand vindicated but are still viewed as curiosities. These are the ufologists and the abductees. People who studied reports of alien contact – or who actually experienced it first-hand. People like Richard Cody and Jenny Thornton, who we'll be hearing from in a moment. It was just three— Hello? There seems to be some activity behind us. Quite a few people have just come out of Main Building. In fact, it's a steady stream now. It may be that there's been some new development, and if that's the case I'm sure we'll hear very soon. Well, I have to say they look rather panicked – let's hope they don't know something that we don't know. I—'. Professional broadcaster though he was, he froze for a few seconds while his producer screamed in his ear and tried to line up another interview.

To start with the presenter just pointed. But his expression had given the game away. A massive diamond-shaped UFO was approaching the crew's position from across the Thames, firing incandescent bolts of energy as it came. There was no cover to be had and all they could do was throw themselves flat on the ground.

'The mothership,' the lighting engineer whispered.

'No – that's the size of a small *moon*,' Cody replied.

'And this *isn't*?'

It wasn't the mothership, but it wasn't one of the fighter craft either. This UFO was the size of a battleship. Though the RAF had tracked a few of these craft over the North Sea in the late 1990s, few people had actually seen one. One had flown over RAF Cosford in 1993 but somehow the story had been killed. This wasn't the sort of scout craft that flitted in and out of a situation in an instant, affording a witness no more than a glimpse – this was a science fiction nightmare come to life.

Cody, Thornton and the BBC camera crew knew that they could

neither run nor hide, so they did the only thing left to them: they watched as best they could from their prone positions. They gazed in awe as the craft moved majestically up the Thames, firing as it came. A couple of RAF aircraft could be seen buzzing around the alien vessel but they seemed to be taking no aggressive action. Cody's first thought was that they were out of ammunition. But then he wondered whether there might be another reason for their restraint as he realized that if the UFO crashed in central London it might very well kill far more people than would die in a surgical strike against MOD Main Building – which was exactly the scenario that seemed to be unfolding.

Even though he was scared, Cody was still analysing the situation. The craft itself seemed to be moving very slowly, while its weapon was apparently quite accurate: bolts of energy were passing well over their heads and Cody's main worry was that they'd be struck by debris from the MOD building itself. He found himself holding Thornton's hand, unsure who had taken this initiative. He looked her in the eyes and smiled.

'We were right all along, weren't we?'

The Alien Mothership

All good commanders are lucky, but *really* good commanders know that you can't rely on luck. Eventually it runs out. This was something Jack West had learned in the Gulf War and had had confirmed to him in Kosovo. And it was something that was about to be demonstrated again.

Death came swiftly and unexpectedly. Just as you thought you'd got away with something, just as the sheer audacity of your action convinces you of your immortality, along comes reality to rain on your parade. So an SAS patrol in the desert is compromised by a young goatherd. And now a mixed pack of military personnel are ambushed far from home, maybe because they had spared a child whom they might have killed. Or maybe for other reasons. They would never know.

Death came at the pilots and SAS soldiers from the rear, mowing down all but those who led the way. Jane Vatch would have been furious if she'd had time to take in what was happening – to be shot in the back would have been particularly galling. She'd have felt she was at fault even though she wasn't – and she'd have liked to have at least squeezed off a couple of rounds. But it wasn't to be: when the alien patrol opened fire they did so with clinical accuracy and efficiency, purple bolts of plasma scything down all but a handful of the fugitives.

West didn't have to tell those left to run, and part of him wondered whether there was any point. They were all dead anyway, he knew. If they didn't die at the hands of a vengeful enemy hell-bent on retribution, they'd die in the fiery aftermath of the nuclear attack he was about to unleash. But run they did, for a while, turning this way and that through the labyrinthine corridors of the alien mothership.

West had a couple of grenades strapped to his person and quickly unhooked one, throwing it back down the passage they'd just run along, seeing it hit the wall at the far end and ricochet around the corner, just as he'd planned. There was a hollow explosion as the grenade went off in the confined space. West heard a scream that sounded human. He knew it wasn't.

Isabelle Bentley found herself caught up in events without having time to take them in or to analyse her own thoughts. She had no plan and simply followed West, knowing that he at least had some idea of what to do. She was no longer scared and though she didn't want to die she had all but resigned herself to that fate.

'What are we doing? What's your plan?' she shouted to West, who was running slightly ahead of her.

'OK, the timer's set on the bomb, but if we're killed they might manage to defuse or jettison it. I'm going to override the timer and detonate the bomb now. You're gonna have to help me.'

Bentley knew that two or three others had survived and glanced back over her shoulder to check that they were following. Perhaps these were the people who could help West fulfil his mission. She wasn't sure she wanted the job.

When someone is running for their life it's funny how little they take in. Bentley heard her own breathing and the sound of her boots on the metal floor. But she never heard the weapon that accounted for the remaining pilots and was unaware that her comrades had been shot in the back until she looked around again and saw nobody there.

West knew it was time for his last throw of the dice. Ducking into an entrance on the side of the corridor along which he'd been running he found himself in a room and determined to make his last stand. The bomb would detonate in fifteen minutes but that was useless if the aliens could make it safe in ten. All he had to do was turn the dial and program in another command. When he did so, the war would be over and the enemy vanquished.

'Take this,' West ordered, throwing his pistol to Bentley – the only other survivor. 'Hold them off, just for a few seconds.' There was desperation in his voice. He had started adjusting the controls on the bomb when a volley of plasma bolts was fired into the room, going wide of West's position but spurring him into action.

'For Christ's sake, hold them off,' he shouted.

Bentley had the pistol in her hand and peered around the doorway. Several people were edging their way up the corridor, carrying weapons and scanning for any movement. Then they fired, filling the air with plasma bolts, a few of which ricocheted into the room.

'Just a few more seconds.' West mumbled. There was the sound of running feet from the corridor outside and West suddenly looked up, catching Bentley's eye. She backed off and took up position in the doorway. He looked at her, a grin on his face. 'Shoot.'

And she did.

West fell forward, over the bomb, a gaping wound in his back.

Bentley wasn't entirely sure what happened after that. She was vaguely aware of hands touching her and the pistol being gently removed from her grip. She couldn't resist and wasn't sure if she wanted to anyway. She was kneeling on the floor and she knew she was crying. But she wasn't sure why.

Permanent Joint Headquarters

'I've ordered our forces to stand down,' Lieutenant General Ball was explaining to his staff officers. 'I'm not surrendering, you understand – I don't have the authority to make that sort of decision. But I can't raise anyone at Main Building and I'm not prepared to let our people carry on taking this sort of punishment. So, for the time being, we're out of the game. Judging by what's happening all around the world, it's all over anyway.'

'Sir?' somebody asked, unsure of what was being said.

'The mothership is in orbit and untold thousands of shuttle craft are bringing their people down to the surface. It's – it's out of my hands.'

The Alien Mothership

As it turned out, one of the US Navy pilots had survived. Badly wounded though he was, he was sent to join Isabelle Bentley. Bentley had been ushered into a room dominated by a viewpoint that ran from floor to ceiling, wall to wall. Through it, looming vast in her vision, was the Earth and heading towards Earth from a point she couldn't see, but which was clearly on the mothership, was an endless stream of craft taking the aliens to their new home.

Bentley was crying. Part of her was crying for West, even though she wasn't sure if he was dead. Part of her was crying for the little girl (*the bad people*), her dead parents and the countless others who, she had no doubt, had died in screaming agony, cut down by the obscenity of germ warfare. But for the most part she was crying at the enormity of what she'd done: history had hit a crossroads and she'd chosen the route, without knowing if she'd chosen right . . . without knowing if there *was* a right choice.

She tried to explain herself to the Navy pilot. 'I – I couldn't kill a *billion* people.'

The Navy pilot grunted in acknowledgement. 'Uh-huh. I understand.'

'Did I do the right thing?'

The Navy pilot looked directly ahead and was transfixed by the sight of so many alien ships making the short journey to Earth. 'I don't know,' he replied, truthfully. 'I really don't know. Time will tell . . . it always does, in the end.'